PRAISE FOR
LARRY BROOKS

"A master of terror and suspense."
—*Publishers Weekly*

"An intoxicating and intelligent tale of corporate corruption . . . entertaining."
—*Publishers Weekly*, for *Bait and Switch*
(Editor's Choice, 2004)

"*Darkness Bound*'s final scenes burst with the intensity of a first-rate horror film."
—*Publishers Weekly*, for *Darkness Bound*

"An addictive thriller."
—*Publishers Weekly*, for *Serpent's Dance*

"Crime novelist Raymond Chandler was widely acknowledged in his day as the Poet Laureate of The Dark Side (he looked about as inconspicuous as a tarantula on a slice of angel food cake). He died in 1959 and ever since there have been many pretenders to his throne. Among the best are James M. Cain, Elmore Leonard, Robert B. Parker, James Lee Burke—all masters of the craft, all wordsmiths of the first order, but none of them had Chandler's gifts. After half a century of being on the lookout for a crime fiction writer with

a voice that rivals Chandler's, one has finally appeared, quietly chugging his way up the bestseller lists with *Darkness Bound, Whisper of the Seventh Thunder, Serpent's Dance,* and *Bait and Switch.* His name is Larry Brooks. The guy has a slick tone and a crackling, cynical wit with lots of vivid descriptions (of both interior and exterior landscapes), and the sparkling figures of speech dance off the page and explode in your inner ear. Though as modern as an iPad 5S, he is truly and remarkably Chandleresque. He's dazzling. Check out his new one, *Deadly Faux*—it's sexy, complex, intelligent; a truly delightful novel with more plot twists than a plate of linguine swimming in olive oil."
—James N. Frey, author of *How to Write a Damn Good Novel,* for *Deadly Faux*

"An absolute must read, *Deadly Faux* is guaranteed entertainment. In Wolfgang Schmitt, Larry Brooks has created a wisecracking protagonist who is witty, resourceful, intelligent, and, most surprisingly, vulnerable. Brooks plunges Wolf into a seemingly unwinnable caldron involving Las Vegas casinos, the mob, and femme fatales, then turns the heat up high. I finished *Deadly Faux* in one sitting, couldn't put it down, and can't wait to read the next book. Step aside, Nelson DeMille and Stuart Woods—Schmitt happens!"
—Robert Dugoni, *New York Times* bestselling author of *The Jury Master,* for *Deadly Faux*

"*Deadly Faux* is a fast, fun read with plot twists I did not see coming and a satisfying ending." —Phillip Margolin, *New York Times* bestselling author of *Sleight of Hand*

DARKNESS BOUND

DARKNESS BOUND

BOUND

A NOVEL

LARRY BROOKS

TURNER

Turner Publishing Company
424 Church Street • Suite 2240 • Nashville, Tennessee 37219
445 Park Avenue • 9th Floor • New York, New York 10022
www.turnerpublishing.com

DARKNESS BOUND

This is a work of fiction. All the characters and events portrayed in this book are either products of the author's imagination or are used fictitiously.

Cover design: Glen Edelstein
Book design: Glen Edelstein
Cover image: Corbis

Library of Congress Catalog-in-Publishing Data
Brooks, Larry, 1952-
  Darkness bound / Larry Brooks.
    pages cm
  ISBN 978-1-62045-455-8 (pbk.)
  1. Sadomasochism--Fiction. I. Title.
  PS3602.R64437D37 2013
  813'.6--dc23
                          2013024445

Printed in the United States of America
13 14 15 16 17 18 19 0 9 8 7 6 5 4 3 2 1

For Laura

Acknowledgments

Aspiring authors hear that no book reaches an audience without many helping hands, and newly published ones, like me, quickly learn how true this is. Heartfelt thanks to my agents, Mary Alice Kier and Anna Cottle of Cine/ Lit Representation, for their faith, talent, and relentless skill; my editor, Dan Slater, for his vision and keen sense of the literary moment; Tracy, Kelly, Lynn, Rick, Robyn, Bernadette, Nadine and Wes for their brave early reads and gracious feedback; Ben Wong and Grey Matter for the assist; Dan Wickenden, my first mentor, wherever you are; PSI, for the tools; and most of all my stunning wife, for everything, always.

PROLOGUE

She sat very still in her husband's favorite chair, sipping an exquisite Pinot Noir as she watched him die. That there could be pleasure in the taking of a life was something she hadn't considered. For all her meticulous planning and diabolical patience, the notion of experiencing some dark shiver of satisfaction had never entered her mind. But here on the threshold of commitment, fully invested and completely immersed in the moment, she understood it instinctively. Whether it was death or power or simply the sweet venom of revenge made no difference, really. Perhaps it was just the intoxicating whiff of impending freedom. For her these things had become a sum in excess of their parts, melting and melding, changing everything.

At first it felt comfortable, like slipping into an expensive designer gown before a full mirror, the moment encasing you and making you understand your feminine power. It didn't take her long to realize, however, that this, like so many fantasies spun into flesh, wasn't the enduring entertainment it had started out to be.

The idea had been born four months earlier while she was scanning a travel magazine at her hair salon. It was a pictorial on the island of Capri in Italy, a place she'd always wanted to see, a place her husband said they'd never go. He'd been there in another life, and he took some ridiculous masculine pride in never covering the same ground twice. She could go herself, he informed her quite seriously, when he was dead and buried. He'd said it with that mean little smile of his, and in that instant the dark idea became an intention that breathed. From that point on, every thought, every agenda, had related to this moment.

Her husband's face seemed younger here on the precipice of eternity. He was sixty, and from the weary way he talked about the world he was quite ready to die. He would accomplish that goal wearing his favorite pajamas, decorated with little faceless golfers swinging tiny clubs. Were it not for the deep and gentle rising and falling of his chest he might otherwise be gone. She glanced at her watch—she had been sitting here for thirty minutes and his lingering was making her late. This was the first night of the rest of her life and she had things to do.

It had been so easy. Wednesdays were golf days. On this particular Wednesday he'd come home much too drunk to drive after gimlets and rib eyes at the club with his peers, a fraternity of CEOs and the prematurely retired who, as a matter of arrogant machismo, allowed their friends to drive drunk. She'd met him at the door with a warm smile and a crystal tumbler filled with his favorite Scotch. The rich flavor would sufficiently mask a substance he could not taste and she could not pronounce. They'd settled in the library, which smelled of his cigars, and as he sipped the potion she'd told him how she had been searching her heart. She wanted him to know that despite the changing of his estate documents, a gesture upon which he had insisted despite her gracious reservations, she would after all give the bulk of his money to his two children should, God forbid, anything ever happen to him. She'd withhold only enough for a nice little house overlooking the Sound and a comfortable and exceedingly quiet lifestyle. Perhaps a new Mercedes every three years or so, an addendum she added with a wink. Two, three million at most. Without him, she had said softly, her life would be forever quiet. She would live on memories. He'd mumbled something about it being his damn money and he'd damn well leave it wherever he damn well pleased. This made her smile, not because of any sentiment in his words, but because the thickness of his tongue told her the potent narcotic was kicking in. By the time she'd asserted her commitment to an ongoing relationship with his alcoholic son and the thrice-divorced daughter who was but a few years her junior, he was nearly asleep. She'd helped him into bed, changed him into his favorite pajamas, and tenderly given him his nightly insulin shot. Except this evening's syringe contained a clear and very-hard-to-come-by fluid that would slow his metabolism gradually until his heart stopped altogether, leaving absolutely no trace for even the most thorough of pathologists. He would go gentle into this good night. She'd waited ten minutes, poured herself her first glass of wine, then shot two more syringes full of his regular dose of insulin into his ample abdominal tissue, which would convince that same pathologist that her husband, a veteran diabetic, had died of insulin shock exacerbated by the presence of abundant alcohol in his system.

A little cleanup and some convincing acting, and she'd get away with murder and a forty-four million dollar portfolio of stocks and real estate.

She squinted, making sure her eyes and the wine weren't betraying her perception. Her husband's chest had stopped moving. She watched for another frozen minute, taking care not to blink, conscious of the total absence of sound.

She went to his side, leaned close, and studied his face. His lips were parted, slightly wider than they were minutes ago. She touched his neck with her fingertips, feeling no pulse. She lifted his eyelid like they did on the cop shows, not knowing what to look for. The pupil was dilated, eerily dry. When she let go it closed only partially, leaving the impression of him winking up at her. She smelled urine and realized it was over.

Goodnight, sweet prince . . .

Something in her stomach growled, an anxiety she hadn't expected. She looked away, drew a deep breath and tried to focus on the why of it all, which justified everything. Change. Outside, through the glass wall that opened to a massive deck overlooking Lake Washington, she saw pinpoints of light dancing on the water. The summer rain had cleared the lake of its abundance of pleasure boats, which on warmer nights cruised the perimeter long after dark in search of romance and, for those with a pair of good binoculars, a view into the bedrooms of the privileged. Their own yacht, a fifty-five-foot Navigator he'd bought and named after her, was a dark silhouette against the silver reflection of the water. She could hear the rain tapping the cedar planks with a

clarity she hadn't noticed sitting in the chair, waiting for
him to die. Hadn't noticed, in fact, in six rainy years in
that house.

She bent down and kissed him softly on the lips. Before turning away to begin her life anew, she closed his
eyelid and gently straightened the collar on his pajamas.

DETECTIVE Tim Rubin stood at the rear of the well-
heeled crowd and watched the rain dance off the bronze
casket like the hood of a freshly waxed car and swore
that someday he'd move from this puddle of a city that
measured its summers by consecutive days without rain-
fall. He studied the mourners, barely hearing the minis-
ter's words, like watching television with the sound on
mute. A lyric from his favorite and long-since archived
hometown rock band suddenly came to him, and he
found himself humming along.

. . . *strange how laughter looks like crying with no
sound* . . .

He wasn't welcome here. The widow had made that
abundantly clear the previous day during the third of
their lengthy interviews. She now stood at the side of
the open grave, which was surrounded by fresh flowers
that hid the black pit from view. He was certain she was
looking at him through the veil of a much too elaborate
hat. She held a handkerchief to her mouth with a black-
gloved hand. Very convincing. Very *Town and Country*.
And hard to look away from. A distinguished older man,
one of the pallbearers who was undoubtedly one of the
deceased's boardmates from Boeing, stood beside her
holding a large golf umbrella, his chin trembling slightly.

The lady was good, Rubin had to give her that.
She'd covered every base, was in command of every

nuance. Her only mistake, the thing that kept Rubin from buying it all, was that her story was just too damn tight. Twenty-two years of listening to stories like this, told under the mirror diversions of grief and fear, had sharpened his nose for the contrived. He'd watched her godless eyes, the too-efficient movement of her hands, the Judas pantomime. And he just knew. She was good enough to fool his lieutenant, who had a weakness for women who smelled like downtown and habitually touched your arm while they talked to you. Which was why Rubin had been told to back off this one, had been assured there was nothing here. This was old Boeing money, entrenched Seattle society, and nothing short of a bloody glove behind the servant's quarters would do. He was on a witch hunt, or so it was believed, because the deceased had been wealthy and everybody knew that Rubin, who would never find his name in that chapter of the social registry, had it in for the rich and their wives. But Rubin's attitude wasn't connected to the golf course he would never play. It was the result of too many years of watching the old-boy network bend the system at someone else's expense. Because he was no fool, he would indeed back off as he was told.

But he would watch. The bitch did it, and she knew that he knew.

The pastor uttered his final words, tossing a handful of what was by now mud onto the casket. It landed with a plop and stuck for a moment before sliding slowly down the side. Rubin lingered at the crowd's perimeter as it began to disperse, positioned for eye contact, wanting her to remember the iron resolve she would see there. As she walked past she glanced over at him, and he saw what no one else could see.

She was smiling. Ever so slightly. A smile meant for him, to test his restraint.

But restraint was the least of Tim Rubin's challenges. This woman reminded him of his soon-to-be-ex-wife and the lawsuit she had filed, that I-got-you-by-the-balls-and-I'm-fucking-my-lawyer smile. The look-at-me clothes. Which is why it was so easy to hate the grieving widow with the smirk that told him everything. He knew her far better than she could imagine. And he would be there when she slipped. No matter how long it took.

And it would take a long, long time.

With his lieutenant's blessing and deepest sympathies, the widow left for Italy the day after the funeral.

DARKNESS
BOUND

1

Four Years Later

The world as he knew it was coming to an end. At least if you believed the midmorning buzz around the office. Simply put, the stock market was crashing. Dillon Masters, stockbroker and reluctant President's Club member, had arrived uncharacteristically late at ten after seven, and already his voicemail had twenty-four messages. He had only to switch on his PC to see why—the Dow had opened down over two hundred points and had since been sliding steadily to hell. The worst of the I-told-you-so doomsayers, including the contrarian asshole in the cubicle next to his, were promising that this was the long-prophesied bull market apocalypse. Dillon's personal accounts—the first thing he checked after he saw the Dow—had already accumulated a collective sixteen grand in losses, the fact of which he tried to ignore as he popped four

Zantac and began returning calls, reaching all but five by eight-thirty. The correction was, like so many market hiccups, simple bullshit and quite temporary, he was certain. Certain enough, he told his clients, to leave his own holdings untouched as he looked for what stocks to pounce on while the pouncing was good. The rebound would be as dramatic as the belly flop, perhaps as soon as tomorrow. And in the meantime, as is the way on Wall Street, there were carcasses upon which to dine.

By the lunch hour, or at least what the outside world defined as such, Dillon realized that the morning had actually been sort of fun. In a business which, for him, had acquired all the meaning and edge-of-your-seat excitement of an Arizona weather report, the ticker had legitimately stimulated a few long-anesthetized adrenal glands. At the closing bell the market was down 554 points, an all-time Dow Jones record. Like all 106 brokers in this Seattle branch of the nation's largest and most respected brokerage institution, Dillon had one of his best commission days of the quarter. His revenue had come from three of his ballsiest clients following his advice in snatching every sagging issue in sight instead of the lemming-like sell-off so willingly facilitated by his peers. In the midst of chaos, a commission is a commission is a commission.

Dillon had no way of knowing that, in spite of the morning's chaos, it would be the afternoon that he would remember most about this day.

THE broker meeting began at one-fifteen in a nearby hotel conference center, complete with catered rubber chicken and a guest analyst from the main office in

White Plains. When the suits from Corporate showed up you were expected to cancel your lunch and your tee time and gather here with bells on. Today's talking head was one of The Street's favorite sons, representative of a legion of Ivy League–bred stock pickers and market visionaries who had never made a cold call in their privileged lives. What they did was author The Company List, grading each issue somewhere between Strong Sell and Strong Buy, with milquetoast intermediate strategies such as Accumulate and Hold. The Company List had a sign-off committee that included some of the most expensive and paranoid lawyers in the land, which meant that it was, if nothing else, as safe as the stock market could get.

Dillon sat toward the back, carving his chicken dijon mindlessly into slivers with his salad fork as he listened to preppy Mr. White Plains dissect the morning's market fiasco. Dillon knew this little faux-crash was like a freak wave at the beach, too high and too sudden to predict with any accuracy, and when you saw it coming, it was too late to get your ass out of the water. Yet statistically speaking, you knew it would arrive sooner or later. And right behind it, certain as the next interest payment, was another wave in an eternal continuum of mostly unremarkable waves, and all the physics of lunar gravity in the NASA library didn't really meant shit. Which was why Dillon was doodling little sailboats onto his napkin when he realized today's luncheon presentation had moved from the rhetoric of fiscal cause and effect to something called the Nomura-America Mutual Fund.

He glanced up and saw several of his peers rolling their eyes.

The Nomura-America Mutual Fund wasn't such a

bad idea if you were wealthy and bored and in need of a little high-risk diversification. It was a collection of up-and-coming Japanese high tech firms, all without existing U.S. brands, none with pronounceable names, who promised to be a thorn in the side of Intel and Microsoft once the new Millennium got its legs. None of the firms paid dividends, meaning they were plowing whatever yen they earned back into R&D and the establishment of global distribution channels for technologies that consumers didn't yet know they needed. Gadgets that would marry the telephone with the family TV and the wristwatch, all under the loving guidance of Bill Gates and friends. Which also meant that these firms were fraught with risk and uncertainty. By lumping them together as a mutual fund and slapping the word "America" on it, U.S. investors could hedge the considerable risk while strapping in for a ride on the old trend machine.

None of that bothered Dillon Masters, who knew how this game was played and had over the years pocketed a buck or two of his own from it. What got his attention today, causing him to put down his fork and listen closely, was the fact that The Company had signed on as the lead U.S. underwriter, and that next month's IPO would be allotted to offices on the same basis as their U.S.-based funds sales performance. Which, in turn, meant that each broker with a significant business in mutual funds, including Dillon, would be expected to schlep this stuff according to some Manhattan marketing whiz boy's notion of a reasonable quota.

Even that would have been tolerable—Dillon had plenty of speculators in his book—were it not for the fact that at the end of his remarks Mr. White Plains announced, "We're looking for a hundred percent participation, so we're giving each broker a minimum three-hundred share allotment, which we expect you to turn in good faith." Good faith. Corporate code for "or else." This was an old sleight of hand, ramming dogs down the throats of the branch offices under the threat of withholding well-deserved allocations of more legitimate IPOs that were certain to be sell-outs.

The broker sitting next to Dillon was twenty-three years old, a freckled redheaded rookie fresh out of Washington State sporting a book with no more than a dozen clients, all of them relatively small, probably retired, inexperienced, and frightened of the very markets their young broker had talked them into entering. Dillon tried to place the name, but rookies came and went like the region's annual salmon run. This particular young man's eyes were closed and he was shaking his head slowly, unaware that Dillon was watching him. At thirty-eight, Dillon was a well-established old guarder who retained the memory of his own rookie pain, and he knew exactly what the head-shaking was about. Freshman brokers are immersed in a paradox: Investors in a position to take a flyer on crap like Nomura-America were the type of people who had the money to lose and already had more than one stockbroker. They were the type of people who wouldn't give this kid or those like him the time of day. That meant the rookie would be left to pitch Nomura-America to little Mrs. Pinkerton, who was most likely his mother's friend or neighbor, with her small utility-heavy account, which along with Social Security was also the primary source of her livelihood. The idea here, as envisioned by the brilliant strategists in White Plains, would be to talk her into boning up for a hundred shares. It was a matter of pairing available cash with stupefying naïveté and then finding a way to sleep at night. Those who couldn't do the latter, even if they'd pulled off the former, usually left the business within a year or two. Dillon remembered that this particular rookie had caught Corporate Holy Hell when a similar situation presented itself just last month. Thinking back on how they'd embarrassed the kid in front of the whole staff, he felt his face grow warm.

"Excuse me," Dillon said loudly, not to the rookie but to the room itself. The entire audience shifted toward him, and he sensed a snicker or two. In a meeting in which 100 of the 106 minds were thinking the same thing, only Dillon Masters had the stones to stand up and say it. Everyone knew what was coming. Suddenly, the meeting was interesting.

The Armani-attired speaker glanced over at the host branch office manager, who was rubbing her eyes in an obvious effort to hide. He whispered something, then squinted and mustered a brave Dartmouth smile.

Dillon stood up, peering down at the napkin in his hands as if referring to his notes. He was tall and athletic, comfortable being looked at. From the podium, the speaker thought Dillon looked a little too much like a Saks window mannequin. Typically, only his MBA peers in New York looked like that.

"Did you say when the offer is effective?" Dillon asked. His brow was creased, as if he were confused or concerned.

"No, I don't believe I did."

Now Dillon looked up. "Is that because you don't know, or won't tell us?"

The room buzzed. One of two things was probably at hand, both of which were, again, familiar Corporate cons—they wanted the brokers to get their clients' money committed now, even though the deal was weeks away from closing, which meant those funds were unavailable for other investments. That, or they were uncommitted on the underwriting side and wanted to get a feel for the volume before they sloughed any extra shares off to other brokerage houses.

The speaker's smile faded as he realized he was about to be called out. "We believe in this underwriting," he said. "We'd like our clients and our registered representatives to believe in it, as well." The man's trust-fund smile remained.

Dillon kept a straight face as he consulted the napkin adorned with three stick-figure sailboats and a doodled pattern of a spiderweb.

"And you would term Nomura-America a somewhat speculative strategy, am I right to assume?"

"No more or less than the bulk of domestic high-tech new money. And you are . . . ?"

"Confused. I'm sort of new at this, as all my clients are either in utilities or bond funds." There were dozens of pairs of smiling eyes and subtly nodding heads. The only person in the room who didn't know Dillon was an experienced pro and a top earner for the firm was the speaker himself.

"Well, our baseline allocation is three hundred shares, and I'm sure you'll be able to find the right investor for them. This is a great prospecting tool. Nobody in town will have this but us."

Someone in the room coughed sharply, and it sounded a lot like the word "bullshit." More snickering ensued. The speaker was getting flustered now.

Dillon pretended not to hear. "Well, excuse me for saying, but all nineteen of my clients are not only tapped out, but they aren't likely to sell off any of their Seattle Power and Light to take a dip in the Pacific Rim. So I'm wondering, because I'm new and all, just what the hell am I supposed to say to these people when I call them on this? And while you're at it, maybe you can explain the realities of brokerage economics to those of us who can't get more than two hundred shares of the next Amazon-dot-com because of this unique and somewhat strained relationship between your quota and my book."

As quickly as it had spun toward Dillon, the crowd now focused back on the speaker, whose smile had faded as he consulted some notes of his own. After a moment he covered the microphone with his hand as he bent to the side to say something to the branch manager. The loudspeaker whined sharply with feedback as the branch manager shook her head, her face suddenly as red as his.

The man returned to the microphone. "And you are . . . ?"

"Outta here," was Dillon's reply, and with that he picked up his notepad and walked purposefully but calmly to the door. The room promptly erupted into applause and laughter. The young broker sitting next to Dillon was clapping loudest of all, his lips pressed together tightly as if he'd just heard General Schwarzkopf personally telling Saddam Hussain to go fuck himself.

The speaker again covered the microphone, but looser this time, loose enough for the entire audience to pick up his words: "Who the fuck was *that*?"

To which an anonymous voice from the audience offered, "He's the *man*, that's who."

2

What to do, what to do . . . buy, sell, hold, call a psychic, down a straight shot? A writer for the *Seattle Post-Intelligencer* was making the rounds collecting quotes— Dillon made sure he was in the bathroom when the guy's route brought him too close. Several concerned clients had shown up, listening intently to their trusted brokers, some of whom were sellers, some buyers, none of whom really knew anything at all except what they read on the wire from the home office, written by people who, like them, really knew nothing at all. Along a wall of eight cubicles you could find eight opinions ranging from divergent to diametrically opposed, with all the informed logic of a daily horoscope.

Dillon's phone was remarkably quiet. His clients had been attended to, their anxiety put to bed, the overly fearful appeased according to their various comfort levels. Nervous clients were like the elderly—you ultimately did whatever you needed to do to calm them down. A couple of brokers came by to offer a high five for the number he'd done on the White Plains analyst. They were old guarders; the newer guys never spoke to the established producers because they never talked to *them*. Today, however, the rookie broker whose anxious expression had triggered it all, risked this social chasm to stick his head inside Dillon's doorway to say thank you. Dillon winked and said, "I'm a professional, kid . . . don't try that at home."

When he was alone again, Dillon leaned back in his chair and watched the wall-to-wall activity with detached amusement. He wasn't sure if he was above it all or simply out of it, and neither alternative felt very good. The place reminded him of a big-city daily newsroom, if not for the intensity and urgency, then for all the pure playacting taking place.

He felt someone grab the toe of his shoe, which was perched on the top of the desk, and shake him back to reality. He looked up to see Janis Dixon, his office branch manager and his boss, standing next to him.

"Having a nice trip?" She was a bulldog of a woman, squat in stature with an unmistakable Slavic profile that had earned her the nickname of Mrs. Yeltsin behind her back. She'd look more at home wearing a scarf, stooped over a stove stirring borsht. The illusion was shattered not so much by her wardrobe of expensive, masculine-cut business suits as by an IQ rumored to exceed 150, and the certainty that she could, if so moved, summarily kick the ass of half of the men in the office while intimidating the other half into silence. Dillon wasn't sure which half he was in.

He smiled up at her. She'd hired him eleven years earlier, mentoring him through the odds-defying survival stage of building his client book. He could usually read her mood, understand every nuance in her tone. Something about her eyes confused him today—this could be a talking-to about the lunch thing, or it could be something else. In either case, Janis would listen to his side and sincerely try to understand his point of view, because normally she shared it, line for line.

"Got a few? Say, in ten?" She raised her eyebrows to punctuate the fact that the invitation was not optional.

He nodded. She squeezed his toe again and moved on to the next cubicle, a mistress of the fine art of management-by-walking-around.

HE appeared at Janis' doorway ten minutes later. She was on the phone, but a flick of her eyes told him to come in and sit. Before he reached the chair she motioned for him to shut the door, which never happened unless something was wrong. People got chewed raw and sometimes canned behind that closed door. He sat and waited, and while he knew he wasn't going to be fired, his stomach ignored the optimism. Maybe he'd done it this time, gone too far, embarrassed her in front of a home office suit. She was mumbling a rhythmic "Um-hum" into the phone in affirmation of the unheard monologue. Her eyes smiled at him, then she silently mouthed the word "asshole" before mumbling another polite "Um-hum."

Finally she hung up and shook her head. "Prick." She didn't say who the prick was, and he didn't ask. She had already leaned back in her chair, clasping her hands over her abdomen in a very male, very executive way.

She just stared at him, a curious look in her eyes.

"Am I supposed to be squirming here?" he asked.

She glared, letting him stew. Finally she said, "You crack me up." Then she smiled; a coconspirator.

"I suppose I owe you an apology," he said.

"For what? Last time I looked this was still a commission business."

"I made you look bad. I'm sorry for that."

"No, you made that pompous jackass with the two-thousand-dollar suit look bad. Hell, I couldn't have said that shit to him. That's why you crack me up, always saying the things the rest of us wish we could say."

"You're not pissed, then."

"Maybe you should be apologizing to *him*. He's the one who's probably pissed. In fact, I can guarantee you that's the case." She was still grinning. He felt himself relax. "That's not what I wanted to talk to you about."

"Okay," he said. He had to avert his eyes from her gaze, which remained locked on him as her smile dwindled away.

"What's up with you?" she finally asked.

"It's that obvious?" he asked.

"Not to anyone else. Then again, nobody else gives a shit. Your numbers are down. You're quiet. You look like hell."

He nodded and exhaled wearily, still not looking back at her.

"Can I help?" Her voice was softer now, sensing he wanted her to probe in the way that old friends just know.

He drew a breath, wondering if he had any Zantac left in his coat pocket. "Karen asked me to"—he caught on the next words—"move out."

Softly, Janis uttered, "Shit."

"That's what I said, too."

"I suppose you did?"

"What am I gonna do, have a domestic standoff in the utility room?"

They both fidgeted, neither of them sure where to take this.

"None of my business?" she asked.

"It's your business if you've noticed." It was true that when no one else in the place gave a shit, Janis usually did. "Of course it's your business."

She nodded. "How long has it been?"

"Six days. I came home to a note."

A pause. Janis always knew how to pace a conversation. "I'm sorry."

Dillon shrugged, forcing a brave little smile that didn't work. "She goes off to some weekend human performance seminar and this is what I get for my four hundred dollars."

"Maybe they give refunds."

"Read the fine print."

"Anything I can do? You want some time? I'd give you some advice, but I don't know shit about marriage." Mrs. Yeltsin had never married. Instead she'd built a book that had made her famous in the industry and revered in the office. Most of the guys thought she was a lesbian.

Time off. He hadn't thought of this. In the brokerage game, time off equated to a pay cut, and that was the last thing he needed right now. He drew a deep breath.

Janis was watching his wheels turn, enjoying the sight. She made no secret of the fact that she thought Dillon looked like a movie star, and got a kick out of telling him so frequently. What she liked most was the fact that Dillon seemed unaware of his looks, of his presence when he entered a room, and she often reminded him that it was her mission to keep him both informed and humble. Dillon certainly had *it*—a slightly cleft chin suggestive of a Florentine statue, a smile that seemed illuminated from within, a youthful charm that only underscored his physical gifts. He was a perfect forty-two-regular who always laughed uncomfortably when people asked him if he'd ever modeled. Now, in his thirties, he retained the window-mannequin face as it took on a certain character, a wisdom around his eyes that made him look worldly and smart and, lately, perhaps a little vulnerable.

"It's just a separation thing," he said, smiling self-consciously.

"That's what the note said?"

"It said she needed space and time to think."

Janis rolled her eyes. She'd never really cared much for Karen, even though she knew this was born of her own lack of confidence. Dillon's wife was a little too quiet and a lot too pretty, allowing you to fill in the blanks. She made Janis face her own insecurities, made it easy to assign her own dark meaning to the aloofness.

"This isn't a surprise," he said, looking away. "The seminar . . . I thought it was a good idea, that maybe it'd help us somehow. Maybe it just woke her up."

Janis nodded, as if he'd stumbled upon a truth she already knew.

"I think she's right," he said. "Space is good right now."

"You're okay?"

"No. Yes. I'm fine."

Janis bit at her lip, thinking for a moment. Finally, she said, "Her timing certainly sucks."

"Uh-oh."

"You remember our conversation last month?"

He did indeed. Janis had dangled a long-sought-after carrot in front of him, a shot at some institutional business that would change both the pace and the potential of his career. It was a reward for those who had demonstrated a consistent ability to generate revenue for the firm, usually attained by all the young lions with fathers who were surgeons. In this business, the pace of success was usually dictated by the nature and breadth of your personal network. Dillon, on the other hand, had built his book and reached the number fourteen slot the old-fashioned way: he'd cold-called. He'd schleped.

She knew she had his attention. "The machinists' pension account popped," she said, referring to a coveted union pension fund, the management of which was spread among all the major brokerage houses. Apparently someone, somewhere, had maneuvered an undefined portion of the account toward their branch.

"I can't give it to you. Not with your head down."

"I'm okay."

"You're a lost puppy. I'm sorry." Janis paused, as if measuring his reaction to the news.

"What can I do?"

"Get some help. You're overmatched . . . she's a woman and she's pissed. She'll eat you alive, burn you down. You won't even realize you're on fire until you smell the singed hair on your ass."

"I can't tell which you hate more, men or women."

"Women are evil, men are stupid . . . it's the food chain of relationships."

She watched him think about this for a moment, then spoke in a softer tone. "Keep me posted. I can hold the account for a while, trade it myself. You'll know when it's time. So will I."

He nodded, knowing she was pulling strings for him.

"I appreciate this."

"I know you do."

He got up, smiled humbly, and turned for the door. Her eyes followed.

"How a woman could walk away from a butt like that, I have no idea."

Without looking back he grinned widely. Had he turned, he'd have seen that Janis wasn't smiling at all.

3

He hadn't planned on missing his exit. Having crossed the floating bridge into Bellevue, he was supposed to exit south onto I-405. But he kept driving east, just as he had for the past eight years. Heading home. As if no domestic hemorrhage had happened at all. Habit has no memory and certainly no pride. Or perhaps it was boldness fueled by the knowledge that it was a Wednesday night, and that Karen would not be there. She'd be at her painting class, nourishing her inner artist.

He felt his stomach twist as the garage door began to rise. He noticed the yard was scattered with debris, and he assessed the pros and cons of letting it go untended. She'd expect him to tend to it, to be the great guy that he was. The nice guy who finished last. The twist evolved into a knot when he saw that his parking spot was occupied by the bicycle he'd bought her as a birthday present a year earlier, defiantly parked squarely in the middle of his side. It was the heart of winter, and unless she had been riding the bike around the garage, this was an overt *fuck you* of the first order. He was amazed at the emotional agenda he was assigning to such things since he'd moved out.

He let himself in, immediately sensing the unique smell of their home, part bacon and part residue from last year's new carpet.

It was a modest house by young urban-professional standards, especially those of his peers. A Stepford home, Karen called it. It was the centerpiece of a cul-de-sac in a neighborhood in which tricycles and summer lemonade stands ruled sidewalks embroidered with brightly colored chalk designs. This was not the house on the water that Karen so desperately wanted, it wasn't "on some land" as she would have preferred. Her ultimate destination, her self-proclaimed destiny, was on the street of dreams. Until then it was these three bedrooms, two and a half baths, twenty-three hundred square feet of comfortable mediocrity.

A smothering quiet accompanied his slow walk through the house. Each change he noticed plunged another needle into the soft shell of his heart. A stack of mail awaited him on his desk in the den, all the bills he was expected to continue to pay. His Nautique windbreaker, normally kept on a hook in the utility room, was no doubt relegated to the guest closet. In the den, his *TV Guide* was missing from its habitual place on the coffee table. Upstairs on the wall outside of the bedroom, the picture of he and Karen arm in arm on their if-you-could-see-me-now honeymoon cruise had been taken down. There was just a bare nail from which he could not remove his eyes.

Somewhere in the distance he heard the muted sounds of the garage door opening. He recognized an overwhelming urge to bolt down the steps and out the front door before she came in. But he stood his ground, not sure what else to feel, or where else he might go.

"**HELLO?**" Her voice rose to him in a lighthearted note, as if the world were normal and his being here were just another night. He said nothing in response.

He could hear her setting groceries on the kitchen counter, the clanking of keys, the rustling of her coat. He could hear footsteps on the hardwood in the entry hall directly below the stairway landing on which he stood, his heartbeat shaking his entire body.

He looked down at her. She had her hands on her hips, looking back up at him, forcing a smile. At least it was that, more than he expected from her at this first meeting of their eyes as a separated couple. It was as if she didn't know the honeymoon picture was somewhere in a drawer. He took note of her business attire, suddenly the consummate real estate professional. Because her new job had coincided precisely with his sudden eviction, Dillon couldn't help but resent it all, the faceless people she worked with, the very ink that displayed her name on her new business cards. He'd found himself flipping off every FOR SALE sign he'd seen since he left.

She was supposed to look harried, burdened by her new life of independence. He had pictured her that way at day's end, eyes closed, her head cradled in her hands, drawing deep gulps of air to recover from the pressure of it all. But that was Karen's gift, wasn't it . . . to always be the coolest one in the room, the perpetual essence of style and grace. Karen's greatest asset wasn't as much raw beauty as it was her formidable femininity, the subtle power of her presence. It was easy to stare at her. He had heard it so many times: "There's just something about Karen." Hers was the kind of attraction that women often noticed before men. They envied her allure, her sense of calm. It was a pure look, a soap ad in a magazine. Men sensed it, too, but only after her smile announced her easy confidence. Karen was completely without the ego that so often accompanies beauty. Her face had a somewhat pixie-like quality, a slightly turned up button nose, porcelain skin with a mother-of-pearl translucent quality. Her eyes, always the source of comment, were the color of polished sapphires in candlelight. She had changed her hair for the job—or was it for her impending singlehood?—cut from its decade-old long and lush to a fashionable shoulder-length, with just the right salon-engineered inward tuck. Shorter now, it appeared thicker than ever, as if it would certainly feel cool and liquid between your fingers. She had even dropped a few pounds. Yet her eyes, upon closer examination, betrayed a trying day, perhaps a slight lapse of certainty and comfort. But he had to look hard to find it, a mere shadow of fatigue.

He drew a very deep breath, not knowing what to say.

"Well, hello, stranger." Again he conquered the urge to charge the door and be gone. "So where's the picture?" He regretted his tone immediately.

He could see her synthetic smile melting slightly, as she considered her comeback carefully. "How are you, Karen," she parodied, "you look great Karen, it's good to see you Karen." The half smile remained, waiting to see how he'd play the moment.

It *was* good to see her, but he couldn't look for long. This was an old and oft-played tape, this need to lash out, to demonstrate that everything inside of him was hurting, and that before any honest emotional exchange, there would be an agenda of payback, the consequences of her heartlessness.

The silence lasted too long.

"If you're going to do this, I'd prefer that you leave." Her voice was controlled, above emotion. He had always thought this tone, when she used it, was more denial than expression, a refusal to get involved. But tonight she had a different power, the proverbial I-am-woman new attitude fresh from the seminar's tool chest of emotional side arms.

He nodded. "I'm sorry. Let's do this right. Like big kids, okay?" He began to descend the stairs. Her smile crept back, beginning in her eyes; she was giving him every chance. Closer now, his suspicions were confirmed—she had indeed lost weight. She'd always had a mother's body, ready to nurse and cook casseroles, despite the fact that she had never borne a child. As their neighbors would too often point out, theirs was the only childless house on the street.

He stopped at the bottom of the stairs, leaving an awkward distance between them.

"Well, come here," she said, extending her arms. He approached, noticing that her perfume had changed, already assigning it significance. He went into her extended arms, realizing immediately that his grasp was too tight, full of desperation. He could feel her start to pull away, and he wanted the struggle of holding her, wanted to show her, once again, that his pain was stronger than his command of his cool.

But he let her slip loose, moving back to arm's length.

"I came by for the mail. Hope that's okay."

She clicked right back into that business-as-usual

tone. "I'm glad you did . . . saved me a trip downtown." After a pause, she added, "It's good to see you." He had left his new address and phone number on her machine, and he took note of her reference to "downtown" as the place to reach him. He took note of everything, because everything seemed like a clue.

"You took us off the wall." His eyes flicked to the empty spot halfway up the stairwell wall.

She looked away. "It was just . . . I don't know . . . too hard, I guess."

This was so much more difficult than he'd imagined it would be. When he looked back at her, she was smiling again.

"You look good," she said.

"Eases the guilt, doesn't it? Knowing I'm not wasting away in a suicidal funk?"

He saw her rolling her eyes as she turned and walked into the kitchen. Once again his regret was immediate, the unexpected ache of a self-inflicted wound. Sarcasm, like self-pity, was a fickle weapon.

After a moment he followed her into the kitchen. She was busy unloading groceries, moving with quick, birdlike movements, the only sign of her controlled rage.

"How goes the real estate wars?" he asked, embarrassed at how contrived the question seemed. Six weeks earlier she'd received her real estate license, the culmination of an entire summer and fall of study. She'd gone after it at the urging of one of her friends who claimed to be making six figures in the luxury residential market. Pocket listings, too exclusive to even advertise. The fact that her friend brought a twenty-plus year apprenticeship to the party seemed to go unnoticed in Karen's zeal to duplicate both her level of income and, Dillon suspected, community visibility. The woman had purchased bus-stop-bench advertising all over town and had succeeded in making her face part of the landscape.

Karen turned toward him and started to answer the question, then stopped. Her hesitance was the collision of her desire to share her day with a suspicion that Dillon truly didn't wish her well in her career. In point of fact, her day had been pure hell, and she didn't really want him to know.

SHE had come close to making her first sale, a houseboat of all things. A call had come in while she was on phone duty, and because floating homes hadn't exactly been the centerpiece of the mail-order exam-prep course she'd ordered over the Internet, she resorted to inviting her supervising broker to accompany her at the showing. The man had consented eagerly, but he said he wanted half the deal if it went down. Business, after all, is business. And showing a houseboat in the dead of winter—it was unheard of and boded well for their chances. The customer—the "fish," in the words of the broker—was fresh off a divorce and had, in Karen's empathetic view, seemed so sad on the phone, so in need of a fresh start. She'd seen and heard herself in him, his need to break with the past and find a small piece of hope. Maybe find enough peace to return to the war for another, and better, try.

During the showing, at which everyone was shivering the entire time, the fish had asked if the houseboat was bank financeable. He had enough cash to avoid a loan if that would help the deal—the houseboat was going for less than a new Beamer—but would probably try for a loan soon thereafter. Before Karen could respond her broker interrupted with the calm assurance that the place was as pristine as the day it was built forty years ago, new stringers and the latest Styrofoam floats, and it would indeed be welcomed at the bank of his choice. He even used the expression "piece of cake." The broker went on to convince the fish to make the all-cash offer in lieu of another bank-dependent offer earlier that week that the seller was still considering. It was a sure way to win the deal with a short closing and be casting lures off the back porch by the end of the month.

But Karen knew something was wrong here. She had read in the listing file on the way out to the marina that a previous deal had fallen through, something about the houseboat being built on a flat deck instead of joists, whatever that meant. Her broker knew it, too, because they'd discussed it during the drive. And if there had been an offer earlier that week, then it was strange that he'd not mentioned it, because that little piece of trivia *wasn't* in the file. When the fish's question surfaced and the broker had answered as he did, so reassuring and strategic, Karen remained dutifully silent, unsure if she was misunderstanding the nuances of marine financing, or if she was perhaps unaware of some alternative mortgage source. An offer was made, a check for earnest money was drawn, hands were shaken.

Karen had her first pending deal. Or half a deal, as it were. She had made her bones, earned her chops. And she'd done it in her first week on the job.

To celebrate, the broker had insisted on a quick drink on the way back to the office at a little lakeside bistro in Kirkland. It was there, just before he suggested that she accompany him to a nearby hotel to celebrate further, that she sought clarification on the houseboat financing issue and the so-called pending offer. The broker's response was a resounding affirmation of his theory of caveat emptor—let the fish beware, especially of any my-word-against-yours assurances that would never stand up in court. It was during the silence of her confusion and emerging outrage that the hotel offer had materialized. She simply got up and walked out, stranding him there. She drove straight to the fish's apartment to return the check and tell him that there wasn't a bank in the area that would touch this turkey. Hope may indeed float, but in this case it was definitely not bank financeable.

On her way home she left a voicemail for her broker, who hadn't returned yet, tendering her resignation from the firm. She left another for the owner of the company, explaining precisely why.

KAREN returned her attention to the groceries, struggling to hold back tears that she knew Dillon would not comprehend. For now, real estate was none of his business. But the question of how her new career was going remained hanging.

"It's giving me some of what I need," she said.

"So who's giving you the rest?" Dillon couldn't help himself. He quickly covered, realizing how transparent he was. "I'm kidding. I swear to God."

She continued to refuse to look at him, so he resumed with a harsher tone, abandoning his excuse-making. He'd opened the can of worms, so he might as well bait the hook.

"What the hell do you expect me to do? Hi, honey, how's the divorce planning coming along? Found a lawyer yet? Maybe your famous bus stop friend can help you out with a goddamn loan."

Now she looked up at Dillon. Her face was different, defiant through a sudden flush. The image of the broker from that afternoon flashed before her, clicking his tongue on his teeth as he waited for her answer to his lewd invitation. For the moment she allowed herself to simply hate the entire species of penis-equipped inhabitants of the planet.

"I think it's you who's going to need a loan." She let her eyes burn into him a moment, savoring the blood she'd drawn, then returned to the groceries.

Women are evil, men are stupid . . .

It occurred to Dillon that he'd not only completely blown the evening, but that he'd also just seen the new direction of his life. He wasn't sure how to react, other than leaving without another word. When he got to the door he heard her voice, full of emotion, almost too soft to understand.

"You should have called."

He turned, seeing that her eyes were full of tears.

"If I *would* have called, you wouldn't have been here. I'll call next time." He paused, then added, "That way you can be sure to stay away."

They stared at each other for a moment before he turned to complete his departure. He hesitated at the door, not wanting to leave. He was surprised, frozen even, when he felt her hand on his shoulder, turning him, her arms encircling him as she buried her now tear-streaked face into his chest. He held her, searching for words, allowing her breathing to return to normal.

He spoke without releasing her. "I'm going to see Ben Carmichael."

Ben Carmichael had been Karen's psychologist. It had been a year since she'd been to him, and Dillon was never sure if she had been cured of her anxiety about "the baby thing" or if she'd simply abandoned the therapy. It had all seemed so absurd to him—what treatment is there for a woman who wants a baby so badly she's willing to hold her marriage hostage to it? All three of them—Karen, the doctor, and Dillon—knew it was *him* who should be in counseling.

He'd chosen Carmichael over cheaper shrinks covered by his HMO simply to please her. Such is the rationale of a man suddenly alone.

She pulled back, looked at him in disbelief. "Really?"

"I don't understand you," he said, lying. "I need to understand *this,* so I can respond to it. Certainly this all has something to do with me, and that's what I don't get. You say it's not the baby thing, so what is it? If I don't get it, then I'll just go on making it worse."

"Sounds like you've already had a session or two." A tiny grin reflected from her moist cheeks. Maybe the males on the planet had a chance after all. "Sounded pretty good, didn't it?"

"I hope he can help you."

"I'm hoping he can help *us.*"

Her smile vanished as she turned away. "When you figure out the difference, please let me know." She was back at the groceries now, moving slower than before.

If he'd triggered this sudden chill, he didn't know how.

"Is this about . . . me? I mean, you know . . . our lovemaking?"

She didn't look up. "We don't make love, in case you haven't noticed. We don't even *fuck* anymore."

It had been seven months, and he'd noticed each and every one of them. As had she. What they hadn't done was discuss it.

A decade of sexual negotiation flashed between them. Dillon had secrets, things that lived in the dark. Karen knew he was no different than most men in this regard, but somehow this was of little comfort. For Karen there was a perverse power in the denial, holding the hope of darkness hostage to her comfort zone. They had never really talked about it, only talked around it, the quiet gulf between their needs and their unwillingness to risk the other's dance.

"Are you seeing someone?" he suddenly asked, jolting her back to the moment. It took her a few seconds to comprehend the question, and when she did, she had to consciously hold back a mean little grin.

"No. This isn't *about* anyone else."

"So what am I supposed to do while you figure out the rest of our lives?"

"I don't know. Go rent *Barb Wire* again."

"I'm serious. What if I meet someone? I'm vulnerable right now . . . you should know that."

She stopped again, looking hard at him. "Is that a threat?"

"No, it's a legitimate question."

"Bullshit, Dillon. It's a threat."

He averted his eyes slightly. "It could happen."

She resumed her work with sharp little motions.

"I'm serious."

"Then I'd have to kill you." She shot him a grin. A very small, ironic grin. This, too, was an old tape between them. Karen's weak link was her jealousy. Raw, out of character, unpredictable. He couldn't look too long, he certainly couldn't say anything. It wasn't about anything he ever did, because he never did anything other than look. It was about his thoughts—she was jealous of what she was certain were his desires when a certain woman with a certain look crossed his field of vision. A woman in black. The dark stuff. She hated it because, to her way of thinking, it wasn't her. It wasn't *about* her.

She came to him again, softening, putting her hands on his shoulders. "I'm not kidding, Dillon. I don't think I could forgive you if you crossed the line. Rent your little high heel movies and go to the bars and watch the painted ladies with their menthol cigarettes . . . but don't cross the line. I mean it. I'll cut your balls off and feed them to my lawyer."

He engaged her eyes for a moment. "You know how unfair this is."

"This doesn't have to be fair. I never said that it would be fair. It just *is*. I'm asking you to give me this time and this space." A pause. "Would you give me that? Please? Without my having to worry about you being around when I finally work this out?"

She touched his face, rising up to kiss him gently on the lips. He was conscious of not kissing back, one more tiny little self-service. When she pulled away she was smiling warmly, the good Karen replacing the bad Karen one more time. The good Karen always made everything okay.

He began to move toward the door. "I should go."

Her face lit up, concerned, as if remembering something that didn't necessarily connect to him. "Jeez, so should I . . . I'm late." She immediately began to tidy up the kitchen. Karen couldn't leave the house with a messy kitchen. Not if Christ came back.

"Aren't you supposed to be painting something deep and beautiful?" It was her painting class night, her favorite night of the week.

"Class was cancelled. I'm having drinks with a friend."

This stopped him cold. He watched her put closure to the space they were in, wiping down the countertop, rinsing the sink, putting a stray fork into the dishwasher. He watched the way she moved, the sudden urgency of it.

A drink with a friend. This was something Karen just did not do. Ever. Coffee during the day, an occasional lunch, certainly the obligatory shopping trip for bonding purposes. But Karen in a cocktail lounge with a friend . . . no way.

"What friend?"

"I assure you, there are no penises involved. Didn't we just discuss this?"

"Is her face on a bus stop bench, too?"

"Fuck you, Dillon." She was almost smiling as she began pushing him toward the door. "She's helping me through this. She's been there, okay?"

She put her finger on his lips as she gave him a final playful shove into the garage. She watched him go to his Cherokee, sulking, and as he opened the door she called out, "This isn't over . . . it's just healing." A pause. "I can't make you wait and I can't give you any guarantees."

He didn't turn around, but spoke loudly: "No way I'm picking up the yard." His grin was for himself as he got into the Cherokee.

Then he remembered what night it was. Wednesday night, paint class night, the day before the morning that the garbage truck came. Like all husbands, it had always been his job to wheel the brown plastic container out to the curb, placing it next to their bright yellow plastic box full of recyclables. The job, which apparently required an X chromosome, always took two trips, sometimes three.

He thought a moment, cursed out loud, and headed back into the garage to do this for his wife.

4

Dillon Masters' journey into darkness began with the simplest of looks. Only later, alone with the truth, would he understand the irony of remembering it as an *innocent* glance. A meeting of the eyes between a man who wore his hunger like a wound and a woman who wore her power like a mask.

Just before lunch he decided to take a walk. It had been a wasted morning, his mind on Karen and the uneasy feeling that his life was at a turning point. The Dow was up nearly two hundred points from yesterday's cardiac arrest, but today he didn't care. A few clients phoned in for quotes and reassurance, which was easy on an up day. On days like this you could throw a dart and be certified a market prodigy.

He was in the designer section at Nordstrom, one

of his favorite routes in the rainy season, when something caught his eye. Something, someone, descending the escalator. It was like the first hint of an approaching storm perceived in the sudden shifting of the wind. An exquisite darkness. A woman, dressed in an ebony black leather suit, exquisitely tailored. Designer stuff from New York or Milan. The skirt hugged the legs and descended to mid-calf, the jacket was snug and accessorized with tiny gold chains and matching buttons. The jacket collar was turned high with significant attitude. Tasteful midheel shoes were accented with a tiny matching gold ankle chain, an ideal balance for the eye. Black gloves, one on, one off and carried in the same hand that held the strap of her bag.

A sensation washed over him, a palpable and familiar physical awareness that was part adrenaline, part testosterone. The rush, the familiar buzz. It was accompanied by an old anxiety, wondering what to do with the moment. Simple appreciation struggled for mindshare with hopeless temptation. The paradox was diabolical and, in his world, very female in nature—being made to want what you cannot have, the torment of someone else's reality passing so tantalizingly close, reminding you of what you cannot touch and cannot experience. Reminding you of your weakness and your need.

It was an all-consuming mind-fuck, one he had learned—like an addict who learns to love the sting of the needle—to simply appreciate for what it was: a moment of fantasy, the dark poetry of desire, with roots too deeply imbedded to be understood. The kind of moment that really pissed Karen off.

The woman was so beautiful that it hurt to look at her. She was the Dark Lady, and she was perfect.

All of this registered in a heartbeat or two, long

enough for the escalator to deposit her into the aisle in front of the cosmetics counter. She looked away from him as if he wasn't there at all.

He moved to a position behind a pillar and watched. She was across the aisle inspecting a rack of new Donna Karan arrivals, using the ungloved hand to feel the textures.

"May I help you?" The voice came from behind him, and he could feel the heat immediately assault his cheeks. His responding smile was contrived and, he was certain, unconvincing. The salesclerk was a young woman typical of the Nordstrom rank and file—sorority pretty, looking to marry money. She seemed somehow hyperaware and suspicious.

He glanced down at the counter with its earrings and gold chains. Looking back up, he saw that the Dark Lady was still across the aisle.

The clerk was staring at him, waiting. He could walk away, find another position, continue the dance. But nowhere else would he be this close, and in this game, proximity was everything.

He pointed at a pair of simple gold earrings.

"I'll take those," he said, reaching for his wallet. Guilt had a price. What it bought was a few more moments of having her in his line of sight.

The Dark Lady was drifting toward the neighboring department, her fingers lightly touching every fabric along the way, her huntress eyes intent on the next approaching rack. This was certainly a rich man's woman. Women who had their own money didn't put it on like this.

When the salesclerk handed Dillon the bag, he turned his attention back across the aisle—but the Dark Lady was gone. He scanned the radius of his vision; perhaps she'd ducked into a dressing room. Perhaps she was momentarily behind a pillar, as he had been.

His breath was short, his skin sensitized with a prickly clamminess. While this was perhaps the best and most electric visualization of his fantasy that he'd ever seen in the flesh, he'd seen others and knew this was a transitory high. The drug usually came in freeze-frames and flashes; this had been an entire short feature. It took only seconds for his mind and his heartbeat to begin its descent to reality, thankful for the hit, committing it to memory.

He turned and began to walk away. As he entered the aisle, the Dark Lady stepped into his path.

This could be no accident. She was looking directly at him. Then again, perhaps he'd stepped in front of her in such a flagrant manner that their eyes naturally locked, a defense mechanism. In either case, the lightning returned with a wave he could feel all the way to the arches in his feet.

She was removing the other glove as she looked at him, plucking at each finger and stretching the thin leather, finally pulling it off. Her hands were slender, with long, French-manicured nails and several expensive gold rings. Hands of privilege.

"You've been watching." Her voice was low, breathy, almost hard to hear. An appropriate smirk acknowledged the awkwardness of the moment.

This was too perfect. The proximity of the woman only confirmed his perception—there were no flaws, no compromises. Her eyes were virtually ablaze with ice blue secrets. She was composed of every dark thought he'd ever allowed himself, packaged within the boundaries of elegance and taste. Sharply angled cheekbones and an ever-so-slightly arched nose gave her a regal air, a look of majesty that was impossible not to notice. She was too beautiful to be over forty and too sophisticated to be younger, creating a timeless enigma that was as mysterious as it was fascinating. Her sly grin was an all too inescapable acknowledgment of what was true between them. Somehow she knew everything. And this, in an instant, made her all the more dangerous.

"I'm sorry . . . I didn't mean to be rude, I just . . ."

"I don't imagine that you were." The grin was deepening now, the eyes full of something beyond intelligence, something intimidating. She was on to him. And from the look of it, if nothing else, it amused her.

The energy of the moment forced his eyes away, and there was nowhere else to go with them other than a luxurious scan of her profile, head to toe. He had no choice. It was tunnel vision, and at the end of the tunnel was the epitome of his fascination, bathed in a soft glow.

She was expecting him to continue. Testing his next move. There were volumes and years of comprehension in the way she looked at him. Or maybe she was just sticking it in his face, this moment of acknowledging the embarrassing truth. Or perhaps it was more. He had no idea.

"I was just . . . I mean I was admiring . . ." He grinned, an intuitive self-deprecation that he knew disarmed any contrivance or perceived ego. He noticed that his nervousness seemed to please her, to change her smile to one of satisfaction. He took a breath as if to signal that he was starting over.

"You look very—"

She interrupted him with a perfectly arched eyebrow. "I know."

The smile faded as she brushed past him, her sleeve barely touching his arm, her perfume rising to confound his senses. What had been so sweet, this mist of heroin licking the open wound of his desire, now hung in doubt. She had dangled a morsel of the fantasy before him, and as his guard began to drop she snatched it away, all for the pleasure of watching the confusion in his eyes.

She had won. And yet, she had left him with something.

This was a woman who was completely, unattainably, out of his league. A woman with the promise of a very palpable and unmanageable danger. A woman with a curtain. An evil woman, in a way that men have found irresistible since Adam succumbed to Eve. A woman who dressed and acted the part, perhaps because it was the color of her nature, perhaps to lure the attention of her prey. Nothing was certain, nothing could be known, it was all his to craft and to savor. The realization gave him an incredible amount of satisfaction, the private pleasure that he'd never been able to satisfactorily explain and that no woman in his life had ever understood.

Except, perhaps, this Dark Lady herself. It had been the hit of all hits, and it had consummated itself perfectly.

5

Stockbrokers inhabit a world that hums along to the ticking of its own clock. On the West Coast the trading day concludes at the one o'clock closing bell. Accordingly, lunch in the West is customarily a one o'clock affair, with tee times and the occasional racquetball court reservation scattered from two to three-thirty. Finding a West Coast stockbroker behind a desk after three or four is as likely as someone at the DMV keeping a window open beyond his shift out of sheer commitment to customer service.

On this day, in this particular office of 106 stockbrokers, only one cubicle was occupied as the clock struck five. Dillon had nowhere else to go.

He leaned back in his chair, feet on the desk in classic tycoon style, fingers laced behind his neck. His line of work generated very little paper. Everything was done on computer terminals and over the phone. What paper there was consisted of analyst reports and magazine articles, both of which facilitated a sort of broker-speak designed to convey the illusion of fluency and inside knowledge about the companies and industries being pushed this week. So while Dillon did, in fact, have a copy of *PC World* squarely in front of him for appearance's sake (most of the brokers here in Microsoftland kept an eye on all the in-vogue high-tech companies), his eyes were glazed, staring straight ahead. On his desk was a picture frame containing two photographs of Karen, one showing her perched on the stern of their twenty-foot Wellcraft ski boat, the other one of those contrived studio glamour shots with Karen coyly clutching the collar of a fur coat with black gloves while wearing too much make-up. That had happened years ago, before black gloves became somewhat of an issue in their relationship.

His telephone rang, jolting him back to the quiet reality of the office. The switchboard operator, who worked until five-thirty, must have remembered he was still there and forwarded the call.

Nobody called at this hour. It just wasn't done. He snatched at the phone, for a moment tempted to answer with something such as, "Dillon's House of Self-Pity . . . whatever it is, it's our fault."

"Dillon Masters."

A woman's voice echoed him. "Dillon Masters."

A moment of silence. He didn't recognize it. Then she went on.

"So you really do something besides cruise department stores looking for women in black leather." This definitely wasn't Karen. This voice was deeper, a sly sneer in it.

"Who is this?" he asked, trying for a nonconfrontational tone.

"Tisk tisk . . . if you can't keep up you might miss the good part."

"So far I like the voice." He did indeed. It had a smoky timbre, a confident sophistication as it toyed with him.

"You liked the outfit, too," she said, softer now. As if delivering on a promise, after making you squirm. It was all too vaguely familiar.

It was her. The tone, the moment, the subtext. The Dark Lady.

"I don't believe this."

"It's virtually impossible, no?"

"How did you—"

She interrupted him. "Scary, isn't it?" A moment passed.

"Very."

A little chuckle. "Don't be too afraid. I know the girl who sold you those awful earrings."

"So who are you? What's your name?"

"Perhaps you should be as resourceful in finding out what you want to know."

"I'll keep that in mind," he answered, immediately regretting it, hoping his voice didn't betray the sudden activity of his glandular system.

"Are we married, Dillon Masters? Or just divorced and full of raging hormones and a few nasty little fixations?"

"I'm surprised you didn't notice the ring."

"You assume I was looking at you closely enough to notice a ring."

"You didn't call because you weren't looking." Dead silence. She was good at this.

He said, "I'll lie, if you want me to."

"Don't ever, *ever* lie to me." She spoke the words slowly, one at a time with a staccato emphasis and a not-so-subtle bitchiness.

He realized she was waiting for his answer.

"We're separated."

"Then you're a bad boy, aren't you?"

"Is that good or bad?"

"Bad can be good, don't you think?"

He wondered if she was smiling, too.

"You sound like an amazing woman."

"I know." It was a whisper. He remembered her saying it that afternoon.

He closed his eyes and drew a deep breath, savoring the moment. He had no idea where to go next, how to finish big. He could tell that she sensed this.

"So now what?" he asked, trying to sound light, failing at it.

"Maybe I'll call," she said with yet another tone change, this time more businesslike. "Maybe not."

The diabolically slow clicking of the receiver was followed by the coldness of the dial tone. Dillon pictured her face, imagining a slightly frightening satisfaction in her dark eyes.

He stared at the phone for another ten minutes, hoping she might call back. His appetite was gone, replaced by chaos. She had seized his evening just as she had devoured his afternoon. All, apparently, quite by design.

This sensation, this being in her power with no clue as to what might happen next, was ecstasy.

6

Dillon was asleep when the machine gun opened fire. He was fully dressed and lying on top of the covers, and they were coming for him. He started to scream before suddenly realizing where he was, here in his colorless room at the Residence Inn, the silent television displaying a weather report under the word mute in red letters. The machine gun sound, even louder now than it had been in his dream, was in fact an enthusiastic and insistent pounding on the door.

It had been an evening spent in a special room in hell, where the house drink is labeled Anxiety. Dillon had dialed his home number too many times, never leaving a message on what was now *her* answering machine. He imagined her "out" with this new friend of hers, probably some bitter middle-aged woman with an expensive boob job and a discreet tuck or two, a survivor of two messy divorces that she loved to discuss over a glass of white wine. She was no doubt providing Karen with the name of her attorney, a domestic assassin who could and would, for a ten-grand advance and the promise of a referral, carve the very heart from a disenfranchised spouse and rent it back to him.

The telephone still rested on his abdomen. With the sweep of an arm he sent it to the floor, where it landed, he noticed with some satisfaction, on top of the Nordstrom bag containing Karen's new earrings.

The pounding continued. Dillon opened the door to see his friend Jordan Chapman standing there with a wild-eyed grin. Jordan was still in his very lawyerlike Perry Ellis suit, desperately clutching an open bottle of Chivas.

"You miserable lonely fuck," Jordan said, bursting inside, putting his arm around Dillon's shoulder. He smelled like a drunk man. "You look like hell. No, you look like shit."

When they had spoken earlier that day—one of their regular "checkin' in" calls after several weeks with no contact—Dillon had confessed his new residential status and the surprising circumstances of his suddenly impending bachelorhood. Jordan was well aware of the back-story leading up to this announcement, and his opinion of Karen's search for herself was a mixture of cynicism and uncompromised condemnation.

"Do you know how long I've been waiting for this night? You and me, out there trolling the great sea of opportunity in a noble quest to stamp out the reported outbreak of sexual frustration that threatens the city's most beautiful women? Shit, this could put an end to the go-ugly-early syndrome forever, I swear to God!"

"The what?" Dillon couldn't help but grin at Jordan's little routine.

"The go-ugly-early syndrome—saves time and dollars, my friend. Believe me, I know. But with you as bait, forget about it. We just sit back and wait for the trophies to swim on by."

Dillon knew precisely what Jordan was referring to, and it made him smile sheepishly. Jordan had for years been a poster boy for the terminally single. He had been married in his early twenties for the humiliating span of eighteen months, something of which he never spoke. Now, like Dillon, he was somewhere in his midthirties and, unlike Dillon, still *out there*. There had to be a name for it, this eternal search for the perfect woman using imperfect criteria and less than noble means. The Asshole Syndrome. The Pathetic Lonely Bastard Syndrome. The Male Pig Syndrome. Something.

Jordan was the Cal Ripkin of bachelors, never missing a night, with a significant batting average over the years in clutch situations. He was fond of saying that he was looking for a *real* relationship, something that would last, say, three or four months. It wasn't his looks that kept him in the game; there were no bedroom eyes, no perfect chin. Jordan was pudgy and a natty dresser, with a frisky beach boy haircut and an infectious grin that had gotten him out of more than one jam. He was the master of the quick comeback, a poet at crafting a strategic line that contained just the right spice of self-consciousness. His money didn't hurt his game, either. He had founded a modest corporate law practice (having been let go as an associate from one of the city's old money firms after being told he wasn't partner material), which had gravitated toward matching rather high-risk real estate deals with surgeons and mid-level executives impatient with their retirement programs. He liked to tell Dillon that he was providing a valuable service to the community, something that Dillon and his stuffy investment outfit could not—a legitimate shot at a financial home rum. He drove a jet black Lexus with plates reading LAWMAN, which always drew attention, if not approval. He and Dillon had met in their twenties playing city league basketball, and had hit it off over half a decade's worth of pitchers of microbrew after the games. When the knees went, the friendship and an underlying barter of legal and market expertise remained.

The running joke between them concerned Dillon's looks. Jordan realized that Dillon honestly wasn't aware of the attention he received from the opposite sex when he walked through a crowded lounge, the way the women stopped moving and then whispered to each other. But Jordan was keenly aware of it. He assured Dillon that he didn't have to say a thing, just stand there and flex his jaw muscles in deep contemplation. Jordan would handle the witty social logistics. Together the two of them would conquer the night.

It had been a joke, a game played over beers. Dillon was married, was happy about it, and Jordan's complimentary taunting was his way of keeping a slice of Dillon for himself. Hell, Jordan was more acknowledging of Dillon's killer mugshot than Karen was. But tonight the joke was center stage, and Jordan wasn't taking no for an answer.

"We're goin' out, pal. You and me. Batman and fucking Robin."

Dillon, though smiling, was shaking his head. "No way."

Jordan was already going through a stack of Dillon's clothes, which were tossed across the back of a chair.

He held up a pair of moderately wrinkled Dockers and a polo shirt, and tossed them to Dillon.

"Add a sport coat, nobody'll know you're clueless." When Dillon started to protest, Jordan added, "Nolo contendere, compadre."

Dillon looked up at the ceiling in thought. Karen wasn't home. He was certifiably hungry, now that he thought about it. Jordan's smile was full of mischief and promise, and once they were hunkered down over two cold beers he'd offer a willing ear to bend when Dillon needed it most. And, from the visual perspective, there were always attractive women where Jordan ended up. Maybe a pretty face and a hopeful smile was just the thing.

He'd go. For all these reasons and simply for the hell of it.

JORDAN was the consummate player. He had different bars for weeknights and weekends, even different ones for daylight hours versus night. In the car on the way to Jordan's favorite weeknight haunt, Dillon found himself talking not about Karen, but about the mysterious woman he had come to call the Dark Lady. Jordan knew enough about Dillon's particular tastes to appreciate the attraction, but they'd never acknowledge the real crux of it, the heart of this darkness. As a rule, men just don't go there.

"I dunno," Jordan said, shaking his head after listening to Dillon relay the details of the Dark Lady's surprise call that afternoon.

"Don't know what?" Dillon had expected more of a "Go get her, cowboy!" response from his friend.

"I'd watch my ass if I were you."

"I intend to."

Jordan gave Dillon a quick look to show that he wasn't joking around. "You've got enough headaches with your wife, pal. There's plenty of time to get your heart broken all over again after she's eviscerated you. Maybe you should just get your pole polished and leave it at that."

"You haven't seen this woman."

Jordan was shaking his head. "Oh, yes, I have. I have her card in my Rolodex. Says her name is Trouble."

"Maybe that's the juice."

"Gee, do you think?" Jordan's grin was back; he knew the basic outline of Dillon's leanings towards the darker side of femininity. "You're a sick fuck, you know that?"

Dillon nodded. They drove on in silence for a few minutes, winding toward the waterfront and its famed restaurant row near the locks. Dillon was regretting telling Jordan anything about the call in the first place.

Jordan broke the silence. "You've got to promise me something, okay?"

"Please don't tell me to use a condom."

Jordan smirked. "Friends don't let friends fuck without a condom, okay?" He glanced over, just to make sure Dillon was in the moment. "You'll keep me posted? Every sick detail, right down to the handcuffs and candle wax, capiche?"

"Capiche, counselor." Dillon flashed the smile Jordan was waiting for.

"You fucking stockbrokers," said Jordan, "you guys get all the skirt."

THE bar was crowded for a Tuesday close to midnight. It was one of those bars for the upwardly mobile, a line of valet-parked egomobiles backed into spots near the entrance. Inside, an experienced eye could easily tell the posers from the players. The geeks and newbies regarded each new entrant as if they were filling out an evaluation form. But the serious catches, female and male alike, were too busy to look, intensely exchanging raging opinions on the economy or the election or why the hell did they let Griffey go, all shouted over vintage 1980s rock. In a city known for its alternative music scene, this was the full circle antithesis. This was where you went to be seen, yet the coolest of the cool pretended not to look.

Dillon leaned against the bar and watched, sipping a Pellegrino. Maybe he'd try a beer later, but he wasn't sure if he was in this for the long haul or not. The tableau before him was surreal, like turning on cable television in the middle of the night. Jordan had disappeared to sign in with some old nocturnal acquaintances, leaving Dillon on his own to behold what he feared might be his future. He was a tourist here, and he desperately needed a map. Yet there was so much to see, women who in another time might have spiked his libido. Here was the heart of Sodom and it was girls' night out, and they were working hard to meet a man who had just taken his dot-com public and wanted to party.

A voice startled him. At first, through the din, he wasn't sure if the words were intended for him.

"You look a little lost," the voice said, a little louder this time.

He turned to see a woman standing next to him, grinning a touch too eagerly as she held the rim of her glass against her lips, leaning in slightly to be heard. She was not attractive enough to simply wait at her table and field inquiries, but she had confidence, and confidence held its own brand of appeal. She had short red hair that made her look younger than she was, huge earrings, and slightly glazed eyes that said she'd been here awhile. Dillon could imagine her working for the utility company, somewhere deep in the bowels of accounts payable.

She was trying very hard and he liked her for it, for seeking him out. He wanted to find a way to flirt back, make her feel attractive. To play this game.

He mustered a smile. "That bad, huh?"

"Not bad, not good. Just obvious."

He nodded, sipped his water, tried to think of something clever to say. He had the momentary notion to offer her a drink, as if it was the next line in this one-act play, but stopped short of that embarrassment. The woman was just starring at him, her grin a contrivance, challenging him to engage. But his mind was blank, and he could feel the heat building in his cheeks.

"You don't do this, do you?" she said.

"No." He gave her his best caught-in-the-act smile.

"You get used to it."

"I doubt that." His eyes assured her he meant no disrespect.

"You're very pretty," she said.

He paused. The woman had balls. No, the woman had consumed four margaritas. "Thank you. So are you, by the way."

"Touché," she said, reading regret in his delivery. She pretended to survey the room for a moment as both of them let the awkwardness pass.

"Would you care to join my friend and me?" She motioned with her eyes to a table. Another woman sat cross-legged, watching them, smiling shyly. He acknowledged the smile with a subtle nod.

"Well, uh, gee . . . I, uh . . . no, thanks." He watched

her smile melt. "It's not you . . . I mean, I'm here with a buddy, and . . ."

"I know what you mean." Her smile vanished instantly as she spun and worked her way back through the maze of tables. He saw her lean down to her friend, who listened for a moment, then shook her head. A wave of nausea crested, sending fingers of ice up his spine.

To make matters worse, he noticed a woman sitting alone near their table, watching him. She had observed the whole sorry moment, and now she was laughing to herself in a way that told him she wasn't here to participate in that level of the game. She was more mature than the others, with stylish short blond hair, an air of money about her. She looked away, avoiding his eyes, freezing him.

Jordan found him like that, cocktail in hand.

"Eyeballs back in, slick. You look like a divorce hit and run."

"I feel like an asshole. I *am* an asshole." Jordan followed his line of vision to the two tables, the one with the two women and the one with the classy woman. A guy was standing next to the two women now, and both of their smiles were pasted back in place.

"We're all assholes. This is an asshole bar. You got your gay bars and your cowboy bars and your Seahawk groupie bars—this is an asshole bar."

Dillon sipped his mineral water and watched Jordan evaluate the landscape, his head bobbing slightly to the sound of an old UB40 tune. It was definitely too late for go-ugly-early.

"You know what I think?" offered Jordan after a moment. "I think what we have here is a textbook midlife."

"Mine or yours?" shot back Dillon.

"Karen's."

Just then two new women walked directly in front of them, weaving through the bodies crowded before the altar of the bar.

"Check it out," mumbled Jordan, barely moving his lips.

Dillon could smell their perfume. These two were not at all like the woman he had snubbed; these were roster players, certified centerpieces. One wore a soft leather miniskirt that hugged her hips deliciously, the other a skintight little black dress. They were so conscious of being watched, so committed to not noticing that they appeared angry, like models on a runway. Attitude was a fragrance—put on too much and you spoil the effect. Get too close and your eyes just might water.

Jordan continued to mumble with minimal movement of his mouth. "What you need, my horn-ball friend, is one of those. Preferably both of those."

Dillon watched the women retreat, appreciating the moment. When they were gone, he continued to stare at the point at which they were swallowed by the crowd.

"Women like that," he said, "always seem to belong to someone else."

As he said it, he noticed the classy woman with the short blond hair, who once again had observed the way he had reacted. And again, her expression registered an amused disapproval as she quickly averted her eyes.

As Dillon and Jordan were leaving the bar, Jordan suddenly announced he forgot something and bolted back inside. Dillon waited at the edge of the parking lot for fifteen minutes, looking across Puget Sound, wondering if he should call a cab. It had rained earlier, and anyone with a clear head could smell the sea.

When Jordan finally reappeared, his face pink and his step cautious, Dillon knew he'd downed another drink. He held out his hand for the car keys, which Jordan had picked up from the valet stand near the door. Dillon led the way to the car, then opened Jordan's door and helped him in. Once inside, Jordan cranked the CD player to code-exceeding proportions for a moment, then turned it back down.

"You are the designated fucking driver of the decade," he slurred.

Dillon backed out, sorry that he'd come.

Jordan was amused with himself. "I never throw up in my own car, so you can relax." A pause, then: "If this was your car, I'd hurl. I'd fucking yak."

Dillon looked over at his friend, who was waving goodbye to the leather mini and the little black dress as they crossed in front of them. They looked away quickly, as if what they'd come to find—a party, some coke, a guy with fuck-you money and a hard-on—hadn't materialized inside, and damn sure wasn't going to happen here in the parking lot. Jordan chuckled, lowered the window and yelled, "Fucking bitches!"

As they drove out of the lot and turned onto the deserted street, Jordan slapped Dillon on the knee. "This singles' shit—it's the fucking best, isn't it?"

Jordan slept on the couch in Dillon's room that night, too sick to drive home. When Dillon's alarm went off only a few hours later, he was already gone.

7

They were several minutes into the session before Dillon took a really good hard look at Dr. Benjamin Carmichael. He wasn't sure if the man was a psychiatrist or a psychologist, nor was he sure he knew or cared about the difference. Either way the man was Karen's shrink, and this was why he was here. It would please her.

Carmichael was in his early fifties with a head completely devoid of hair. His scalp looked moist, even greasy, as if a fresh sweat had just emerged. Dillon wondered if this sheen required a daily shave. Carmichael wore his glasses halfway down his bony nose, a pair of frontier-era reading specs that conveyed a very professorial air. Khaki slacks were worn over spanking new Nikes (a strict Karen fashion no-no), and Dillon wondered if Carmichael was indeed a runner or just a fashion disaster. His was the face and neck of a veteran distance man, a fast-forward metabolism and a wouldn't-quit-if-I-was-vomiting-blood competitor hiding behind colorless gray eyes.

"Tell me what was so perfect about her," Carmichael said without looking up from his notepad, which after ten minutes was still blank. Before this question they had been chatting about Karen, about the black-and-white nature of their separation and Dillon's sense of losing control of his life. Dillon had recalled as much of the dialogue as he could, filling in with what he realized was his own armchair analysis. For the past several minutes, coprocessing with the story, he'd been inspecting Carmichael and his tiny office. It was on the twelfth floor of an old building, complete with a classic pipe radiator and no view. There were two leather chairs—he was surprised and disappointed to find no couch upon which to recline. The leather on the arm rests was slightly discolored under the pressure of decades of confession. There was a rather unremarkable end table next to each chair, one of which had a fresh box of Kleenex on it. On the doctor's side of the room was a cheap digital clock. On one wall hung a pastel watercolor print of flowers, and on the other a framed poster showing the Bridge of Sighs in Venice. In the corner was Carmichael's desk, behind which were mounted several diplomas and certificates.

The session had opened with the doctor asking Dillon what he had on his mind.

"Well, there is something," he'd said, trying for a smile. The doctor's eyes were waiting. "I trust everything we say here is confidential? Doctor-patient relationship kind of thing?"

Carmichael didn't smile back. "Nothing we discuss

will leave this room. And for the record, nothing that Karen and I discussed last year will be revealed, except for purposes of context or when I feel it will move us forward without compromising her privacy."

He wondered what this meant, what little secrets they had shared. The thought passed quickly, and he proceeded to tell Dr. Carmichael about the coincidence of meeting a woman who had seemingly stepped right from the sticky pages of his most private, unspeakable thoughts.

And that's when he'd asked what was so perfect about her.

"There are a lot of answers to that, I think," he said.

"Choose one." Carmichael was writing something now.

"Her eyes." The image came to him. "Her knowing that I was looking at her, knowing what I was thinking."

"I see." Carmichael wrote. "What else?"

Dillon shifted in his seat, realized he was frowning now. "Did Karen tell you about our sex life? I mean about me . . . what I . . . *like?*"

"Your tastes in women, or the things that turn you on?"

"Aren't those the same thing?"

Carmichael didn't look up from what he was writing. "Not always." This was followed by a moment of quiet. "What else about this woman?"

"The way she was dressed. Definitely that."

Carmichael only nodded slightly, writing it down. Dillon felt he was expected to continue. He described the leather outfit in some detail.

When he was done, Carmichael gave a small nod. He'd been studying Dillon while he talked, as if looking behind the words. Then he began to write again.

Dillon went on, nervous now. "It was the whole image, I guess. I could psychoanalyze it for you if you want, but then you'd have to pay *me*."

Now Carmichael looked up, pressing the end of his pen against his lip, his eyes continuing to travel toward the ceiling. "Why do you think you're drawn to these images of femininity?"

"Aren't most men drawn to femininity? I mean, most straight men?"

"You don't need to convince me of your heterosexuality."

"I wasn't." A moment. "Was I?"

This one finally caused Carmichael to crack a minuscule smile. "I was referring to these darker images of femininity. To these classic erotic icons. We sometimes refer to them as fetishes, but that's a nebulous term."

They locked eyes. Dillon got the feeling that nothing he might say in this arena would be remotely creative or new. The thought made him relax. He was in the company of a veteran who'd heard it all before.

"You think there's a connection here? I mean, with Karen?"

"The road to understanding has no map. You try a street, see where it takes you, turn around if you end up going in the wrong direction. Some of the streets are scary and dark."

Dillon slowly nodded, realizing there would be no quick diagnosis today. Not before a thorough tour of the metropolis of his mind.

"Our fantasies are the windows to our soul," said Carmichael.

"I'm here to save my marriage. Throw in my soul, I'll take that, too."

Carmichael nodded slightly as he jotted more notes.

Dillon wondered what could be remotely noteworthy in what he'd said. After a moment Carmichael continued speaking without looking up.

"We'll come back to this. We should talk about your mother. That's always a good starting place. . . . I bet we'd find a dotted line somewhere."

"Dotted line to what?"

"The way you feel about women. Which is an important factor in your marriage to Karen." He looked at Dillon. "Wouldn't you agree?"

Dillon nodded with one of those you-got-me-on-that-one grins. But Carmichael wasn't giving up his own smile easily, reciprocal or otherwise.

"Did Karen ever play out these fantasies with you? For you?"

Dillon hesitated before answering, a thin library of choices flashing through his memory. Of course she'd tried, especially at first. In fact, in the first few years she'd wear anything he'd wanted to bed, usually with a self-conscious obligatory joke, then with an even more self-conscious this-is-crazy attitude that threw the proverbial bucket of ice water on the whole affair. Each time it had been *his* idea, *his* selection, and he quickly realized that his appetites, his desire to make the fantasy real, were growing stronger from starvation rather than proximity. All he wanted was to taste her power, to bask in the heat of her sexual greed. It took more than a fashion show, and he could never make her see it.

"It isn't as good if you have to ask." Dillon looked away as he answered, his voice slightly lower.

Carmichael wrote for the longest time. Finally, he said, "You want her to read your mind."

He could feel himself nodding slightly. "She knows. You don't live with someone and not know."

"Maybe she felt the same way . . . that you didn't know what she needed."

Dillon thought for a moment. "Are you suggesting she asked me to move out because of my needs, or because I didn't know about hers?"

"Interesting question, isn't it?"

"Not particularly."

"Let's assume the former, that it's your needs that are the problem. We'll come back to the other."

This, Dillon sensed, was a flyer, one that grossly missed its mark. He'd stopped the sexual campaign several years ago, signing out his secrets to the unanswered yet uncompromised visualizations of his mind. It was easy to do, because his imagination offered so much more than Karen's tentative playacting.

Carmichael shifted. "Sometimes things like that fester, you know. It's a seed that grows into something that no longer resembles what you perceived it to be, and it affects behavior in ways that you neither recognize nor understand."

"Dotted lines and side streets," said Dillon, smiling self-consciously.

Now Carmichael almost grinned back. "Precisely."

"You tell me."

"Tell you what?" asked Carmichael.

"Which one it is. If she booted me for my shit, or for hers. I mean, I certainly can't see it, either way. Maybe you can." Dillon frowned as he spoke.

Carmichael's eyes went to the ceiling again. Then he said, "It's been over a year since I've spoken to Karen, if that's what you mean."

Dillon nodded. A side street ending at a brick wall.

"I think this has more to do with her than it does with me." He realized as soon as he'd said it how naive this sounded. "I'm not in denial or anything . . . it's just that there's a bunch of stuff going on for her that I don't think I can change, or that she really wants to share with me. What's behind that, I have no idea."

"The baby thing?" Carmichael said it quietly.

Dillon's eyes drifted to the window. Six feet across a twelve-story abyss was an aging gray brick wall. This was her Pandora's box, the cracking open of which was one of the things that had driven Karen to see Dr. Carmichael in the first place. It was the classic paradox—Karen's maternal clock was exploding in a rage of impatient hormones and fear, while Dillon was clinging desperately to some testosterone-induced resistance to growing up. He'd said it was his career, but they both knew this was bullshit and for the past two years had directly avoided confronting the truth. Dillon just couldn't do it. Without an explanation, his resistance forced a wedge into their relationship that grew through the years like the child they'd never had.

"If you mean has she been on me about it again, the answer is no."

"I see."

"Maybe she just doesn't love me anymore." Dillon raked his fingers through his hair, realized he was perspiring slightly. "People change. They get older, they get crazy. They get . . . honest with themselves."

He watched Carmichael writing notes and took a deep breath.

"She went to one of those seminar things," said Dillon.

Carmichael looked up, his interest obviously piqued. "What was it called?"

"I don't remember. But nobody was wearing pink robes or anything."

Carmichael nodded, wrote something down. Then said, "You think something happened there that broke the dam?"

"I think that's exactly what happened."

"Whether it was the seminar or not, if there was enough pressure building to cause this, it would have happened sooner or later."

"So a refund is out of the question then?" Carmichael grinned without looking up from his notes.

"There's something only counselors and divorce lawyers seem to understand. It's the key to understanding what Karen is going through."

"What is it, for God's sake?"

Carmichael looked up and slowly, almost smugly, removed his glasses, full of himself, as if he was about to slip the key to life into the door of the future.

"Men leave women for other women. Women leave men for another way of life."

8

The boy was six when it happened, an only child. He awoke in darkness to a symphony of shattering glass. A still moment passed before he heard their voices. His hand searched along the bedspread for his stuffed panda bear named Sammy, which he found and pulled under his chin and listened to words a six- year-old boy should not know. The sound of hearts broken too long ago to ever mend yet far too weak and codependent to ever part.

After a few minutes the boy swung his legs to the side and padded from his room into the stairwell, protected by shadow as he crouched behind the bars, a tiny face framed like an inmate, watching without knowing that tonight his world was about to shift on its fragile axis.

He saw his father lying on the sofa, eyes clamped tightly closed, a hand covering his eyes. A white strip of plastic from the hospital was still wrapped around his wrist. Thirty-three surgical stitches were still raw and oozing on the back of his neck, the result of a fusing of two herniated disks.

The television was on. A man called Palladin was squaring off in front of the saloon with an unshaven cowboy. What used to be a familiar glass ashtray lay in scattered pieces before the hearth. A haze of smoke hung in the air.

His mother was standing over his father, hands on her hips, bending low. The boy imagined that his father could smell her breath, and the thought made him shiver. She was shouting thick words and jabbing her fingernail into his father's chest. Her other hand held a glass that splashed brown liquid onto his father with every joust. In the same hand was a cigarette, the too-long ashes destined to fall at any moment. His father began swiping up at her with his arm, screaming, "Just shut up, please, for God's sake just get out of here!" at the top of his lungs. His voice didn't boom tonight like it usually did.

His mother was a tall woman with jet black hair that never changed its form. She had cold dark eyes that pierced him and made him want to look away. Her swollen red lips left wet smudges on his face when she kissed him, which she did a lot. He hated it when she kissed him, mostly because it was always wet and her lips were cold, like a dead person's, and she smelled like medicine and cigarettes. She had a yellowish nicotine hue about her, every pore oozing the scent of something sour and foul.

Suddenly everything stopped. His mother had said

something that made them both freeze, some unspeakable violation now spoken. She began to smile, as if realizing she'd stumbled across an elusive raw nerve. His father was gazing off into space, totally motionless. The path of a tear appeared, reflecting the television's light. His mother began to laugh now. As she took a swallow from her glass, his father awkwardly tried to sit up as he lashed out with his arm to backhand the glass away. She blocked the advance with her arm while stumbling backward, and his father, with the thirty-three stitches and the fused disks in his neck, fell face first across the coffee table in slow motion, crying out when his chin hit the floor with a thud that would echo for decades.

The boy would remember everything about this moment, the smell of the room, his father reaching back to clasp his neck, the sound of his moaning, his mother stooping low to say something else, her face boiling with slobbering glee. He would remember the cigarette ash dropping into his father's hair.

She turned toward the stairs, seeing her son there behind the bars. As she approached, her steps slow and unsteady, he was praying that he wouldn't have to feel the cool stickiness of her cold flesh, that he wouldn't have to smell her.

She sat down on the stairs and pulled his head tightly to her breast and began stroking his head slowly and rhythmically. The odor was suffocating, stale perfume mixed with the sharp scent of bourbon. Yellowed fingernails tracing ever so lightly across his face, sending shivers up his back. She tugged his Sammy out from between them and cast it aside. The dry black eyes looked back at his best and only friend and pleaded helplessness. A Pall Mall commercial played, a gentleman holding a lighter for an elegant lady with full red lips.

Something in the microcosmic mystery of his psyche was forever branded then and there, a million vulnerable synapses and neuro-pathways gelling in ways never to be fully understood, a doorway of darkness pushed open and inviting him inside with the sickly sweet scent of some urgent and primal need.

One day he would sit in an office and pay a man to ask him about this night. He would suspect but never fully understand that this was where it all began, or at least it somehow exemplified the layers of sculpted impressions that would combine to mold the lens through which he saw the world.

He would pursue it, but he would never quite be one with it.

On this night he knew only that he wanted his mother to go away, that he wanted her to be dead, that he wanted to somehow help his father struggle to his feet but was too afraid and too unsure to move. Instead he cried himself to sleep in her unyielding clammy arms, breathing through his mouth.

9

The day after the appointment with Dr. Carmichael went slowly. Other than a tasty buy order for a balanced-growth mutual fund from a bargain-hungry anesthesiologist Dillon had been hounding for a year, the phone barely rang. His outgoing calls went unanswered; Jordan was out of town and Karen, whom he'd tried to reach three times, was off looking for a new real estate gig.

He left the office at three-thirty, intending to go to his athletic club, whose door he hadn't darkened in six weeks, the longest sedentary spell of his adult life. When he reached his car he immediately noticed that a note had been slipped under his windshield wiper.

It was folded once, written on expensive stock the color of mint. In thick black felt-tip ink was written:

"6:30, Ray's, near the locks, tonight." No signature. Just a hand-drawn sketch of a rose, rendered with remarkable detail. On the stern below the bud were several pronounced, sharp thorns.

RAY'S looked out over Puget Sound at the point at which the locks released an unending stream of boats venturing forth from Lake Washington. It was two doors down from where he and Jordan had partied the night before, and he entertained that this might be more than a coincidence. He'd already accepted that very little was beyond the Dark Lady's definition of the possible. His instincts, rusty as they were, told him to take nothing for granted with this woman.

He also realized that this was not a particularly wise choice for a clandestine meeting. Clients, peers, friends—hers and his—they could all be here, any night, any time. That hadn't bothered him last night, but now the thought sent his stomach into a spin. But neither the risk nor the nausea turned him back.

She was sitting in a corner by the window, looking thoughtfully out at the lights reflecting off the water. This was a dark and quiet bar, filled with a couple of parties waiting for their table and a few stag suits tossing down their day's pay. Elegant, brass-accented antique lamps on each cocktail table cast a warm glow through the room.

Anyone asks, she's a client. That would go down easy, because anyone who saw them here together would notice immediately that she simply reeked of money.

She looked up at him and smiled, the effect of which created a diametrically opposite essence from the wicked woman he'd seen in Nordstrom. He was sure he saw genuine pleasure in her eyes, not a role being played. Her smile revealed impossibly white movie star teeth framed by pouting lips painted the color of a fine cabernet. Her raven hair fell perfectly straight on either side of her face, tucked slightly inward at the jawline, very L.A., with a gothic essence. She wore a crisp white blouse that highlighted her breasts and had full blossoming sleeves buttoned tight at the wrist and the collar. The top was tucked into a pair of pleated glove-leather black slacks, which reflected the lamplight in compelling ways. The fact that she had mentioned his eye for leather and then worn it for him told him this evening had an agenda. His eyes lingered there a moment too long.

She offered her right hand up to him with an unashamedly royal air. Her skin was startingly warm and scented, and he found himself simply holding her hand instead of returning the handshake. He was tempted to bend low and kiss the back of it, a winking gesture of romantic humor with a serious intent, but decided better of it. Cool was always the wiser default posture, especially this early in the dance. She wore a gold cocktail ring that was tastefully surrounded with tiny diamonds; not so showy but definitely uptown. Her long fingernails, formerly a French manicure, tonight were a deep and dangerous burgundy matching the richness of her lips.

As he sat across from her she said, "I ordered you a drink—mineral water, twist of lime." Her own drink was a martini.

He tried to combine a smile and an expression of confusion, but failed in favor of the latter. She read the look and giggled a little.

"How could you possibly know that?"

"There's an explanation for everything, you know." She was coy, playful.

"I can't wait." He paused. "Really."

She just stared at him with a teasing expression. There was something about a woman who didn't have to try too hard, one who enjoyed knowing things you couldn't possibly know. Like the fact that he wasn't drinking anymore, other than the occasional beer with Jordan.

"You're not going to tell me, are you?"

"Call it a hunch."

He drew a deep breath, conceding the moment, diverting his eyes. No familiar faces were there tonight, at least that he could see.

"Are we a teensie bit nervous?" she asked.

"A teensie." He took a sip. "Maybe even a tad."

He watched her hands as she reached for her purse. Pulling out the pack of Virginia Slims. Shaking one out. Holding it in one hand while digging in the purse with the other, withdrawing a black Bic lighter. Handing it to him.

His stomach ignited with the flame. His fear was that his hand would be trembling when he held it for her. He'd done this so many times in his mind. It did tremble, ever so slightly, and as she cocked her head slightly to the side as she leaned in, he could tell that she noticed.

As she exhaled toward the ceiling, all style and femininity, she asked, "Do you mind if I smoke?"

He shook his head, trying for nonchalance as he handed the lighter back to her. She set it on top of the package of cigarettes and pulled in another puff.

He was writhing now. He could feel the familiar old chaos beginning to kick in. Her eyes and her smile were both fixed and distant, as if she was contemplating an abstract painting. As if she had pressed his start button just to see what would happen.

He shifted in his seat. "What do I call you?"

"You don't. I call you."

"I mean your name."

Her grin widened. "I know what you mean."

He nodded appreciatively. "You like to mess with guys, don't you?" He said it more as a compliment than an accusation.

As if his statement cued the move, she took another slow, perfectly choreographed puff on her cigarette. She took her time with it, striking a perfect balance between camp and ballet. Her eyes remained on him the entire time as she exhaled, slowly and luxuriously.

He nodded in the same way as moments before. "Yes, you do," he said with a softer voice.

She grinned her acknowledgment.

"So. You're a stockbroker and you prefer your women in black. Other than that I really don't know much about you except that you're gorgeous and you say you're separated."

The comment surprised him. In his mind this had been a one-way attraction. It had to be. She was that kind of woman. His fascination had been so all-consuming that, despite her call and her presence here, it had never really dawned on him that she might find him attractive in return.

"Thank you. You also know I like lime in my mineral water."

He took a sip, watching her smile change form again. He realized that many of her answers were in her eyes. He also noticed a significant diamond glittering from her left hand, the one with which she held the cigarette.

She noticed him looking at her ring. Or perhaps the Virginia Slim.

"We have matrimony in common," she said. She held the ring higher.

"Nice."

"It is, isn't it."

He leaned forward slightly, more focused. "Tell me about him."

"Tell me about *her.*"

Another puff. Her movements, her command of the ritual, froze him with a complete inability to tear his eyes away. Karen claimed she never understood this one, even though there was a time years ago when, as a joke at a party, she handled a cigarette with the onstage confidence and pure eroticism of a fetishist. So she really *did* know. But they never talked about it. It was one of the unspeakable things, even in its relative silly harmlessness. The bad girls were so much more interesting, and the good ones who played at being bad were even better. They made promises, they had secrets the others didn't.

"I already know about you," she said in response to his comment, using the ashtray now for the first time. "We can sit here and wonder what our respective spouses are like . . . or we can burn that little bridge right off the bat."

"Me first . . . right?"

"Dillon's catching on. That's good."

He smiled as he drained his glass, hoping the cold liquid would quench the broil in his stomach. "Well, she just passed the real estate exam and now she thinks she's Donald Trump. For some reason she's convinced that because I choose my battles, and the ones I choose aren't always the ones she would choose and are far less frequent, I'm letting the world walk all over me. She figured she might as well join the club, something about needing to respect the man she lives with."

"Don't we all," she said with deadpan sincerity.

He looked away, sorry he'd said this much. "I moved out a couple of weeks ago."

"So *are* you?"

"So am I what?"

"Letting the world walk all over you?"

He looked back at her. A breath helped him add some punch to his answer. "Respect and simply wanting someone to see the world exactly as you see it aren't the same thing."

"Your wife's a control freak."

"Aren't you all?"

The twinkle returned to her eyes. "I bet she's pretty."

"I suppose. In a wholesome sort of way."

Another puff. They both watched the stream of smoke she expelled into the air. "Well, somebody's got to do it." She watched him watch her, comfortable with it. "How about smart?"

"Getting smarter all the time. Can we adjourn to a new topic?"

A moment of quiet followed. He tipped a few ice chips into his mouth and tried to chew them without noise. He hoped he was only imagining this sudden chill, as if this little game, this meeting, was too contrived and therefore beyond any real hope of easy intimacy. Fantasy and intimacy, he had concluded, were mutually exclusive. This was the great deception, the Faustian punchline. Dillon, for all his twists and fascinations and little-boy embarrassments, wasn't interested in a fictional coating as much as a very real and very intimate exploration of things he could never admit. He wanted to embrace the ridiculous with utter seriousness.

She put out the cigarette, her eyes on the task. Dillon watched her fingers, and he thought to himself that this was precisely what the marketing boys at Virginia Slims had in mind.

"So why are you here?" she asked.

He shifted in his seat before answering, letting his eyes drift for a moment.

"I see a woman who takes my breath away. I make a fool of myself and she sticks it in my face. Then she calls me up out of nowhere and sets my brain on fire . . . like she knows me. But she can't possibly know me. I find myself thinking about her, asking questions, making up little movies in my head. I wonder what else she knows, what scary little secrets of mine are secrets of hers, too."

He waited for a reaction and was rewarded by that dazzling smile, inviting him to continue.

"And then I realize that maybe they are."

"Scary secrets are the best kind."

They locked eyes. Whatever awkwardness had been there was now gone. A barrier had been crushed under the admission of attraction and the acknowledgment of hope. The air was warm again, the game afoot once more.

Dillon spoke. "I've been walking away from opportunities like this all my life. You . . ."—he searched for the words, letting her feel his courage—"are too incredible to just let go by." His glass was empty, but he feigned a sip anyway.

"Why risk it now, if you've been a spectator all your life?"

"I have the feeling you're the personification of risk. I also have the feeling that you're absolutely worth it." This pleased her. He saw a genuine shyness fighting for airtime with a sense of victory, as if this was just the response she had hoped for as she'd slipped into her leather earlier that afternoon.

"Not worried about moving too fast, are you," she said. But a glimmer in her eyes told him he hadn't crossed any lines.

"It's really not like me," he answered, realizing how he'd sounded.

She lifted her glass, nearly empty now, for a toast. He touched his own glass to hers with slow deliberateness, keeping the rims in contact. A toast full of innuendo, like a first kiss.

"To scary little opportunities," she said, her voice lower, silkier.

She grinned at this, draining what remained of the martini. The waitress came near, and Dillon signaled for the next round.

"So why are you here?" he asked.

She gave him a look of mock disapproval, her eyes playful, unpredictable. Hidden behind the pleasure was a distinct sense of intelligence and control. "Out of sequence, Dillon. You're supposed to ask me about my husband."

"Maybe you'll tell me *his* name." His grin was mischievous, having snuck one in.

Her eyes averted ever so subtly. Apparently this was a topic that bored her. "You've heard it. He's rich, he's powerful, he's moderately competent in bed . . . really quite a nice man. We're *not* separated, by the way."

Her eyes returned and held, as if to catch every nuance of his reaction.

He held her gaze, then said, "I see."

"I don't think that you do." She looked away again. Dillon took the moment to search for the waitress, hoping for a momentary reprieve.

"What does he do?"

"In bed, or for a living?"

"Which is more interesting?"

"Depends on what gets you off."

He wondered what this might mean. "For a living," he said.

"He used to be a software prodigy. Now he acquires desperate little companies and sucks the life out of them."

"Which one of you gets off on that?"

Her eyes were suddenly intense. "I do."

The waitress arrived out of nowhere, setting the drinks down in front of them. Dillon reached for his wallet, but the Dark Lady instructed the girl to add the drinks to her tab. They both took sips, grateful for the pause.

IT lasted another thirty minutes or so. It was a conversation unique to the sexual joust, spiced with veiled hints and body language. Every eye movement and every expression was a riddle and a recipe. Anyone watching would have known this was a first encounter, seen the energy colliding in the air between them. She was a mistress of the dual arts of listening and provocation.

He told her more about Karen and their current situation. He hadn't intended to get into this, had in fact promised himself that he'd steer clear of the topic despite the natural inclination to expose these wounds. She seemed genuinely interested, even hungry for it. He got the feeling she was relating to his story of spousal familiarity and its predictable breeding of contempt. No good guys or bad guys, just two human beings yielding to their imperfections. The Dark Lady's eyes were magnetic as she listened, burning into him with a heady combination of empathy and fascination. Almost as if she were studying his words, making him feel like the most interesting man in the world. She'd shift positions slightly, holding her chin one minute, toying with her hair the next, always with what seemed to be an attentive look and an occasional nod.

He told her how changes had crept into his and Karen's life like a slow, insidious cancer. How the strong and independent woman he'd married had become isolated to a world that didn't meet her particular standards. It was her fierce independence that had attracted him to her in college—she was the vice president of a sorority she'd rejected as a freshman because she didn't believe in the politics of rush week. A profile in the student paper had painted her as a hero, an idealist, and an intellectual representative of a new student elite. The piece was so complimentary that the sorority pursued her into the next school year and virtually redefined itself around her leadership. Dillon had skipped rush himself, only his choice was born more of shyness than political bravado. He'd met her through a friend at the paper, and they'd quickly fallen into a pattern of late-night studying, political discussion, and frenzied morning sex before class. She preferred being on top, which suited him nicely. Academically she was pushing him harder than his parents or his teachers had, pushing him with her own easily intellect and uncompromising work ethic. She nurtured in him a potential he'd never acknowledged and therefore never challenged. Karen was the girl all the other girls wanted to be, and the girl all the boys simply wanted.

She continued to push him after they were married, but gradually the fierce energy of her standards took on an air of disapproval as he settled into his career as a stockbroker, a place where ethics and profits were too often a nodding acquaintance. In the worst moments she labeled him a sellout. As for Karen, her view of the world kept her from the longterm commitment necessary to a professional career of any substance. She had inexplicably abandoned her plans to become a lawyer during her senior year of college, and since then had shown no real interest in anything remotely corporate. She wanted a baby instead.

But parenthood never arrived. Her career was on permanent hold pending a call that never came. Instead there was a series of time killers and passing fancies—sponge painting, writing children's books, selling long-distance telephone cards, distributing therapeutic magnets on a multilevel plan. Instead of a career, *change* arrived, inevitable and fair, and change without conversation was a recipe for erosion. Apparently they had reached a fault line in the terrain of their relationship. A place where all the little things became land mines and the echoes of dying dreams yearned to shout and dance again.

Dillon was uncomfortable in this conversation because most of what he told the Dark Lady was a lie of omission. How could he tell her that Karen was finally stepping into the self-respect he'd denied her all these years? That the fuse he'd unknowingly lit with his own career focus, sparked by her unflagging support, had finally burned to the explosive heart of her own agenda? How could he admit that this was all his fault?

He couldn't, and still keep the evening's dance of seduction and positioning alive.

"You really are uncomfortable talking about her, aren't you?"

He suddenly wished he hadn't come at all.

She continued. "It hurts, doesn't it . . . the rejection?"

He looked away. Every time he did, he found himself

noticing how the soft light played off the smooth and buttery ripples of her leather pants. It was a safer and darker place for his mind to hide.

"There's a lot more to it, isn't there?" she asked. She was reaching for her purse, fetching her wallet as the waitress approached. The end was near.

"Not really," he said. "It's sort of sad how little more there is."

He wasn't sure that she heard this as the waitress arrived. The girl took the empty glasses and asked if the tab should remain on the card, to which the Dark Lady said no and held out two twenties. When the waitress was gone, the Dark Lady reached around and pulled her designer leather coat into her lap. She withdrew her gloves, which had been folded neatly in half.

"It's amazing how intuitive you are," he said, trying not to be too obvious that he was staring at the way she put on her gloves, that it was fascinating him.

"Isn't it," she said, picking up the innuendo and running with it. She'd caught the line of his sight and instinctively understood.

They just exchanged smiles. It was what it was.

SHE'D asked him to meet her in the parking lot, preferring that he stay at the table until she was gone. The better to witness her exit, he assumed.

She was against the side of her car, arms crossed, enjoying his approach. He had no place to hide as he crossed the open parking lot toward her. The Mercedes SL 500 was jet black, like her coat, both of which were bright with reflection from the spotlights illuminating the parking lot.

He was all too conscious of his awkwardness when

he reached her, his hands in his pockets. His stomach was twisted, pulling at his throat from below. He just stood there, waiting for something; a word, a move. For a moment all pretense was gone, the game no longer a casual amusement. He was tempted for just an instant to pull her to him, kiss her with abandon, a Hollywood kiss. Instead he grinned like a child and moved to the side. He ran his finger along the hood of the car and whistled.

"Very nice."

"Very expensive," she countered.

Her gloved hand covered his. He looked at her. The smile was gone and she was looking right into him, all awkwardness cast aside.

He turned, put his hands on her shoulders, locking eyes as he pulled her in. Her hands dropped to her sides, letting him take her with a look of amusement in her eyes. He leaned in, very close, when she suddenly raised a hand and put her leather forefinger on his mouth. She toyed with his lips a moment, her eyes darting between his lips and his eyes. He inhaled her scent, the essence of her proximity. Then, very deliberately, she took a firm grasp of his chin and pulled his mouth to hers.

It wasn't the pounding kiss he had fantasized as he'd walked toward her, but a slow dance of lips and tongue-tips lasting half a minute or so. He tried to penetrate more assertively, but she bit his tongue playfully, and he could feel her giggling. He never closed his eyes, not wanting to miss a moment of her. She tasted of gin, of smoke, of woman. He realized she'd freshened her lipstick, and it was at this moment when the electricity of the kiss set his libido ablaze. It was the first kiss he'd had in fourteen years other than with his wife, and along with his churning stomach and his emerging erection, he felt a lightness in his temples.

She pulled back enough to whisper, "My husband is afraid of the dark." Her lips brushed his as she spoke, and he could feel the heat of her breath. "Are you afraid of the dark, Dillon?"

Now she kissed him again, deeply this time. Her tongue was quick and probing and delicious, and then it was gone.

"I think maybe I should be," he whispered back.

She pecked his nose with a playful and concluding kiss, then pulled away, her expression smug and private. Without another word she opened her car door. He watched her curl into the seat, pulling the tail of the coat in behind her.

She didn't look up at him as the door closed and the engine fired with the sweet music of German precision, never looked back as she reversed into the street and then drove away. He saw her license plate and smiled. It read: HERS. He could hear his own breathing under the purr of the Benz as he watched, motionless. He had no way to contact her, would have no control over the torment of waiting for what would be next.

It was all so perfect.

10

Dillon watched the clock far more closely than the digital stock ticker the next morning. He was waiting for the rest of the world to arrive at work when Janis stopped by, asking how he was, and if there was anything she could do. He was tempted to ask about the pension fund, but it was too soon. Instead, he was too eager with his assurance that life was suddenly looking up, and her don't-bullshit-me smirk showed him she knew better.

He called Jordan at precisely nine o'clock. Lawyers' hours, nine to nine.

"How's your head?"

"Head's fine. I'm more worried about yours, frankly."

"You'll like this," Dillon said. "Things are heating up."

"The market or your sex life?"

"Our analysts have a strong 'buy' recommendation on both."

"I'm two-forty an hour, if you want to spill it."

"What I need from you is a favor."

There was the slightest hesitance. "You mean, like, for free?" Jordan held that for every legal opinion he offered he was entitled to three solid market tips, given that lawyers were worth more in this economy than stockbrokers. Dillon's usual response was to ask when was the last time you heard a stockbroker joke.

"You still friendly with those guys over at the DMV?" In addition to his real estate ventures, Jordan did a good business in whiplash litigation, for which his cultivated connections at the DMV were a solid strategy.

"Oh, shit . . . you sure you want to do this?"

"Mercedes SL Five Hundred, license H-E-R-S."

"Oh, that's cute. Wonder what she puts on her towels?"

Dillon told him what had happened, omitting certain subtleties that Jordan wouldn't appreciate. The lack of specificity, the focus on the flavor of the communication, was all in contrast to what women assumed was the universal nature of male sexual gossip. He often assured Karen that men don't fixate on breasts and blow jobs, and she assured him that this would be both surprising and disappointing news to the women of the world.

"Take it from an old country lawyer," said Jordan when the story concluded with its parking lot kiss. "A pound of flesh does not a settlement make."

"Just check the plates, counselor."

When he hung up, he realized he was feeling better than he had in days.

*   *   *

DILLON spent the lunch hour at his athletic club. It felt good to sweat again, though the scale bore evidence of the layoff. His old routine was a challenge now: forty minutes on the Lifecycle reading the latest *Men's Health* cover to cover, followed by free weights in moderation (he secretly believed the Nautilus machines were for pussies), and a few minutes of jump shots and free throws in the gym. He timed the latter for when the lunch basketball crowd was thinning, freeing up a hoop. Unlike the obligatory tee times of his peers, basketball was still his game. It occurred to him that it was nearly a year since he'd actually been in one.

In deference to the scale he grabbed some yogurt and went back to work, promising himself to never let his edge slip away like this again. And in the same thought he pictured the Dark Lady looking him up and down with hungry eyes, a woman who surely appreciates a man who takes care of himself.

Upon his return to the office the receptionist called out to him as he entered the office lobby. Sheila had been there since he started and unlike most of the brokers, he enjoyed her company. Sheila had a soul. Dillon fed her hot speculative stock tips, and she owed her IRA performance to him. He'd always wondered about her life outside of work, what a chubby but competent woman did with her time and her dreams, but he had never really inquired about either.

She was holding out a long gift box.

"This came for you." Her eyes twinkled.

Dillon took the box from her, obviously embarrassed. Sheila knew he was married, and his guilty expression made the moment unnecessarily awkward.

At his desk he opened the box, holding it in his lap so that no one could see what he was doing. Inside, he encountered tissue paper. There was no card. Pulling it back, he saw a single stemmed rose.

The rose was black, and it was made of leather.

As he climbed into bed that night he could feel the onset of the repercussions of the afternoon workout in his muscles and joints. Tomorrow there would be pain, and he would be in close communication with every major muscle group for the entire day, reminding him of his impending middle age. But tonight he wanted the pain, the ache that announced he was challenging his limits. Though he was exhausted, sleep was sporadic, not so much for his aching muscles as his nerves and his reeling mind, which broadcast a hellish newsreel of his life.

Only when the telephone rang did he realize he'd actually been asleep. Instinct made him glance at the clock—it was precisely midnight.

His voice cracked as he mumbled a hello.

A velvet feline voice responded. "The witching hour," it said.

He cleared his throat unsuccessfully. "Well, hello . . . "

"What were you dreaming about?"

"I think maybe you know," he lied. He had been dead to the world.

He could hear her small chuckle. "I have a question for you."

"All right."

Her voice shifted, lower, softer. "Do you still want to play, Dillon?"

His stomach registered an answer. It took him a few seconds. "Yes."

A few more perfectly timed seconds passed, then she

said with a near whisper, "That's good. Sleep well. If you can."

The line went dead. He kept it to his ear for at least another minute before he moved. The way she'd said "if you can" kept dripping in a dark corner of his mind like some cerebral water torture.

He didn't fall back asleep until nearly three o'clock.

11

It was Saturday. Dillon arrived unannounced at the house at mid-afternoon, but of course Karen was not there. So he'd sorted the waiting pile of mail, putting a stack of monthly bills in his pocket. He found a Seahawks special on the television—*his* television—but he couldn't keep his mind on anything for more than a few minutes. He kept hearing things, kept going over to the drapes to peek outside in hopes of seeing Karen's BMW sitting there in the driveway, waiting for the garage door to open. He did this too many times between three and six o'clock. Each time, he felt a little more foolish than the last.

He knew he should leave. But he had nowhere else to go, nothing meaningful to do. He needed to connect with Karen, check in with her temperature where he was concerned. Only in the wake of her continued coldness toward him could he justify and then pursue this thing with the Dark Lady.

At six-thirty he went out and cleaned up the lawn. It was dark outside, the winter air thick and smelling of wood fires. He took his time with it, as if lovingly tending a grave.

At seven-thirty he cracked one of Karen's favorite books and finished it by ten. His stomach was too upset for food, so he'd passed the evening in the silence of the living room, listening to the occasional creaking of a house still settling after eight years. Probably the ceiling beams adjusting to the crisp fall air. The book was about a barnstorming pilot's close encounter with a would-be messiah, written by the same guy who heard voices telling him to turn seagulls into raging spiritual metaphors, and in doing so resurrected Neil Diamond's career. Ever since, Karen had been on an eternal search for her own personal messiah, looking for love in all the wrong places. It had led her to the seminar.

Dillon threw the book against the far wall and closed his eyes.

There was so much he didn't know, didn't understand. And all of it boiled down to the simple one-word question: Why?

In his heart he knew this was a dumb question. It was more than the baby thing and the chilly sex life with its underlying divergence of appetites. It was the simple nature of boredom, an untended forest of childless domesticity left to evolve and decay. It was, in part, the predictable textbook predators of money and family. Karen spent their money with relish, as if the things she bought with the money he earned were as much his quest as hers. Dillon couldn't shake the foolish conviction that it was his money, too.

Then there were the quieter changes, dueling sets of inner demons, that had eaten away at the foundation of their marriage. It was the simple fact that he and Karen had both changed, and that those changes had different compass headings and variable rates of acceleration. He could tick them off, see the tracks of their descent into apathy. What he didn't understand and wanted to discuss with Karen tonight was how she *felt* about it all, because they had never really talked. To talk was to argue, to confront the abyss, and arguing was harder than remaining silent. So they hadn't shared a real conversation in what he recently realized was years. She had simply thrown him out when she understood she had forgotten what it was that had made her ever notice him in the first place, and then, in spite of her own whisperings, try to love him.

Neither of them were sure anymore which promises had been made by whom, much less which had gone unfulfilled. She claimed it was the seminar that had awakened her sudden and now raging independence. But in his heart Dillon knew it had never been asleep . . . it had been watching, keeping score.

He fell asleep on the couch around midnight. Any remaining self-respect had been stowed away with the lawn rake, and like a protester awaiting arrest, he would see this day through to its ugly and inevitable conclusion. He had, after all, already invested his pride in it, sold it cheap.

The distant sound of the garage door bolted him upright. It was ten after one in the morning, and Karen was finally home.

SHE was drunk. It was an easy diagnosis, even through the mist of his sleepy eyes. He didn't get up. He remained on the couch, waiting for her to come to him. She clanked around in the kitchen for a moment, a rather obvious gesture of acknowledgment that he was there, in her house, obliterating what was left of his pride. When she emerged into the dining room she cut straight across to the stairs.

"How long have you been here?" she asked without even looking at him. She was climbing the stairs slowly and carefully. Her tone was as if they'd already started arguing.

She didn't wait for his answer. When he saw the light pop on in the bedroom he followed, eager for a return on the investment of his self-respect.

She was undressing in her walk-in closet. He could smell the faint trace of smoke-saturated clothing that is unique to bars. His Karen, out drinking and smoking, carrying on, being a bad girl in the night. The irony almost made him smile.

"I thought we should talk," he said.

"I asked you how long you've been here." She emerged from the closet, walking past him without looking up, wearing only her bra and panties. She went into the toilet alcove and sat, leaving the door open. This had never happened. It was a Karen law, now forgotten.

Suddenly, as if she realized what she'd done, she reached out with her foot and kicked the door shut. He could hear the sound of her urinating, then flushing. The door opened and she marched out of the bathroom, turning off the light, leaving him there in the shadows.

The house was as quiet as a tomb.

He followed her into the bedroom. She'd flopped onto the bed, already under the covers. When he approached she reached up and turned off the nightstand light, again without looking up. She didn't move when he sat next to her, and after a few moments he wondered if she'd already fallen asleep.

"Did you drive?" His voice was soft, avoiding judgment.

"Of course I drove." Hers was impatient and too loud.

He let another quiet moment pass. It was like trying to defuse a bomb—every move had to be perfect or the ensuing explosion would send your face spiraling into the neighboring county.

"I really wanted to talk to you tonight," he finally said.

Her silence mocked him. He chuckled, loud enough for her to hear.

"I hang around here for nine hours, and now I don't know what to say."

"You're pathetic," she said wearily.

He stood up. "You're right about that."

He walked to the doorway, then stopped. She still hadn't moved, and he could only make out the silhouette of her under the covers.

"Your little strategy is backfiring," he finally said.

"My what?"

"This absence-makes-the-heart-grow-fonder, hard-to-get bullshit. This silent-treatment crap that's supposed to make me realize what I'm missing and come crashing back into your life with a bunch of promises and regrets."

He allowed her a moment to consider this, then added, "It's not working. It did at first . . . but now you're starting to piss me off."

Her voice had a fresh tone of maliciousness in it. "That's why you waited here all fucking day? To tell me what I'm not doing is not working?" She allowed a disgusted chuckle. "You truly *are* pathetic."

He felt the old rage then, the urge that always knocked but could never be allowed to enter. He clenched his fists, remembering what their first counselor had told him in those days, about making choices and listening to the voice of reason even though the screams were too loud to endure. About just turning and walking away.

He drew his breath in slowly. Karen turned over, her back to him.

"I've met someone," he said.

She didn't move. He waited at least two minutes, just staring at her form, realizing that this was it, that he no longer had choices that mattered to her. Her silence was her letting go.

He went downstairs, pausing to turn out the reading lamp in the living room before he left. At the door he stopped, looking around the house that seemed to have already changed and decayed. It was no longer his.

He kicked at the base of the brass coat tree next to the door, an absolutely necessary and nonnegotiable six-hundred-dollar concession to the last time Karen had cooked Thanksgiving dinner. It crashed to the stone floor of the entryway with a satisfying clang, coming to rest in the middle of the living room.

If the Dark Lady wanted to play, then let the games begin.

12

"How many times have you been with her?" asked Dr. Carmichael.

"Just once," replied Dillon.

Carmichael kept his eyes on his notebook, writing furiously. It occurred to Dillon that these walls knew no time, that this place was an eternal Rod Serling moment that never changed. It was as if the doctor never left, never changed his clothes or his position in the chair, his pen never running dry of ink.

"There's been a few times on the phone, too."

"Why did you cancel your last appointment?"

Dillon felt himself look away reflexively, as he always did when someone created an awkward moment. "I don't know." He was lying. He knew damn well it had to do with Karen, with rebellion. Seeing Dr. Carmichael had been about engaging, about getting Karen back. For the last two weeks that objective had diminished under the weight of his anger and the intoxicating promises of the Dark Lady's game. Engagement could wait.

"Why did you decide to come back?"

"Because I feel myself moving away."

"From the therapy, or from Karen?"

"From Karen. I still love *you*, Doctor." It was an attempt to get Carmichael to grin. It didn't work.

"Your heart is growing cold."

"Sounds like a bad song lyric." Another swing and a miss.

"Are you falling for this woman?"

"I'm not sure I'd put it that way."

"How *would* you put it?"

"I'm . . . intrigued by her."

"Intrigued by what, specifically?"

Dillon thought a moment. "By her game. By the way she plays."

Carmichael finally looked up and engaged Dillon's eyes. "She's fucking with your head, and you like it."

Dillon nodded. It was strange to hear a doctor use the term in such a clinical way.

"She likes making me react. She likes to observe what she creates."

"And you like that."

"Yeah. I like it."

"Is it what she does, per se? Or the fact that you believe she gets off on making you react to it?"

"That's an interesting question."

"Isn't it." He scribbled notes for nearly a minute before saying, "Tell me more about what she does."

"How she fucks with my head?"

"Precisely."

Dillon got to his feet and walked over to the window, with its view of the neighboring wall. If you looked to the side you could see the real world far below, the place where time ran in its logical sequence, where people hid their illogical secrets behind facades of good taste and good sense.

Dillon began telling the doctor about the calls.

THE first came late Monday, two days after Karen's big night out. Dillon had left Karen a voicemail message apologizing for the coat tree, but when she never responded he promised himself he wouldn't call again.

The Dark Lady made that promise easy to keep.

Once again, the call came precisely at midnight. He noticed the digital clock—his own, despite the fact that the Residence Inn next to I-5 provided one of comparable effectiveness—as he bolted upright, somehow knowing it was her instead of Karen.

"Miss me?" were her first words.

He couldn't believe the instant chemical reaction in his body. It began deep in his stomach, and before he could answer the electric sensation crackled across the palms of his hands.

"Of course. We need to talk."

"Really? About what?"

"About what's going on here."

"Why don't you tell me what's going on here."

"You're driving me crazy is what."

"Hmmm. I like that."

He savored the tingle, which had now spread to his lungs and was making ever inhalation thick and warm. His head was light, and he flopped back down on the mattress.

She broke the silence. "I'm calling to invite you out." Her voice was low, difficult to hear, and full of a seemingly contrived but overtly deliberate sensuality.

"Okay." His voice betrayed his eagerness.

"It's not what you think." This was amusing her.

"Of course it isn't."

"You have to watch."

"Another game? I can do that."

"You *will* do that."

"Okay."

She chuckled, then said, "I have something else I want you to do."

"Okay." He wished he could come up more scintillating banter, but she had a way of rendering him speechless, like a child receiving a scolding.

"I want you to look up a stock for me."

"Don't tell me I get to open an account for you."

"I already have a stockbroker. Two of them, in fact."

"They're not as good as I am."

"They don't have to be good. They just have to do what they're told."

"Like me."

"They're nothing like you."

"Is that a compliment?"

"Neurotronics Technologies . . . N-R-T-T."

Dillon jotted down the symbol on the notepad next to the phone.

"I'll check it out. What do you want to know?"

"The question is, what *do* I know."

"Now you're making me nervous."

"I want you to watch."

"The stock? Or you?"

He visualized her in her own bed, head back on the pillow, enjoying the game as much as him.

"Were you sleeping?" she finally asked.

"I was dreaming."

"Tell me."

"I can't remember it."

"I know people who think our lives are like that. That when you go on to whatever is next, what happens here just fades away like a dream, sometimes with a trace of a memory and a vague regret that grows fuzzier over time. Very soon it's all gone and nothing that happened here matters."

"Do you believe that?"

"No."

"What do you believe?"

"That everything matters."

"I believe that, too."

"I believe that we take every memory and every moment with us, and that whatever those memories are become our heaven or our hell."

He took that in. "You are an amazing woman."

"I'm so glad you think so."

There was an awkward pause as he scanned for something to say.

"How is it that you can call me at this hour? I mean . . . you're alone a lot."

"Who says I'm alone? Who says I'm even home?"

"I just assumed . . ."

"Never assume anything."

"I'll remember that."

"Please do."

"Then maybe your husband's asleep, dead to the world. You're downstairs, speaking very softly."

"Maybe he's on the bed right next to me, right now. Hearing everything I say to you."

The words hung, suspended, reverberating.

"Now why would he do that?" he asked.

Her voice was very low. "Maybe he has no choice."

They were dancing. "That would be quite cruel."

Her voice was nearly a whisper now. "Exquisitely," she said.

He realized his breathing was loud enough for her to hear, glad that it was.

"I want to see you," he said.

"And so you shall."

"I mean, I want to be with you. Touch you." His own voice lowered huskily. "Taste you." The rhythm of their speech was steady, like soft sex.

"It's working, then."

"What is?"

"My wicked spell."

"Yes."

He could imagine her smiling, too.

Her tone was bolder when she asked, "Are you ready for what's next?"

"That depends."

"Does it?" The question elevated and hung, and he realized from the subtle shift in her tone that his answer was important. He would either play her game or institute his own.

"You've trapped me, haven't you."

"Do you want to escape?"

He took the slightest pause, then answered, "No."

"I have a new dress."

"I'm sure it's beautiful. Let me guess . . . black?"

"I think you'll like what you see."

"When?"

"Tomorrow night. At the symphony."

"I prefer Aerosmith."

"So do I, actually. My husband has season tickets. I

do try to be a good wife, you know."

"Are the three of us sitting together?"

"Wear a tux for me. I've imagined you in one."

"I can't rent one overnight."

"You can if you want it bad enough."

"I do. I hope I can live up to your imagination."

"That's a tall order . . . my imagination is out of control."

When she broke the moment of silence that followed, her voice had changed again, more deliberate now, with a trace of humor. "He who plays by the rules live to play another day."

"Your rules?"

"There are no other."

He closed his eyes, as if she were rubbing his neck. "You're diabolical."

"I know."

The line clicked and went dead.

DILLON wasn't kidding about Aerosmith. He'd seen the band four times, but had been to the symphony only once. It was a "pops" concert dedicated to Andrew Lloyd Weber musicals that, despite the multimillion-dollar acoustics of the Paramount Theater renovated by Microsoft baby boomer benefactors, fell far short of his Michael Crawford CD from K-tel.

It felt strange to be in a tuxedo and alone. He wasn't sure if this self-consciousness stemmed from his stag status or the fact that he was one of only a few penguin suits in the place. He quickly considered that this, too, was part of her plan, her conspiracy to make him feel awkward, and this made his anxiety easier to accept in an even more twisted way. There was no sign of her before the program began. He spent the time milling about the lobby trying to blend in, recognizing several faces from his office while successfully steering clear of their line of sight. His seat was in the second balcony, far above where she certainly was sitting. He scanned the crowd, but the house lights were too low to differentiate one profile from another. Perhaps this was all another game, but without her here to observe and relish his confusion there would be no point.

She didn't disappoint. At the intermission Dillon returned to the lobby and quickly spotted her, standing with another couple in front of the bar. She was indeed the lady in black, wearing an obviously expensive gown with clean tailored lines and a scandalous plunging neckline that framed a classic strand of pearls. Her husband wore a tuxedo very much like his own rental, which he'd paid a ridiculous rush charge to get on such short notice. He was short. As a couple they looked like first-time nominees negotiating the press line at the Oscars. He had a leading man sort of presence, too—dark, a subtle Roman profile, an easy smile, and an air of complete and utter confidence. The kind of guy Dillon could like at first glance, the kind of guy with self-made money and the keen instincts of a cheetah. A hunter, relaxing tonight, sure of tomorrow's kill.

All four were drinking champagne from the cheap plastic cups common to concert hall lobbies. Dillon took a position directly in the Dark Lady's line of sight, leaning against a column as if scanning the evening's program. She noticed him right away, her eyes fingering to acknowledge him. He thought she even smiled, but she was good and quickly blended the moment into a response to something one of her companions had said. They all laughed easily, sipping their champagne. She held on to her husband's arm, and it anchored him to an old feeling, watching the girl he couldn't have with the guy he'd never be. He wondered if the gesture was for him, if she understood the impact of the pose. And in not knowing, Dillon realized yet again that this was a woman he'd notice anywhere, a woman who'd completely filled his mind and displaced whatever faceless image he'd had of his composite ideal. She was exquisite.

And now she was his playmate, his special friend with the promise of something yet to come. For once, one of the women who always belonged to someone else belonged, in a secret way, to him.

He was close to smiling at this thought when the house lights flickered to signal the end of the intermission. He held his ground as the crowd began to move, sweeping her along with it, directly toward him. She was the last of the four of them, and he could tell she was falling behind on purpose. This was it. The other couple passed, then her husband, all without a glance. Dillon looked away nonetheless. Then, as the Dark Lady herself passed close to him, she held out her champagne glass without meeting his eyes, an obvious gesture. He took it from her, amused at the way it happened, so quick and natural and without drawing attention. He held it and watched as she followed her group into the crowd toward the doors to the auditorium. She never looked back, but he knew she could feel his eyes on the bare skin of her back.

He grinned, then swallowed what remained of her champagne, noticing that the rim was smudged with her lipstick. He feigned another final sip, this time using the tip of his tongue to wipe it clean.

*   *   *

"**YOU** like the idea of being her victim." Carmichael had stopped taking notes during Dillon's story, sitting motionless, chin in hand.

"I don't feel like a victim."

"But you like the idea of it."

Dillon didn't say anything. Carmichael stared for a moment, then went on when he realized no response was coming.

"That's the real kick, isn't it, a woman who openly enjoys manipulating you, who wallows in her own power and savors your suffering like a fine wine. She's every broken heart you ever had . . . every unspeakable desire that must go unanswered in your life."

Dillon noticed Carmichael's intense staring as he talked, and that his voice was a touch louder now, with an urgency to it.

"We of the weaker sex have always been fascinated by feminine evil. The siren, the witch, the succubus . . . they lure us to our doom, we are allowed to abandon our guilt as we suffer for them. We feed their need, our pain is their pleasure, and it is in the bondage of their wickedness that we are set free, because what we see as dark in our own hearts becomes theirs. Suddenly we are without guilt or will or accountability. Suddenly, we are liberated."

Carmichael's eyes had wandered as he spoke, almost as if this were all a recital of some dark poetry, memorized and romanticized. Then, as if he caught himself, his eyes returned to Dillon.

"Nobody in my business would ever advise you to engage in an extramarital affair. You hear about it, but it's usually a lie fostered by patients lacking accountability. But I can say with some authority that the discovery of one's desire and the facing of one's demons is an exercise that can have a beneficial impact." He paused, reflecting. "Perhaps your desire and your demons are one and the same."

Dillon sat up a little straighter. "So what are you telling me?"

"When a man has a chance to save his soul, he should take it."

Dillon just stared, unsure of what he was hearing, whether he should run screaming into the flames or away from them.

Carmichael grinned a father's grin.

"This is about intimacy, and intimacy is precisely the need and the hunger that is missing from your relationship with Karen. Your fascination with this woman is as much about the hope for intimacy as it is about your sexual fantasies. Hope feeds the soul. Intimacy gives it wings."

"You should write that shit down."

It appeared that this pleased Carmichael, perhaps in a sad, small way. The misty look he had been wearing morphed into what seemed to be a memory, his eyes locked on his window with no view. Dillon wondered what images were there, what woman had shown him his own demons.

Carmichael suddenly returned to the room and said, "There is no desire as strong as intimacy. Nothing so intimate as a dark secret between lovers."

He paused, and Dillon nodded slightly. For the moment they were friends who shared the same secret.

"She's fucking with your brain, Dillon. It's the best kind of sex there is."

CARMICHAEL stood in the doorway to his office and watched Dillon depart down the hall. At the elevator Dillon turned, wondering why the doctor was watching him this way. The elevator arrived and took Dillon away.

Carmichael went back inside, closing and locking the door after him.

He went to his desk and opened a drawer. He withdrew a handheld cassette recorder and examined it, checking to see that the spools were still turning. A cord was plugged into the unit, which led back into the desk and connected to the hidden microphone mounted in the corner nearest the chair where his patients sat. Where minds and hearts bled. He pressed the stop button, then the reverse button, commencing the squeaking sounds of rewinding tape. Then he pressed stop again, followed by the play button. Dillon's voice could be heard amidst a fog of ambient audio noise: "You should write that shit down."

Carmichael stopped the tape and popped the cassette out. He put the recorder back into the drawer and glared at the cassette for a moment, motionless. Then, purposefully, he picked up the telephone and began to punch a number from memory.

13

Dillon came back from a client lunch to find a note requesting his presence in Janis's office at two o'clock. Janis was unique in that she never went out for lunch unless one of the New York suits was in town or unless she had an agenda with a broker. Obviously, today's agenda had his name on it.

"Close the door," she said without looking up. As he sat down she finished her paperwork and put it in a drawer, which meant whatever she was working on was a personnel matter. His, perhaps. The brokers weren't reviewed because their production meant everything. They could phone in orders from Maui between drug deals and it wouldn't matter to management.

She took off her reading glasses and rubbed at her eyes wearily.

"You look happier," she said.

"Last time we met you said I looked like shit."

"I said you looked like hell. You never look like shit."

She grinned. It was an amazing sensation, flirting with a Ukranian linebacker wearing Italian design couteur. "You're getting laid, aren't you. I'm jealous."

"I'm not."

"Bullshit. Tell me it's Karen. Then I won't be jealous."

The way he looked away from her said everything.

"Oh, boy," she said quietly. "I just assumed."

"Karen and I aren't talking. I can't even reach her. Our voicemails are getting very cozy."

"Has she filed?"

"No." He noticed himself avoiding eye contact.

Janis put her reading glasses back on and looked at something on her desk. "Your numbers are up again."

He nodded, smiled modestly. It was all bullshit once you had your account base and you stopped active prospecting—the phone rings, you make money. The market pops, the phone rings off the hook. Someone at the Fed sneezes, your month sucks.

"Our machinist friends want a meeting," she said, referring to the union pension fund she'd wanted to turn over to him a few weeks earlier. It was a small union and a relatively small fund, about eight million, with discounted commissions and an outside consultant who managed the assets. All they needed from a broker was execution—an order taker.

Dillon nodded. Janis sat back in her chair and just looked at him. Pretty soon a sneaky grin, the kind exchanged only between confidants, returned. He was forced to grin back at her.

"The broker of record needs to be there," she said.

"Which means, it happens now or it happens to someone else."

"I'm okay. I hope that's obvious to you."

"Your numbers are good, you look healthy, and you deserve this. But I'm worried about something."

"I can handle it."

"You're having an affair."

"You don't know that."

"You're not denying it."

He looked away. "It's not an affair, exactly."

Janis' grin was now a don't-bullshit-me smirk. "There *is* someone," he said.

Janis just stared as her grin melted away.

"She's a friend. We've been spending some time."

"Will you admit it's an affair after you fuck her?"

Dillon looked at her quizzically. He wished he could be outraged and say that she didn't know him that well, but she did.

"That's sexual harassment." He made sure his smile made misinterpretation impossible.

"Yes, it is. But you've got enough legal troubles, I think."

"I can handle it."

Now she snorted and shook her head, a gentle rebuke.

"I've seen affairs turn perfectly sane people—men, usually, but there are exceptions—into raving lunatics. I've seen devoted fathers and Christian elders and heads of empires reduced to blubbering fools who show up drunk on your doorstep wanting to talk and cry in your arms. I had one guy in the Cleveland office collapse in the lobby and to this day he's still on Prozac. All because of women they called friends. All because of affairs. The fact is, men *can't* handle it. They can't take the heat when it gets ugly, and it always gets ugly. Women, on the other hand, band together in the face of pain. They get strong. And then they get even." She paused, her eyes boring into him. "At least you don't have kids. That's the worst part of it. Men deserve what they get—their kids don't."

"What's your point?"

"They all thought they could handle it, too."

He drew a deep breath he hoped would quiet his sudden nausea.

"I appreciate your concern." He realized he sounded a little too cold.

She looked back at the report on her desk. "I'm going to give you the machinist account because I want you to have it." She looked back up again. "I'm trusting you, Dillon. I don't deserve to get fucked on this and I'm counting on you to make it happen straight up."

Dillon felt an electric tingle, not dissimilar to the afterglow of an orgasm. Combined with the nausea, it was a dizzying effect. The account was worth over thirty grand a year in commissions, just under half of which would be his. Karen had made sure that he knew he'd be needing it. Which is why he'd try to figure out a way to somehow keep it under wraps.

When he got up to leave Janis had a peculiar look on her face. His system had calmed down a bit and he suddenly wanted to be somewhere else.

"What?" he asked.

"I'm not one to give advice," she said, her voice uncharacteristically soft.

"Of all the people I know, it's okay. Please."

She nodded appreciatively. "In the end, when the door closes behind you, you have to ask yourself if you've done everything you can about Karen, if you went the whole nine yards for her. Because when it's over you can't go back, and you need to be sure you haven't left anything behind that you'll need in the next life. All you'll have left is the truth, and you're stuck with it."

He was amazed to see that her eyes were moist. As he departed, his smile was as gracious and grateful as he could muster.

And then, on the walk back to his cubicle, something amazing and completely unexpected happened to him. Something out of the ethereal left field rocked him to the point where his vision blurred and he feared he might vomit. His mind filled with Karen, with missing her, with an urgent need to talk to her and make sure she was okay.

He called the house, but the answer came from her inevitable answering machine message. She'd changed it again, and it was not lost on him that her voice sounded so completely calm and happy.

JORDAN called at four o'clock, just as Dillon was shutting down his computer for the night. Most of the brokers left their screens untouched, but Dillon's screen was home-paged on his own IRA account, and the place was known for its snoops.

"You're there," opened Jordan.

"Where else am I going to be?"

"I'm calling with reason number seven why people hate their lawyers."

"Seven out of, what, several hundred?"

"As a species, we usually gloat when we pull something off."

"And you're gloating."

"Like a motherfucker."

"You got the DMV."

"Of course. That was never in doubt."

"Talk to me."

"You sure you want to do this?"

Dillon paused. He wasn't nearly as sure as he was before.

"It's my funeral. Please do come, by the way."

"H-E-R-S, Mercedes SL, model year two thousand. Registered to one Hamilton J. Wallace, two oh one Vista View Court."

Dillon was writing it down. "Got it."

"You're porking the first lady of venture capital, pal."

That made the name sound vaguely familiar.

"Not yet I'm not."

"Wife's name is Veronica. I asked around . . . she's a piece of work."

"How so?"

"Foxy, rumored to be smart as a whip. Personality of a cobra. Keeps her husband on a very short leash."

"Literally or figuratively?"

"You tell me, tiger. You tell me."

DILLON was almost out the door when something he'd intended to do earlier came back to him. The news about the Dark Lady's identity had jolted his memory— Hamilton Wallace was a big cheese, a power guy with his paws on every local venture-capital deal in town. A couple of days earlier Dillon had looked the name up in a local who's who directory used by the newer brokers as a prospecting tool. Wallace had made his chops early as a big dog at Microsoft and was one of the first to bail with eight zeros and an appetite for software start-ups. Some said he'd shown Bill Gates and Paul Allen how the

game was played, but like many of the founding generation of Microsofties, he was content to let the kids take
center stage. Within ten years one would own two major
league sports franchises and a private 757, and the other
would simply be the richest and arguably the most powerful man on the planet.

Dillon returned to his desk and re-booted his PC
and waited for his stockminder screen to appear. He
punched in four letters: N-R-T-T. Neurotronics Technologies, traded on the NASDAQ and mysteriously recom-
mended to him by one Mrs. Hamilton Wallace, a woman with some serious connections. It took about three
seconds before the readout appeared. It had closed at
17½, up 4½ on the day on heavy volume. Nearly double
from when he last checked it.

A blinking icon signified there was a news release
within the past twenty-four hours. Dillon clicked on
the icon and waited about ten seconds for the story to
download. When it did, the headline read: "Affinity Offer Accepted by Neurotronics." The story went on to detail how a holding company by the name of The Affinity
Group had been accumulating shares of Neurotronics
Technologies for some weeks now, eventually control-
ling nearly twenty percent of the outstanding shares.
When the company began buying back its own stock as
a defensive measure, thereby driving up its own price,
the Affinity boys came out of the closet and issued an offer of $17.75 per share, nearly double the street price of
only a month before. The Neurotronics Board, consist-
ing of some legitimately dumbfounded doctors anxious
to turn their self-made paper wealth into beachfront
property, acted quickly to accept the offer.

Dillon went to fetch a book that would tell him what
he already knew, thumbing the pages quickly. It was just

as he'd suspected, just as he'd both feared and secretly hoped. The Affinity Group was owned, operated, and ruled with an ingenious and legendary ruthless hand by an ex-Microsoft executive named Hamilton J. Wallace.

14

In his new bachelorhood, Dillon began to indulge in a sentimental little habit of which both Jordan and his shrink would highly disapprove. On his way home from work he had taken to traveling several miles out of his way to stop for orange juice and ice cream at the new neighborhood megastore he and Karen had frequented. It was the old neighborhood, and these aisles were a comfort.

He was standing at the frozen case trying to decide between a Swanson's chicken experiment and some mystery-meat-filled burritos, when he heard a familiar voice behind him. A woman's voice.

"Slumming, are we?"

He turned to see Karen, pushing a full cart and looking years younger than their last episode at the house.

She was in her newest and best real estate finery, accented with a colorful scarf that kept it all from having too much business bitchiness to it. Her hair was even shorter than before, more stylish than usual.

She was grinning mischievously as she snatched the frozen dinner out of his hands and turned it over to read the nutritional analysis. She was a notorious and enthusiastic fat Nazi who used Dillon's love of Dreyer's Grand Chocolate as proof of his ignorance and sloth. Frozen dinners were the root of all evil.

"With all this fat and sodium you'd think it'd taste better than an old Reebok, wouldn't you?"

She handed it back to him, eyes twinkling. He wondered if she was really this glad to see him or glad to see him eating like this.

"You look good," he said, meaning it.

"Don't act so surprised."

"I'm not. But really . . . wow. You look absolutely fantastic."

"Okay, you can move back in." Her expression strained at the quick realization that the humor was distastefully black. She rolled her eyes, took a deep breath and said, "Oh, boy."

He put the frozen box back into the case. "Old habits die hard," he said.

"I never considered your giving me compliments a habit, actually."

"I meant coming here. To shop."

"They let anybody in."

He nodded. Her tone was aggressive, as if she'd rehearsed this moment. As if it didn't bother her in the least. If only he'd have laughed at her little joke.

He looked down at her cart—fresh shrimp, Brie, some expensive crackers, and several bottles of wine, all mingling with toilet paper and sanitary napkins.

"Dinner with a friend?"

"Hot date." This time she was smiling, but it was a cruel smile meant to confuse and confront. "I'm not *doing* anything, Dillon, for chrissakes."

He nodded. It felt ridiculous to draw a blank when so many hours of contemplation and so many dry-runs had been invested for this moment.

Karen cracked the moment open. "Speaking of . . . how's *your* new little friend?" She was referring, Dillon had to scramble to realize, to his mention of meeting someone during their last sparring match.

"Foxy. Smart as a whip. Personality of a cobra."

Karen arched an eyebrow. "How nice for you." There was a lot going on behind her eyes. She began to move past him. He knew he'd crossed the line, and he was not sure how he felt about doing so.

"We should talk," he said quickly, not wanting her to get so far away that he'd have to add an embarrassing level of volume.

"Oh, we'll talk." The threat in her tone was unmistakable.

"When?" This one was too loud.

She didn't turn this time. It was such a deliberate dismissal, as if he simply bored her and it was time to move on. Any remnant of his afternoon attack of warm sentiment was gone, frozen in her arctic wake. It was getting easier to go back to the Residence Inn every night, to his television and his burritos and the fresh half gallon of Dreyers that he decided right then and there to pick up and eat in one sitting. And of course, there was always the chance that his phone would ring at midnight.

But the telephone would not ring tonight. The Dark Lady was out with her own new friend.

*   *   *

KAREN placed the groceries onto the backseat and quickly folded herself in behind the wheel, slamming the door a little too hard. The woman in the other seat who had been waiting while Karen shopped immediately registered something, an energy that wasn't there when Karen had gone into the store minutes earlier. She reached out her hand and touched Karen's shoulder.

"You're upset. What is it?"

Karen didn't answer at first. She just stared ahead, drawing a deep breath, centering herself. Finally she turned to look at her friend, with her understanding blue eyes and perky-short California blond hair, her beautiful new friend who knew and understood so much and had supported her since her separation from Dillon.

"I ran into Dillon inside." She paused, not sensing the very subtle tensing in her friend. "I think he's seeing someone."

The hand tightened on her shoulder. The other woman now looked straight ahead as well, as if the answers were out there somewhere and would reveal themselves if she looked long and hard enough, like an image embedded in a computer-generated design. Then she offered a brave smile, the same brave smile she'd had for Karen since she'd put the idea of this separation into her head on the last day of the seminar where they had met.

"In that case," she said, "I suggest we start drinking as soon as possible."

With that Karen shot her friend an appreciative glance, not realizing she was looking at the woman her husband referred to in his mind, often and with escalating delight, as the Dark Lady.

15

The group was separated into pairs. Fifteen twosomes sat in facing chairs, knees touching, awkwardly holding hands. Nobody in the room had known anyone else in the room two days earlier, but by this midpoint in the four-day personal growth and human performance seminar, certain secrets had emerged, and the facades behind which most people hid were growing porous. The lights were completely off, and the hotel conference room where they convened was without windows. Cracks of light emerged from around the edges of double doors, allowing the facilitator, an attractive forty-ish woman with a calm, angelic voice, to wander safely through the maze of pairings as she guided the group through this exercise. Everyone's eyes except hers were tightly closed.

Karen Masters and Veronica Wallace held hands. They hadn't said much more to each other than hello during the first day and a half, but Karen had noticed the woman attached to her now, her confident manner, the obvious money, the telltale hints of a story beneath the Tiffany's veneer. When the exercise had been introduced and the moment came to select partners, Veronica had purposefully and quickly sought out Karen.

The instructor's voice was barely a whisper in an otherwise quiet room.

"Imagine you are sitting with the person in your life with whom you need to share your innermost thoughts, your private truth. It could be your life partner, your spouse, a parent, a child, a friend, your boss, an employee, a coworker, a hero you never met, or anyone else who occupies not only your mind, but your heart. Feel this person's hands in yours . . . they are with you now, and they are listening to you." Karen felt her hands being squeezed reassuringly, felt unfamiliar thumbs lightly caressing the back of her hands. It felt good, inviting her honesty.

"There are things in your heart that trouble you, things they need to know and understand but have never heard from you. These are issues that might frighten, embarrass, or confuse you. They might be an admission of resentment. You may seek to clarify a question or demand an answer. You may need to bury something in your past or resurrect something already buried. The person holding your hands is listening . . . and because we are all connected, they are the pathway to the unloading of your burden."

She paused. Karen felt emotion rising in her throat.

"Begin now. Partners, say nothing, but communicate what you hear with your hands. Be there for your partner, invite them into your own heart."

It was quiet at first, and then the room began to fill with the sound of mumbling, fifteen separate confessions and inner dialogues unfolding like prayers. The facilitator continued to stroll among her subjects, a collector of souls, peeking into dark corners of the human heart.

Karen began with a low voice. "I want to say I love you so desperately, Dillon. I want what we had to come back into our lives, but as much as I try, I can't remember what that was. It was as if all we ever had was hope, that somehow it was always going to change and we'd fall together in a way we hadn't yet connected, but looking back I realize that this hope was always bigger than us, that it was a dream that never came true."

Karen felt her hands being squeezed again, held more firmly than before. It was easy to imagine the hands as Dillon's, and she went with the moment.

"I know you say you love me, and in your own way I do believe that you do, but you must know that saying it isn't enough. I'm so confused by what I feel, because what I feel seems to shift and change. One day I'm bored and blaming you and the next I'm ashamed and blaming me. Sometimes I tell myself that we can work on this, but I can't compile the list of what it is we need to work on; it's just a blank piece of paper. I just know that my life is so empty and that somehow, it is because of you. Whether that missing element is because you can't give it to me, or won't, or you simply don't have it to give, or if it's because I don't know what to ask for . . . I don't know. It hurts me because I truly want what we promised each other and have never seemed able to find it."

By now her voice was trembling, tears streaking her cheeks. If she had opened her eyes she'd have seen her partner gazing at her with a fixed and somewhat intense expression as she gently caressed Karen's hands.

It went on for three more minutes. Karen talked in circles, about the man she fell in love with, a man who had the promise of wings and a smoldering fire within him, but how it all seemed to remain a dream, how the reality of his career and her own search for fulfillment outside the home seemed to smother everything else. She talked about her desire for them to conceive a child. She knew that if they were in love, truly in love the way she'd dreamed of being, his fears would be conquered. Children had became part of other people's dreams, not theirs, for reasons she could understand but could not accept. And for this she had, insidiously and covertly, started to resent him. The circle of pain had begun, and in the circle everything must remain symmetrical and balanced.

The instructor broke the trance with her voice. "You have thirty more seconds to say what you need to say. Partners, open yourselves up, pull the demons out with your empathetic energy."

Karen sniffled loudly, her makeup descending her cheeks in gray rivers. Her partner's grip was firm and full, like a parent guiding a child across an intersection.

"I don't know what to do," she said, her voice steadier now. "I just know that I've been expecting you to fix it, to fix *me,* and that's unfair. Whatever happens needs to come from inside me, from a place I've never been. And I need to find that place before I can find *us,* whatever it is *us* means." She paused, fighting back emotion. "I'm scared, Dillon. So fucking scared."

And then she wept openly, unable to continue speaking.

When the instructor announced a switching of roles,

Veronica Wallace told a story of her quest to find the woman inside of her that was too fearful to emerge from her husband's shadow. She spoke of her husband in glowing terms, of her own unworthiness, and how this unworthiness kept her inner self imprisoned in a luxurious private hell. She was afraid to ask for permission to emerge, unsure how to enlist him in her unfolding, afraid she would be cast out if her true face were to show. She wept softly several times—strangely, always without visible tears—and Karen tried as hard as she could to channel her empathy through her hands, to tell this women who would become her newest best friend that she was there for her, that she understood.

They embraced as the exercise concluded. Veronica whispered, "We can help each other. . . . I can help you discover your life, Karen. I want to be your friend. Let me into your heart." When Karen pulled back, she looked into the woman's impossibly blue eyes, misty with sincerity. She decided then and there that her journey of discovery, whatever it might entail, need not be taken alone.

16

It was almost a shame the two women were not lovers, because the setting was perfect. Karen had crafted a fine fire in the family room, and she and her new friend sat before it sipping wine. A green throw blanket was spread across their collective feet. Kenny G played softly, as if the piece had been composed with the crackling of a fire in mind, and the buzz of the wine seemed to impart a romantic surrealism that separated them from time and reality itself.

Her new friend had a soft way of leading Karen to truths she'd formerly kept locked away, hidden behind a wall she had mistakenly thought was her strength, but now realized was her prison. The tears were welcome, because they washed away the wall like a cleansing rain.

"He doesn't deserve this," said Karen after a particularly quiet moment.

"Neither do you," shot back her guest, almost as if she'd been waiting for this to surface. "Nobody said life or love is fair. Or that either is easy."

"He just . . . he didn't *do* anything, that's all."

"Bingo," said Veronica, grinning, assigning a deeper meaning to the word.

Karen frowned slightly. "One day he's just cruising through his routine, dumb and happy as always, and he comes home to a note."

Veronica now frowned as well. "I really hope that's not guilt I'm hearing. You didn't do anything either. Except realize that the rest of your life is at stake." Her smile was gentle.

"I know . . . it just . . . doesn't seem fair." Karen's tears were welling up again. Her friend slid the box of Kleenex closer, remaining quiet. "We both go from numb to miserable," said Karen, continuing. The tears began to spill now. Her voice lowered. "I don't know if I can go through with this."

Veronica leaned across the space between them and began to massage the tension from Karen's shoulders. Karen closed her eyes, moving slightly back and forth under the steady pressure of soothing fingers. The fire crackled and Kenny G's saxophone played, and for a while the moment was perfect. Veronica spoke softly, almost motherly. "Someday, no matter how this turns out, you'll realize you're doing him the biggest favor of his life."

Karen looked up as she blotted her cheeks. She tried for a brave smile.

"He'll either change or he won't. At least you're giving him the chance. This is his wake-up call. He's a man, Karen, for chrissakes . . . you've got to hit most of them between the eyes with their three iron to get their attention."

Karen moved away ever so slightly, a cue to stop the massage, accompanied by a weak thank-you smile. Veronica left her hands on her shoulders a moment longer than Karen would have preferred.

"He used to be so . . . focused," said Karen, trying to regain the rhythm of their previous conversation. "I loved that intensity, his passion." She paused, replaying some private silent movie in her mind. Veronica watched her eyes, wondering what she was remembering. "I don't know what happened to him. Or to us."

"Life happened. If you don't fight it, it wins."

Karen nodded, trying to understand. "Maybe it was me. Maybe I'm the part of his life that smothered his fire. How are you supposed to fight that? Maybe it's me who needs the wake-up call."

"Well, it was you who woke up, wasn't it? We'll see how he responds, see if there's any fight left in him. If there isn't, then maybe you're better off without him."

Karen suddenly looked at her new friend, a puzzled expression emerging. She was aware of a coldness she'd not sensed before but realized had been there all along, a black-and-white sensibility that bordered on cruelty. It was a feminine thing, and she wasn't sure if she was frightened or attracted to it. Perhaps both.

Veronica leaned back against the couch, having just drained her glass, aware that Karen was studying her. She stretched her hands high into the air and closed her eyes, a moment's departure from the intensity of their exchange.

"It's moments like these when I'm sorry I quit smoking," she said. "Hamilton made me stop . . . Sometimes I hate him for it."

This brought a grin to Karen's face. Veronica raised her eyebrows, wanting to know the story behind the smile.

"It's just . . . what you said," she said.

"Well, if I said it then at least you can let me in on it."

"It's kind of embarrassing." Karen was genuinely girlish.

"I bet it's not."

"Well . . . it's about Dillon. What you said, about Hamilton making you stop smoking. Dillon actually thinks it's sexy." She paused. "I told you."

"You're kidding."

"Nope. He never actually tried to get me to do it for him . . . he just hinted at it, let me know early on that it rang his chime. You know, right woman, right time, right place, you've come a long way, baby, and all that crap . . ."

"So *did* you?"

"Me? No. Well, once. It was never my thing." Her smile faded. "It was *his* thing."

Veronica grinned. "Where do they come up with that shit? What's sexy and what's not?" She was pouring more wine now. "Hamilton likes to tie me up with my panty hose. Only it has to be right when I take them off, while they're still warm. It doesn't do it for him if they're fresh out of the drawer . . . the heat is the thing."

Karen watched her friend's own silent movie flicker behind glistening eyes. She held her glass out and Veronica emptied the bottle into it.

Veronica spoke softly as she sipped. "They have these buttons, you see. All of them do. Some want them stroked, some want them licked . . ." She raised her eyes to Karen's now. Her voice changed slightly. "Some even want them whipped." She paused, as if to see if this caused a reaction, however subtle. "Men are so . . . easy."

A tiny, evil smile appeared on Veronica's lips as they touched her glass. It was the same kind of expression, complex and dark, that would trigger some inexplicable fascination in Dillon.

Veronica set the glass down on the coaster gently. "Let me tell you something. I can make a man do anything I want . . . if I know what his buttons are." Her expression widened to the near proximity of a smile.

But Karen didn't smile back. She just stared, as Dillon might have stared.

"I do believe that you can," she said.

THEY popped another bottle—a Merlot this time—and settled in to peel back more of life's little layers. It was well after midnight now, and the index of their evening was long and varied, covering everything from sororities to classical music to the exquisite curvature of Matthew McConaughey's ass. But they always returned to this thing between women and men, this game of power disguised as intimacy. The more they drank, the more honest the game became.

"You first," said Karen. Veronica had challenged her to describe the strangest sexual desire her husband had ever brought into their bedroom.

The smile on Veronica's face was full of delicious mischief. For a moment her gaze drifted slightly, then she said, "Okay," almost shyly. "This one I think is pretty common." She shifted, and their eyes locked. "He wants me to make love to another woman. He wants to watch from the foot of the bed with a Cuban cigar and a glass of Courvoisier."

Now Karen's eyes drifted, unable to hide a discomfort born not from the visual, but from the sudden sense of proposition that hung between them.

Veronica sensed the tension and grinned. "I haven't wanted anything that badly. Not yet."

"What do you mean?" Karen felt a cool sensation she recognized as relief.

"I mean, when there's something I want from Hamilton, I give him what *he* wants. Then I get what *I* want."

Karen could feel her friend watching her, searching for a reaction that she knew she couldn't hide simply by looking away.

"Haven't you ever done it? Wanted something from him, so you fuck him in a way that makes him happy about giving it to you?"

"I never thought about sex as an instrument of negotiation."

"Maybe you should."

They sipped their wine thoughtfully, both of them staring into the fire.

"Your turn," said Veronica at the precise moment the silence became heavy. "The weirdest, freakiest thing."

Karen leaned forward, picked up the poker and began to prod the half-consumed logs back to life. Veronica watched, allowing the time to pass patiently as the answer took shape.

"There *is* something."

"Tell me."

Karen shifted her position. "He used to talk a lot about me getting a tattoo. A little one, on my breast. Too big and it wouldn't work for him. Like the Virginia Slims thing . . . it has to be just right."

"A tattoo of what?"

"He never said. I don't think it matters."

"That you would *do* it is what matters." Veronica allowed her to ponder before adding, "Men are so fucking weird."

Karen nodded, but not from agreement. "He said it drove him crazy thinking about it. It was something he only talked about . . . when . . . you know . . ."

"When he was inside you," said Veronica. "Hot talk . . . whispered friction."

Karen's nod was very slow, remembering. It had been such a long time since they'd shared any hot talk, or friction for that matter, in their bed.

"He had a real thing about it, I think."

"Sounds like your Dillon has lots of *things*." Another moment of tense quiet caused Karen to look at her friend, seeing a you-know-I'm-right smile. "If you wanted him back, you'd give them to him."

"A tattoo? Oh, I don't know . ."

"Why not? I mean, if you wanted him back."

"I don't think it's as simple as that."

"If you want him to be the man you need, then perhaps you should consider becoming the woman he needs first. It's really very simple." Veronica's smile was a little too full of teeth. "Driving him crazy could be fun."

Karen poked at the fire, too obviously with an absent mind. "Maybe I should introduce the two of you. You'd be perfect."

"I wouldn't be perfect, Karen . . . I'd be perfectly smart. You don't need to understand what he likes. The key is understanding yourself and what *you* want. When you do that, it's not prostitution and it's not selling out. It's power. In the end, that's what the war is all about. Power."

"I never thought of it as a war."

"Then wake up, girlfriend. I'll tell you something

that I've learned and that not enough women understand. They underestimate the enemy. They think that
for men it's all about their dick when for a lot of them
it's really about something else entirely."

"I can't wait."

Veronica just grinned patiently. "You don't get power
over him by fucking his brains out. You get power over
him by fucking his *brain*."

They locked eyes, Veronica's very sincere, Karen's
a bit bewildered. After a moment she nodded, as if she
understood.

Now it was Veronica's eyes that drifted toward the
fire. "It's so ironic," she said, her voice much softer than
before.

"What is?" answered Karen.

"What you want, what I want. How we're so different yet the same."

"I'm not sure what you mean."

"You want a man who rules your heart with his
strength, who commands your loyalty with his gentleness. A man you could kill for."

Karen smiled because her friend was right.

"And what do you want?"

The Dark Lady looked up with an expression that
sent a sprinkling of ice through Karen's spine.

"I want a man who would die for me," she said.

17

Her voicemail instructions were to be on the dock at eight, waiting in his car in the lineup for the last Bremerton ferry of the day. "I miss watching you squirm," was what she said, along with instructions to bring champagne and a basket of gourmet picnic goodies, most especially caviar. As he waited he watched dots of red lights crisscrossing the Sound, remembering how his father had brought him to the waterfront in the summers for fish and chips.

Suddenly his passenger door opened and the Dark Lady slipped into the seat with the fluidity of a ballet dancer. Her raven hair was pulled back and secured with a large clasp, and the combination of her earrings and her black fur was more suited to the symphony than a picnic in the car. She grinned at him and leaned close for him to kiss her cheek. He inhaled, the sharp scent of a nameless perfume mixed with the cold evening air. He made a mental note to ask her what it was.

He caressed the coat, then whistled softly.

"Please don't ask me if it's real," she said.

"Aren't you afraid some environmentalist will hit you with a can of paint or something?"

Her eyes twinkled. "I only wear it to clandestine liaisons with men with whom I'm having affairs, none of whom are environmentalists."

"Are we having an affair?"

A gloved hand reached for his face, pulling him toward her. The kiss was soft and probing, her lips cold from the night. Both kept their eyes open.

As they pulled apart she whispered, "You tell me."

They shared their picnic in his car as the ferry crossed the sound for forty minutes. All the cars around them were empty, their occupants having gone topside for a drink or to wait it out in the warm passenger cabin. It was a brilliant choice for their rendezvous, out here in the netherworld between two shores, moving through the night to instrumental music from his CD player. The engine ran to keep them warm, and the Dark Lady had pushed her fur down over her shoulders, revealing creamy shoulders and a black evening dress.

"You haven't told me where we're going," he said as he unwrapped the foil from the stem of the champagne bottle. She was surveying the contents of the picnic, which was held in a brown grocery sack instead of the basket he was actually tempted to buy for the occasion.

"We're going to bed," she said without meeting his eyes.

He froze, his hands now motionless. He realized his breathing was audible and that his mouth was forming into a huge smile.

Dillon popped the champagne cork with perfect timing, which made them both giggle. She held the bottle close to her face as visible wisps of mist flowed from the top. She parted her lips, inhaling as if it was smoke.

"Wow," he said quietly, "never seen anybody do *that* before."

Her smile was smug as she withdrew two crystal champagne glasses from her purse, unwrapping them from a sheath of deep burgundy velvet. She held one glass for him to fill, which he did with great care.

"To us," he said, signaling a toast.

"To pleasure," she countered as the crystal touched with a crisp tone. They sipped without speaking.

After a moment she set her glass on the open glove compartment door and picked up the opened jar of caviar. She scooped some out using her index finger, the blackness of the sturgeon eggs matching the leather of the glove to which it clung. She brought the finger slowly to his mouth, depositing the caviar onto his outstretched tongue. Then she began painting the residue of it across his bottom lip with her fingertip. Her eyes focused on this work, again the detached scientist at work. It was this look, despite the utter kinkiness of it, that was the most intoxicating of all to Dillon.

Without removing her fingertip, she leaned closer and began to taste the juice on his lip with the tip of her tongue. They played at this for a while, sparring tongues and caviar-salted lips and fingertips, until the momentum escalated into a deep, churning kiss.

After the kiss had run its course they pulled apart, washing the moment down with champagne. He spread some caviar onto a cracker, and as he handed it to her she felt his bicep, squeezing hard.

"I bet you were a big jock," she said with a touch of

sarcasm. She didn't seem like a woman who would be attracted to the athletic type. More like the mogul type, the self-made billionaire.

"Thank you."

"It's not necessarily a compliment."

He looked embarrassed, his eyes straying.

"You're a humble man. People mistake it for softness." She paused, watching him, and his eyes told her she was right. "But you have so much more going on than most men. You needn't be quite so humble. It's not all that attractive to most women."

"Really? You live in a world where men spill more in cocktail lounges than I make in a year."

"I'm not talking about money. I'm talking about your heart. Something most of those guys don't have. You have a good heart. A rather gentle heart." She paused. "People mistake that for softness, too."

"Well, I like animals and I always buy the candy when the little-leaguers come to the door." He paused, then said, "How can you tell all this about me?"

"It doesn't matter. That's one of the reasons I'm here."

"My heart."

"You have the heart of a warrior and the spirit of a dreamer . . . perhaps one whose heart has been broken. What you don't have anymore is the hunger."

"I'm suddenly famished again."

Her eyes narrowed slightly, as if seeing something in his expression that fascinated her. "And you're honest. That's harder to intuit."

Suddenly an obnoxious public address voice blared their approach to the Bremerton terminal. The speaker was right next to where they sat, and the volume was startling. She sat upright and collected herself.

"Now what?" he asked, not hiding the tone of expectation in his voice. He could feel the champagne thickening his tongue, and when he turned to look outside through the openings in the ferry's hull, the lights from shore were slightly blurred.

"I need to freshen up," she said as she began tidying their picnic mess.

"So . . . are we getting off?"

She was gathering her purse. "I guarantee it," she said.

BREMERTON wasn't part of her plan. She told him they'd be staying on board, that he should meet her up on deck in ten minutes for some air after the turn. Then she disappeared in search of a ladies room.

She was on the aft deck, standing alone at the rail watching the Bremerton terminal recede into the night. He approached her from behind, encircling her waist with his arms. He could feel her warmth through her coat and his own jacket. He nuzzled his face into the hair at the side of her neck, and from the corner of his eye saw that she was smiling, her eyes closed, her head thrown back to accept his gesture.

She turned toward him, her eyes locking on his for a moment before she pulled him slowly down for a deep and rhythmic dance of a kiss. It was a bizarre and heady sensation, the taste of a bad girl's lips. It was intoxicating, and he felt himself getting hard.

"You're amazing," he whispered through the kiss.

"I'm so glad you think so. A woman likes to be appreciated."

"Tell me what else this woman likes, so I can give it to her."

She pulled back to look at him, not disapprovingly, but with a trace of surprise that gave way to mischief. "You don't have enough money for that," she said playfully.

"You already have all the money you need, so it must be something else."

Her grin melted, and as she turned around to face the water again, holding his arms in place, she said, "It must be."

He held her like that for a while, his face in her hair, luxuriating in her, sinking his hands into the fur of her sleeves, pressing himself into her. He wasn't sure which one of them began to move first, but soon they were swaying back and forth together, very gently. The only sound was the steady churning of the water below them.

"It's okay if we like each other, isn't it?" he asked.

She turned to face him again. "You be sure and let me know when you don't like me anymore," she said, her eyes on fire. They kissed again, more soft and playful than urgent or hungry. Time was standing still, at least until the ferry reached the line of city lights on the horizon ahead.

"This could get scary," she whispered, closing her eyes as she buried her head into the nape of his neck.

"It's already scary."

Without looking up she said, "One learns to love the fear."

They said little else until the ferry reached the Seattle waterfront. They held hands in the car as they drove to the Olympic Hotel and the suite she had reserved for them in his name earlier that afternoon.

18

Before the madness there was the game. The name of the game was control, and the winner was never in doubt. Only the rules remained to be negotiated, a discarding of expectation and assumption that would define the playing field.

He let her off in front of the hotel while he parked the car, electing not to utilize the valet. He was to meet her inside in front of the elevators, which he did with both heart and stomach pounding, again beating back the pesky notion that she wouldn't be there. But she was, card key in hand, looking somewhat nervous herself. They said nothing as they rode the elevator alone to the top floor. Midway up she stopped tapping the card against her knuckle and reached for his hand, holding it tightly until the doors opened to the concierge.

At the door to the room she slipped the magnetically-encoded card into the lock and waited for the green light to appear, then pushed it open. But instead of going inside she suddenly turned to him and put her hands on his shoulders, as if she were about to lecture a child or perhaps confess some great and meaningful secret.

She just stared at first, her eyes sincere, filling him with even more anxiety than was already coursing through him. She looked younger like this, more vulnerable than he'd seen her thus far, and he wondered how many sides of this woman there were to discover. And, how many times she had stood here before.

The more complex she became, the more bewitched he was.

"I need to know something," she said. "I need to know that you're okay with this, and this isn't about just getting laid or getting back at your wife. And if it's neither of those, I also need to know that you're not so full of guilt that you can't get her face out of your head."

He started to speak then paused, not sure what to say. Guilt, or some cousin seed of discontent, had indeed been gnawing at him the entire evening, a quiet war between his notions of propriety and reality. The reality was that Karen had left of her own will, not driven off as much by him as by her own confused muse. In the echo of her declaration of independence he was innocent and free. His personal definition of ethics would allow him to pursue this. It was time to be strong again, to take control of his life away from Karen's and her inequitable rules and the yoke of his own limits. It was time to move on.

"You'd know if I was lying," he said.

"That's precisely why I'm asking. There's something in your eyes. I feel something in the air between us. I just need to check in with it, with you . . . give you a chance to rethink this. We can just have a drink if you want, talk to each other. Or I can just go away. There's no need to rush, Dillon."

He looked at her with as much sincerity as he could muster. "What you feel is simple electricity. Frankly I'm nervous as hell but overall I'm fine." He hesitated, using his eyes for emphasis. "I want this . . . I want *you*."

Her face softened as her hands began to toy with the buttons on his jacket. He knew this was a critical moment and that they'd moved successfully past it. This had more to it than just getting laid. It was about *something*. Whatever it was she needed, he wanted desperately to give it to her.

"That's good," she finally said.

"That's the truth," he replied.

"Because once we're in that room on those terms, your wife and my husband do not exist. Not in our hearts or our minds or in this world. They are dead people and they are forgotten. I need all of you, everything in you. That's how I make love." She paused, her eyes meeting his. "That's how I fuck."

She pushed the door open and went inside.

DILLON reclined against the headboard and surveyed the room, which was bathed in the candle's faint light. He could hear nothing from the bathroom as he tried to picture her there, tending to lipstick or feminine primping or perhaps just making him wait.

Finally the bathroom door opened and for an instant the hallway filled with light. Then the light went off and he stared at shadow, waiting with held breath for her to emerge from it.

When she did she was as perfect as he knew she would be. She wore a low slung black bra and panties with a matching black garter belt and nylons. And of course, heels. He was not surprised when he saw that she had kept her leather gloves on. He watched her, afraid to breathe, as she moved with sure feline grace to the nightstand. She set her purse down there and took out her pack of Virginia Slims.

"My God," he heard himself say.

"Hardly," she responded, leaning down to him with perfectly pursed lips and hungry eyes, telling him that she knew and relished his every weakness.

And then the madness began.

HE had never known such intimacy. His mind had been pried open and licked until it screamed.

When it was over they remained entwined, their heartbeats and rate of breath slowly returning to normal. Her head was on his chest and her fingers, still gloved, circled lazily back and forth against the moisture on his shoulder. One of her legs was thrown over his, and he could sense the dampness between them. His hand rested on her hip, his fingertips softly stroking the strap of her garter belt. She was beautiful and perfect and warm and wicked.

They had done things, the secret things, as if she knew his dreams. She had talked and whispered through the whole thing, instructing him to touch her just so, how to use his lips and the tip of his tongue. She had four orgasms, each one more shudderingly powerful than the last. The last had occurred in precise accompaniment to his own. Both of them had cried out, a chorus of insane pleasure. Along the way she had played erotic games, putting the tips of her leather-clad fingers in his mouth and grinning devilishly as he sucked, biting his nipples until he cried out. She cupped his face with her palms while she told him how he filled her and made her wet. And how, at the end, she had pushed him to his back and mounted him, how she had reached down and put him inside her with a confidence and dexterity that made him feel owned, how her movement was slow but unrelenting and full of destiny, how she instructed him to hold back, not to come until she commanded it, how the very essence of the instruction was the thing that pushed him over the top, and how her sly smile told him she knew precisely that this would be so. She kept her lace black bra on the whole time, and when he attempted to remove it she had stopped him. She had pulled one side of it down to allow his suckling, which again was performed according to her narrative, and then at the climax she had used both hands to thumb the straps and pull the entire garment away.

In that instant his eyes went to a black spot on her breast. There was a tattoo the size of a quarter, a black rose with a red serpent entwined about the thorny stem. He raised his head up to see its detail. She allowed this for a moment, but he was very close to the end and she had something else in mind. She firmly grabbed his face with both hands and lowered over him, the pace of her dance escalating now, her eyes inches from his, and she breathed, "Stay with me," as his orgasm crested. When his eyes started to flutter she plunged a black thumb into his mouth and said it again, "Stay with me!" holding his head firm so their eye contact was maintained. He could tell from her voice and the tension in her thighs that she was cresting atop her own wave, ready to tumble with him. He exploded with a sensation that froze time and, he was sure, rendered him unconscious for a perfect eternal moment.

Now, lying here with her and remembering all that she did and said, he realized that it was her eyes he would remember most, the fascination in them as his climax took command of the moment away from her.

"Tell me about the tattoo," he said. They remained still.

"You like? My husband hates it."

"You have no way of knowing how much I *like*."

They lay very still. Then she spoke softly, a wistful memory.

"I had a lover . . . he had a thing for tattoos. And I believe in giving my lover what he or she wants."

He or she. She was licking his mind again. He would ask about that later.

"Most people don't understand that," Dillon said, "especially men."

"But we understand, don't we Dillon."

She still hadn't moved, he couldn't see her face. "What's it mean . . . the tattoo."

After a pause, she said, "It's me."

"Tell me."

"Enigma and mystery . . . the beauty of the flower and the risk of the thorn, dancing with the serpent."

She shifted her eyes, alive and on fire and locked on his.

"Read your Genesis. Women were the conduit for evil in the world. It's in our DNA."

She wasn't smiling, and he found himself responding, a twinge of arousal. His finger traced the moist tattoo lightly.

"His design or yours?"

"Mine. I knew it would be with me after he was

gone. The mystery of femininity was something beyond his understanding."

"Not all men are alike."

Now she grinned. "Never confuse understanding with appreciation, Dillon."

His mind tasted every word, and he knew he wanted her again. Already he was different, beyond what he was.

"You're diabolical," he said, his tone husky and sensual.

"I know," she responded.

"You know what I like about you?"

"I'm pretty sure I do."

"Your ego . . . your confidence. You just *know*."

"Yes."

He rolled to his side to prop up his elbow, and used his palm to support his head. They were facing each other, legs still entangled, arms still loosely around each other.

"I have a confession," he said. "I think about us . . . together." He waited for her response, which didn't come. "After tonight I'll think about us even more."

"That's not what this is about."

"It is for me. Call me romantic."

He saw something in her eyes, evidence that what he'd said wasn't okay. She sat up and turned, putting her feet on the floor. He reached over and rubbed her back, marveling at the incredible silkiness of her skin, and she shifted slightly, enjoying his touch.

"That's nice," she said.

He continued the massage. "I don't mean to frighten you. I get pushy when I'm passionate about something. You're just . . . addictive."

"Be careful you don't get hooked."

"I think I'm already there."

She moaned at his caresses. "I love your passion."

"You make it easy."

He could tell this made her smile. "Someone once described me as the hard stuff."

"Tattoo boy?"

A pause. "Someone else."

"Tattoo girl, then."

She didn't respond. After a moment she leaned down and kissed him. It was a sensual kiss, still tasting of lust and sex, and he knew his renewed desire would be reciprocated. This, too, was different and unexpected for him.

"You have no idea what you're saying," she said, suddenly serious. He assumed, incorrectly, that she was returning to the topic of their being together. "There's a prenuptial. I thought I was in love . . . desperately, foolishly in love. Ironic. It took me precisely six months to realize I was more in love with what he could do for my wardrobe and my tan."

Her eyes were moist. This confession moved him, a peek behind the Dark Lady's shadow. It made him feel special, and he stroked her hair, urging her on.

"He's impotent, Dillon."

He didn't know what to say, so he shrugged sheepishly. She looked away, moving on.

"He likes me to masturbate for him. He says he wants me to be satisfied, that it's a form of sex that we can still share. He won't even touch me, do it for me . . . he just likes to watch. Sick fuck."

"I really *am* sorry."

Looking back, her eyes bore into him with a fresh intensity.

"I need the heat, Dillon . . . the passion and intimacy of *fucking* . . . I need a man inside me, someone I care for." She kissed him again. "I need you, what you give to me." Now a deeper kiss, hungry again.

Then, using a new tone intended to titillate, she said, "Sometimes I watch him sleep . . . pretend he's gone. I imagine that he's dead."

He pulled away awkwardly. Her eyes glistened as if this was precisely what she had in mind; a jolt, a response. He tried to analyze her expression, seeing many women there, especially the one that liked to observe the outcome of her provocations.

"That's a little scary," he said.

Her smile broadened and she pulled him back into her, close enough to feel the heat on her breath.

"One learns to love the fear," she whispered into his mouth.

He pulled away gently, saying nothing, eyes drifting.

She took his chin in a firm and motherly way and turned his gaze back to her. "It's just a game, lover boy."

"Right now, right this second, it doesn't feel like playing."

"Then I'm winning, aren't I."

Victory filled her eyes, and he realized he was certifiably bewitched by them, unable to look away. Having won the moment, her attention then shifted to the nightstand. "Hand me those, would you please?"

He handed her Virginia Slims and her lighter over to her, wondering if this was part of the game, too. She extracted a cigarette, slowly and deliberately, then asked for the ashtray. The decorative glass piece was heavy enough to require both of his hands to lift at his reclined angle. He set it on the bed beside her.

She held the cigarette at the ready, knowing he was frozen in the moment. Without looking away she held out the lighter expectantly, a little nibble on a secret corner of his libido. He took it. The game was on again.

He watched the way she leaned in and inhaled, slow and elegant and excruciatingly feminine. As she exhaled the smoke, her eyes staring deeply at his, her other hand reached for his sex, finding him, taking him firmly. His response was immediate and grand, more grand than even he could have dared promise.

Feeling his response, her eyes widened and she smiled ever so subtly.

"Behold," she said. "The resurrection."

And again, the madness came.

19

The boy was eight when he told his father that he wanted to be a pilot. They were sitting in his father's Ford Torino in a gravel lot next to the runway at Sea-Tac, where an airliner either took off or landed every thirty seconds. It had been awhile—close to a year, in fact—since they'd spent a Saturday this way, the way they used to when he was younger. The boy ate a McDonald's cheeseburger while his father drank a six-pack of Schlitz. They would stay until the beer was gone, and then they would leave.

His father didn't say much. He sat slouched behind the wheel so that the back of his head was square against the headrest. When he was done with a can he'd crush it with one fist and toss it out the window. Then he'd pop the top of the next can as he rolled the window back up. The boy had always observed this ritual as closely as he

did the airplanes, only now after a year he found himself interested in the silence as much as the rhythm of it.
Because the silence meant something, an untold story.

Things were different than the last time they'd come
to watch the planes. His father's hair was whiter, and
his tummy was beginning to tumble over his belt as he
slouched. The clothes were the same though, dull green
pants and a solid color flannel shirt, his weekend uniform. But his eyes were the most different of all. Before, when a big Boeing would power down the runway
and lift into the sky, the boy had seen a fire there that
told him this was one of the best things you could ever
see. Today his father's eyes remained fixed, staring at
something straight ahead, never once even looking up
at the planes. The boy's notion that he was witnessing a
preview of his own destiny seemed a touch unsettling.
Which was why, when he thought about it later, he decided right then and there that he wanted to be a pilot
when he grew up.

"Fuck," was what his father said in response to the
announcement. A 747 had just landed, gear extended
like the talons of a massive bird, moving as if in slow
motion with its magnificent wings flared and its engines
filling the atmosphere with a glorious swarm of noise.
What better thing to be than the person in control of all
that choreography.

"How come?" the boy said.

His father turned his head to the right to look at his
son, his forehead creased with disapproval. "How come
what?"

"How come fuck?" answered the boy. There was no
sarcasm in his voice.

"Don't use that word, goddamn it! Or I'll kick your
puny little ass."

The boy stared a moment, then turned his attention back to the runway when the sound of the next plane landing reached his ears. It was a 727 this time, and he wondered where it had come from, what adventures those on board were either beginning or concluding.

"Do pilots have to go to college first?" asked the boy.

His father said nothing.

The boy watched another landing and tried again.

"I mean, is there like a pilot school or something where they learn to fly?"

"Of course there's a goddamn pilot school." His voice was harsh. The boy stared at his father for a moment, wondering what he'd done to warrant this tone.

"Are you mad at me, Dad?"

The father's head flopped to the side, not lifting from the headrest. His eyes were red, and he awkwardly tried to smile.

"Do I seem like I'm mad at you?"

"Sort of."

"Well maybe if you didn't ask me all these dumb-ass questions about pilots and shit I'd be in a better mood."

His stare returned to the previous mode, straight ahead and empty. The boy quietly watched three United jets take off, thrilling to the sound. He fought back the urge to cry. . . . His father hated it when he cried, called him a little pussy and told him to grow some balls before he turned into a fag. He didn't know what this meant, but knew his father wanted nothing more than for him to not be one, because this was what he always said whenever he cried.

"Michael Carlson's uncle is a pilot," he said.

Suddenly his father spun in his seat and grabbed his son by both shoulders. His eyes were dull and his face was flush with sudden color. When he talked, the foul smell of beer filled the car.

"Listen to me—get that shit out of your head, hear me? Talk like that will give you nothing but heartache, because shit like that just does not come true. You understand me? Just get it out of your head and worry about getting through school in one goddamn piece."

"But, Dad . . ." he whined, needing to explain that he wasn't trying to be bad, that he just wanted to do something someday that was an adventure and not a plain old job, and he thought his dad thought airplanes were cool because why else would they be sitting here together like they always used to be.

The man shook the boy hard, which shut him up abruptly.

"I mean it! Dreamers don't get *anywhere*, goddamn it! You want something in this life you got to work for it! Nobody ever got nowhere sitting around talking about what they wanna be. Shit like that just happens, and it doesn't happen to people like us, okay? It happens to people with brains and money and connections and . .

He stopped in mid-sentence and drew a deep breath, gently releasing his grip on the boy, who quickly slid toward the door. The man slouched back into his familiar pose and looked straight ahead again, except his expression remained contorted in disgust.

"Nothin' I'm gonna say to you is gonna make jackshit of a difference anyhow." He drained his can of Schlitz in one pull. "Just don't let me hear you with any more pilot talk or I'll kick your little pussy ass."

He rolled the window down, crushed the can, and tossed it out.

"I wanna go home now," said the boy very quietly.

"What?"

"I want to go home."

His father just stared at him for a moment, scowling. After a few seconds he began to shake his head.

The boy began to cry. He couldn't help it.

"Fuck," muttered his father, starting the engine and backing up fast enough to send gravel and dust flying everywhere. "Goddamn faggot."

The boy held his chin in his hand and pressed his forehead against the window the entire way home, imagining that he was flying a 747 to someplace where the sun never went away.

20

Lunch at McCormick's in downtown Seattle was the place to be seen if you were upwardly mobile and proud of your wardrobe. A town full of alternative musicians, software nerds, and the terminally hip, Seattle was also a nexus of fashion and ambition that rivaled Manhattan. People moved here to live in the rain to simply be among it all.

Dillon and Jordan lunched here often, in Dillon's case because it was close to his office and the crab cakes were delicious. Jordan simply liked the women. You didn't enter this establishment without the type of self-confidence that overcomes what God forgot. The two men were hunched over a table set for four, and Dillon was finishing bringing his friend up to date on the elusive fantasy that his life had become.

"You're the last guy I'd peg for something like this."

"Something like what?"

"Like being a chump." He leaned in, lowered his voice, keeping humor in it. "I mean, you're a nice-looking guy and all, we all know that for chrissakes . . . but shit, Dillon, she's married to one of the richest assholes in the city, and you expect me to believe that she's putting it all at risk because you two have something *special* between you? That you give her something nobody else can?"

He sat back, one eyebrow raised in a sorry-the-truth-hurts way.

"You're a cynic. That's why you're alone."

"And you believe in love. So we're all idiots." He grinned mischievously. "She's using you like a tampon, man."

Dillon winced. "Come on, Jordan."

"I mean it. And that's okay. I mean, shit, hot sex with a woman like that, who wouldn't want to get used up? Where do I sign on? It's just that you sound like, you know, like it all *means* something."

Dillon drained his Pellegrino. "I couldn't do this if I didn't believe that."

"Oh, that's right. Mr. I'm-not-like-other-men."

Dillon fought off a surge of defensive emotion with a calm grin. Janis called it "living in the pause," and it worked.

"Give me a little credit, would you?"

"Shit, you get all the fucking credit in the world, pal. You get the Bill Clinton Big Cigar award. I mean, I'm not playing doctor with Mrs. Rich-bitch-scratch-my-itch in riding gear. Hell, I'm just a guy trying to get by."

"Don't you think I haven't been down that road already? That I know I'm lonely and vulnerable—"

"The perfect antidote," interrupted Jordan.

"Let me finish. That I'm lonely and vulnerable and in a position to lose a lot with Karen, emotionally *and* financially. It's just that . . . you've got to *meet* her, man. I mean, what began as all this chemistry opened both of us up to what we really want. Maybe her husband just doesn't appreciate her the way I do . . . and God knows I do. Women put a high price tag on that. Maybe I'm the guy she's been thinking about when Venture Capital-boy has his mind on the next round of financing. I'm not saying it's going anywhere. I'm not that naive. But it's here and it's real and it's powerful. Call it serendipity or divine providence, but it's just the ticket for two needy people, right here, right now. Give me a little credit for understanding what I'm getting myself into. Maybe if you understood it better yourself you'd find your own dream shot."

"Like you have."

"Like I have." He paused. "What am I supposed to do, sit home and wait for Karen to wake up? I don't even know if I want her to wake up."

The ensuing moment of silence was appreciated by both men. Then Dillon continued, his voice a different pace and tone. "Women want a *lover*, Jordan. Not just a fuck and a flower. They want to connect."

Jordan grinned as he pushed back his embroidered Dior cuff to look at his watch. "Look at the time. So where is she?"

Both of them glanced at the entrance, which was crowded with clusters of suits waiting for tables. Dillon had called Jordan midmorning with this idea, to surprise the Dark Lady when she arrived, to show her off for his best and most pessimistic friend. The original arrangement, the one between Dillon and the Dark Lady, had been another game—both were to arrive alone, and he was to try to pick her up in the bar. She would resist his charms and finally agree to a drink, which would lead to lunch and whatever else the afternoon had in store. It would all be done her way, as usual.

"She won't like it, man," said Jordan, still watching the doorway.

"It's kinky. She'll like it."

"It's *too* kinky. For a guy who claims to understand as much as you do, you're taking a lot for granted. You'll be history."

"I don't think so."

They waited another minute before they both checked their watches simultaneously. She was ten minutes past the appointed hour, and Dillon realized the game might involve her not showing up at all.

His heart seemed to stop when he finally saw her. She looked like a business executive, a ball-busting bitch, in fact; conservative hair, dark suit, briefcase, matching purse, expensive sunglasses. The look didn't really work, because she was far too beautiful to pull it off. Sophia Loren as a patent attorney—women like that don't have jobs, they have manicurists. Nearly every man in the place looked up and took notice. You could almost hear a hush come over the room.

Jordan saw Dillon's smile emerging, then turned to look for himself.

"Jesus." Jordan's voice was low and respectful.

"Do I get that credit now?"

"Jesus," he repeated, softer this time.

The Dark Lady took off her sunglasses and squinted into the restaurant as if looking for someone, as if she didn't notice the wave of turning heads and supposedly nonchalant glances. Women like her had the move down, the perfectly normal acceptance of their power to command a room.

Dillon raised his hand to get her attention. None of this was according to plan, because none of it was planned.

When she saw him her face remained stoic. As she quickly but smoothly put her sunglasses back on, a bolt of ice shot up Dillon's spine and exploded into his limbs. He was smiling, waving her over, but she didn't move. After a moment her shaded eyes began searching the restaurant again, as if he was *not* the lucky lunch date at all. He felt his face go flush, wondering if anyone noticed, knowing that Jordan certainly had.

"Houston, we have a problem," said Jordan.

"She's fucking with me," said Dillon. "I'll be right back."

When she saw him coming she turned and left the restaurant, heading into the adjacent galleria mall. Dillon trotted to catch up, grasping her arm when he did. She shook it off and kept walking, all without looking up. Her face was red, her forehead tensed.

"I wanted him to meet you," he said.

"Give him my apologies," she said, her pace swift. He matched her stride, forced to weave through a sea of shoulders to keep at her side.

"Listen, I'm sorry . . . I thought . . ."

She stopped, turned to him. When she removed her sunglasses, her face was cool, almost amused. For an instant he felt a glimmer of hope, that the game was adaptable. He was wrong.

"I know what you thought, Dillon. I just don't *care* what you thought." Her voice was smooth and calm, controlled.

She held his gaze for a moment, her eyes burning

with a confusing mixture of rage and dark glee. She was letting it sink in, branding him with the fire of her independence and her will. When she was certain he'd seen the face of hell, she replaced her sunglasses, pivoted, and headed away.

He started to speak but stopped, realizing he'd have to shout over the heads of the crowd. He watched her departure, the feline way she angled her shoulders to adapt to the flow of the hustling crowd.

When he returned to the table Jordan was shaking his head in solace. "My bad," he said. "Saw it, knew it, should have protected you from it."

Dillon sat back down, raised his eyebrows, and puffed out his cheeks in a now-what-do-I-do sigh. "Shit. I don't get it."

"You're not supposed to get it," said Jordan. "She's a woman, for chrissakes." Jordan's eyes went to the doorway where she'd been, and his voice lowered. "And, if I might add, every bit the woman you said she'd be."

JORDAN was propped at a forty-five-degree angle in bed, his eyes heavy behind reading glasses that had slid almost to the tip of his nose. A thick case file rested facedown on his abdomen. The television was on; Letterman was bantering with his first guest, one of those unbearably cute women from the television program *Friends*, which he'd never seen. Tonight's chatty guest was the one with the great hair.

The telephone rang. He jolted upright, all systems scrambling, reflexively glancing at the clock before answering. It was midnight, straight up. Either his mother had died or one of his clients was having a meltdown.

"Hello?"

He could hear music coming over the line, the faint sound of a radio or stereo somewhere in the room with the caller.

"Hello?" he said again, a little stronger this time.

Jordan could sense that someone was there. He could perceive the soft echo of breathing. He waited ten seconds.

"Last chance," he said. It could be one of a hundred possibilities—a cadre of discarded one-nighters and old girlfriends, a pissed off client nursing a bottle of gin, someone on the losing end of one of his real estate deals. Hell, maybe it was Dillon and his mysterious new friend, playing a little joke after a round of kiss-and-make-up.

"Asshole," he mumbled as he hung up. But instead of placing the receiver in the cradle, he depressed the button with his finger for several seconds, then listened for a new dial tone. He pressed the star key, then the number 69. When told that the number of his last call was unavailable, he hung up, pushed his reading glasses back into place, and returned his attention to the file in his lap.

21

Dillon drove by the Dark Lady's house after work, but when he got there he regretted the impulse and quickly drove on. The place seemed abandoned, no cars, no activity. Not that he'd have known what to do if he'd have seen signs of her there. There was no way to call her, the lifeline of their relationship had been secured to her end. Her rules. Her game. Her exile.

He slept fitfully, not sure how long at a stretch he was actually under. When dawn arrived he felt drugged, actually anxious to get to work to get his mind on something other than the mess he'd made of things.

The kick-off meeting with the machinist pension fund management committee was held in a conference room at the airport DoubleTree. The presentation involved a slide show about the union and its mission of brotherhood and support of its members. Dillon felt his eyelids sagging, a nearly impossible urge to resist, which brought a stiff elbow to his ribs from Janis. With her eyes she indicated a man standing to the side of the room, observing the crowd. The client. Better not let *him* catch you nodding off with the hard-won savings of his constituency at stake. He was a frail little man with thick glasses and a shirt collar several sizes too large.

"I really like high tech," said the little man as soon as they were introduced. "E-commerce, chip stocks, and the like."

"Risky ground," said Dillon, sipping ice water.

"That's why they call it a growth fund," replied the man, grinning as if he understood Dillon's obligation to remain the voice of caution.

"You tell me to buy something, I'll give you my opinion, and then I'll buy it for you anyway." Dillon was serious. "But I *will* give you my opinion."

The man grinned, sipped his gin and tonic, and cast a glance back at Janis. "Your boss says you're the best."

"I do a little more than just read the hot sheet and place orders. Not much genius in that."

"I didn't say you were a genius. I said you were the best." There was a cockiness in his voice that was too obviously linked to his physical stature.

Dillon just nodded.

The little client lowered his voice. "Take care of me. I have aggressive goals for this fund and I intend to out-perform the market."

"What are you saying?"

"You see something, you jump on it. I'm saying that between the two of us, we can kick some serious ass."

He looked over to see that Janis had been watching their exchange, and that she was greatly amused.

*   *   *

THE call came shortly after midnight at the close of his third day in exile from the Dark Lady. Ironically he had been asleep, the result of complete exhaustion and his decision to simply let it go. Moving on would be painful, the loss of a brief dream, but it appeared he had no other choice.

"You won't get another chance," was the first thing she said to him.

He bolted upright, took a deep breath, alarmed at the intensity with which his heart was pounding in his chest.

"I fucked up," he said. "I'm sorry."

"Royally." Her voice was almost sympathetic now.

"I understand enough about women to know that saying I'm sorry won't get me anywhere. It may even piss you off. But I am sorry."

"Maybe you don't know as much about women as you thought."

"Enough to know that what you want to hear is that I learned a lesson from this."

"Maybe I want to hear *how* sorry you've been, about your misery."

"I can tell you, if you want."

"No need. I can hear it in your voice."

"I didn't think you'd react this way."

"The first part was right."

"The first part?"

"You didn't *think*." A pause. He could hear her soft laughter. "Get out of bed and go to your window," she said.

He set the phone down and did as instructed. Across the Residence Inn parking lot was her black Mercedes

500 SL, its lights off. He could make out the silhouette inside, holding the cell phone to her ear. He went back to the phone next to his bed.

"Come in," he said humbly.

"Trust is everything, Dillon. The more dangerous the game, the more important it is."

"You can trust me."

"You haven't shown me that I can."

"Come in here and let me show you."

"I have another idea." Her voice had shifted. The playfulness was back.

"Another game?"

"This one has a name."

"What is it?"

A perfect pause.

"Punishment," she whispered.

THE game she had named Punishment was to occur the next night at eleven o'clock. Her instructions were to bring a pair of powerful binoculars and to find the dirt road that skirted the hill behind her house. The Wallace estate was on a steep butte with a million-dollar view of the city and the Sound. The hill continued to rise sharply behind the house, which had been cut into the terrain with enough room for a tennis court and pool. The dirt road led to a meteorological station at the crest of the hill and was marked by No Trespassing signs.

He found the road and parked directly behind and above her house. Looking down at a distance of about sixty yards, he could see that an upstairs light was on, very dim. The sky was sprinkled with stars on an uncharacteristically clear evening, the temperature crisp and biting on his cheeks. Beyond the house the city sprawled like a cheap black velvet painting, the downtown skyline rising from a blanket of diamonds.

He trained the binoculars on the second-story bedroom window. The drapes were open, and he could see a slice of the master suite illuminated by flickering shadows—probably a television playing in an otherwise darkened room. Or perhaps candles. He couldn't tell which.

He checked his watch. It was precisely eleven.

There was nothing to see at first. He was leaning against his car, the engine still running, not quite drowning out the crisp sounds of the clear night or the distant hum of the city below. He had played through all the outcomes of this game, assuming it would be a bizarre show-and-tell meant to ring his chimes and prime him for their next encounter.

He would be right about that much.

Somewhere inside the house a door opened. There was a reflection, from the bathroom, perhaps. A set of bare feet appeared, stepping out into the main bedroom area, walking slowly, almost seductively. Stalking. Then he saw a full silhouette, not a reflection this time but the real thing, a perfect female form framed in the window. The source of the light, most certainly candles, he had decided, bathed her in a warm yellow hue, reflecting off her skin almost as if it were wet. It was most certainly her, the Dark Lady, those perfect breasts, hair tied back. The only thing she wore were earrings, which winked when the angle caught the flame of the candles within.

She appeared to be talking to someone there in the room with her. Someone lying on the unseen bed, perhaps. As she spoke she ran her hands over her hips. After a moment of this she began touching her breasts, still talking, locking eyes with whoever was there. Then she leaned forward, propping her weight on her hands on the bed, her feet still visible, one of them kicking back at a ninety-degree angle. She stayed that way for a few moments, and his mind filled with an image he could not see.

And then she was standing again, still touching herself, still talking. This went on for several seconds before she walked out of his line of sight.

Suddenly his heart froze at an unmistakable sound. An approaching car. Tires crunching on frosty gravel. He lowered the field glasses, seeing approaching headlights.

Glancing back at the window, he saw the woman standing there now, looking directly at him.

The car emerged from the blackness of the hillside, filling the night with bright beams of light. He could see red and blue fixtures on top of the vehicle. After a moment a spotlight near the driver's side mirror flicked on, pointing at him with blinding intensity.

Dillon lowered the binoculars to his side. He considered dropping them, trying to nonchalantly kick them down the bluff, but the spotlight had frozen him like a deer. He had to remind himself to breathe.

Thirty seconds passed. Nothing moved except the nearly audible percussion of Dillon's throbbing pulse.

Finally the door opened and the officer got out, leaving the door open as he approached, training a flashlight on Dillon's face. When the officer was close enough for Dillon to see around the light, he was surprised to look upon the face of a woman, her warm breath like smoke in the night air.

"Evening, sir," she said with surprising good cheer. Dillon swallowed, struggling for some semblance of cool. "Evening officer," he said, still squinting from the flashlight.

"This is private property, sir."

"I didn't know. I'm sorry."

"There are signs."

"I didn't see them."

"Mind if I ask what you're doing up here?"

"It's kind of embarrassing," said Dillon, putting as much smile into his voice as possible.

"Why don't you tell me anyway."

"Well, my wife, she sort of threw me out. I'm just, you know, cooling off. You know how it is. Nowhere else to go."

"Can I see some identification, please?"

He tried to discern her face as he fished his wallet out. He opened it to his driver's license, handed it over, and saw her eyes for the first time. She reminded him of Janis, only much younger and trimmer, someone you wouldn't want to piss off.

The flashlight's beam cut to the wallet.

"I understand how this looks," he said. She didn't look at him or respond. "Nice view up here . . . that's why I came." She continued to study the license, glancing up to see how well the photo matched the face. "Nowhere else to go to think," he repeated.

He felt the urge to vomit and concentrated hard on swallowing it back.

"Wait here, please," she said, again fixing the flashlight beam on his face as she backpedaled toward her car. He noticed that the hand holding the wallet was resting on the gun in her belt as she executed this obviously textbook move.

It was perhaps the longest two minutes of his life. Only now did he notice the closed shades in the house below, the lights all off. He took deep, measured breaths, the cold air an effective counter to the nausea, and cursed himself for being here, for playing these games which had suddenly become as dangerous as the Dark Lady had promised.

One learns to love the fear . . .

The officer returned, wallet in hand. As she handed it back to him she said, "Best cool your jets somewhere else, Mr. Masters. Lots of significant taxpayers in this neighborhood who value their privacy and get nervous easily. I think you understand."

He smiled, trying to elicit the same from her, but the best he got was an obligatory and highly professional tightening of her lips.

They got back into their vehicles at the same time. The police car didn't move as Dillon jockeyed the Cherokee back and forth across the width of the road to reverse his direction, and as he drove down the hill he could see the squad car's bright red taillights in his rearview mirror.

On the freeway going back to the Residence Inn he remembered what the Dark Lady had called this game, and after a moment's reflection it made him grin slightly.

The name of her game was Punishment. And she had won again.

22

Dillon was studying the asset list from his new machinist's union pension account when the Dark Lady called. The fund was mostly old industrial dogs and commodity blue chips going nowhere. Anyone looking at him would have wondered about the sudden smile, the relaxed way that he slouched back into his chair when the call came in.

"Sleep well, did we?" she began.

"*That* was interesting," he said.

"I thought so."

"You're dangerous."

"You have no idea."

"Who was that with you?" he asked.

"Who do you think it was?"

"I never take anything for granted with you."

"Smart boy."

There was a brief pause. Then she said, "It's exciting, isn't it, Dillon?"

"Yes, it is," he said with equal restraint.

"How badly do you want me?"

"How bad can you be?"

She laughed softly, but said nothing.

"Test me," he said. "See how badly I want you."

"All right. I'm going up to Vancouver on Monday. I go shopping there every season for the spring sales. They get some of the younger and hipper designers that we don't."

"I don't think you need any fashion tips from me."

"There's a three-fifty flight. I want you on it. There'll be a ticket for you, prepaid." She allowed him a moment to respond, and when he didn't she said, "Are you with me?"

"You know I am."

"Wear your gray double-breasted suit."

He pictured her stalking him, and the notion was exciting. His silence brought another inquiry.

"Do you want to play?" she asked.

"What's the name of *this* game?"

He heard her soft laughter, as if his every response were coming from her own script. "Take a taxi to the Fraser Hotel. Have a drink in the bar. I promise you, you'll need it."

"Will I be drinking alone?"

"Order Scotch. I like the taste of Scotch on a man's tongue. Sit at the bar. The bartender's name is Rick. He's gay. . . . I want you to flirt with him."

"You'll be watching us, then."

"I'll know if you do as I ask or not."

They listened to their mutual breathing for a moment, staring into their mind's picture of each other's eyes.

"What if the flight is late?"

"I'll know that, too."

"You seem to know everything."

"I want you squirming, imagining what I'm going to do to you."

He just moaned softly, slightly contrived for her benefit.

"At eight o'clock take the elevator to the top floor. Not a minute before."

"How will I know the room?"

"You'll know. Don't turn on the light. Come in, sit on the bed, and wait."

"I'm not sure I can wait."

"But you *have* to wait, don't you, Dillon."

He closed his eyes, swooning with the rush. "Yes," he whispered.

"By the way . . . I have something for you," she breathed.

"I have something for you, too," he countered.

"Punishment and reward go hand in hand." Her voice was delighted with itself.

"Are you near your computer terminal?"

"Of course."

"Punch in A-S-T-S," she said.

He did as he was told, and after a moment's search the computer screen filled with data.

"I have it," he said.

"It will look a lot different in a day or two, I guarantee." An appropriate pause, then she said with velvet promise, "I'll see you in Vancouver, Dillon."

And the line went dead.

He stared at the terminal for nearly five minutes, not

seeing the readout at all. He was allowing his body chemistry to return to normal, feeling the drug of her subside while imagining himself playing the role precisely as she'd scripted it. The precision of her instructions made him smile.

Then it dawned on him what he was looking at. He was looking at a fortune. Neurotronics Technologies, the company she had alerted him to a few days earlier, had doubled overnight on the news that her husband's company, the Affinity Group, was engaged in a takeover bid.

Something inside him went off like an air horn. Any information from her was insider information. And judging from Neurotronics, any information from her was golden. Her husband was the insider's insider, the man who moved mountains. He was looking at a windfall here.

When a man has a chance to save his soul, he should take it.

He studied the screen. ASTS—Applied Software Technology Systems. It was traded on the OTC Bulletin Board, which meant it was a small cap company, not yet large enough to reach the NASDAQ. In the high-tech world this could mean one of two extremes: feast or famine. The fact she had mentioned it, however coyly, surely meant a feast was at hand. Her husband was circling over Applied, fangs bared, ready to devour it. The price was only a dollar a share, give or take a few cents. It was up fifteen cents already on the day, on surprisingly heavy volume. Whatever the news was, it was already leaking into the market.

Dillon had seen small cap stocks rocket to the moon before. They could double or triple on breaking news, sometimes overnight. On more than one occasion he'd watched it happen and wished he had been on the inside, sitting on the news yet insulated from the core transaction and the eyes of the Feds.

Like he was right now.

He closed his eyes. It was a victimless crime. Not a crime at all, actually. People traded on inside info all the time. Good people, people with respectable careers and genuinely good souls. It was really just a matter of proximity. The nature of the business. A rotten game. His proximity to Applied Software smelled like money.

He punched in his IRA and 401K accounts, which he had configured onto one screen. They totaled $105,000. With any luck they could be at two hundred grand in a week. But he had to act. He had to act now.

A shiver slithered up his spine. Any late-morning hunger was gone, displaced by adrenaline.

Grow some balls, Masters. Just do it. Just fucking do it.

Within the span of a minute he placed sell orders for nearly all of his holdings in his IRA and 401, twelve mutual funds and stocks in all. Within the following minute, having calculated the proceeds, he placed an order to buy over one hundred thousand dollars worth of Applied Software Technology Systems.

The high was electric. It was sexual, and he wanted his Dark Lady in his arms right then, to ravish her, to make her feel his courage and his power to break free of the rules and howl at the moon.

He took a walk, the buzz only escalating. The world looked different today. He was the lion king, in command of his jungle empire.

When he returned just before the lunch hour, he called his new client at the machinist pension fund and pitched him on ASTS. After going through the fundamentals on his screen, supplemented with several favorable but obscure analyst reports he'd dug up on the

Internet, the man rolled over on it.

It was already up three eighths from his purchase price.

"There's nothing in the fundamentals that smells like a play," the client said.

"I'm not looking at just the fundamentals," said Dillon, his voice clearly full of subtext.

"It's a hunch, then."

"Better than a hunch." He put just enough nuance in his voice to make his point.

The ensuring moment of silence signaled that the little CFO understood.

"You're a bad motherfucker, aren't you, Masters."

"You said to let you in. The door's open."

After a long pause the client said, "We're in."

"How much?"

"A third. Dump the regional bullshit." A third of the account, presently invested in long-dead local timber and aerospace companies, was nearly half a million dollars. Dillon checked the ASTS volume for the day—nearly four million shares had traded. A halfmill buy order would goose the market like a sharp poke in the ass. And since his own order had already filled at one and three sixteenths, he would be the beneficiary. It was the paradox of a gold rush, feeding off its own momentum. Let the games begin.

"You've got it."

"This better fly."

"It'll soar."

DILLON left for lunch at twelve-thirty, his stomach still churning with excitement. In fact, he was ravenous. On his way out he stopped by the desk of the young broker who had been the catalyst for his confrontation with the visiting corporate suit who had tried to ram the Nomura fund down their collective throats. Since then, he and the kid had connected in a subtle way, trading morning hellos and the occasional professional aside. Like most of the young guys, the rookie looked at Dillon as a role model, a man who made his own way in a business full of sheep. Today, that view would be reinforced.

The kid was on the phone when Dillon arrived at his cubicle. He motioned for him to wait, but Dillon grabbed a pen and scribbled "ASTS" onto a notepad. Without hanging up the young broker, who reminded Dillon of a paperboy he'd known in his youth, picked up the notepad and stared at the letters before looking back at him. Dillon grinned and gave the young man a thumbs up, a veteran's quiet "trust me." There would be no possible misinterpretation.

The young broker grinned, realizing what had happened. Money had happened. Dillon left, heading for his favorite deli for deep fried chicken livers and strawberry soda, his ritual celebration of good fortune in the market.

Shortly before one, when the rookie finally got off the phone, he hastily called his only two active trading accounts and talked them into buying all they could of a little-known high-tech issue called Applied Software Technology Systems. "Just trust me on this," he'd said to both of them, and they did.

The kid's final order of the day, which he snuck in just before the closing bell, was a sell order for everything in his own retirement account, some eighteen thousand dollars, and a corresponding buy order for ASTS.

For Dillon, the weekend would be eternally long. But at the end of it there would be Monday. And at the end of Monday there would be Vancouver.

23

The Fraser Hotel in the heart of downtown Vancouver was very much like the Olympic Hotel in downtown Seattle. Both were proud Westin properties with lobbies finished in finely polished imported wood and accessorized with gleaming brass. Both laid claim to hosting presidents and prime ministers, as well as countless thousands of secret couplings like the one he was pursuing.

The flight had been uneventful, a short Air Canada hop that cost as much as a well-planned trip to Mexico. Just as she'd said, an E-ticket was waiting in his name, prepaid, an exit row window seat.

The bartender didn't seem all that gay or all that interested. Dillon sat in his gray double-breasted suit and sipped Dewar's, trying not to squint with each swallow. The hotel in general was strangely vacant, and for the life of him he could see no means for her to observe him. Perhaps she had enlisted an accomplice for this task, since there were a handful of well-suited patrons sitting in pairs, deep in conversation, perhaps headed for their own night of unspeakable delights upstairs.

At precisely eight o'clock he went upstairs. The elevator door opened and he stepped into a brightly lit hallway. He was grateful no one was nearby, for he had no idea which way to turn. He studied both alternatives, noticing the carpet design, seeing a few spent room service trays on the floor awaiting pickup.

With no other choice, he decided on one of the corridors and began to walk, studying each room number and brass fixture, not sure what the sign would be.

At the very end of the hall he found it. The door on the left was ajar, open several inches. Attached to the knob was a single red rose. It was dark inside.

After a reflexive look down the empty hallway he pushed the door open and stepped inside.

He listened for a moment, hearing nothing. The bathroom door was closed, but there was no light coming from beneath it. When he put his ear to the wood he again heard nothing.

He closed the door behind him and waited for his eyes to adjust to the complete and perfect darkness. The only light emanated from digital numbers on the television console somewhere within the room. He was conscious of a faint smell, something old and musty.

It took a full minute before his eyes could comprehend a faint square outline of light around the drapes. He felt his way into the room, reaching down to locate the edge where the bed should have been, and finding it, he sat down. He wondered what would happen next, how long she would make him stay like this in the dark, what he would see when the door opened and her sil-houette filled the hallway.

Three minutes passed. He could hear very faint sounds, traffic twelve stories below, a distant door slam-ming somewhere on the floor, the occasional tick of a building still settling after four decades. And his own heart, thudding relentlessly and expectantly within his rib cage.

He leaned back on the bed. Something was there. A lump beneath the covers. His hand felt along the bed-spread, encountering the soft, slightly pliable shape. His mind leapt to the conclusion that it was her, that she'd been with him this entire time, listening to his thunder-ing heart.

He smiled. His eyes were used to the dark by now, and he navigated around the bed to the nightstand, where his fingers found the lamp switch.

He flipped it on and squinted toward the bed.

There was a mound under the bedspread, roughly the size of a person curled up in a fetal position. The cover was perfect and without wrinkles, as if this bed had been made with military precision even though someone was still in it. You couldn't crawl under the covers and leave them this smooth . . . someone else had to have done it.

His smile unwittingly vanished as he stared at the mound. Nothing moved. The scent he had noticed ear-lier was stronger now. He gripped the corner of the bed-spread and threw it back with one bold motion.

He gasped aloud. He began to shake, and he felt the Dewar's beginning to rise in his throat. He didn't realize he was backing up as he stared at the bed, and he crashed into a glass coffee table and tumbled back-ward to the floor, certain the racket could be heard all the way to the elevators. He remained on the floor, feeling nothing, his eyes riveted on the ghastly scene before him.

The cream-colored sheet was spotted with red stains. It was blood, dark and sticky and glistening. A body, a very naked and very dead body, was in the middle of the bed. A man, lying on his side in an impossible position. Something heavy and sharp had put a dent into the man's head, which was the source of the blood. His ankles were bound together with panty hose, as were his wrists, which had been pulled and tied behind him. An electrical cord was tied to the juncture of his ankles, one end of which was pulled excruciatingly taut up along his buttocks and his spine to the point at which it was wrapped several times around the throat. His eyes were bulging, about to pop out of the dead skull, and the skin there was a deep burgundy in color from vessels that had burst during the death struggle. The man's tongue protruded, almost a child's sassy pose. It had been a slow death, forcing the victim to arch his back to an extreme angle to lessen the pull from the electrical cord that connected his ankles to his throat. After a few moments, when the back muscles spasmed and grew weak and then cramped, the body naturally straightened, pulling at the bindings around the throat, crushing his windpipe. A man's back couldn't sustain the unnatural backward arch necessary to survive for more than a minute or two. The man's own reflex to relax his back muscles ultimately strangled him, certainly after agonizing minutes of trying to alternate between separate and equally excruciating hells.

Satan himself couldn't have devised a more ingenious form of human bondage and hopelessness.

Or *herself*. Because the dead man on the bed was Hamilton J. Wallace, the Dark Lady's husband.

AT first Dillon couldn't take his eyes off what the Dark Lady had left for him. He realized his perception of time was warped—it could have been minutes or only a few seconds that he gazed at what he knew represented the end of life as he knew it.

He would call someone, tell it all straight. The forensics were too easily exposed, there was nothing here to tie him to this—no DNA, no bloody glove. As he looked around the room, however, he realized how very wrong he might be about this assumption.

There was an open bottle of champagne on the desk. Next to it was a glass. A strangely familiar glass, exactly like the one the Dark Lady had brought with her on the ferry picnic and then to the hotel room. He closed his eyes and tried to remember everything, and he quickly realized that his kinkiest memory was perhaps also the deadliest. The leather gloves. She had not taken them off. Not during their entire time together. What he had assumed was a secret and harmless little fetishistic treat was something infinitely more sinister.

He began to search the room. He was on his hands and knees, looking under the bed, when he saw something. Glass. An ashtray, which quickly sparked yet another dagger of a memory to go with the champagne glass and the gloves. It was the ashtray from their night at the Olympic Hotel, and it had been left here for someone to find, along with his fingerprints.

Then, as he flashed back to that night, a new and even more frightening image filled his mind. It was that of the Dark Lady, sitting cross-legged in a chair at the foot of the bed right here in this room, wearing her gloves, watching her husband struggle and bleed, sipping the champagne.

Suddenly his heart froze. Someone was knocking at the door to the room. He heard a voice, but could not make out what it said. He walked to the door with numb legs and trembling hands. The knocking repeated.

"Room service!"

Through the peephole Dillon saw a young bellman standing next to a cart containing several covered plates.

"Room service, Mr. Masters!"

Dillon's chest was heaving. He clamped his eyes tightly closed.

"I can't open the door right now!" he said loudly, certain his voice betrayed his panic. "Can you just leave it there?"

"You have to sign for it, sir. I'm sorry."

"I'll come down in a few minutes to sign for it. I'm not feeling well right now."

"I'm not supposed to leave the cart, sir."

"You'd leave it in the room anyway, right?"

The bellman grimaced, thinking it over. Then he mouthed the word "shit" and moved the cart next to the wall, out of the center of the corridor. Already this was unusual enough to ensure that the young man would remember everything for the district attorney's tape recorder.

"I'll leave the food and the check, Mr. Masters. Just call when you're ready to sign for it. I hope you feel better, sir."

Dillon turned his back and leaned heavily against the door. How could it be? This was madness.

Another thought popped into Dillon's reeling head, one that chilled him to the core. He walked briskly over to the television, finding the remote control. He pointed it at the TV, waiting an eternal few moments for the

screen to illuminate. A menu of choices soon materialized, one of them labeled "Guest Services." He punched
in the code—88—and was greeted with another screen
reading: "One moment please."

"Come on!" he said aloud, glancing at the dead eyes
and the oozing dent in the victim's frontal lobe.

And then he saw what he expected to find and feared
most. The television displayed the current status of the
account for the room. The meal outside the door was
already there, right under the room charge and the appropriate taxes. At the top of the screen was the name of
the guest to whom the room was registered.

The name was his own.

24

He had never truly known helplessness. Not like what he was feeling now. In this moment, standing in the naked gaze of the dead man on the bed, he realized that in his past, during times he thought were indeed hopeless, he always had options. Even now there were options—two of them, in fact. Flee and be crucified, falsely accused. Or call someone and throw himself on the mercy and wisdom of a judicial system he knew too little about and had learned from the media to distrust. Both options sucked.

He processed the alternatives for about twenty minutes. He had few connected thoughts, none that moved him any closer to a concrete plan. He had even reached for the phone to call Jordan, friend and lawyer, both of which he needed desperately. Halfway through dialing, however, he realized he was acting out of panic, that the call would commit him to one course of action over the other. The best Jordan could do would be to refer him to someone else. He slammed down the phone, cleaned off his fingerprints, and began to pace.

His thinking was distracted by the corpse, whose tongue, lolling out between blue lips, seemed to be mocking him from the bed. He couldn't concentrate, and he needed to more intensely and clearly than ever before. After many minutes of trying he threw the bedspread back over the body and sat down to work out his destiny.

There was another nagging distraction that nibbled at Dillon's mind. The betrayal. Its pain was almost louder than his fear. She had played him like a master puppeteer. He had been so easy, a classic fool wearing a sign that read: "Fuck me over." If he ever got out of this he'd challenge Carmichael to explain it, because right now it seemed beyond understanding. Right now, getting out of it didn't seem a likely outcome. She had covered every base, anticipated his every reaction.

And then it hit him. A possible crack in her armor. She had been so *arrogant*. So vain and assumptive. Her vanity was certainly part of the costume, the shiny black catsuit of seduction tailored specifically for his tastes, which she seemed to understand so completely. But the arrogance and the vanity were real. A woman can't fake such self-confidence, the utter acceptance that the world revolved around her ability to gather attention and get her way. This was the part of the game she liked best.

Perhaps it was a fatal flaw, one that gave him a third option after all.

He knew instantly what he must do. What he didn't know was how to do it, and if he had the stones to pull it off.

No one was in the hall when he opened the door. He pulled the room service cart inside and began putting the plates of food onto the dresser. She had ordered him seafood pasta, two Pellegrinos, and an ice cream sundae. The bitch. They were his favorite dishes—even the food would be incriminating.

Once the cart was empty he threw off the white cloth and sank to his knees to examine it closely. The cart ran on rollers connected to a framework of legs and cross-supports, all of which were normally covered by the pseudo-tablecloth. He visualized what had to happen, and realized that what he was considering was as grisly as it was most likely impossible. A live body couldn't possibly assume the shape required to pull this off. But a dead body wouldn't argue. It would simply bend, even break if it had to. And it would have to for this insane idea to work.

IT took half an hour to complete the nightmare task. First he cut the panty hose and the electric cord away, fighting back the gag reflex when the limbs, now free, barely moved from their unnatural position. The smell was getting worse, as human waste oozed from the corpse at the pace of gravity.

He dragged the body to the room service cart and literally stuffed it into the web of legs and cross-supports. He had to tie the wrists to the legs just under the tabletop, using the same panty hose and the electric cord that had brought about Hamilton Wallace's death. The bulk of the weight rested on the cart's bottom beams, which crossed in an X formation near the floor between the four legs. The corpse's eyes remained open, a dry and distant stare, and Dillon tried closing them, using a technique he'd seen a hundred times on television. It didn't work. The touch of his fingers on the cold and open flesh of the man's dead eyeballs made his stomach twist.

He retched again when he had to push on a knee joint so hard that something snapped. It was a wet pop, surprisingly loud. He had known the sound would come, because he was pushing on it with his shoulder like a lineman pushing a blocking sled, trying to fit the dead frame into the unforgiving geometry of the space beneath the cart. The sound made him jump back, and he used the moment to catch his breath.

It was the sound of commitment. He had only one option now.

He'd had the foresight to move the body with the sheet still under it, sliding the entire affair off the bed with a sickening thud. He now used the sheet to help secure the body to the cart, wrapping one end around the head. He was also smart enough to remove his own shirt and pants before beginning the job, and now, upon completion, he looked at the blood on his hands and on his body and again felt the urge to vomit. It was a process of focus and determination, because anything less would have allowed him to consider the horror of it.

He showered quickly, cursing when he saw that there were no clean towels remaining. Perhaps the Dark Lady had cleansed herself of the crime before leaving. He used the bath mat to dry himself, noticing that his hands were still shaking. Then he quickly dressed before spending ten minutes restoring the room to some semblance of normal use.

It was done. It was time.

Details would make or break him now. He looked around the room yet again, seeing something he'd noticed but not attached any importance to. Wallace's clothes were neatly folded on the floor next to the desk. Odd, how someone about to be tied up would take the time to fold them this way. Dillon went through the pockets of the trousers, made of fine Italian linen and costing three to four hundred dollars, and found what he was looking for.

Car keys. A familiar key chain logo.

The last thing he did was drape the cloth back over the room service cart. It reached nearly to the floor, completely hiding the hideous sculpture beneath it. As an afterthought, he spooned a couple of bites of the ice cream into his mouth, which was dry and tasted of bile. The coldness was soothing, and he hoped it would quiet his raging nerves.

He put the plates of food back on top of the cart. Then he opened the door and pushed it out into the bright lights of the hallway.

25

The worst thing Dillon could do now was look nervous. He had to appear as if he had the world by the balls and intended to squeeze. He had to look like anything other than how he felt. You didn't mess with someone in a hurry and on a mission, even if they were pushing a room service cart.

There was no one in the hall. Just before he reached the bank of elevators he noticed a door without a room number, and he sensed it had something to do with housekeeping. He stopped, pushed the door open, looked inside, and saw the service elevator.

It took forever to arrive, which made sense for anyone who had ever ordered a meal sent up to a hotel room. When it did, the car was empty—so far, so good. He pushed the cart inside and studied the button panel, and was relieved to find a P button there. Somewhere in the bowels of the building was Wallace's Jaguar. If there was more than one Jag, he'd simply try the key. If he was wrong, he'd have to listen to the car alarm's wail as he continued his search.

As the door slid shut, he saw a single drop of blood on the tile floor of the room. He tried to stop the door, but it was too late.

Looking down, he saw another drop of blood on the floor of the elevator. The tile floor was a highly scuffed mess, so he took the sole of his shoe and spread it thin until it virtually vanished into the grungy ambiance of the tiles. He'd have to take his forensic chances with the droplet left behind.

His heart stopped when the elevator slowed to a halt on the fourth floor. The doors slid open and a tiny Hispanic woman entered with an arm full of towels. Her eyes immediately registered confusion, but she came in anyway and hit the L button. She glanced at him and then quickly looked away when he nodded a greeting. He watched her eyes, seeing if they ever lowered to the cart. But the cart wasn't the anomaly in this elevator. He was.

The doors opened on the L level. The woman moved out into a service hallway, avoiding his eyes. As the elevator doors closed, he saw that the little housekeeper had turned to regard him a final time, and that her eyes were now fixed on the cart. He had to get the hell out of there fast.

The elevator doors opened out into a glass lobby that led to the parking garage. He could see the traffic through openings of the distant walls. The pavement was sloped, leading down into two more levels of underground parking.

Dillon checked the floor under the cart. There was no blood this time. But there was no way to know how many drops of Hamilton Wallace's essence had marked his journey.

He started to push the cart through the glass doorway, then stopped. He was sweating at the exertion of pushing the dead weight of the cart through a warm hotel, exacerbated by the fact that he was fleeing for his life. He used the moment to think, considering his next move. He'd have to leave the cart behind and go look for the Jag first.

HE found the Jaguar after several brisk minutes of walking through the hotel garage. It was on the second level, a brand-new champagne XK8. He hit the remote key button and was relieved when the taillights flashed and the horn issued a friendly little toot. He shook his head at the irony—it was his dream car. An issue of *Car and Driver* with one on the cover was somewhere in a desk drawer at work. Now he'd get a test drive with the owner's body stuffed in the trunk.

He got in, started it up, and wound his way back up to the street level.

HE had left one of his shoes in the door of the glass-walled elevator lobby, keeping it open several inches in anticipation of his return. It was a security door; one had to buzz the front desk to gain entrance, or use a room key, which he didn't think to bring. There was nothing else there to use as a doorstop. His heart pounded as he pulled the car into the garage entrance, praying he would see the glass door ajar from his shoe and the cart still there.

He'd left it unattended, though realizing that the first employee to pass would grab it and head upstairs for the kitchen. They'd notice how heavy it was, stop, and look at the wheels, then pull up the white cloth for a peek underneath. They'd see Wallace's naked torso with its swaddled head between its knees, one of which was bent at an impossible angle. They'd see ankles and feet tied to the cart with panty hose. And then they'd scream or faint dead away. Luckily, the cart—and his shoe— were still in place.

He stopped the car, got out, and opened the trunk. Ninety grand and the trunk was no bigger than a Geo Metro's. In the trunk were Wallace's golf clubs, a ridiculously expensive set with his name embroidered on the side of the bag, as if he were a pro. Then again, Wallace had been the kind of guy who probably shot scratch golf and would do anything to win. Dillon pulled the clubs out and stashed them behind the bucket seats.

Almost home now.

Several drops of blood were visible on the concrete floor. Dillon grabbed the dinner napkin from the tabletop, which he'd unrolled to get to the spoon for his medicinal bite of ice cream. It was still there, too, half melted now. He wiped up the blood and pulled the cart through the doorway.

There was a wooden strip at the bottom of the door. When the cart's rear wheels bounced over it, the panty hose gave way and one of Wallace's naked and alarmingly white legs shot out from under the cart.

Dillon moved fast. A car could pull in at any moment. The elevator doors could slide open and Mr. and Mrs. John Q. Public from Peoria would get the surprise of their lives. He yanked at the remaining knots and freed the body's wrists and ankles. He lifted the torso from behind, underneath the arms, not having the time to take care that blood didn't get on his shirt. There was no alternative. Wallace's heels dragged on the pavement and off the curb as he backpedaled toward the open trunk. He'd heard somewhere that dead weight was the heaviest of all, and he'd heard right—Dillon felt like he was moving an outside linebacker.

He dumped the body facedown into the trunk. Then he went back to the cart for Wallace's clothes. It was then that he noticed the blood on his shoulder. A huge stain, the size of a softball.

Part of Wallace's wardrobe consisted of a sports coat. Linen, designer name, very billionaire-appropriate. He was much smaller than Dillon, but this was his only choice in the closet. Dry cleaning was not an option here. Still sweating, he worked his arms into the jacket, already uncomfortable, but grateful.

There were always options. Sometimes you just have to invent and then stretch them in creative ways.

THE Jag's cornering was all that he'd fantasized in calmer times. As he rounded the final one with a squeal, he saw that a toll booth stood between him and the street. Inside the booth was a bearded man watching a hockey game on a portable television, the stub of a fat cigar in his mouth, nearly burned down to his beard.

Dillon pulled up, rolling down the widow. The attendant slid open the glass partition and looked at him expectantly.

"I, uh, lost my ticket, I guess. Sorry." Dillon patted his pockets as he spoke, trying to appear casual—not an easy task when the sports coat you're wearing is two sizes two small.

"You a guest of the hotel?"

Dillon hesitated, and the man's forehead furrowed. Finally, he said, "Yes."

"Name?"

He hesitated again.

"Name, sir?"

Panic came and went. He almost said the wrong name.

"Dillon Masters."

"Nice ride."

Dillon just nodded.

The clerk entered the name into his computer terminal, waiting a moment as he gave his attention back to the hockey game. Then, seeing what he needed to see, he pressed a button on the cash register and the partition raised.

ONE more hurdle and he could relax. The U.S. border. Sometimes they checked you out, sometimes they didn't. What triggered an inspection was as fickle as the guard's mood. If he got the wrong man-hating bitch at the wrong time of the month, he was dead. If he got a five-foot-four minimum-wage Clint Eastwood with a face like a bulldog that had been beaten one too many times, he was finished. Guys like that hated guys like Dillon on sight. It was all in the hands of God now. What had transpired thus far had been the work of the other team.

The border was twenty miles or so south of downtown Vancouver, giving him time to think. Nothing he had done would protect him if the heat kicked on. If Veronica Wallace told the police her husband had gone to Vancouver and not returned, they'd find what they needed to find. If she told them about Dillon and their affair, twisting it to position her own innocence, he was toast.

The only way his efforts to remove the body from the hotel would benefit him was to somehow convince the widow that it was in her best interests to consider another outcome. Because without a body and a complaint, then what he'd done to cover his tracks just might work. The room was his, and he had trashed it. No big deal. Hotel employees have seen the aftermath of everything of which human beings are capable, because they've had to clean it all up.

Short of the realization that his only hope rested with the Dark Lady, he had nothing. No plan, no square one. All he had was his awareness of her single weakness, which she perceived as her strongest power—her feminine ego.

The U.S. border loomed ahead, glowing in the night like a neon oasis. One of the stalls was open, and he saw a female guard step out of the booth, clipboard in hand. He stopped next to her and lowered the window.

"Evening. Late drive home?"

She looked like a woman who had dreamed of this uniform all her life. She could have been attractive, and if uniforms were your thing, then this was your gal. But instead of coming off as feminine she was all business, her hair regulation short, her eyes cold and probing.

"Saves a fat hotel tab," he said. When her eyes surveyed the Jag, he realized how ridiculous this sounded. Her expression confirmed his realization.

"In Canada for business or pleasure tonight, sir?" She was still looking over the car, he hoped longingly rather than skeptically.

"Depends if the deal closes."

This made her look back at him. A slight smile appeared. Then her eyes went to the tiny backseat where Wallace's golf clubs were resting. It wasn't exactly golfing weather outside. He saw her eyes narrow. "What's in the trunk?" she asked.

Heat assaulted his face. "Samples. I sell commercial carpet . . . airports, hotels, things like that. Oughtta be driving a van, I know."

She as checking out the Jag again, her face softer than before.

"Business must be good." She wrote the license number down on her pad. Without looking at him she said, "Have a good night, sir."

She stepped back, allowing him to drive through, into the land of the free and the home of the best legal defense money could buy.

26

At the precise moment Dillon was passing through the security checkpoint into the United States, Jordan Chapman was calling out to a God he had never before acknowledged except with profanity. The woman straddling him was in the midst of her third orgasm in what had been the most amazing sixty minutes of athletic sex he had ever experienced, and now he was joining her in heaven. He'd been close several times, but the woman had an uncanny sense of his urgency, and managed to slow down to a safe speed moments before the inevitable came to pass, riding him softly until he was in control again, licking the sweat from his nipples, then assuming her frantic pace and what seemed like an almost angry pummeling. He normally didn't prefer the submissive posture, where control of pace and angle was less available to him. But she'd insisted, not with words, but with the physical persuasion of a wrestler. Were it not for the Viagra he'd popped as they were leaving the bar, Jordan knew he would have missed this train, because there was no denying her need to control the dance.

He'd gone to his favorite quiet bar after seeing a movie alone, not really in the hunt tonight but hopeful for a bit of conversation. Romantic comedies made him lonely. He'd noticed the woman immediately upon his arrival. She was sitting at a corner table away from other patrons, nursing a martini while studying what appeared to be an annual report. Her reading glasses gave her an executive aura that matched her tailored business suit and Mont Blanc leather briefcase on the floor at her feet. A cell phone was on the table next to her glasses case. The ashtray was clean, always a good sign. Her short blond hair was stylish but conservative, and her fingernails were perfect but understated.

It was as if she'd stepped right out of the screen of his own romantic comedy, scripted and directed for his solitary viewing pleasure. It's title was *The Business Bitch*, and he'd been viewing the trailer for years.

Eye contact was achieved within minutes, though she looked away as if to dismiss any notion that she was there for conversation. He quickly abandoned all hope, content for the next ten minutes with stealthy glances using the mirror behind the bar. After a while, when she returned from the rest room, he was surprised when he heard the words "excuse me," coinciding with a light tap on his shoulder. He turned to see her standing next to him.

Without the reading glasses her face had a sort of Grace Kelly perfection. An embarrassed but confident little grin put him immediately at ease. He raised his eyebrows, trying to look responsive yet cool.

"I bet you're as tired as I am of this little mirror game we're playing, so I thought I'd come over and say hi."

He glanced at the mirror, where her empty seat was clearly in the line of sight. "You play it better than me, obviously," he said, feeling the heat descend on his face.

She extended a hand. "I'm Ronnie."

"Jordan." He returned that handshake, noting that hers was firm and masculine.

"Would you care to join me?" She nodded to the bartender, who understood that two fresh drinks were required at her table. "My tab," she said to the man, who smiled back at her.

Ninety minutes later she was in Jordan's bed, and her black Mercedes SL 500 was parked in the driveway to his condo.

"**WE'RE** terrible," said Jordan. "We haven't even exchanged last names. Mine's Chapman."

She was sitting on the edge of her bed, her eyes searching for her clothes. A CD of a classical guitarist played softly in the background.

"You are assuming I remember your *first* name."

It had a cold ring to it, and he grimaced. He started to speak, but stopped when he saw that she was gathering her things from the floor.

"You can stay if you want. I'd like that."

"I have to go home." She didn't look at him as she spoke. "My husband might call."

"Holy shit."

She had been so perfect, so full of sophistication and bubbling enthusiasm for his stories. They had touched hands over drinks, the outcome quickly inevitable, and it had been her idea to come here, to see where he lived. He'd been swept up in the momentum of it, the romantic comedy of it all. They'd talked about movies and about business, interrupted only by a quick call with the cell phone to leave an obscure message about her being out later than expected. He hadn't asked for details.

"You're brutal," he said.

"That's how I fuck," she replied. "Any complaints on your end?"

She shot him a quick grin as she wiggled into her skirt.

"I mean, slow down here, okay? What is this?"

"Exercise," she replied.

"You're kidding me."

She didn't respond, slipping into the suit jacket now. He'd never seen a woman dress so efficiently. After seeing to her hair in his dresser mirror, she turned to him and said, "It was really very nice." She came to him, bent low, and kissed him on the forehead. He tolerated the moment, then pushed her away, as if her touch was suddenly toxic.

She grinned down at him. "You're better than your friend Dillon."

Jordan felt his jaw fall open, and in a flash it was all clear, the fragmented color of a shattered crystal. Her grin remained in place, allowing him the moment to put it all together. In his mind he saw the dark hair, the sunglasses, the silhouette of the woman who stood over him now.

"Holy shit," he said again. "You're . . . *her*."

She turned now, her grin wider, affirming his query. After adjusting her skirt and jacket, she plucked her purse from the dresser and left without turning back, without saying another word.

*   *   *

THE next day at his office, a midmorning delivery arrived. It was a bouquet of red roses, addressed to Jordan. His secretary seemed amused, assuming something close to what the truth actually was—a one-nighter, a new flame, someone smitten with Jordan's car and attitude. Jordan had kept his cool as he read the card in front of her, but when he left for lunch early she went into his office and read the card for herself.

"Thanks for the romantic comedy. I so adore affairs, don't you? V."

27

The boy was twelve when he first confronted courage. His parents had been fighting, a particularly long binge this time, so when he arrived home from school to find his mother drunk and on the telephone, he was not surprised. It was like a Polaroid in his mind, her standing there still in her pink bathrobe, the house choked with stale smoke and overflowing ashtrays, one in every room. His mother's dark eyes were framed with shadowed circles, her hair stringy and uncombed, a glass of pungent brown liquid in her hand. The faint smell of vomit was in the air, mixed with the smoke and the morning's stale perfume.

He went right to his room and shut the door, donning a headset and trying to lose himself in a flying magazine.

It was only a matter of time before his door opened. They'd go through the usual charade, her asking if she could talk to him, her voice more than slightly slurred. He would pretend, very politely, that this was a delightful idea. She would want to talk about his father, and he knew better than to try to derail her intent, because this would put him smack in the center of her fickle target. It was nothing particular about the man—whatever set her off on these binges quickly faded to a detail in the big picture of their matrimonial misery—just the continuing state of his complete and utter ineptitude as a husband and a human being. She wasn't looking for dialogue with her son, yet sooner or later in the script she expected sympathy or agreement. When it didn't come quickly enough she would turn on him, reminding him how he was just like his father, how neither of them deserved her, how all her work was what kept the family strong and how she should be treated with some goddamn respect.

But today was different. Today she talked about her fear. Last night his father had thrown her to the ground as he stormed out of the house. Because he had seen it, the boy knew it was just a stiffer than necessary shoulder to move her out of the doorway as he stormed out, and her drunken balance betrayed her. A couple of days earlier his father had backhanded her and then shaken her until she threw up. Between retches she was screaming that he was trying to kill her, though the boy knew his father was simply trying to get her to shut her mouth. Yet it was her version that the neighbors would hear, as would her sisters and even his friend's parents. Tonight she omitted the fact of her taunting, challenging him to hit her, assuring him that this would be the only way he could ever get her to stop speaking her courageous truths.

Today her agenda had a new wrinkle. Today she would challenge her son to protect her from her husband. Today, she advised him, he would understand what it meant to be a man.

She was still in his room when his father got home. "There he is," she said when the sound of the front door reached them, her voice low and conspiratorial. "A woman shouldn't have to be afraid in her own house. It's not right. You need to put a stop to this. You need to do the right thing. You're big enough now, and you can't hide from what's right in this house any longer!"

His father appeared in the doorway to his room, his expression showing full comprehension of the evening that awaited him.

"Jesus Christ, leave the boy alone," he said with a depth of sincerity that unmasked a broken heart.

She went after him with a vengeance. The sheer volume and tone of her voice would be enough to break any other man, at least that was what the boy had used to rationalize his father's inevitable and unavoidable violence. His father almost always endured it quietly at first, sitting motionless with his head in his hands as she bent over him, screaming the utter injustice of her world. The soundtrack was the same from fight to fight. The boy could feel the tension building, see it twitching in his father's neck, and then the explosion would come, his father springing upright, the next move in question. On most nights he would storm off to another room and slam the door with enough force to splinter the wooden frame. Sometimes he would leave the house altogether, and she would follow him outside in the rain in her robe and stand on the sidewalk, screaming at his car.

On some nights his father would take hold of his mother's shoulders with both hands and slam her into the nearest wall. There they would both scream at once, neither hearing the other, nose to nose, saliva and tears mixing in the air between them. Occasionally the shouting would end with a slap to her head, or her being thrown to the ground, or both. Never a clenched fist or an outright attack. Just a spilling of pain that overpowered his mother's rain of venom and his father's restraint.

This would be one of those nights when the pain would win.

Tonight it took about fifteen minutes of screaming for his father to react. She had followed him as he fled the family room where he had tried to watch the news, turning the volume up full. He was in tears, his eyes terrified and terrifying, and the boy knew the man was near some sort of breaking point.

He didn't really want to intervene. He just wanted to watch with detachment, observe the inevitable and natural outcome of opposing forces colliding. It wasn't his moment, it was theirs. But tonight he knew his involvement was precisely what his mother was vying for. He knew this was the moment when he had to do something, to be a man, unsure of why.

So he acted. Nothing too dramatic, just a timid hand on his father's arm as it held his screaming mother motionless. He remembered the look in her eyes at that moment, a wild glee, and he instantly understood the manipulation, how she had put him into the play as her advocate, simply with this feeble and misappropriated touch. He drew back his hand, but it was already too late.

"Dad . . . don't. Please." It was a twelve-year-old's voice, unsure and already sensing this was the wrong thing to do, the wrong place to be. He was nearly as tall as his father by now, but with a child's body.

His father swung out his arm, the wrist connecting to the boy's forehead. The rage had overridden any sense of strength or degree. The blow turned the boy's vision white, a flash of nothingness, staggering him backward, and his father's screams to stay out of it sounded as if they came from a distance. The boy toppled against the opposite wall and slinked to the floor, one hand holding his head against a swirl of pain and the suddenly distant and hollow shouting.

One of his father's hands was pinning his mother's throat against the wall, while the other pointed at the boy. "You want some of me, little man? You think this is your goddamn fight? You *don't* want this fight, goddamn it! Just stay the fuck out of my face, you hear me?"

At the same time, his mother was shouting, "Don't let him do this! You have to stop this! This is wrong, it's sick and wrong!"

The boy never told anyone about that evening, which ended with his father threatening yet again to blow his own brains out with his service revolver, which he kept loaded in the nightstand. That and only that would finally make his mother happy when all of his other efforts have so obviously failed. The boy spent his adolescence trying to analyze his father's failure that night, as well as his own, his inability to protect his mother and his equal inability to comprehend why he should.

His mother never asked for his protection again, even when she needed it, which would be often. And if she had, the boy had decided that he had no place in his parents' dance of rage, and that whatever happened between them, be it her submission or his service revolver, was in some way what they had chosen for themselves. She did on occasion, however, use what had happened that night as a point of reference during the years that followed, proof and validation of how he, like all men, had failed her when she needed him most. How he had failed himself, as well. It would be decades before he would understand that this was precisely what she had hoped for when she came into his room that evening, that he and his father were nothing more than props in a one-woman, one-act passion play. And that its outcome, which changed everything forever, was never in doubt.

He decided that night that if he was ever going to act against either one of them, he'd have to do it in such a way that they'd never see it coming.

28

Veronica Wallace opened her eyes the next morning and smiled. She was alone in her bed, and as she fanned out her limbs she enjoyed the coolness of the sheets. Hamilton had been a bed hog, all knees and elbows, and even though she had awakened alone on many mornings when he traveled, today's freedom was different. It was . . . significant. Rare winter sunlight illuminated the sheer opaque window coverings, and as she stretched she marveled at the complete and utter absence of any emotion other than pride.

She could do anything. Absolutely anything.

And now all of this was hers.

She got up and yanked open the curtains, looking out at the covered pool. The patio looked lonely without its furniture, which was stored until spring. Beyond, the dark green tennis court surface had turned almost black from the rain, and it was reflecting the low winter sun like a pool of ice. Where normally the grounds were alive with color, everything was barren and brown. Today's unexpected brightness made it all look abandoned, a sepia-toned photo from another time.

She would sell the house. Move to Grand Cayman and find a young hard-body banker who liked to get high and swim naked in the ocean.

She padded into her bathroom wearing a peach satin nightgown, leaving her robe draped over the bedstead on top of the one-thousand-dollar handmade quilt Hamilton had brought back for her from the Amish country two years ago. She looked at herself in the mirror, her blond hair short enough to remain stylish even in the morning. It was the kind of thing a man—the *right* man—would appreciate. Her eyes were a deep emerald green, as striking as the ice blue lenses she'd been wearing whenever she donned the dark wig for her games with Dillon.

She ran the sink full of cold water, staring at the smoothness of her skin while she waited. She remembered her plastic surgeon's smile, the way he stroked her neck as the anesthesia rushed down the IV into her mind, and how the laser burns took forever to heal. She lowered her face and lifted the water to it with cupped hands, enjoying the frigid jolt and the soothing of her eyes.

When she straightened up she patted her cheeks with a hand towel. Upon lowering the towel she looked into the mirror and into the face of a man standing right behind her.

Dillon.

Her gasp was remarkably subtle. She just stared at

him in the mirror, both of them completely motionless, and it occurred to her that she was imagining the moment. She blinked, but Dillon remained in the mirror, his face grim, slightly threatening. After a moment she could sense his body heat and the sensual electricity that comes with proximity.

"You look like you've just seen a dead man," said Dillon. Already his tone was different, calmer and stronger than before.

Something was terribly wrong here.

She just stared. Dillon could tell her mind was racing, carefully side-stepping mistakes born of emotion, in no hurry to commit. She was good at this. In an instant, witnessing her cool, he realized what he was up against. His plan was going to be impossibly difficult to pull off.

"I've been watching you sleep," he said.

They locked eyes, a world of possibilities reeling like fruit and sevens in a slot machine window.

She drew a deep breath. Her grin was forced and unsuccessful in masking her confusion. "My housekeeper will be here. I'll scream."

"Now why would you do that?"

She didn't answer, instantly sensing that a play was at hand, and that her initial assumption was possibly invalid. Instinct had always served her well, and it was yelling at her now. She would wait, see what he did with his cards.

"I like your hair," he said, acknowledging its different color and length. "That must have been where you were last night . . . changing your hair."

She blinked. "Last night?"

"When you were supposed to be meeting me. In Vancouver. You were getting your hair done."

He moved closer, feeling her stiffen at his touch. He

encircled her waist with his arms and put his chin on her shoulder, a lover's gesture, keeping eye contact in the mirror. They were gunfighters, waiting for the other to flinch.

"You're a very bad little girl, aren't you, Mrs. Wallace?"

He could see something akin to fear creeping into her expression. He kept his arms around her, surprisingly calm.

"I don't know what you're talking about," she said.

"Your games . . . sending me to that hotel and then standing me up like that. Making me your fool. You are so very wicked."

She didn't know what to say. Her eyes wavered, flickering to the side, before she caught herself and again locked into his gaze, defiant now.

What had gone wrong?

His grin melted away and he narrowed his eyes. "We need to talk."

"What are you doing here, Dillon?"

"I like it when you say my name like that."

"Don't fuck with me."

"This isn't how the game is played, is it? *You* do the fucking, I do the squirming."

She started to respond, then changed her mind. She turned when their eyes met, and she saw a resolve there she'd never noticed before.

"Something happened last night," he said. "But then, you already know that, don't you?" He paused. "Or, do you? I can't tell . . . you're acting very strange."

"Tell me what you want."

He looked puzzled. Then he smiled again, enjoying fucking with her.

"I want to talk."

She paused, squinting, analyzing options. "I need a minute."

His smile held, commanding the moment.

"I'll be right outside. Take your time."

He backed out of the bathroom, reaching for the knob and pulling the door closed behind him.

When the latch clicked the Dark Lady covered her mouth with her hands and stifled a sob, slowly sinking to her knees.

29

Dillon sat on the edge of her bed and waited with his eyes fixed on the bathroom door. He'd already checked the room out—there was no other exit. While she was still asleep he'd gone through every drawer and every nook of the bathroom's cabinets—there were no weapons, no telephone.

He was in no hurry to take the next step. It had been the longest night of his life, and now the weariness was settling into his joints and muscles in a most palpable way. He drew slow, deep breaths in an attempt to force a sense of calm.

First he'd stopped at the Residence Inn to change into a T-shirt. The blood on his dress shirt had dried stiff, and the trace scent was making him queasy. He'd forgotten to check for messages, but that could certainly wait.

Getting into the Dark Lady's house had been as simple as using Wallace's garage door opener and strolling into the utility room. The house was big enough that the noise was sufficiently distanced from the third-floor master suite, where he assumed she was. Her car was in the garage, so he intuited she was home, sound asleep upstairs. He'd arrived shortly before five, when the night was still motionless under a shroud of lawn-hugging mist.

He'd removed his shoes and searched for the stair-well. He took a moment to check out the geography of the main floor, as much to take in the excess of it all as anything else. He was strangely light and free, as if having nothing more to lose. There was a righteousness to his trespass, a vindication in his impending treachery.

He'd climbed to the third level and found the master suite. He stood in the double doorway, allowing his eyes to acclimate, eventually seeing that she was alone in her bed. He'd half expected otherwise, and was ready with a wrench he'd palmed from the garage on his way in. A quick peek into the second level bedrooms had assured him that the house was otherwise empty.

Then he'd gone into the bathroom and completed his checking, finally settling in behind the marbled glass shower door, which allowed him a clear view of the bed. If he'd had any doubts at all, they dissolved when he watched her stretch out on the mattress, then get out of bed and stand before the window with her short and perky blond hair flat against her head.

She didn't look at him when she finally came out of the bathroom. She crossed through the master suite into the huge walk-in closet as if he were part of the decor.

The closet was the size of a normal living room. She took off her robe and began to dress with a casual indifference that was remarkably ineffective. He followed and stopped at the entrance, not sure what she might have hidden there, a weapon or an alarm of some sort. He leaned against the doorway and watched as she pulled on a pair of black leggings.

"You're angry," he said. He waited for a response, but she didn't so much as look up. "I don't blame you. I break in, catch you without your makeup . . ."

"Tell me what you're doing here," she said without looking up.

"See, you *are* angry."

The action behind her eyes was amazing, filling him with confidence.

He went on. "Aren't you going to ask me how I knew your husband wouldn't be here? I mean, why would I break in, if I didn't already know you'd be alone."

He could almost hear her heart pounding.

"I assume you're going to tell me," she said.

He nodded, his own eyes hiding stories. "I had a client dinner last night. An emergency meeting. I had no way to call you. Supposedly you were already up in Vancouver shopping. What could I do?"

She stopped what she was doing, looking up at him with those curiously squinting eyes. Behind them, he could see, was a storm of activity.

He went on. "I couldn't get out of the meeting. Believe me, I tried. When I couldn't reach you I waited until six and started calling the hotel."

He could tell her searching eyes were looking for a crack, the slightest weakness, something upon which to pounce.

As was he.

"You called the hotel?" she finally said, her voice distant as she returned to dressing.

"Oh, yeah. At least eight times. Got pretty chummy with the receptionist. Asked her to page you, asked her to talk to the bartender, I even asked for your room."

Her eyes shot to him again. "And what did they say?"

He had obviously touched a nerve.

"They said they didn't have a room registered to you."

He saw her relax a little. "Of course they didn't," she said.

"That's what I finally figured out. It takes me awhile sometimes . . . all this sexual arousal, it takes the edge off." He paused, his grin almost friendly. "You weren't there. That was the game."

"The room could have been in another name."

"I thought of that. There was nothing I could do about it anyway . . . because, you see, I wasn't there either."

He watched the fly hit the water and waited for the fish to hit. If she bit, he'd have to play the line with a deft touch, just enough tension to keep the hook in place. He wasn't all that sure she would go for it.

After a frozen moment a playfully cruel smile emerged on her face as she stepped into the role.

Fish on.

"It would have been an interesting evening, don't you think?"

You like to mess with guys, don't you . . .

He returned the grin, a challenge met. "You get me up there, stand me up, no room on the top floor, just me wandering around like an asshole looking for some sign, not finding anything, mad as hell, embarrassed, maybe even a little afraid . . . that's some game. I'm really sorry I ruined it for you."

She continued dressing, a stylish tennis sweatshirt over her leggings and straight-out-of-the-box tennis shoes, as if heading out for a jog or a spin on the old StairMaster. Her movements were abrupt and clipped, her gaze too steadfastly fixed on the wall.

She was good. He shivered with the thought of how good she might be, the calculating sociopathology of her. For all he knew she was putting it all together at this instant, way ahead of him, already well into her next move.

When she turned to him they locked eyes, this time for at least thirty seconds, an eternity of considering the unsaid. All the smiling and posturing had vanished. It was just them, naked of their fraud, trying to read the other's intent with everything at stake. He sensed a fresh confidence in her now, as if she believed she had her hands back on the reins.

Which was exactly what he wanted her to think.

He moved closer, reaching for her. She didn't respond at first, then slowly came to him, allowing his touch. They embraced, holding each other, using the moment to calculate the next move.

"Don't be angry with me," he said convincingly. "I'd have come if I could, you know that." He pulled back to look at her, lowering his voice. "I wonder what dark little surprise you had for me in that room . . ."

She squinted, then quickly returned to the vixen grin. "You'll never know, will you, Dillon."

Hook set.

He pulled her closer. Now it was *his* grin that was cruel, and it wiped her face clean with sudden confusion.

"I had to see you this morning . . . tell you what happened . . . make things right. When I saw that your husband's car was gone, I slipped the lock and came in. You don't know how that feels, the helplessness, the anxiety, wondering what you'd be feeling and thinking, how furious you might be. I need to put it all back the way it was . . . you and me . . . the game. I need it all back. I need *you*."

He held her shoulders firmly, like an adult scolding a child. He mustered all the earnestness he could and said, "Even after what you tried to pull, how you tried to hurt me—I want you even more."

She peered at him, as if trying to see inside. "You still want to play. Even after . . . this."

His smile was vague. "I'm not playing anymore." He let his eyes burn into her for emphasis, then pulled her to him again. Holding her, he tried to imagine the pace of the thoughts that filled her head. He whispered into her ear, "You read me wrong, Mrs. Wallace. I'm just getting started with you."

The embrace held, like two lovers reuniting at the airport. Then he pulled back to see her eyes once again. "Now that you have what you were after, you *do* want things back like they were, don't you?"

"I don't know what you mean." She was asking him what this was really about. First he intimated he was there, then he intimated that he wasn't. His weapon was vagary, and it was working. She wasn't sure if he knew or if he didn't. Which meant she didn't know what to do with him.

"I think you know," he said. "I think you know how completely and utterly vulnerable I am to you now." She broke away, shooting him another tormenting smile, the kind that used to raise his blood pressure. He followed her into the bedroom, where she opened a jewelry box and held up some earrings in front of a vanity mirror.

"You like it this way," he said. "Me, hopeful and eager, waiting for what's next. That's how you like your men, isn't it?"

For a moment it was as if she were alone in the room as she primped.

He came to her again, spinning her firmly and taking her chin in his hand. He saw the surprise in her eyes as he lowered his face to kiss her softly, teasing at her lips. Through the kiss he whispered, "Not knowing . . . that's the drug."

Then he pulled back, waiting for her reaction. It seemed to fluster her, and she turned back to her mirror and her earrings.

"You have to leave," she said coldly. "I have things to do."

"I want what I've always wanted. Even now. *Because* of now."

She stopped, as if suddenly seeing through this entire charade. Her eyes squinted up at him. "I can't believe you're saying this to me."

"After all you've put me through."

She just looked at him. One moment she was sure, the next she wasn't.

His smile softened. "You should give yourself a little more credit."

"Stop fucking around, Dillon. Tell me what this is about. I mean it."

He forced another kiss, which she resisted at first. Finally and gradually she submitted, melting into his mouth.

"I already told you what I want . . . I want you. You make me crazy, you're everything I've ever laid awake at night and dreamed about. You're my darkest desire, and now that I've tasted how truly dangerous you are, what you're capable of, I want you more than I thought I could want a woman. No matter what you've done, it only makes me want it and want you more. I thought it was all a fantasy, but the reality is so much more powerful. I'll do anything you want, but I must have you . . . I *will* have you . . ."

He grinned with just enough ambiguity to confuse her.

"You have to leave," she said, her countenance suddenly changing.

Still grinning, he moved toward the door.

"There's a phrase in basketball after you hack someone really good and get away with it—no blood, no foul." After a moment he softened his voice and added, "I cleaned up all the blood, you see. So there's been no foul."

He waited for a response, which came in the form of her solemn stare.

"Game over, sweetheart. There's a whole new ball game now. Which means you still have a shot at the big win. *If* you're as smart as I think you are."

Then he turned to leave, wishing he could see the look on her face.

SHE waited until she heard doors closing from somewhere in the house below. Her heart was racing, her mind trying to keep up. Then she went to the window at the end of the hallway, the one overlooking the front of the estate.

Her breathing caught in her throat and her knees weakened when she saw her husband's Jaguar XK8 backing out of the garage, then heading out of the gates and disappearing into the neighborhood.

Now she understood.

More than anything, she understood that the man she had set up to be her victim was far more dangerous than she had anticipated. Perhaps as dangerous as her.

But it hadn't worked. It was he who was doing the underestimating. Whatever he'd tried to do, he'd failed. She wasn't sure what his game was, but it didn't matter because everything she'd put in place was still in play. Her husband was dead. Someone would have to pay.

She smiled as she picked up the telephone and dialed 911. When an answer came, she said, "Yes . . . police department, please."

30

After he had left the Wallace estate, Dillon began to head back to the Residence Inn to check out. He was still driving the Jag, a situation he knew had to change fast. His Cherokee was at the airport where he'd left it, so for now he had no choice. The Residence Inn parking lot was almost empty at that hour of the morning and there was no other choice but to leave the Jag exposed while he went inside and packed everything in a frenzy of mind-dulled urgency. He had the phone in his hand, ready to call the front desk and inform them that he was checking out, when his heart froze with realization. What he was doing could be a fatal mistake. He'd intended to call in sick at work, but realized that would be a mistake, too. None of this was a good start . . . he needed to be smarter than that. Outwitting the Dark

Lady would be challenge enough, and now he realized he had to stay one step ahead of his own impulses.

The smart play would be to create and maintain a facade of normality. It had to appear to the world as if nothing out of the ordinary had happened. To move out suddenly with no notice and nowhere else to go, to simply disappear from work, would be to step into the shoes of a fugitive. But there was no body to find—it was still in the back of Wallace's car, and thank God it was barely forty degrees out. Still, that had to change, too, and soon. With no body there was no crime—no blood, no foul—and therefore no reason for the people at the Fraser Hotel to call in the Mounties. The worst that could happen would be that someone out there would begin to miss Hamilton Wallace. The trail from that point would take a long and winding road before it led to him.

Unless the widow hadn't been convinced earlier that morning.

He couldn't worry about that now. He had serious work to do.

He opened his suitcase back up and took out his suit, which hadn't yet wrinkled beyond acceptance. A few minutes later he was driving the Jag through downtown side streets, finally parking it and its coagulating payload in an obscure lot near Pier 39, blocks from his office.

Once at his desk, the first thing he did was call Jordan's office. The secretary would only say that Jordan was in court and would get his messages. He told her he'd try later, that he was unavailable during the day. When asked if it was urgent, he calmly replied, "No."

He called Karen right away, leaving a calm message at the house and at her new office, to get in touch with him, which she rarely did in response to many such messages over the past weeks. He thought about confiding in Janis, but she was in conference all morning.

He slipped out half an hour before the market closed, walking to a parking structure on the waterfront across from Pier 39 and its famous attraction called Ye Old Curiosity Shop. Then he walked the tourist route to collect his thoughts, looking into the green water and wishing he was far, far, forever away. He came across an ATM, from which he withdrew his daily limit of $200, then used a credit card to withdraw $200 more. If he needed to disappear, cash would be required.

At mid-afternoon he took a cab to the airport, taking care not to let the driver have a direct view of his face. Thanks to traffic it was after four when he arrived at Karen's house—his house—in the Cherokee, hoping to find her there watching Oprah. He went inside, noticing more changes to the decor, a level of uncharacteristic disarray and the scent of Mexican food. He drank some orange juice and channel surfed for a few minutes, hoping she'd show.

Then he remembered it was Wednesday. Spa day.

One of the ways Karen had changed her life since the seminar was joining a health club. Driving there now, Dillon was filled with a sense of guilt, remembering how he'd laughed when she'd called the office to tell him she'd enrolled at a spa. Not a real athletic club with courts and leagues and Lifecycles equipped with Internet terminals. A fucking *spa*. She'd hung up on him for it.

Dillon couldn't remember the name of the place but he remembered where it was. It was one of those outfits whose name changed annually in a musical chairs game of buyouts and mergers. In an earlier incarnation it had been a women's-only spa, painted all pink.

He saw her BMW in the lot and felt a simultaneous sense of relief and terror.

Dillon talked his way past the receptionist pleading an emergency and found Karen seated in the weight room, doing shoulder presses with the awkward movement of a beginner. She wore a black leotard he'd never seen before, fitting in nicely with the five o'clock crowd. She looked good. Serious about the task at hand. Many of her peers wore yellow headsets connected to tape players, few talked to anyone else. The entire club buzzed with the sound of spinning machines and clanking weights. Standing behind Karen was a muscular young man in a polo shirt embroidered with the club's logo. Conan the trainer was holding her elbows lightly and telling her with a European accent what a great job she was doing.

Dillon could tell right away that Karen wasn't pleased to see him. The trainer's expression showed confusion and a quiet disapproval of this intruder in street clothes standing before them.

"This better be good," she said. Both she and the beefcake seemed impatient for his answer.

"Quite the contrary." He looked at the trainer and grinned. Then he offered his hand, which was accepted with hesitance and the suspicion of impending attitude.

"Dillon Masters . . . how are ya? She's done for the day."

The trainer looked at Karen, waiting for an indication of what was next. She glared at Dillon, then touched the trainer's arm lightly, flirtatiously, telling him she'd be just a minute.

Dillon followed her to the drinking fountain, waiting until they had some space to begin talking. Her neck was moist, something he couldn't remember seeing on his wife in a long time. She'd lost a few noticeable pounds for her trouble, too.

She raised her eyebrows impatiently, signaling him to explain.

He looked around quickly, not wanting anyone to hear this.

"Someone's been killed."

Her jaw fell open. "My God . . . who?"

"Me."

HE could feel her staring at him as he drove.

"What have you done?"

"It's a long story."

"I think I'm afraid to hear it."

"I'm afraid to tell it."

They rode in silence for a few moments, but the worry kept nagging at her. Finally she said, "What the hell are you so afraid of, for chrissakes?"

He looked at her, his eyes full of emotion. "You," he said.

Minutes later the Cherokee pulled into the Pier 39 parking structure. Dillon recognized the same ticket taker from that afternoon, hoping the guy didn't recognize him in return.

He'd left the Jag on the second floor, facing the waterfront. He parked right next to it and turned off the engine, commencing an awkward silence punctuated only by the ticking of the Jeep's engine. Then he reached into his pocket and withdrew the key ring with the distinguished Jaguar logo, looked at it for a moment, then held it out to her.

"Open the trunk." His eyes indicated the Jaguar. She looked over at it, then back at him.

"You bought a fucking Jaguar?"

"Open the trunk."

"Whose car is it?"

"Just do it. You said I was melodramatic . . . get ready for the mother of all melodrama."

"Why don't you just tell me?" Her eyes were alive with suspicion now, an evolution of confusion and distrust. There was nothing fun about his tone.

He bit at his lip and stared out at the lights of the waterfront. The Seattle aquarium was right across the street, and he imagined the seals playing in their pools to the delight of children and families who had simple lives and peace of mind. He feared he'd never know that feeling again.

Finally he turned to look at her, taking her reluctant hand into his. "Because if I told you, you'd go off on me. You'd react to me and to the story. I want you to react to what you see first."

She was squinting at him, trying to see behind the words. It reminded him of the way the Dark Lady had squinted at him at her house that morning. The way a woman who doesn't need a man regards a man who desperately needs a woman.

He went on. "We're either in this together, or I'm in this alone. I need to know. We can pound through the details later. I just need to know."

She held his eyes, then opened the door and got out. He watched her walk to the rear of the Jag, saw that she was fumbling with the keys. Finally the trunk popped open, obscuring his view of her.

It remained open for too many seconds. He could feel his heart pounding with what had to be medically hazardous ferocity.

When the lid lowered she was holding her hand over

her mouth. She seemed pale and frozen, staring down at the trunk lid as if it was still open. After several seconds she walked slowly back to the Cherokee and got in, eyes straight ahead.

Her voice was very low and even. "Who is it?"

"A friend of a friend."

There was a long silence.

"We have to go to the police."

"I don't think so."

She looked at him for the first time. Her expression was complete incomprehension, fueled with outrage.

He took both of her hands in his. She resisted at first, as if she feared him. But he insisted, and finally she kept them limp within his urgent grasp, his thumbs caressing as he spoke.

"Listen to me. He was killed in a hotel room registered in my name. Not by me, in case you're wondering, which I hope to God you're not. But if anyone looks close enough they'll find a motive and a story that goes something like this: I'm obsessed with the man's wife. I've been following her around, taunting her, making an ass of myself. She can prove it . . . she has witnesses."

Karen's eyes narrowed as she slowly pulled her hands away. "What are you saying to me?"

Emotion overwhelmed him now, seeing how this was affecting her, realizing the scope of the price he must pay for his sins.

"I've been set up. I'm basically fucked."

Nothing was said for half a minute.

"Why are you dragging me into this?" she asked, crying now.

Her tears made his own eyes spill over. He tried to reach for her, but she turned her shoulder to him without removing her eyes from his. It was a most fearsome image, tears and rage entwined, exposing her pain but keeping it from him.

"I need your help," he said.

She slapped him across the face. She'd never done that before. She'd been angry to the point of vomiting, but never this. The sting jolted him, burning his cheek. For a moment, staring at her sizzling rage, he wondered if she might do it again, secretly hoping she would. She needed to vent before the work of salvation could begin.

After a moment he touched his mouth and checked his fingers for blood.

"I brought you into this because I need you. More than ever before. More than I've *ever* needed anyone."

She stared straight ahead, drawing deep breaths, holding a hand over her mouth as she wept quietly. An occasional shudder escaped her lips, and he watched it all, knowing that to look away was to hide from what he'd done. If he looked away, it was all over.

The Cherokee's engine ticked.

"I don't have much time," he said.

She was very still. Then she looked over at him.

"You have to tell me everything," she said.

31

Somehow he talked her into driving the Cherokee back to their house while he followed in the Jag. He thought about this as he drove, remembering the way she'd looked at him, as if something in his eyes was what made her consent to it. Everything he knew about her pointed to a different outcome—the old Karen wouldn't have budged until she knew every detail. He also thought about his cargo, feeling ghostly touches on the back of his neck, unable to stop himself from visualizing what was seeping in the dark of the trunk.

Karen was already different. Living without him all these weeks, he could sense her new awareness of herself, a confidence and a softness that wasn't there before. Somehow the two qualities were linked. The combination was as confusing as it was intriguing. All this time, as their marriage slid toward hypothermia, he'd assumed she was the victim of her own atrophy, when perhaps it was he who had been holding her back.

But none of that mattered now. What mattered was that he convince her to help him save himself. What mattered was the dead guy in the trunk.

WHEN they arrived at the house he told her everything.

She didn't move during the entire story. As she listened she stood in front of the picture window and its panorama of the cul-de-sac. The street reflected a granular sheen unique to that magic moment when the night air dropped precisely to the freezing point. The window was dotted with raindrops and smears of reflected night. Karen's arms were crossed, her face remaining stoic through the whole saga, as if this were all a memory being recalled from behind the safe cushion of years. Even the details of his betrayal, the way this woman, this Dark Lady of his, had seized his most private desires, caused not so much as a blink, not the slightest flaw in her silence.

God, she looked so beautiful to him now. Aloof, untouchable, holding all the keys. He was ashamed to notice, because it acknowledged both his present need and his past ignorance.

Dillon sat on the couch, leaning forward, pulling at his fingers. He went through it all, from the first glimpse of the Dark Lady at Nordstrom and her unexpected call that afternoon, to the revealing of the tattoo at the Olympic Hotel. He found himself providing details that somehow rationalized what he'd done. Karen knew his secrets. How, in the quiet truth of her own heart, could she begrudge him his weakness when, after her own lack of interest, it passed within his grasp? He tried to position it all in context to his entrapment, how the web had been cast and how it affixed itself to a wall of reason.

Karen's eyes held to a distant reference point as she said, "Someone is in this with her. She'll have an alibi, so who killed him?"

He could see the analytical part of her mind working furiously behind the fire that raged in her eyes, and he took momentary comfort in it.

Dillon nodded his agreement. "Somebody killed him while she had drinks in some very public place with some very public friends. Somebody wrapped that electric cord around his throat and just sat there and watched."

Karen seemed not to hear. She was somewhere else, no doubt a place in which the world stroked her pain and told her this was unfair, that her husband deserved what he had wrought. All of these people whom she did not know but who were crashing in on her life deserved what *they* had created. The notion made him angry. The way her face appeared to be made of stone, cold and dead, made him feel supremely alone.

"Excuse me," he said, his tone reflecting the perceived rejection. "Am I keeping you from something? I mean, I'm fucking drowning over here. . . . I can't do this by myself! Do you hear what I'm saying? I *need* your help."

She still didn't move. It was as if he'd said nothing, as if it were she who was alone in the room. He sat back, amazed at her resolve, wondering what it was that held her mind so focused in the face of his humiliation. He'd never seen her like this before, so calm and so cold. So . . . *cruel.*

When she finally spoke, her voice was matter-of-fact.

"I remember what Trish Burke said when this happened to her."

"Trish Burke's husband got framed for murder? I don't think so."

She took a breath, then started again, still not looking at him.

"I remember what Trish Burke said when she caught her husband with that bimbo from his office. The one with the big hair and the fake nails. She said that she wished he was dead. I've heard other women say the same thing when it happened to them. What they'd wear to the funeral . . . how they'd rush home from the cemetery and burn all of his clothes over a glass of wine. I've seen the look in their eyes. It always kind of frightened me, the way a woman's heart can turn to ice. I remember thinking it was a terrible thing to say, that it was an evil and unfair thing to wish on someone you thought you loved just the day before. How can you love someone one day and wish them dead the next? It used to trouble me, thinking about those women. I believed that even when you're hurt you don't stop loving, that you *can't* stop loving. I believed you started lying to yourself. So I never believed Trish Burke and all the others who knew that pain."

She stopped, appearing as if she had nothing more to add.

"Until now," said Dillon.

A bitter smile appeared on Karen's lips. "Love and hate are mutually exclusive things, I think. That's what it has to be. You can't love yesterday and hate today. You can't have them both at the same time. They cancel each other. What's left behind is dead. It's cold, it feels nothing."

The room became very quiet as a tear appeared on Karen's face, sliding slowly across her skin.

Dillon's voice was very soft. "I don't believe you feel *nothing*."

She quickly wiped the tear away. He waited for words, but she remained quiet.

"This has nothing to do with not loving you," he said.

She turned toward him, the calm already gone. "Fuck you, Dillon. Just don't say anything, okay? Just . . . fuck you."

He watched her sob quietly, under control, still staring at that same place outside. Several times he started to speak, but nothing seemed right. Finally he said, "I'm asking you to forgive me."

When she looked at him her face had completely changed. Her control was gone now, overwhelmed by something primal and suddenly in command.

"You're asking me to help bail your ass out! This has nothing to do with me *forgiving* you! This has nothing to do with *me!* Spare me the hearts and flowers, you self-serving hypocritical flaming chickenshit asshole!"

Her tone danced with his own sudden anger now.

He got to his feet and leaned toward her. "You put *me* out on the street, remember? I never would have—"

Her hand was quick and unseen, slapping him squarely. The palm cuffed his ear, the acoustics of the blow adding orders of magnitude to the intended impact. He covered his ear reflexively, his eyes welling at the sting. She was breathing hard, staring at him, ready to crack.

When he lowered his hand she smacked him again, exactly the same as before. This blow doubled him over slightly, and he closed his eyes until the ringing stopped and the sting had evolved into what he already knew would be a headache that would last until dawn.

When he opened his eyes she was exactly as before, poised, ready to strike again. He kept his hand over his throbbing ear.

"I'm dead if you don't help me," he said.

The same bitter smile emerged on her face again. He watched it melt away, like a love note thrown into a fire.

"Maybe there is a God after all," was what she said.

SHE threw him out. He hadn't expected an invitation to her bed, but he was surprised at the look in her eyes when she told him to leave.

It was nearly nine o'clock. There was so much to think about, so much to set in motion. There was a body that would begin to smell. There was a trail, only partially covered, that led from a botched frame-up to a botched cover-up, and the discovery of both was just a matter of time. And lurking nearby was a woman capable of unthinkable treachery, a woman who knew his every secret because he had invented her.

And more than anything, there was a wife who at this moment would relish the sight of him burning in a hell of his own design.

As he was leaving he noticed how out of place the gleaming new Jaguar looked here in his garage. The sight reminded him of his smallness, of dreams that now seemed forgotten and lost. He ran his hand along the hood as he walked through the garage en route to his Cherokee, which was parked in the driveway. Once there, he punched the garage remote and watched as the door lowered, eclipsing the Jag's rear quarter.

He sat quietly for a moment, an idea emerging. Then he pressed the remote again. His eyes had taken in more than Wallace's car. He'd also seen the ancient 1960s vintage freezer that had once belonged to his parents and now held an entire side of year-old frost-encased beef. The summer had come and gone without a single barbecue.

It took him ten minutes. When the freezer was empty he hauled the body from the trunk of the Jaguar and stuffed it inside. It had stiffened considerably, and he had to compress the angle of the legs to wedge it into place. Then he arranged as many of the butcher paper-wrapped sirloins as he could over the top of the corpse. The rest, well over half, went into plastic garbage bags that he'd take with him in the Cherokee and throw into a Dumpster behind a 7-Eleven somewhere. He hid the racks from the freezer under a workbench, well out of Karen's routine line of sight. He prayed she wouldn't have a sudden urge for a flank steak.

This would have to do. There was no telling how long it would take for the world to end.

Once he was finished he drove to Jordan's condo. It was a development in Bellevue, populated with single lawyers and divorcees of lawyers, with units cascading down a hillside toward a private dock populated with Ski Nautiques and small cruisers. His first thought of Jordan had related to his own salvation—Jordan had seen the Dark Lady, could testify that they knew each other in defiance of her forthcoming allegation that Dillon was in fact some anonymous stalker. Then again, their illicit relationship might be the centerpiece of the Dark Lady's plan, an affair driven over the top with lust that got the best of him and caused him to off the rival husband. In that case Jordan would be corroborating her fiction. There were any number of variances on the theme, each of which she could twist into a nest of deceit and incrimination.

As long as she held the trump card, he was fucked. His only play was to change suits and up the ante. To bluff his way out of this.

Jordan's condo was dark and his Lexus was gone. There were two papers on the welcome mat in front of the door, both still in their blue plastic wrappers. His secretary had said he'd been in court that day, and would be there again the next day as well. Maybe the courtroom in question was in Tacoma and he'd stayed down there. Maybe he was sound asleep in the arms of his latest lady friend somewhere in a loft downtown.

Dillon drove home carefully, passing two squad cars along the way. By the time he pulled into the lot at the Residence Inn he knew what his next move would be. There was only one place left to turn, one more ear to light on fire.

THAT same evening, in an old-money downtown steak-house, Jordan was nursing an after-dinner drink with some out-of-town clients. The check was being delivered to him in a black leather folder, and as he opened it he saw a handwritten note along with his credit card and the slip. The note read: "Look up." A little smiley face was drawn under the words.

He looked up. Sitting at the bar was Veronica Wallace, dressed in a gray business suit, her leather overcoat still on. She was smiling, motioning for him to come to her.

"Excuse me," he said to his guests, who by now had noticed the woman with the short blond hair at the bar. The two men were not unaware of Jordan's lifestyle, and despite Jordan's apparent concern they reacted with quiet smiles and slightly sarcastic shrugs.

He approached, getting close before speaking. "What are you—"

She rose on her tiptoes and placed her hands on his shoulders. Then she kissed him, the greeting of a lover. His reaction was to freeze, to not make a scene and let the moment play out. But he was obviously uncomfortable, ever the shy kind of guy to anyone looking on.

"What the hell is this?" he seethed through a phony smile.

She moved her mouth close to his ear and whispered, "We're having an affair."

She took him by the arm and practically dragged him back to the dinner table, where Jordan's two clients quickly sat upright. One of them reflexively straightened his necktie.

"I'm sorry to interrupt," she said. "I won't steal him from you. I was nearby and I just wanted to surprise him. I'm Veronica Wallace." She conducted businesslike handshakes with both men, then turned back to Jordan and kissed him quickly on the cheek.

"Call me in the morning, sweetheart." Then to the men she said, "Nice to meet you both."

As she left she waved and pursed her lips in an air kiss for Jordan. All three watched her departure quietly, then Jordan took his seat at the table.

The men just smiled at him, not familiar enough to comment. Jordan continued to look at the door, biting his lip, feeling the color still in his face. He drew a deep breath and turned to his guests.

"Sorry about that," he said, offering his best lawyer smile as he drained what was left of his cocktail.

32

Death visited the boy twice in this fourteenth year. Not with a pointing finger, but with a conspiratorial wink.

The first occasion honored his father, who crept into his room in the middle of an icy February night, kissed him on the forehead, and then departed forever. At first he had been unsure if the creaking floorboards signaled the presence of his mother or his father, but the familiar scent of beer and stale work clothes was unmistakable, distinct from his mother's sweet poison stench. It had been an evening of screamed obscenities and hurled ashtrays downstairs, though it had been quiet now for about an hour. The boy pretended to be asleep, having over the years mastered the illusion through the deep rhythm of his breathing and the complete and utter stillness of his eyes beneath their lids. There were several long minutes of quiet prior to the lingering touch of dry lips above his eyes, and later the boy would realize that his father had stood in the shadows and simply gazed down on him.

At the moment of the kiss, the boy felt an object being pressed gently into the palm of his hand. Minutes later, when he was certain he was alone, he'd flipped on the reading light next to his bed. In his hand was a keychain with a tiny metal airplane attached to one end.

The next morning an official-looking car arrived while he was dressing for school. Two men in suits declined his mother's persistent offers of coffee and gave them the news of his father's accident before dawn on a two-lane mountain highway near the coast. The car had gone over an embankment at a high rate of speed. Given the weather conditions it was assumed that he'd lost control of the vehicle. The car had exploded at the conclusion of a two-hundred-foot, end-over-end descent to the bottom of a canyon where—in what seemed like a tragic coincidence to all—his father often fished for steelhead. There were no curves at the point at which the vehicle left the road, nor were there any tread marks in evidence, the facts of which were still under investigation. But considering the number of empty beer cans in the vehicle and the presence of ice on the pavement, the sequence of events seemed a foregone conclusion. The boy's mother sat with her face buried in her hands as she listened to these details, her long red fingernails perfectly aligned. It was a pose that lasted until the precise moment that the official-looking car containing the two men in suits had cleared the driveway. When she finally looked up, her face reminded the boy of a statue, bone dry and cold, completely gray as the sky.

At the funeral she was attended by her brother and

a neighbor, who escorted her down the aisle and back again because she was having trouble walking on her own. She had gauged her funereal drinking binge to the very precipice of consciousness with the precision of a seasoned anesthesiologist. All who attended, some twenty people from his father's insignificant slice of the world, had a warm look or a kind word for the boy, who sat next to his mother during the service, inhaling her pungent scent, fingering a keychain while silently wishing it were her who was dead.

His wish was granted on Halloween night, long after the children of the neighborhood had been put to bed with their sugar-induced nausea, after eight months of a living hell, the nature of which he'd never spoken to anyone. Somehow, his mother was convinced, the death of her husband was to be attributed to his vast disappointment in the boy.

The investigation confirmed the boy's story, that his mother had passed out in her bed after three-quarters of a bottle of Seagram's, a cigarette still burning in her hand. It was a miracle the young man had escaped without injury, given the rage and urgency with which the fire had consumed the upper floor where the bedrooms were located. The final fire inspection report stated that the blaze had indeed been caused by a cigarette left unattended on the bed, creating flames that spread rapidly due to the explosive effect of large quantities of what was probably a highly flammable liquid near the source of ignition. It was an odd circumstance that seemed to puzzle the investigators, who quizzed the boy with what seemed to be a curious doubt. The boy told them that his mother always kept a large stash of liquor in her bedroom, and that he had been unable to reach her through the blinding smoke and a thick wall of flames. They'd looked at each other when he'd said this, but the boy kept his breathing normal and his eyes steady. He'd had the presence of mind, he told them, to toss a handful of precious possessions from his bedroom window before jumping to safety himself, severely spraining an ankle in the process. He had not, however, had the presence of mind to call 911. The possessions he'd saved included school clothing, some books, a box of his father's favorite records, a poster of Bette Davis from the movie *Hush, Hush, Sweet Charlotte* and a tattered stuffed panda bear. Everything else had been destroyed.

Through the ordeal of his mother's funeral—attended by only ten folks, all relatives—and his ensuing placement into a nearby foster home, several people commented that he'd behaved with uncanny strength and reserve. Others, teachers mostly, observed that he seemed unmoved—bone dry and cold, completely gray as the sky.

Several months later, during a scheduled follow-up session required by the state child welfare division, a counselor had asked the boy about the night of the fire, how he held it in his memory, if it was vivid and therefore a constant nightmare, or if he had compartmentalized and rationalized it in a way that made the world safe again. The boy's eyes had grown distant, and it took a long time before he answered.

"I remember it as a night with no dawn and no God," he'd finally said. The counselor didn't know how to respond, and given that the boy had nothing else to say on the subject, he wrote in the report that he was doing just fine.

No one ever asked him how he felt about that night again.

33

Dr. Benjamin Carmichael listened to Dillon's tale as if this was just another patient confessing the anxiety of the week. He took a few notes, asked for a little clarification, and nodded on occasion. But mostly he just stared off into space, taking it all in, as if somehow searching for meaning.

"They'll want you to testify," said Dillon, using the line to signal that there was nothing left to tell. He'd been in the hallway when Carmichael arrived that morning at a little after nine with a surprised and troubled expression upon sighting Dillon. He'd protested that an appointment was necessary, but Dillon said the emergency was of the life and death variety, quite literally. Carmichael's reaction was puzzling—strangely placid, as if he faced such situations on a regular basis. Just another morning at the office with the wackos. Luckily for Dillon, there was no one else waiting for an appointment this morning.

Carmichael was writing something on his pad as he responded to Dillon's comment on testifying.

"They can't make me do that."

"You can back her story—I've been following her around, just like she'll say I've been. I'm obsessed with her, I'm a bona fide stalker. I've got all these little stories and fantasies . . . you don't even have to lie, and you'll be reading her script for the jury. For all you know I really did kill Wallace and everything I've told you about my version of reality is the delusion of a psychopath."

"Interesting theory," said Carmichael.

"Movie of the fucking week," replied Dillon.

"Sounds like you're adding paranoia to your dossier."

"Hey, why not? Maybe I really did the guy. Maybe we were lovers and this whole thing, all my little fantasies, is a cover. Maybe this is a crime of passion. Maybe I tied him up that way, like he likes it. . . you can testify about my fascination with that shit, can't you, Doc? You could tell them I was into that."

Still writing, Carmichael said, "Why do you think I would betray you?"

Dillon looked away. His voice lowered as he said, "Somebody did." When he looked up Carmichael was staring at him. Dillon added, "Otherwise, how could she know what she knows?"

A trace of a grin hinted at the doctor's eyes. "Men are easy, Dillon. Especially men like you . . . men with a vulnerability, a weakness."

"No one, no woman, could know what she knows about me. Unless somebody *told* her. And that narrows the field, don't you think?"

Carmichael put down the notepad and folded his hands in his lap. He glared at Dillon, squinting over his spectacles.

"What are you saying to me?"

Their eyes locked until Dillon finally looked away, feeling ridiculous. Nothing was connecting. There were too many options and too little light.

"I'm not as weak as she thinks I am."

Carmichael rubbed his eyes and nodded, as if he knew Dillon might say this. "I'm afraid I really must quit early today. I need to take some medication. I hope you understand."

Dillon's face was contorted with surprise. "I'm afraid I don't, actually."

"I'm sorry?" Like most doctors, Carmichael wasn't used to push-back. They said cancer, and they expected you to roll over and die without a second opinion. Preferably quickly, so they can make their tee time.

"I mean, you act like this is just another jerk-off fantasy with some connection to my potty training, for chrissakes! I need *help* here, goddamn it!"

"Dillon, calm down." His voice was sharp, fatherly.

Dillon stopped himself, realizing that he was on an edge he didn't want to fall over. He nodded, drew a deep breath, and sat back on the sofa.

"I could use a little medication myself. I can't sleep. I have no appetite."

"I can give you something, if you want." The doctor was already writing a prescription. "You want something for your stomach, too?"

"Yeah . . . absolutely."

Dillon accepted the slip of paper the doctor handed to him.

"So what now?" asked Dillon.

The doctor's smile, an attempt at calm, was instead infuriating in its patronizing transparency.

"You do nothing. There is nothing to do until something happens."

Dillon squinted. "You don't believe a word of this, do you."

"I can't help you solve your problem if it's what you say it is. In that case all I can advise is to call the police. And if it isn't, then I can only help if you let the story play itself out in your mind. In the meantime, take the pills and get some sleep."

The doctor was on his feet, extending his hand cordially. Dillon felt like he'd been auditioning for a community theater project.

"I can't afford to sleep," said Dillon, ignoring the hand and scooping up his jacket as he turned for the door.

FIFTEEN minutes later Dr. Benjamin Carmichael's Cadillac STS pulled out of the parking garage beneath his building and into the downtown traffic. Heading north, it merged onto the 520 and joined the flow of midmorning commuters heading for points west, toward Microsoftland and beyond.

The Caddy took an exit, then wound through the heights until it arrived at a gated neighborhood with a perpetually empty guardhouse. Moments later it pulled confidently into the driveway of an elegant-looking estate nestled into the base of a wooded hill.

Carmichael's habit of rarely using his rearview mirror was only one of the reasons he'd not noticed that a car had been following him. The other reason is that the car had shadowed him with care and strategy, hanging far back on the freeway with plenty of other vehicles between them, then staying an innocent distance behind when the chase had entered the neighborhood.

Had the car been Dillon's white Jeep Cherokee, Carmichael might have noticed. Somewhere on one of his yellow legal pads full of notes was the scribbled fact that Dillon drove such a car, and the good doctor was a stickler for details just like that. Details, he had told many a patient, were salvation. Rumor held that God lived there.

But the car was not a Jeep Cherokee. Following the session, Dillon had driven straight to his office and was at his desk at the moment Carmichael turned off the engine there in the Wallace driveway.

This car was a BMW.

Looking through the lens of a video camera from a distance of two hundred yards, Karen watched Carmichael emerge from the Cadillac and stroll toward the front door of the Wallace residence. When the door swung open she saw the outline of a woman, but it was too shadowed and dark in the rain to see clearly through the viewfinder. Pulling the camera aside, she tried using her own eyes with no better results.

She had really wanted to see the woman who had taken her husband's heart from her and shredded it into hamburger. Maybe then her hatred would have a face, something she could picture as she helped her husband escape the frying pan. Maybe the hatred would push her over the line, make her feel good about saving Dillon's ass.

Right now she didn't know how she felt. Right now, the jury was still in the next room weighing the evidence.

She could always change her mind later on.

34

He could feel trouble in the air like the scent of Obsession in a singles' bar. His first clue as he walked into the office was the lack of eye contact. He noticed that several people turned away when he scanned for someone to whom he might utter a casual "Good morning" on this day when an appearance of calm, however contrived, might allow him one more day of freedom. His peripheral vision, however, picked up a preponderance of incoming signals—nearly every eye in the place was on his back as he strolled through the lobby toward his cubicle.

He had barely removed his coat before Janis showed up in his doorway wearing a no-nonsense expression. "My office, now," was all she said, confirming his sense of something headed terribly south. Somehow it had all detonated during the night, and somehow the shock-wave had reached the office before it hit him. Yet there were no detectives waiting, no squad cars out front, no mobile news vans in sight.

His stomach resumed its status as a toxic hazard zone.

"Shut the door," said Janis, not looking at him as she seated herself behind her desk.

He did it, then took the hot seat in front of her. Her arms were folded and she was staring at him. It reminded him of his mother's expression when he had displeased her for reasons he could not comprehend. He shifted uncomfortably, not able to hold her intense gaze without looking away.

Finally she said, "What the fuck were you thinking?"

He bit his lip, unsure now what she was talking about. She could read his expression, not liking what she saw. The room was suddenly hot, and he could feel a droplet of sweat skating down the indentation of his spine beneath his dress shirt.

She waited an eternity of tiny moments without blinking. His expression began to turn more helpless than clueless.

"Don't fuck with me," she said.

"If you weren't so obviously pissed off, I'd say the same thing to you."

Her eyes narrowed at this. Then she looked at some data in front of her, shaking her head. A bad report card. A note from the teacher. A dirty magazine discovered in his jockey drawer by his mother.

She looked up again. "Do you have any idea how much shit you're in? Do you have any idea what kind of position you've put *me* in here?"

He was too confused to speak. This had to somehow link to his current situation, but it didn't feel like it did.

What possible position would it put *her* in? No, this was something else, and he had no idea what it could be. In his gut he knew that, whatever it was, there would ultimately be a connection. But the lid was still on this cauldron of chaos, and what he smelled here was fumes, nothing more. The scent of a brush fire beginning to spread.

"Don't you have anything to say to me?"

"I need to make some calls," Dillon said, trying for a hook that made sense. He realized he didn't sell the line. Janis knew he was bullshitting.

Now she turned her eyes away from him, a dismissal. As she began collecting the paper on her desk into a folder she said, "You're suspended from trading until further notice. You can come in, have Thomas do your trades for you . . . we'll adjust the numbers later. Or take a few days, whatever. I don't particularly give a shit right now. If you don't hear from me on this in a few days then you'll surely hear from White Plains, and if I were you I'd be rooting for it to be them." After a pause, she looked back at him a final time. "If you hear from the union lawyers first, you're to hang up on them and call me in. Is that clear?"

He just nodded.

"That's it. Go make your calls or whatever it is you need to do."

At his desk he switched on his computer and immediately discovered what had happened. Everything made sense now—the collective cold shoulder, the peripheral glances, Janis's wrath. It had nothing to do with dead bodies.

Applied Software Technologies had opened the day's trading at fifteen cents on several million shares. Down over eighty cents. A complete and utter crash the likes of which he'd seen only a few times before. His personal IRA had been virtually wiped out. Whatever his young broker friend had bought for his clients and himself on Dillon's winking recommendation had probably cost him half his meager account book and the bulk of his infant son's new college fund. Not to mention a career-threatening inquiry from the boys in White Plains.

And worst of all, the machinist union pension, for which he was the genius steward, was basically in the toilet. Like his own career, as of right now.

Applied Software Technologies had announced at the close of the previous day's business that it was filing for chapter 11 protection. Banko. Tits up. There was no takeover bid. There never had been.

Like his wife, like his life, the money was gone.

35

The club called Sloan's overlooked the waterfront, and for twenty years had been notorious for its moneyed crowd and its dedication to decadence. Standing outside in the inevitable line, you could hear and feel the pulsing music from within, the kind of place where conversation was conducted with eyes and hips, where the visual reigned and attitude made up for what that money couldn't buy. A few miles away in the downtown clubs the alternative hangers-on were still searching for the next Pearl Jam, while the urban vampires gathered here, the cocaine and Cristal crowd, still looking for their own flavor of kick.

Dillon knew she was inside because he'd followed her here. Standing in the line, dressed in obligatory black under an umbrella, he pictured her dancing, wondering who she'd be with, what she'd say when she saw that he was there. It took only twenty minutes, and when he was allowed inside he realized the waiting was part of the schtick, that there was plenty of room for swinging elbows and swiveling pelvises looking for a partner.

He saw her right away at a cozy corner table. She was blond tonight, her short hair styled ten years too hip for her age. She wore a black Lycra minidress and enough eye makeup to render her nearly unrecognizable as the Dark Lady he knew. Tonight she was over the line. He realized she could walk through her own class reunion in either of these contrasting looks without being recognized, and that this chameleon quality was always at the heart of her boldness as she seduced him.

She was with a Latino man who, if not young enough to be her son, was at least young enough to still mow her lawn for a living. Most likely he was either her narcotics connection or her hairdresser. He wore tight black leather jeans and a Calvin Klein white ribbed tank top framing tight strands of arm and shoulder muscles. The edge of a large tattoo was visible on his shoulder, a wing of some sort. Both ears bore gold hoop earrings, and his eyes were the crackling black of freshly polished coal. He was almost prettier than her, and just as dangerous looking.

She looked up at Dillon with intoxicated eyes that were far beyond the ability to show surprise. Instead he saw glazed amusement when she realized who was standing there next to her. Her young companion instantly sized Dillon up, testosterone simmering, waiting for her reaction before moving to claim the territory. The two of them continued to cuddle and giggle, even more so now that he was here to see it.

"How did you find me?" she asked as she brought her glass to her lips.

"How does any self-respecting stalker find the object of his obsession?"

Her smile was appreciative. He was still playing the game.

"This is David," she said. David didn't smile as he met Dillon's eyes. "David, this is my stalker. He likes tattoos."

Dillon tried a little nod of acknowledgment, but David wasn't having any. David, he could tell, was more likely visualizing cutting Dillon's heart out of his chest in a corner of the parking lot later on.

"You have an interesting way of mourning," said Dillon.

"Mourning?" Her eyes were an act for her new friend. "My husband's out of town. He's with his favorite hooker in Vancouver right about now. I thought you knew that."

"I assume he's buying your crap, too," said Dillon, referring to David.

She grinned, drunk. "You assume too much."

The Dark Lady reached for a pack of cigarettes on the table. They were Marlboro Lights tonight, and Dillon was suddenly anchored to her betrayal, to the fact that the woman who had seduced him had not even been real. She shook one out and pulled it from the pack with her teeth. So very un-Dark Ladylike. David took the candle and its holder from the table and held it for her, his eyes still very much on Dillon, his patience quietly growing thinner. Her fingers never touched the cigarette as she lit it.

Dillon took in the crowd for a moment, his presence intrusive. He didn't want to watch what she was doing.

"What I assume," he said, "is that you still want what I have."

Her grin was full of conceit. "What I assume is that what you have is a slow burning ulcer."

"Had that before I met you, sweetheart."

"Yes, but now the credit is all mine, isn't it."

He grinned with equal cockiness and nodded. They were debaters respecting the other's move, engaged in a private and cryptic dialogue that was making David visibly restless.

She leaned over and touched David's face, whispering something that Dillon could not hear. After a menacing scowl for Dillon, the young tough got up and disappeared into the swarm of black-clad players crowding the bar. Dillon saw her eyes drinking in his exit, focused on his ass, seeing a hunger there that was as unappealing as it was obvious.

"Let me tell you about ulcers," he began, sitting down in David's seat, settling in with the false confidence of a man who had just won the girl. "I'm an expert, so pay close attention here. Ulcers are when your husband is gone and no one knows where the fuck he is. Ulcers are when an entire estate is tied up in legal toilet paper while the authorities try to find some evidence that you whacked the guy. Ulcers are what happens when they never find a trace of him, not a goddamned pubic hair, and while you're waiting years, I'm talking *years,* for his money to materialize, there's this pissy little voice that keeps reminding you that it could have been different . . . *if* you'd have been just a little bit smarter when you had the chance."

He kept his eyes on her, watching the words drill home. Her stare was fixed and distant, and he could tell she was trying it on for size, getting a feel for this unexpected seizure of the game. She remained that way for several seconds before her eyes settled on him and her lips betrayed a tiny smile.

"You're not this good."

"Amazing what the trump card does for your confidence."

Her smile widened. "You're not who I expected you to be."

He waited long enough to make his response poignant. "But *you* are."

"Whatever does *that* mean?" Her voice was softer, back in attack mode. Her fingertips alighted on his wrist, her nails moving back and forth slightly.

He looked down at where she was touching him. He issued an ironic little snort of a laugh before pulling his hand away.

"It means you're fucking with the wrong stalker."

He gave her his best narrow-eyed Clint Eastwood glare as he got up and walked casually through the crowd toward the door, narrowly avoiding David's protruding shoulder as he passed.

VERONICA Wallace caught up with Dillon just as he reached his car in the parking lot. He could hear her heels rushing up behind him, and he smiled to himself when he heard her call his name. He made sure the smile was gone before he turned around.

She was breathing heavily as she stopped in front of him. She put her hands on his shoulders, rose onto her toes, and kissed him, pulling him down with a firm grip on the back of his neck. The kiss was raw and probing, not at all the controlled cool of the Dark Lady's teasing lips and whispered promises. The taste of her mouth was sour.

"Tell me what you want," she said, punctuating the request with another long kiss commanded by a whiplash tongue. He felt himself getting hard now in defiance of his mind, in spite of the taste of her, perhaps because of it.

He took her face into his hands and pushed her away. Holding her head firmly, he narrowed his eyes. "What I want . . . is you. Not your bullshit, not your money, not your treachery. Just you. All of you." After a pause, he added, "Now you tell me what *you* want."

Her smile was pure and irresistible evil, tinged with the spice of victory.

"I want my husband's Jaguar back."

She let him enjoy her expression, knowing how it fascinated him, before she melted into his arms. They mashed for several minutes, sensing people passing them on their way to their cars. It was an asphyxiating kiss accompanied by probing hands, each touching the other's face and neck, entwining fingers in each other's hair, returning the other's urgency and anger.

But the smile hadn't fascinated him. It had jolted him into clarity. It only fueled his realization that the fire he had been playing with was about to consume his soul. Like a drug, it whispered promises he knew were false.

He knew he had to choose. As he kissed her he chose life. In the arms of the woman of his dreams he confessed his sins and committed himself to penance. Whatever it took, he would choose Karen now.

"Who's fucking who now, is the question," she said, kissing him yet again before he could respond.

KAREN watched from the quiet of her BMW, which was parked along the street in the shadow of an overpass across Elliott Street. She was pointing her video camera at Dillon and the woman—her idea, hatched as they'd planned the evening's strategy—but they were mostly viewfinder silhouettes in the night. The camera's zoom feature didn't help clarify the images, it only made them harder to watch. Celine Dion sang to her softly, reminding her of many lonely nights, recent and otherwise. She wanted to look away but couldn't, driven to watch by some selfish need to keep her anger and her hatred inflamed. Because in the end it would be the dark power of those emotions that would allow her to do what she needed to do. Courage alone would not be enough. Something much more passionate would be required to put the world back in order.

Dillon's plan to save himself is as desperate as it is doomed. He was right when he said he needed me. He needs me to save him from himself.

This tape, provided there was enough light, would be his salvation. It would tell the world that Dillon and Veronica Wallace were indeed having an affair, that Dillon wasn't the unknown stalker the new widow would have the world believe he was. And Karen had control of the tape. Which meant she had control of Dillon's life.

But videotapes wouldn't be enough. It was half a plan, a pathetic plan. Desperate times call for desperate measures. Dillon wasn't up to this. But she was, because she was angry beyond comprehension, and that made her strong.

Only at the end of it, as Dillon got into his car and left his companion with the short blond hair and the even shorter black dress standing there alone, did Karen recognize her adversary. Looking through the zoom lens, she felt a rush of nauseous adrenaline followed by stinging tears.

Any doubts that she could finish this her way were gone.

36

Karen drove around Seattle for nearly an hour before going home. She headed south along the waterfront through the industrial district, past the site of the recently imploded Kingdome and it's gaudy replacement, all the way down to the Boeing complex, itself a respectable metropolis of sprawling warehouses and loading docks. She stopped next to the Air Museum and stared at the massive white-and-red hulk of what had been the very first 747, now engineless and relegated to an adjacent boneyard. She remembered being there nearly thirty years ago when it had lifted so gracefully from the ground for the first time, its wings like the outstretched arms of a great angel. She remembered dreaming of it taking her away, commencing a new life, representing her unrequited quest for the romance she would never quite find. Since then she'd never failed to notice the giant Boeings on their slow-motion approach to Sea-Tac and think about dreams she barely remembered, the angel that never quite smiled upon her. Now the dream machine was sitting cold and forgotten behind a fence, never to fly again. Tonight she wept for a dead airplane, a ghost with no crypt and no memory of the sky.

Dillon was waiting for her at home. He was sitting in darkness in the living room, still wearing his jacket as if he knew he'd be asked to leave. She came in through the kitchen, seeing his silhouette there, and after taking off her coat took a seat across from him on the sofa, keeping the lights off. It was better this way, not seeing each other's eyes.

Nothing was said for a full minute before Dillon said softly, "It's too much. I know that."

"Yes."

"That must have been hard to watch."

"Harder than you can comprehend."

"I don't . . . I mean . . . I'm sorry."

She let that one linger a moment before replying. "Yes, you are."

"I didn't plan it. It just happened. I had no choice." She said nothing. He was a convincing actor, her husband. For both women. It wasn't that she doubted him now. It was that she doubted her ability to forgive.

"I should have never asked you to get involved," he said.

"You have to trust me. I wonder how that feels, after what you've done."

"It feels good, trusting you again."

"You may want to rethink handing me your balls for safekeeping."

The air was thick with tension. Then she said,

"There's something I have to tell you."

He just raised his eyebrows, waiting.

"I know her," she finally said.

He looked back up and made a sound, a sudden exhalation.

"She was in the seminar with me. She was my partner for some of the exercises. We got close. Real close. It was like she'd been where I was heading, like she knew what was next. Since then we've become friends."

"Friends. That explains a lot."

"More than you know." She took a deep breath, then went on. "We went out, talked, drank a lot of wine together. It was very intimate, she made it easy to be vulnerable."

"I know that feeling."

She glared at him, and he was sorry he'd said it.

"I told her things about us," she said. "About *you*."

"You served me up. Like a duck on a fucking platter."

More silence ensued with the oppressive realization. "That's what you talk about with girlfriends," said Karen.

"I thought you talked about funerals."

I want a man who will die for me . . .

He rubbed his eyes. "You must have laughed your asses off . . . all of Dillon's little fetishes and fascinations."

"We didn't laugh."

"Of course not—she was taking notes."

"I think she liked what she heard."

I can make a man do anything I want . . . if I know what his buttons are . . .

"Obviously."

Karen's voice changed suddenly. She turned and looked directly at Dillon. "I'm not the only one who knows."

A pause, then Dillon said, "Say that again?"

Karen shifted in her seat, feeling the weight of the exchange shifting onto her shoulders. "I'm not the only one who knows . . . what you like."

"But you're the only one who knows *her*, aren't you?"

She drew a deep breath and said, "Dr. Carmichael knows her, too." In the shadows she could see his face twist with confusion and surprise.

Dillon brought his hand to his temple, his eyes now wide. Karen waited for him to speak, but he said nothing.

"Your little leather goddess is fucking your psychologist."

"That's impossible."

"On the contrary. . . . It explains everything."

"Jesus Christ . . ."

"This morning, when you went to see him, I followed you. I wanted to see where you went, if you were with someone, with her. When I saw where you went I was ashamed. I just sat there and cried. I couldn't move, I didn't have anywhere to go. When I saw your car leaving I started to follow you again, but I broke down. It all seemed so . . . so *dirty*. So I just sat there, not sure what to do next. Then I saw Carmichael in his car, and the way he peeled out of the garage . . . it was just so *odd*. I had a strong feeling. So I followed him."

"To her house."

She nodded. "I didn't recognize her when she opened the door . . . I was a block or two away. Then tonight, when I saw her with you, I knew."

"This is insane."

"Brilliantly so. Think about it, Dillon. It was Carmichael who got me into that seminar in the first place. If you were going to arrange two people meeting each other and have it seem natural and spontaneous, what better and more vulnerable place to do it?"

He remembered how it happened, how Carmichael had called the house one night out of nowhere, months after Karen had stopped her sessions with him. He said he'd come across this personal growth seminar that changed the course of the lives of the people who took it. He'd taken it himself, and he felt it was a perfect place for Karen to continue "her journey," as he put it. He said he had thought of her throughout his own experience there, and couldn't shake the idea that this would bring Karen the clarity of vision and peace of mind he'd not been able to facilitate for her in his treatment. It was an easy sell, given the emotional chill in the household and the fact that Karen had just abandoned another new career start-up. He'd even offered to advance her the tuition if she didn't want to ask Dillon for it. She declined the offer but not the seminar. She liked the notion of finding support as she set about changing her life.

Dillon's eyes were on the carpet, and he still rubbed at them. "What could be in this for him?"

"She's one of the richest women in the city." She paused for effect. "I can call 1-800-PSYCHIC to help you understand, if you want."

Dillon remembered Carmichael's face, the look in his eyes when he was talking about a man's vulnerability to a woman who embraces his weaknesses as if they were her own.

Her name is Pain, Dillon. . . . You kneel before her gladly, if only for a single touch, a moment's grace from her indifference . . .

This had to be the explanation. Or at least, connected to it somehow.

"Why you?" he asked. "Why get next to you if she had a pipeline into my sexual closet through Carmichael?"

"Think about it," said Karen, her patience born of the fact that she'd already thought this through. "I met her at the seminar before you even started seeing Carmichael, before you even met her. The whole thing started with me, when I told him all about you and your little weak spots. He's already doing her, and they're looking for a way to put hubby's estate planning into effect. When he hears my story, up pops the idea—the perfect plan for the perfect patsy. Then he sends her in, dressed to kill."

Karen only paused a moment as Dillon pondered it.

"Then you show up as a new patient. That must have thrown a wrinkle into things, but obviously, it wasn't a deal killer. In fact, it made it easier for them."

"Why not just send her straight at me? Why bring you into it?"

She thought a moment before answering. "Maybe she needed more of the nuances to pull it off, to really get her claws into you. Things only a wife could know and a woman could understand."

"Or not understand," he said, which earned him a dirty look.

"Why not just push the guy off a cliff?"

"Maybe the game's the thing for them. Then again, I wouldn't understand, would I?"

It is in the bondage of their wickedness that we are set free . . .

A chill shot up Dillon's spine, as if just now realizing how close he was to the heart of pure darkness, the static electricity of human evil.

"There's something else," he said, his eyes fixed. "I never told Carmichael about the tattoo thing," he said. He remembered the moment, her black gloved fingers tugging the cup of the bra down to reveal the entire breast, the tattoo of the rose. He remembered the sensation of his rapidly engorging manhood, the crackling link between his eyes and his brain and his genitals. He felt it again now, just thinking of it, visualizing the flame in her eyes as she watched his fascination wash through his skin like heroin.

Karen said nothing.

"Did you hear what I said?"

"Yes."

"*You* told her about that."

Her voice was barely audible. "Yes."

Karen began to cry, turning away. He went to her and put his arm around her shoulders. She immediately buried her face in his chest, and they embraced, saying nothing for several minutes.

She stiffened in his arms just before sitting suddenly upright, creating distance between them.

"You're asking too much of me, Dillon. This is too crazy. . . you need to go to the police and do this right . . . and you need to leave me *out* of it!"

His response was barely audible. "It's way too late for that."

Both of them knew he was right. His taking of the body, combined with her story of his obsession and the trail of public witnesses to support it . . . he'd be laughed right into the courtroom. And then there was the stock thing, a motive strong enough to nail him on its own merits.

"I need you to forgive me." He didn't expect a reply, and didn't get one. "There's no reason for me to do this if you don't."

Her eyes grew cold. "You need me to do a lot more than forgive you."

Then she headed for the stairs, the conversation

over. He waited until he could see only her feet before blurting out what he knew he had to say.

"You have to disappear," he said loudly.

She stopped, didn't move.

"You can't help me anymore. It's too dangerous."

She backed down the stairs.

"What are you talking about?"

He cleared his throat, the meaning of his words catching in his throat. Then he said, "She has to kill again. And when she does, she'll come after *you*."

He noticed the curious look that came across Karen's face.

"Not if I kill her first," she said before climbing back up the stairs and closing the bedroom door behind her.

37

Dillon drove to his office in the morning as if the world were as it should be. What little night there had been after leaving Karen's had been surprisingly restful, due mostly to the fact that he was as physically exhausted as he'd ever been. And despite the lack of sleep his stomach was calm enough this morning to try a Starbucks latte and one of their overpriced scones.

As he pulled into a stall in the parking garage adjacent to his office building, he was immediately aware of another car, a late model Mustang, pulling to a stop directly in front of him, blocking any sudden change of mind he might have. At first he didn't get out of the Cherokee, instinctively waiting for the car to move on. But it didn't. The man behind the Mustang's wheel just stared at him, looking neither menacing nor particularly out of his mind.

They locked eyes for a while before the man motioned for Dillon to get out and approach him. No one else was in the vicinity, and it was a great day for a robbery. Or a contract hit, perhaps. Instead of being frightened, Dillon realized he was ticked off and ready for a confrontation. The guy had picked the wrong day to piss him off. Dillon got out of the car with the thought that nothing could get any worse than it already was.

The man in the Mustang was about fifty or so, wearing an expensive leather trench coat. His face was weathered and a bit sad, as if he'd seen too much of the things from which most people choose to turn away. His moustache was peppered with gray and in need of a trim, giving him a sort of Jerry Garcia huggability that Dillon sensed was a facade. The man didn't exactly smile, but there was a curious look of cordiality in his eyes as Dillon stopped several feet away.

Only then did the man lower his power window. He held out his wallet, which was open to reveal a badge. Dillon leaned in and saw the word Detective embossed into the gleaming silver.

"Dillon Masters?"

Dillon nodded, distracted by the shield.

"You don't look all that surprised to see this," the man said.

Dillon was still studying the badge, saying nothing.

"You don't have to talk to me. But I hope you will." The detective's smile was almost empathic. "Detective Tim Rubin, Seattle P.D."

Their eyes connected. Dillon knew this would be a no bullshit conversation.

Rubin reeled in the wallet. "I didn't think you'd appreciate me bothering you at home. Or at your office."

"You seemed to know where to find me."

"If I were you I'd be more concerned with *why* I found you."

Dillon nodded for the man to continue, feeling his stomach twist.

Rubin grinned slightly. "Your tax dollars have provided us with computers that know things you wouldn't believe. I like to tell people I have good instincts, but that's bullshit. It's all in the software."

The detective's smile widened. He seemed sincerely interested in making Dillon relax.

Then the grin faded away, very suddenly. "One week ago your car was reported stopped on Vista View Crest."

Dillon didn't respond. Rubin's eyebrows were raised, as if expecting something back. Seeing that it wasn't coming, he continued.

"At ten fifty-five a woman in the neighborhood called to report someone loitering behind her house. Wednesday morning that same woman called in a missing person report on her husband. He was a no-show for a meeting in Vancouver and still hasn't returned home."

He watched Dillon closely, and Dillon knew there was no hiding.

Again Rubin gave Dillon a chance to say something, which Dillon started to accept but stopped.

"You don't have to say anything."

"You already told me that."

Rubin nodded slightly, then raised his eyebrows again. "Yesterday when I came to work I didn't know you from Adam. Today I know that your credit card was used to charge a round-trip ticket to Vancouver and that the return portion of the ticket was never validated. I know that this same credit card was used to pay for a room at the Fraser Hotel in Vancouver that night, and that you left with one of the sheets without checking out.

We know it was you because the bartender remembered you from your picture, which we pulled from the DMV."

Rubin's eyes narrowed. There was no smile now.

Dillon felt his stomach cramping and wished he could double over or simply lie down. Heat was assaulting his face, a trickle of sweat already running behind his ear. This was what it felt like to die.

"Amazing goddamn technology," added Rubin.

Dillon covered his face and closed his eyes, no longer caring what Rubin saw and what he thought. Part of him was on the brink of relief that this insane game was over. He wanted to tell the truth again, bathe in its cleansing fire.

"Do you have an attorney, sir?" asked Rubin.

"I did. I can't find him."

Rubin nodded. His eyes drifted, and his expression took on a curious glaze, as if confronting something confusing and beyond his reach.

"She's an amazing woman, isn't she?"

Dillon's eyes popped wide and his jaw opened. Rubin didn't look back at him at first, knowing he had the man's full and complete attention.

"This is the hard part, Mr. Masters. The waiting. Trying to put on a normal face, living your normal routine, wondering what happens next, when the hammer will come down. This is where most of us crack."

His eyes, which had been alternatingly twinkling and emphatic, were now gentle, sending a message.

"I don't know what to say to you," said Dillon.

Rubin just nodded, a little sadly. He handed Dillon his card. "For when you change your mind about that."

The power window raised and the Mustang moved off. Dillon stood rooted to the spot and watched until the taillights disappeared around the corner.

38

An hour later Dillon was calculating the exact damage to his retirement funds when he looked up to see Veronica Wallace standing at the doorway of his office. He was conscious of his heart stalling momentarily, and even with their present state of war he realized he was drinking in the sight of her. This morning she had melded Veronica Wallace and the Dark Lady into one extraordinary package, street-legal yet treacherous. She wore a fashionable business suit under her long black leather coat, collar high, one glove on, the other off. Today she was a striking blond, making far more impact than the previous morning with her made-up eyes and expensive earrings. It was a dose of reality in the fantasy that seemed to suggest permanence, as if nothing about her darkness had been a facade. In real life she was every bit as wicked and irresistible as her fantasy counterpart.

The old chemistry knew neither pride nor guilt.

Her expression was smug, reading his mind, the confident alchemist. She made a production out of crossing her legs as she sat down in the chair next to his desk. He could hear the gentle friction of her nylon hose in the movement, and he could smell the lethally sweet scent of her perfume.

"You look like you've just seen a dead man," she said.

She sat with her back to the office. Dillon sensed that a few dozen pairs of eyes were on them. Maybe this was good. Maybe he could use this.

"I'm here to make an investment." She was grinning as she methodically plucked off the glove, finger by finger.

Dillon shifted in his seat, daring not to look. "I had a business meeting this morning with a Seattle police detective who has an intense interest in your husband's whereabouts."

"Don't we all." She inspected her fingernails, which were dark maroon and perfect.

She was actually enjoying this. No one was this cool.

Dillon chanced a glance out at the terrain of the office. A quiet giddiness came over him, because this was exactly where he wanted her—on his turf, out in the daylight. By being here she was handing the keys over to him, thinking it was her only shot at the money.

It had worked. A new game was on.

"What are you doing here?"

Her look was sensual, full of mischief. She leaned forward and spoke the words very slowly and with a low volume, conscious of her full, pursing lips.

"Driving . . . you . . . crazy."

She untied the belt of her coat and pulled it open. Underneath she wore a buttery black leather vest with a high neckline, unabashedly over-the-top. Her fingers moved to the zipper and began to pull it down, keeping her eyes riveted on him. He noticed the sound and realized that the desired effect was at hand.

"Having a tiny change of heart, are we?" he asked, deliberately not allowing his line of sight to follow her zipper.

"Precisely. Now . . . I want you to tell me what you have planned for us."

He narrowed his eyes for emphasis. "I want my life back."

He took a deep breath, holding her stare. She was perfect, sculpted from shadows of dreams that had haunted him since his first rush of hormones. The zipper had stopped in the middle of her chest, revealing foothills of porcelain skin. To look down at them was to crash on the siren's rocks.

Her grin invited him to loosen up. This was their game, seductress and victim, the sparring made all the more gratifying when both acknowledged the play of the other.

"You're quite the surprise, Dillon."

"To risk a world-class understatement, so are you." He still wasn't smiling back at her. "Tell me what this is really about. We can't go backward from here, you know. You're committed now. You've committed both of us."

"I like how you're handling this."

"Yeah, I'm James fucking Bond, aren't I?"

"I never considered this as a potential outcome."

"Neither did I."

"It's really very . . . intriguing."

Their eyes locked, each of them sensing the other's thoughts. After several frozen seconds she shifted and cleared her throat, leaning in.

"I want to negotiate. Think of it as a settlement."

"Gee, are we getting divorced?"

Dillon opened his desk drawer, fumbled a moment, and withdrew a pen, as if to take notes. He closed the drawer and resumed his pose.

"Who are you working with?" he asked.

She raised her eyebrows. "I thought you'd have learned by now not to underestimate me."

"That would be a fatal mistake, I'm sure."

"It almost was."

This made her smile. "What makes you think I'm working with someone?"

"Because you can't be in two places at once."

"Two places?"

"In Vancouver playing with ropes and here cementing an alibi."

She held his gaze for a moment, then her eyes drifted slightly.

"It's ironic, really. I was going to watch you go down. . . . I was going to walk away with everything." Her eyes returned and she practically winked at him. "But you turned out to be James fucking Bond."

"So where's the irony?"

"That you end up with precisely what you were looking for . . . and I end up with precisely what I never thought I'd find."

"What might that be?" he asked.

"A man more dangerous than me."

Her grin was smug, watching him chew on her words. The old addictions were blind to logic. She was pornography—she commanded his eyes in spite of everything that was good and true. The cost of submission would be his soul. It occurred to him that it might just be worth it.

He forced the image of Karen into his mind. Karen, good and true.

"Perhaps you assume too much," he said.

"You want it too much."

"It?"

"This." She ran her fingertips down her cleavage and over the leather bustier.

He refused to look, which seemed to amuse her.

"So negotiate," he said.

She straightened her posture and dabbed at the corner of her mouth, as if choosing her entry point.

"We need a story."

"Try me."

"You and I have been having an affair for a month now. My husband suspects something, he's seen you hanging around the fringes of our life, so rather than deny it I tell him about a man who has been following me. We get into a terrible fight because he doesn't believe me. He thinks we're playing some twisted game with him as the puck. He's brilliant and he's paranoid . . . a formidable combination. So to appease him I call the police, report that some creep is watching me. A very handsome creep. I mean, that would prove there's no game, that I don't know the guy. He still doesn't buy it, so he splits for a couple of days. I get worried, I call the police, report he's missing."

The leather creaked audibly as she shifted, leaning in closer. Dillon didn't move a muscle.

"Here's the brilliant part. The new twist."

"I'm all ears."

"He comes back."

She studied his eyes, looking for them to flinch. They didn't.

"I call the police again, tell them he's back home safe

and sound. The slate is clean, they call off the dogs . . . you have your cozy little life back."

After a few moments of holding her gaze, Dillon said, "You have my attention."

"He's still pissed off about it all, though. By now I've had enough, the arguments, the paranoia, the abuse . . . so to hurt him I tell him everything. I'm a certifiable bitch, you see, and hurting him is my hobby. So I tell him about you, about us. I tell him that everything I've been saying, all my stories, have been a he. That we've been fucking and your dick is much bigger and prettier than his. His worst nightmare turns out to be real. He can't handle it, goes off the deep end, disappears again."

"And this time he really doesn't come back."

The Dark Lady nodded, pleased that he understood. It was amazing how comfortable she was with evil, how well it suited her.

She went on. "He turns up a few days later, very dead. They find a note—suicide. Poor man died of a broken heart. Meanwhile you and I have come out in the open with our relationship. It's cruel, we're not proud of what it caused . . . but, hey—it's nothing we can be arrested for. Love is war, people get killed. They stopped executing people for adultery a long time ago."

"How lucky for us. There's just one problem."

She answered with her eyes, curious.

"The medical examiner is very good at what he does."

"That assumes they'll find a body, doesn't it?"

He tried to return the same expression. Cat and mouse, mouse and cat. "That assumes you even have a body to work with," he said, "which at the moment, you do not."

"Which is precisely why I have to negotiate. You want something . . . I want something. May I?"

She reached across his desk, pivoting the telephone toward her as she raised the receiver to her ear. Her eyes alternated between Dillon and the keypad as she stroked in a number from memory, then waited.

She spoke into the phone, keeping her eyes locked on his now. "Yes . . . whom do I talk to about a missing person report?"

She covered the receiver, and spoke softly to Dillon. "I'm giving you your life back."

Then she returned her voice into the phone. "Yes, my name is Veronica Wallace. I called yesterday morning to report my husband missing? Thank you." She sounded to Dillon as calm as someone calling for dinner reservations.

On hold again, she covered the receiver. "I'm asking you to give me mine."

She started to smile, then someone came back on the line.

"Yes, thank you . . . . Listen, I am so embarrassed. . . . My husband came home late last night." After listening for a moment, she said, "Yes, everything is fine. We had an argument . . . he's never done anything like that before. I guess I overreacted. I feel like a complete fool. You must think I'm crazy."

Her smile was widening now. "I appreciate that, Officer. Thank you. . . . I'm sorry to have caused you any trouble." A beat. "Thank you . . . and you, too. Bye-bye."

She replaced the receiver then leaned back, folding her hands in her lap.

"Now," she said, the tip of her tongue flicking at her teeth for a moment, "why don't you tell me what you've done with my husband's body?"

*   *   *

DETECTIVE Tim Rubin was hunched over a computer keyboard, using both index fingers to peck in the final paragraph of a murder-suicide report. Boy hits the bottle, girls hits the roof about it, boy hits girl upside the head with said bottle, girl clobbers boy in his sleep with a metal softball bat, boy comes to and whacks girl with the ass-end of a nearby hand tool, boy shoots self with handgun. Rubin loved his job but truly hated computers, in part because he lived in a city that defined itself by the software that ran it, and he had a thing about software. It wasn't the technology—which made him feel inadequate and old—as much as it was the politics of it all. It had bred a new bloodline of techno-snobs, and a strain of criminals that was beyond his reach. Like the subjects of the report he was typing, both of whom were in the software industry. Rubin worked for the dead, bringing justice to their families and to the people. The computer was, in his opinion, guilty of kidnapping souls, of displacing God.

A uniformed officer, a young woman named Roderick, stuck her head into his cubicle. She'd played basketball at Washington State and could look him straight in the eye and just possibly kick his ass if so moved, which was part of her charm. Rubin had long ago given up an awkward campaign of coffee and lunch invitations, settling for simply having her around within visual range.

"Your lady friend just called. Hubby's home, safe and sound."

He looked up to see her shrugging, beats-me expression before she ducked out as suddenly as she'd appeared.

He spent the next ten minutes with his chin on his hand, staring out the window, remembering.

*   *   *

LIKE most men, he had been fascinated from the first moment he laid eyes on Mrs. Veronica Stanich, whose friends called her Nicki. His fascination caused no anxiety, because he was as much repulsed by what he saw as he was drawn in. The woman was a magnet with two poles, and unlike some men, he had never been tempted by the negative side of love.

The call came on a rainy Thursday morning—one of the big cheeses at Boeing woke up dead in his bed at his lake estate. The ambulance boys, who liked to play detective and often did so with great success, said it looked like a routine upper-middle-class medical fuck-up—insulin poisoning. The deceased was a dead diabetic. One should never drink and drive a needle into one's ass. Procedure called for a detective to check in before the coroner took the body away, and it was Rubin's turn on meat-wagon duty.

His first clue that something was wrong was purely a product of his instinct. She was too nice to him. Most new widows, distraught and afraid and most of all confused, resented his unexpected appearance because it implied the suspicion of impropriety. Grief was rarely strong enough to conquer indignation. But this woman, whose grief was as contrived as a detergent commercial testimonial, was ready for him, not at all surprised to see him and not at all in a hurry to see him leave. It was as if she knew that the harder he looked, the less he'd find, and she was gloating about it. She was *inviting* him to look.

So he did. He'd started to peel back the lives of the Staniches, who moved about in the stratosphere of Seattle society, where there was no shortage of co-occupants with an opinion. With the lack of any forensic evidence he was forced into a mode of psychological autopsy, looking for motive where there appeared to be no crime. His superiors called him off, as much as anything because of the twinkle in his lieutenant's eye for this woman and the fact that the chief of police and the mayor all belonged to the same country club as Stanich. The widow was entitled to be spared the embarrassment of an unnecessary investigation. These people watched one another's backsides like siblings.

But for Rubin, the investigation was compellingly necessary. Because he knew what had happened. Knew it as certainly as he'd known his wife was having an affair months before he could prove it. Nicki Stanich had given her husband the double dose of insulin that killed him while he was drunk. Chances are she had given him something else, too, to help it along, something the coroner could never find. There were a hundred anonymous ways to stop a human heart.

When he was challenged by the suits to produce something more admissible than his gut feeling, he couldn't. He was ordered to go back to his day job, and to stop watching so many movies of the week. But his gut had served him and the city well until now. So he did as he was told, always in his heart knowing he was right.

He believed he was right even when the most obvious potential motive for the murder turned out to be precisely the opposite of what he expected. Stanich left his money to his children. His wife got a car and a hundred grand in cash and all the jewels she could carry. She also received clear title to the family yacht, a fifty-five-foot Navigator cruiser cleverly and, Rubin surmised, accurately named after his wife: the *Picki Nicki*. Stanich's three children from a long prior marriage, losers all, divided forty-four million dollars in stock, real estate, and personal property, the latter commencing a fight that over the years would never reconcile. When Rubin interviewed each of them unofficially several months after the ritual reading of the will (a career risk that thankfully never came back to haunt him), they told him their stepmother got more than she deserved, that she didn't even like the boat, and that their father had died a lonely and miserable man. Leaving her the boat was, in fact, his final fuck-you. One even confessed that they believed she had indeed killed him, but feared any push for justice might get in the way of their proximity to the money. If it didn't raise the dead, why stop the machine? Fact was, she had done them all a great service. The old man had been a consummate meglomaniacal asshole.

All of this had happened during the same spring when Rubin's own wife had confessed her complete and utter distaste for his physical presence and inaugurated an ugly campaign of divorce. She didn't even wait until the hearing to go public with her affair with a famous local car dealer who starred in his own TV ads. She refused to marry the schmuck until all three years of Rubin's alimony obligation had been fulfilled, the economics of which could only point to her desire to prolong his suffering.

He wasn't sure which woman, Nicki Stanich or his own wife, haunted him more. In either case he had seen the face of Satan, and saw that it wore eyeliner and lipstick.

In Rubin's line of work, life and death went on with equal dispatch. Over the course of the four years he'd made it a point to check in on Veronica "Nicki" Stanich from time to time—traffic tickets, credit reports, and the occasional drive-by just to see what she was driving these days. The *Picki Nicki* had gone unmoved since its arrival shortly after the funeral at a posh moorage just north of town. He'd been amused when her wedding to Hamilton J. Wallace hit the society column two years ago, noticing that the man was several years younger than her and cut from a different cloth. He was rock climbing and half-marathons, she was white wine and liposuction. He was philanthropic with a preference for anonymity, she would have the city council name a building after her for a sufficient donation, which was actually a rumor at one point in some circles. He was self-made, the real deal. She was simply dealing.

Then her latest husband was gone, now suddenly and inexplicably back again. And here was this new player in the game who had no idea who and what he was dealing with. Something was up. If Rubin were a betting man, his bet would be that Hamilton Wallace was already dead. His gut was telling him this was so.

He would have to wait less than an hour to find out.

39

Dillon was sitting in the lobby of the Seattle Police Department's headquarters twenty minutes after the Dark Lady left his office. He announced himself as there to see Detective Rubin, no, he didn't have an appointment, and no, he didn't care to state the nature of his business.

The wait lasted nearly half an hour. This surprised him; he would have thought his appearance would have turned the homicide department on its slightly cauliflowered ear. But it was easy time to pass—his pocket was full of salvation and his heart was full of truth. Karen was his truth. He'd seen it in her rage and in her pain the night before.

The Dark Lady had ended her visit to his office with an offer. She wanted to seal their dark alliance with something more than a kiss. She suggested the Westin or someplace equally close, and promised him she'd show him things about himself he'd be too afraid to face in a mirror. Lines were made for crossing, she'd said, and she was in the mood for some nonlinear creativity.

He'd turned her down. It was easy, because it played so nicely into his new man-in-charge persona. He'd watched her eyes when he said no, at first surprised, then angry, then hurt, then intrigued, then finally satisfied. She was testing him and he'd aced the exam. In point of fact, however, his response was a product of something else altogether. Dillon was married again. He'd deal later with the shame and guilt of what he'd done, but for now he had his life to save and his marriage to reupholster. There was another wake-up call, too: the way Karen had rallied to overcome her own righteous indignation after a couple of pops to his temple. She'd shown him what unconditional love was all about. To betray her now would be to betray himself and all that he was struggling to resurrect. Dignity, hope, self-respect, love . . . these were the prizes that hung in the balance. To lie with darkness now would be to surrender his soul.

An extremely tall female officer, black and lovely in a very unpolicelike way, finally summoned him from the lobby and led him through several hallways into a large room that looked like a cross between his own office and a metropolitan daily newsroom. Walking behind her, he found the journey intimidating and more than a little humiliating. He wondered if this was the idea, if the police were indulging in a bit of strategic mind-fucking.

Rubin's office was a cubicle with chin-high walls covered with beige fabric. A picture of a boy and a girl was framed next to a PC monitor, nice looking early-teenaged kids with their father's thick chin and jolly eyes. He wondered how old the photo was, where those children were in their lives as fledgling adults, if they loved their father more now than they did then. Most kids did it that way, sometimes too late, almost always with regret.

Rubin was on the phone. He motioned with his hand for Dillon to take a seat. He was listening, responding with an occasional affirmative grunt, scratching notes. Dillon noticed his cheap shoes, which were probably from a discount chain in a suburban mall. Finally Rubin hung up with a terse "Okay" and finished his notes before looking up.

"Sorry about the wait," he finally said, extending a hand.

"You don't look at all surprised to see me," said Dillon, remembering Rubin's opening line from that morning.

"Not this soon, at any rate."

The detective leaned back, put his hands behind his head, confident and smug. The pitch of the chair was severe; Dillon wondered if he'd ever gone over backward in the thing.

"What can I do you for, Mr. Masters?" The look on his face indicated he already knew the answer.

"I'm taking a very big chance being here," Dillon said.

"That so?"

"I can't find my lawyer. He's dodging me, in fact. My guess is, when I tell you what I've got, you'll recommend I don't proceed without one."

Dillon had tried Jordan's office again, but this time the secretary wouldn't say if she knew where he was or not. He'd left another message on his home line, stressing that they needed to talk as soon as humanly possible, that the big turd had hit the propellers. The fact that Jordan had actually laid eyes on Veronica Wallace, that he knew Dillon was telling the truth, or at least that her story of his stalking from afar was bullshit, made him the only legal option Dillon would consider.

"I can already recommend that," said Rubin. "In fact, before we go any further, if you want to talk to me I'm going to have you sign a waiver telling the world that I didn't coerce or otherwise mislead you into saying anything. Do you agree to this?"

"I'm hoping the fact that I agree to it tells you something."

Rubin looked at him suspiciously, then asked Dillon to sit tight for a moment and disappeared. Dillon closed his eyes, tried to will his stomach toward a reprieve, wondering when the acid would eat completely through his abdominal wall. He tried to picture Karen's face, but he couldn't focus.

Rubin returned very quickly and read the disclaimer out loud to Dillon. He signed it without hesitation, hoping to make a point with his assertiveness.

"Must be some story," said Rubin.

Dillon held his eyes for a moment, hoping his perception of the man as being highly intuitive and sensitive was accurate.

"I'm here because of something you said to me this morning. You said, 'She's an amazing woman,' as if you *know* her. If you do, then you know what she's capable of, and how someone like me could get sucked into something I had no idea was going down."

"And if I don't know her?"

Dillon's face was cold. "You know her."

Rubin resumed the same pose, dangerously close to toppling backward. He was a big man, a barrel chest over an all-you-can-eat tummy, and the chair seemed to strain under the weight. He didn't respond, the fact of which made Dillon more nervous than he already was.

"Do you have a tape player in here?" Dillon asked.

"I can get one." Rubin didn't move.

Dillon dug a cassette tape from his jacket pocket, held it up.

"Did she consent to being recorded?" asked Rubin, eyeing it.

Dillon bit at his lip. Several seconds passed before he said, "This is a mistake." He pocketed the tape as he started to get up.

"Tell me what I'm listening to and I'll be the judge of that. I'm big on context, you see . . . it's one of my favorite words, actually."

Dillon settled back into his seat, realizing Rubin was fucking with him, and that on the other side of his cool veneer there might be a sympathetic ear. Some people required their pound of flesh before indulging you.

"Context is what makes one and one equal five. See, one and one with a little intuition equals three. One and one with intuition and a little luck equals four. But context . . . that's the magic pill. Most people don't understand that, and even fewer have it mastered."

"I can see that you do."

"It's the business. Without context we're a bunch of clock punchers in suspenders. With it we can sometimes work miracles." Rubin opened a drawer to his desk and pulled out a portable cassette tape player. He fumbled with the plug, finally having to get down on his hands and knees beneath his desk to plug it into the combination power strip-surge protector that supported his PC and clock radio. Dillon stifled a grin, wishing he had a camera.

Rubin brushed off his knees as he sat back down. "I

have to tell you, I doubt any of this will be admissible in a court of law."

"This is my court of law," said Dillon. "Right here, right now."

Rubin narrowed his eyes and leaned forward. Whatever this guy was up to, it was working, because in his eyes Rubin could see a sincerity beyond contrivance. His gut was telling him that he should listen closely.

"I'm here to convince you that you need to believe me, that everything I'm going to tell you after I play the tape is the absolute truth."

Rubin nodded, implying a commitment to give it a chance.

"If you don't, then I have to rely on the evidence and the work of you and your esteemed peers . . . and to be honest, that doesn't exactly make me want to engage in any long-term life planning."

Rubin didn't think that was so funny.

He put in the tape and pressed the play button.

40

They listened in silence. Rubin's eyes never moved. Dillon studied them carefully as the Dark Lady's voice once again seduced him. His own voice, sounding like someone else on the tape, shamed him.

He turns up a few days later, very dead. They find a note—suicide. Poor man died of a broken heart. Meanwhile you and I have come out in the open with our relationship. It's cruel, we're not proud of what it caused . . . but, hey—it's nothing we can be arrested for. Love is war, people get killed. They stopped executing people for adultery a long time ago.

HE let it play right up to the part where she called the police department and reported that her husband had returned home. Then he hit the stop button and waited for Rubin to say something.

"As I said, I'm not sure this is admissible," was what he said.

"I'm not trying to admit evidence. I'm trying to get you to believe me."

"You're not on trial. But I'd talk to an attorney if I were you."

"I'd rather talk to you. I have video, too. You can see the truth with your own eyes."

Rubin's body language became animated, as if his clothes suddenly didn't fit. His eyes wrestled with temptation and his mouth betrayed the fact that he'd rather be somewhere else entirely, somewhere where the choices were easier and no careers and no lives were at stake.

"I offer you nothing," he finally said. "No promises, no tomorrow."

Dillon nodded. And then he told him everything, except for the location of the body. An ace is often most useful when left in its hole.

WHEN Dillon was finished, he realized how exhausted he was. There was no peace in telling the tale, no cathartic unloading. Instead there was the worst kind of shame, the inability to make someone feel the same sense of hot breath on his most secret desire, the song of the siren. He had exposed his weak link, and because he did not fully understand it himself, how could anyone else be expected to somehow justify what he'd done?

Rubin was frowning. Not so much from disapproval, but from the complexity of it all. From the way Dillon's story connected to a secret he'd been carrying around in his gut for the last four years.

Dillon realized he needed to sell it harder. "Whether you believe me or not, this tape proves something."

Rubin nodded slowly. "It proves you are conspiring to break the law."

"It proves she's lying, goddamn it!"

"Does it?"

"You heard it! He's not back at home safe and sound, he's fucking *dead!* Her whole story hinges on me being some obsessed asshole with a hard-on! On me not *knowing* her!"

Rubin just stared, squinting.

"It's rather obvious that this woman and I know each other, isn't it, Detective? If you have any doubt, I have video footage that will take care of it."

Rubin's only move was to rub the stubble on his chin absentmindedly. His stare was intense, laced with many layers.

"Would I be here if I was in on this?" said Dillon.

"Maybe. You look like a smart guy to me. Maybe smarter than me."

"I don't think so."

"You're right. I'm not the schmuck with a hook in my mouth," said Rubin.

Dillon nodded, realizing this was a good sign. A connection was being forged here. Rubin was at least acknowledging Dillon's status as a victim.

Rubin went on. "So far all I've got is a bunch of nothing from a bunch of people who keep changing their minds."

Dillon looked away, out across the room, which was strangely quiet, not at all like the police sets in movies he'd seen. Every police drama had a grouchy lieutenant who hadn't slept in a week and tried to hide his respect for the lead character beneath a curmudgeon's wrath. Dillon wondered where this guy was today. Rubin was a candidate for the job, to be sure.

"I need a crime before I can start an investigation, Mr. Masters."

"I confess, goddamn it."

"To what? The man's wife says he's at home. You say he's dead. Not that you don't have my attention . . . but until a body turns up or we have reason to believe that Mr. Wallace is indeed among the nonbreathing, that's all you've got."

"Call his office."

"I may do that."

They locked eyes. There was more to this than his words.

"You don't believe me."

"I said I need a crime. All I have now is a story. A very tall tale, at that."

Dillon changed his tone, lowered his volume. "You said she was an amazing woman. Somehow you know who she is, and if you do, then in your heart you know why I'm here, handing you the rope to hang me with. In your heart you know I'm telling you the truth. You wouldn't have the job you have if you didn't possess that kind of sensibility." Dillon paused. "Look at the context of it, Detective."

Rubin chewed at his lip, his eyes drifting slightly. As if facing the moment when he must reveal that which he had sought to keep hidden. As if facing a choice of his own.

"Let's just say, hypothetically, that I believe you. And just as hypothetically, that I know this woman and what she's capable of. Just for grins, let's say she's done it before and got away with it. Now, if you were me, and you've got another shot at busting her, what would you do? Jump in, fuck it all up because after all these years you can't wait to slap the cuffs on this bitch? Think about it, Masters . . . nothing's changed! All you've got is your story and not a shred of evidence to contradict the very accusation she started with. I jump now, she gets exactly what she set out to get."

Dillon frowned. "What's that?'

"She gets *you.*"

He watched the wheels turning behind Dillon's eyes before continuing.

"I could arrest you right now, you know. You've just confessed to about fourteen crimes, and you're admitting you've got a dead body stashed somewhere, and I've got to admit that worries me. But what good is that? Because if I act on what you've just told me—hypothetically speaking, of course—then the game is over. And this is the part you don't seem to understand—*she* wins."

He paused, letting it sink in. Then he leaned closer and lowered his voice.

"I just bought a ticket, pal. I'm here to see the good guys win."

Dillon drew a deep breath. "What should I do?"

"You know I can't answer that."

"Shit," mumbled Dillon under his breath as he closed his eyes. He wasn't sure what he expected out of Rubin, but this wasn't it.

"My advice to you is to find your attorney. When evidence surfaces, if it surfaces, I have to act on it. If it points at you, it's you I'm coming for. If it points to her . . ."

Dillon's eyes popped open, finally comprehending

Rubin's game. Rubin let the sentence hang unfinished for a moment. Then he finished it.

"Let's just hope the evidence points to *her*. You get my drift?"

Dillon didn't exactly grin, but a new light shone in his expression.

Rubin just stared. After a moment Dillon nodded, realizing Rubin would offer nothing more.

"Ask her about her tattoo, Detective. In case you aren't sure who to believe, hypothetically speaking. If I were you, I'd want more, too. So ask her about it. Watch what she does. Watch how eager she is to prove to you that I'm out of my mind."

A twinkle of acknowledgment flashed in Rubin's eyes as Dillon turned to go.

WITHIN the hour Dillon had removed Wallace's body from the freezer in his garage and rolled it back into the trunk of the Jaguar. The limbs would no longer bend—Wallace had been pickled in somewhat of a fetal position—and he had to try several angles before everything fit and the lid could close. After carefully wiping down the interior of the freezer and replacing the steaks, he drove the Jag to the airport and parked it in the long-term lot, the only place he could think of where a car could remain overnight without attracting undo attention. Wallace's Jag, every inch a traveling executive's car, would fit right in. If Rubin had been straight with him, nobody would be looking for it . . . yet. And if he hadn't, there would be no stiff in his freezer to confirm his story.

He took a taxi back to within half a mile of his and Karen's house. He walked the rest of the way there to pick up his Cherokee and drive to where he and Karen had agreed to meet over dinner to discuss what might happen next. When he had made the date he had no inkling what that might be. But now he had an idea.

It was time to break a few more laws.

41

There was no guarantee that the Dark Lady would leave her house that evening. Dillon and Karen were sitting in her BMW, parked strategically half a block away. A neighbor was having a party and the street was choked with cars, providing all the cover a stalker could ever ask for as long as his or her own car had a sticker price in excess of sixty grand. They said little to each other as they waited.

It was after eight. Dillon was already thinking of calling it off when he noticed that the upstairs light in the Wallace house suddenly went out.

He had no idea that Karen was of the same mind. But until her own plan crystallized, a process which was already well under way, she'd go along with this and whatever else Dillon needed to do.

Less than a minute after the light was extinguished, the garage door began to elevate to reveal the red glow of waiting taillights. Veronica Wallace's black SL 500 backed out and started down the drive, passing between the twin brick pillars flanking the driveway and turning into the street, heading directly toward them. They both slouched low, hiding from her line of sight.

A moment later Dillon grabbed the small overnight bag at his feet and opened the door, squeezing Karen's hand as he got out. He was dressed all in black, having to resort to a pair of dress slacks and Ecco loafers to achieve the requisite fashion of those who break and enter for a living. The night air was markedly colder than when they had left home, reminding him how alone he was with the consequences of his impulsive passions.

As he walked briskly down the sidewalk he unzipped the bag and took out his portable cell phone, flipping it open with one hand and punching in a number with practiced fingers.

Inside the BMW, the portable cell phone in Karen's hand began to ring. She pressed the button but said nothing.

He held the phone to his ear as he walked, neither of them saying anything. They had agreed to keep the line open to warn him of the Dark Lady's unexpected return.

He glanced about and took a sudden left turn through the pillars into the Wallace driveway. He began to jog now that he was off the street, heading around the garage where he knew there was a door. Decorative landscaping lamps cast enough light to keep him on a concrete path, which was wet and slick.

"I'm here," he said, realizing that in a perverse way he was enjoying the urgent rhythm of his chest, the flush of his cheeks, the buzz in his gut. It was the rush of survival, the high of hope, the supporting touch of his wife's eyes and ears.

He tried the knob. The door was locked. It occurred to him at that point that he could have brought the garage remote along, but it was in the Jag, right where it should be if anyone with a badge happened upon it.

"I'm doing it," he said into the phone, waiting only a moment for a response, which didn't come. He positioned his elbow at the center of the glass window in the door and punched it in.

The glass shattered at his feet with much more noise than he had anticipated.

"It's done," he said, knowing she'd understand what he meant.

"Five minutes . . . go." She was referring to the assumption that what he had done had triggered a silent alarm. In a moment a telephone inside the house would begin to ring, and the person on the other end of the line would be staring at a PC screen upon which was shown the password the Wallaces had selected. Something like "leveraged buyout." When the call went unanswered, the security officer would immediately notify the police, providing them with the name and address of the home and his company's clearance code. A police operator would forward the information to a patrol dispatcher who would then radio the nearest squad car with the same information. Depending on where the squad car was or what the officers were doing—Dillon pictured them sitting at the counter at a nearby doughnut emporium—it would take from two to five minutes for them to arrive in the driveway. Hell, Dillon and Karen had friends who claimed it took the police over thirty minutes to respond to an alarm. In the meantime the security dispatcher would continue to ring the Wallace number. Worst-case scenario from Dillon's perspective was five minutes.

Then again, maybe Veronica Wallace didn't bother with the alarm at all this night. He'd never know. He'd be in and out before it mattered.

Dillon fished a flashlight out of his bag and scanned the far wall for the door that led to a utility room.

This door was unlocked, as it had been two mornings ago. Only the truly paranoid locked the inside door to the garage when there were automatic openers on the big outside doors.

"I'm in," he said as he closed the door behind him, already noticing the smell of the house, the scent of a hundred lush fabrics and imported hardwoods and years of privileged occupancy.

"Go," was all that Karen said, alternating her scan between the road ahead and her mirrors. If the Dark Lady returned now Dillon would have to cross her path to escape. In all likelihood she wold produce a gun and shoot him, and it would be the perfect climax to her contrived story. She would have a huge grin on her face as she pulled the trigger. Karen almost admired the pure poetry of it.

Inside the house Dillon slipped off his shoes and put them into the bag, which he then slung over his shoulder. It had been Karen's idea—dirt tracks from outside would never do. There was a chance the alarm would go unexplained and that the backdoor glass would go unnoticed until the next morning. The more likely outcome was that Veronica would see the broken window when she pulled into the garage.

As Dillon rushed through the kitchen and into a hallway it occurred to him that someone else might be there. Several lights had been left burning, and his ears strained to pick up a distant echo of a television or running water. But he suddenly heard something else, and even though he had known it was coming it still sent a bolt of electricity through his skin.

The telephone.

He vaulted up the curving staircase three steps at a time, buoyed by adrenaline. He went straight into her bedroom, where the ringing continued with a different tone from the nightstand.

"I'm in the room," he said into the cell phone.

"Four minutes," she said. "Move."

Dillon took a moment to size up the room. In the shadows it appeared smaller than before. The bed was perfectly made with what seemed like dozens of pillows stacked in some mysterious magazine-layout sort of way. He went to the window and looked up at the hillside where he'd watched this very spot through binoculars before Ms. Police Officer had arrived.

He dropped to his hands and knees and lifted the dust ruffle, shining the flashlight under the bed. There were two department store boxes and something with a coiled cord. He squinted—it was one of those Brookstone handheld massage devices that doubled as orgasmatics. He reached for one of the boxes and slid it out, but from its weight he could tell it was empty. The other box was heavier—it contained a cookbook and an oven mitt, probably an ungiven or unwanted gift of some kind.

This was too obvious. This wasn't where she'd hide something that was critical to her scheme.

The telephone had stopped momentarily, then resumed its ringing. It was louder than any telephone he'd ever heard. He looked up—it was a concept phone, in the shape of a golf bag.

"Do it!" Karen said. Her voice was calm and confident, like an air traffic controller talking down a civilian who had assumed the controls after the pilot collapsed with heart failure. Dillon heard competence in her voice, wondering why he'd never noticed it before.

"Still looking," he said.

The first nightstand yielded nothing but a few paperbacks and documents he didn't bother to examine. This wasn't where she'd put it either.

The plastic golf bag stopped ringing as he reached the other nightstand.

He could hear Karen through the cell phone—"Go go go go go . . ."

Dillon opened the other nightstand drawer. It was as much from curiosity as it was a hunch, neither of which pertained to his mission. Inside was a box full of cassette tapes, each bearing a label. Next to it, on top of a Bible, was a small cassette tape player and headphones.

And next to that, a gun. It had been a good hunch.

"Got something," he whispered into the phone. He picked up the gun and put it into the bag.

It was then that Karen noticed headlights approaching in the mirror. She didn't respond to Dillon's words.

With the tiny flashlight clenched in his teeth, Dillon held the box of cassettes with one hand and flipped through the tapes with the other. The cell phone was tightly wedged between his shoulder and his head, the required angle making his neck cramp. Each cassette label showed a handwritten name and a date. They were all women's names. He looked through them, wondering what this could mean. Finally, remembering the clock was ticking, he put the box down and closed the drawer.

Then he froze as a new thought licked at him.

He opened the drawer again and picked up the tape

player. At the touch of the proper button one of the sides popped open, revealing the cassette. It had Karen's name on it. The date was last summer, coinciding with her sessions with Carmichael.

As he popped out the cassette and put it into the bag, the telephone began ringing yet again, slicing the thick air like a sonic razor. He grabbed several other tapes and stuffed them into the bag before closing the drawer.

The SL 500 glided past Karen. The brake lights came on as it slowed for the driveway. It was going too fast, braking abruptly . . . something was wrong. She had only been gone for a couple of minutes, not long enough to do anything except drive around the block. None of this was Veronica Wallace's style.

Then it hit her. When no one answered the phone in the house, the security company probably had a cell phone number on record. They'd called it, reached Veronica, told her about the alarm at her house. And now she was back.

Karen started to say something. But there was the slightest hesitance, and for a moment she felt the power of her position, realizing she liked the feeling. Dillon's balls were in the palm of her hand. All she had to do was squeeze. All she had to do was keep quiet, and this would be over.

She hadn't known how she'd react to this moment until it arrived. Now, tasting it, she still wasn't sure.

There would be other moments. His balls were going nowhere.

"Dillon, she's back. Get moving. Right now."

Dillon put the flashlight and the cell phone into the pocket of his coat and sprung for the door. Then he stopped cold, a deer paralyzed by death's sudden headlights.

He closed his eyes, feeling his nerves twitching. He had known fear before, the kind that comes cloaked in shame and guilt or shrouded in pain—but never a moment like this. Suspended between past and future, between right and wrong, he realized that this decision would define him. If he turned away from it, even if in the end he somehow survived, he would always know. This was where he chose to be the man the Dark Lady had picked as her prey, vulnerable and weak, or the man his wife had married. Karen had stepped up, now he had to, as well.

He opened his eyes and decided, turning his back on the hallway that would lead him to freedom. He had to finish what he'd come to do.

He approached the darkened double doorway of her closet. Feeling for the light, he found the switch and flipped it on. The room was amazing, a surreal snapshot from an Orwellian *Architectural Digest*. The clothes were in perfect array, the hangers evenly spaced, as if a servant had been assigned full time to manage the symmetry of it all. The fabrics appeared as blocks of colors—blacks with blacks, reds with reds, whites with whites, a cold and inflexible code.

All this was registered in a quick flash of surprise. He saw several round boxes on a shelf above the clothes, perfectly aligned. He reached for one.

Karen kept saying Dillon's name into the cell phone, nearly screaming it now. The taillights were still on as the Mercedes stopped near the mansion's entrance without raising the garage door. Of course . . . if she knew an alarm had been tripped she wouldn't simply drive on in. She'd be cautious. She'd wait for the security people or the police to arrive. Or, if she assumed—even hoped— that it was Dillon, she'd rush inside, withdraw her handgun from her purse, and shoot him in the head.

Dillon opened the hatbox and saw a black hat inside, a perfectly funereal Dark Lady accessory. It smelled of his grandmother's sache. Moving quickly, he reached into his bag and withdrew a heavy object wrapped in newspaper. He uncovered it—the ashtray from the Fraser Hotel. The object that had collided with Hamilton Wallace's forehead, now wiped clean of any fingerprints. Only a half-inch square section of glass, a sharp corner, had gone uncleaned, where a dried smear of blood was still visible.

The lack of fingerprints would make sense. Just as the presence of *his* fingerprints had been the reason for leaving it in the hotel room in Vancouver. The Dark Lady was, after all, most fond of wearing gloves. He quickly put the ashtray into the hatbox and replaced it on the shelf. This would be right where Rubin would want to find it.

Halfway down the stairs he heard something, a tone at the very edge of perception. It was more a presence than a sound—a car outside, motor running. He squinted through the foyer toward the entrance. A trace of red, diffused through leaded glass—taillights from outside.

At the base of the stairs Dillon headed in the opposite direction from the kitchen, toward the other end of the floor plan. There had to be a back door, and he had to find it.

There was, and he did.

42

They were sitting in Karen's BMW in the lot of the Residence Inn, parked right next to Dillon's Cherokee. She'd taken him back to pick it up after his escape from the Wallace house. She'd followed him here, expecting to go inside and face the next chapter of this saga. But instead he'd asked if they could sit in her car for a while and talk. He'd held her for several minutes, still breathing hard, letting the tension melt into the comfort of her embrace. She could feel his need, sense that she was his anchor now. It felt good to have him needing her this way, and the memory of how it felt back there at the Wallace estate, with her linger on the trigger of his fate, rushed back to her.

But there was more to this than Dillon's need for comfort. He wanted her to listen to the tape he'd found in a cassette player next to Veronica Wallace's bed. A tape with Karen's name written on it.

When Dillon inserted the tape she recognized her own voice and then Carmichael's, immediately remembering the conversation from nearly a year earlier. It had been one of her last sessions, one that had changed her world. It made her conclude that she'd be more comfortable talking with a woman, that no matter how hard she tried to explain her feelings about her husband and her life, Carmichael seemed to always push for some sort of capitulation. There was always a subtle call for an allowance for the way men operated in general, as if his sort of womanly tolerance was, in the end, the source of marital peace and fulfillment. She'd decided it was mostly unenlightened bullshit from a man who couldn't understand what women needed, regardless of his training. Carmichael's testicles were blocking his vision.

She'd had no idea the session was being recorded. Now, a year later, her sense of violation was no less severe than if she'd found the hidden microphone that very day.

Someone would pay for this.

Karen and Dillon stared at the dashboard stereo, listening to the tape, completely still.

"**MORE** men are into this type of thing than you can imagine, Karen."

"Type of thing?"

"The fascination, even the obsession, with feminine power. With an interpretation of femininity as inherently evil. Think about children's literature for a moment. . . . Isn't the evil queen usually hypnotically compelling and often beautiful? Isn't her darkness confusing to almost all little boys, beckoning to them while frightening them at the same time? Isn't she the character they lie awake at night and think about, afraid to sleep for fear she might be in their dreams? Isn't that the same dance we embrace as adults, cloaked in metaphor and social niceties? Some men, because of their experience with women as a child and later in adolescence, never lose that fascination and that association. It torments them and delights them for their entire lives."

Karen could be heard taking a deep breath.

"I just can't be his evil queen, Doctor. I've tried, I swear to God I have. I just can't shake the feeling that it's all about someone else. It's . . . it's just not about me. It's not who I am. I need it to be about *me*."

"Then perhaps you both have something to work on."

The rustling of bodies shifting in their chairs. Then Carmichael again.

"A sexual fetish is really just a form of crying out. It's the voice of childhood abuse or neglect . . . some unfilled need or insecurity. It's not right or wrong, good or bad. It just *is*. If we don't listen to it, we can't comfort the child within. The child needs to be held, and through the filter of adult hormones and the complex wiring of the male sexual circuitry, that embrace takes on darker implications. Don't ask the man to explain it, because he can't. Don't ask him to simply deny it or rid himself of it, because he can't do that either."

"I'm going to lose him, aren't I?"

"If the two of you don't decide to start fulfilling each other's needs—his dark, yours poetic, whatever—then you leave yourselves open to . . ."

A cough, unclear as to whose. Then Carmichael continued.

"You leave yourselves very vulnerable."

"Vulnerable to what?" A hint of defiance in Karen's voice.

"To someone who will."

A long pause.

"The key, Karen, is not simply to make love to Dillon, or even to screw his brains out. The key is to screw his *brain*. The woman who figures that out in her life, in her marriage, can have absolutely anything and everything she wants . . . from any man she chooses."

KAREN reached out and turned the player off.

"I'm so sorry," she said.

Dillon started to say something, but found the words blocked by an unexpected emotion. The collision between what seemed to be her sudden acceptance of his need and the realization that Carmichael had used that same need as a stolen weapon was beyond his words. So he just drew her against him and held her, his anger and his sadness and his guilt melding as one, wondering if either of them had the strength to do what had to happen next.

It wasn't the right moment to tell him that she didn't think his plan would work. Or that she had her own notion about how to end it once and for all.

43

Karen spent the night with Dillon at the Residence Inn. They went to bed naked and in silence, returning to an easy embrace that had been forgotten long before she'd asked him to move out of their home. Spooning was her word for it, with him behind, enclosing her within the curve of his body, holding her with an encircling arm. He was amazed at how warm her skin felt, and long after she'd drifted to sleep he remained awake, listening to her breathing, watching the line of her closed eyes in the dim light. Despite the proximity of their bodies, lovemaking had not been an option or even a notion. Yet watching her sleep, thinking about her new strength of will and commitment in the face of danger, he realized he wanted her, and that, precisely because of the proximity of their bodies, he knew she was aware of his desire. She was more beautiful and powerful than he remembered her ever being. She was even slightly dangerous in a way that appealed to the same place within him that had been vulnerable to her coldness.

The next morning he left her in his bed and went to the office. It was nearly an impossible place to be, given the state of his life, but there was no other place he could await the next chapter and remain visible to the world. Karen had a mission later this morning, the outcome of which would define their next move and possibly the rest of his life. As they kissed goodbye, the first real kiss they'd shared in many months, he'd handed her the loaded gun he'd taken from Veronica Wallace's nightstand.

He wouldn't see her again until this was over. But they would talk. The plan depended on their leaving the lines of communication open at all times.

This morning, when the plan kicked in, there would be no turning back.

When he arrived at work he was greeted with a message to call one of the company's compliance executives in White Plains. The machinist union had filed a grievance and asked for a full investigation of the Applied Software Technologies fiasco, with a view toward a settlement based on a breach of fiduciary trust and responsibility. Janis was out of the office all morning tending to an unrelated legal matter, so Dillon saved the message and tried to put the stock market out of his mind.

Her call came in just before nine. She was sitting in the parking lot of a marina on Puget Sound just north of the city, the most expensive and distinguished nautical address in the metropolitan area. Super-yacht city.

"Is it there?" asked Dillon.

Karen once again looked through her binoculars to be sure. It was raining, the sky as gray as Mt. St. Helens ash. She focused on the stern of a high-profile yacht and read the name imprinted there.

"*Picki Nicki*. Very cute. If a boat as big as a building can be called cute."

"You're sure you're up to this?" he asked.

"I sort of have to be, don't I?" She didn't sound as confident as he'd have liked.

"You have to trust me."

"I *did* trust you." This was followed by a long silence, during which he wondered, if they should survive the day, how many years he'd have to pay for his sins. "Now you have to trust *me*," she added.

After another pause, he said pointedly, "I do trust you."

She was glad he couldn't see the bitter expression on her face.

"You won't hear from me for a while."

"I love you for this."

"I know," said Karen softly as she punched the cell phone off.

The words echoed familiar in Dillon's ears. He grabbed his overcoat and left the office, wondering if he'd ever be back.

IT was a garden club with no garden. The women who lunched here belonged to men whose blood was blue and whose money was old. No Microsoft fortunes within these halls. The Boeing bloodline, which was well represented here, was about as contemporary as the money got. There were timber and shipping legacies and a handful of diversified portfolios with no roots. Primary club activities included lunch and civic service, with millions funneled into the community on both counts. Several public buildings and a few streets in town bore the names of the families who formed the club's membership.

Veronica Wallace had been a member here for nearly a decade. It had nothing to do with her present marriage to one of the new generation of high-technology millionaires, even though he was now a venture capitalist, a much more acceptable avocation. Secretly the women referred to her present husband as her "boy toy," given that he was six years her junior. No, Veronica had been embraced by these ladies in a prior and more appropriate life, when her then husband had been part of the inner circle of Boeing executives. In those days she was the youngest inductee ever accepted into a Seattle institution that had its roots in the late 1800s, and she was still among the youngest who came here to be seen. For over a hundred years these women had taken care of their own—when the spouse dies and the money remains, you get to remain here with it.

Veronica Wallace had taken great care to see that these women didn't find out that her late husband's money never found its way into her bank account. The boat helped establish the facade, especially with her name on the stern and its residence at the best and most visible marina in town. Appearance, she had learned long ago, is an easy thing to create and maintain. It was appearance that brought her here today to drink martinis and play cards with women who politely called each other friends. She was the center of attention this morning, because the word was out that someone had broken into her house the night before while her husband was away on business, and that she'd returned in time to scare the criminal away before anything was stolen.

Like Dillon, the Dark Lady understood the value of maintaining the proper illusion in a time of crisis.

The garden club's building was an ivy-draped stone mansion located in the heart of downtown, with a killer view of the Sound and a parking garage that offered free privileges to the membership. Dillon rang the doorbell and waited, pulling his collar high against the morning chill.

He knew she was here because it was Friday, and he recalled her saying that Friday was pitch day at the club, which included lunch and an optional massage from a delicious Spanish boy named Armande. Dillon had called to confirm that she was indeed present before showing up, telling the club receptionist that he had a delivery to make and needed to confirm her presence.

The maître d', a surprisingly young man with an effeminate manner and a harsh scowl, told him to wait in the lobby. Nonmembers weren't permitted beyond the foyer unescorted, for which Dillon was profoundly grateful.

Veronica was staring at a king-high hand of four spades, an iffy three-bid, when the young man leaned close and told her there was someone to see her in the lobby. Her first thought was that it had to be Carmichael, who had been frantic to be with her as the heat began to mount. The thought made her smile. Or perhaps it was that nice patrolman from the night before, with his soft blue eyes and strong arms, who had taken so much time checking the house for her. When he left she knew he'd be back, no matter how contrived the excuse.

Dillon was not who she expected to see. She thanked the maître d' and took Dillon's arm to move him away. She wore a taupe linen pantsuit that seemed to flow with her as she moved.

"This is not acceptable." Her tone was as stern as it was quiet.

"I think you'll change your mind about that."

"How did you find me here?"

"That's less important than *why* I found you."

She glanced to the side instinctively. His presence would be hard to integrate into any version of a story concocted to serve her original intent, which was to sacrifice him for her freedom.

He read her mind. "No going back now, is there, Mrs. Wallace?"

She looked up at him, saying nothing.

"I have a plan," he said. And indeed he did. He and Karen had spent the entire morning pounding out its details. She hadn't seemed convinced, but she said she'd go along with it. If nothing else, Karen was proving to be a team player.

Veronica Wallace's eyebrows elevated, inviting him to continue. She seemed more interested in him getting on with it than in what he might have in mind.

"Everything we've wanted . . . everything *you've* wanted all along, can be summed up in two words." He was smug, his smile sharp and a little mean.

He watched her take a deep breath, waiting. It felt good to have the hammer in his hands instead of hers.

"Salt water," he said, enunciating the syllables clearly.

Her eyes narrowed, then slowly came alive with comprehension. A smile emerged on her face, the kind that reached down beyond his mind and stroked the most mysterious and fragile part of him. He felt the effect of it and remembered why he signed on with the Dark Lady in the first place, why he was in the situation he was in.

It was a witch's smile, delighting in the darkness, inviting him to dance.

44

Veronica hadn't seen the vessel that bore her name since the end of summer. That event had been a cocktail cruise on a summer evening with clients just in from New York who thought Seattle was a marvelous wilderness. Hamilton had hired a fit young captain to ferry them around the sound—he'd never bothered to learn to steer the boat himself. She assumed it was because it was her boat, sentimental baggage from her previous widowhood. She'd had some helm time years ago when her late husband had bought the yacht for her on their second anniversary, and had actually liked the feeling of power in her hands almost as much as she liked the look of her name on the stern. It was easier to drive than it looked.

Now it was the dawn of another lifetime, and once again the *Picki Nicki* would carry her over the horizon to something better. A mechanic had pronounced the craft seaworthy, if not a little lonely, just a few months earlier in conjunction with its annual service. She hoped this meant the engines would fire for her tonight.

They did. Marine batteries were one of the technological wonders of the world. Blowers on for a full minute, throttles set on idle . . . then a marvelous roar that, for a moment at least, had always made her feel sexy and wild. The *Picki Nicki* was ready for sea at the hands of her namesake mistress.

She glanced toward the parking lot, unable to see the cars because of the angle of the shoreline. Hamilton's Jag had been there when she arrived, just as Dillon promised. It was unlocked, also according to plan, allowing her to leave the white envelope with her name on it on the driver's seat. Inside the envelope was salvation, followed by liberty. Before going down to the boat she'd checked the trunk, just in case. It was empty, smelling slightly of Pine-Sol.

Dillon's plan was indeed under way. It was a brilliant strategy, confirming him as a worthy adversary. And because of this, perhaps, a delicious partner. Either way she played it, things would turn out in her favor.

It was dark by now. Veronica tried several switches before finding the running lights. She let the engines warm thoroughly, waiting until the temperature gauges were well past their center point before going on deck to cast off lines. It was cold on the water, and the ropes were stiff and snug after months of tugging against the elements. One of them required her to fetch a crowbar to finally loosen it sufficiently to lift it off the cleat.

The dock was completely deserted. Owning a yacht in Seattle, especially at this marina, was a fair-weather hobby indeed.

Returning to the helm, she realized she was as nervous about her role now, in this moment, as she had been about any of the otherwise more distasteful elements of her plan. She looked about to make sure no one was watching. She had to slip out of the marina unnoticed, or at least without becoming noteworthy.

She clicked the twin handles down into the reverse position. The hull shivered beneath her feet, and by looking at the lights on the dock she could tell the ship was sliding aft. After a moment she pushed the handles back into the neutral position, letting inertia glide the fifty-five-foot Navigator from its berth. When the bow cleared the mooring walkways she spun the wheel hard to port, momentarily kicking the port lever back into forward and the starboard to reverse position to tighten the turn. Looking back, she saw there was plenty of room behind. Only a hard wind, thankfully absent on this night, would make the task even a modest challenge.

When the ship was perpendicular to the dock from which it had just disengaged, she pushed the levers into the forward position and eased the throttles forward just a hair, and the yacht began to slide toward the blackness of open water. In fifteen minutes she'd be abreast of a designated point of land north of the city, where Dillon would be waiting for her.

DILLON sat a few hundred feet off a black shore, glancing at his watch. A mist that couldn't quite qualify as fog slid slowly through the night like smoke, its chill penetrating his ski jacket. He shivered, looking at his watch yet again. The tiny Wellcraft bobbed like a wine bottle cork in a Jacuzzi on the sound's pulsing water, forcing him to hold tightly to the windshield when he stood up to scan the horizon for approaching lights.

Behind him, in the middle of the deck of the ski boat, was a mound covered by a canvas mooring cover.

Ten minutes after the appointed hour he saw lights approaching. He started up the engine and shoved the throttles forward, lurching momentarily over the crest of a swell, landing with a bone-numbing thud.

It was the *Picki Nicki,* all right. He could see Veronica's silhouette at the inside helm.

He flashed his running lights, and the yacht's engines cut to idle, the bow immediately settling into the icy water.

He moved the ski boat to the stern. When he was ten feet away Veronica appeared on deck, dressed in black from head to toe, including a baseball hat with a Planet Hollywood logo on the front.

"Give me a hand," he called out, tossing a rope up toward the deck. He had to nearly yell over the sound of the idling engines and the open sea. He noticed how awkwardly she moved, unaccustomed to catching and pulling ropes. She secured it loosely to the ladder leading down to the swim platform. Once she had it tied, she climbed down and stood there, holding the rope in her hands to keep the tiny boat steady.

The water was choppy enough to cause the ski boat to pitch and yaw dramatically. If it got too close to the *Picki Nicki*'s swim platform, the target of this exercise, a swell could lift the bow right up onto it, possibly breaking it off.

Dillon threw the canvas back to reveal the body of Hamilton Wallace, still almost completely frozen from two nights in a freezer and a full winter day in the trunk of the Jag. It was naked, starkly white in the dim illumination of the yacht's deck lights. Its fetal position was similar to that in which death had occurred, head thrown back, mouth impossibly wide, legs bent backward, arms pulled behind. The hair was perhaps the most chilling sight of all, sticking straight upward from the scalp, as if composed of clay. The deadly bonds had been long removed, but the muscles had fixed this way, in a silhouette of agony. The eyes were still open, like a salmon's glassy gaze in a grocery store freezer case, devoid of memory.

There could be no peace in death. Not if death looked like this.

When Dillon looked up toward the deck of the ship, he saw that Veronica was holding her hand over her mouth in what seemed like horror.

"What did you expect?" he asked.

She didn't answer. She just turned her head to the side, keeping her knuckles in her mouth. Her reaction surprised him.

He tugged the body up onto one of the seats of the ski boat. It was incredibly heavy, nearly impossible for one man to move. But he had moved the impossible before, several times in the past several days, in fact.

"The clothes?" he asked, barely looking at her.

"In the master suite," she said, her eyes still fixed on her dead husband.

They had talked this through, covered every moment of it, so that now, with the act at hand, there would be no need for discussion. Dillon was tying a rope around the body's throat, covering the ligature marks that had already marked the flesh there. Once secured, he leaped from the side of his boat across three feet of black Puget Sound water onto the *Picki Nicki's* swim platform and began tying the other end of the rope onto a mooring cleat.

"Go and cut the engines," he barked.

"What for?"

Now he looked up, his expression urgent and intense. "First of all, because I *told* you to. And I told you to because the prop might cut the rope, or the wash might tangle it, in which case we're fucked. The slack needs to be gone before you start her again. Stay there, I'll signal you when to fire it up again."

He watched her climb up onto the deck. When she was out of sight he frantically began to pull Wallace's body over the rail and onto the swim platform. It landed with a thud and nearly rolled off into the water. Dillon lunged for it, his feet slipping on the fiberglass decking. After a doubtful moment he steadied himself and began to roll the body away from the edge.

Once there, he untied the knot around the corpse's throat as quickly and as quietly as he could.

He had less than a minute before she might sense something was wrong.

TWO minutes passed. Veronica Wallace stood at the helm in the cabin, wringing her hands and pacing, her eyes fixed on the stern. Something was not right. Just as she opened the sliding glass doors and stepped out onto the deck, she saw that Dillon was climbing up. She noticed that he was now wearing a pair of thin rubber sanitary gloves.

"It's done," he said, his face soaked with sweat.

He brushed past her into the cabin, heading straight for the controls. He cranked the first key, listening for the engine to catch. When it did, he turned the second. The *Picki Nicki* hummed, low and guttural.

Dillon pushed the yacht into forward gear and turned the wheel toward open water. His eyes watched the compass until the needle was centered over a carefully planned heading—340 degrees, straight toward the mouth of the sound, directly into the San Juans a hundred miles to the north. If the yacht didn't hit an island, it would disappear into an endless ocean night. Either would be fine.

He locked the autopilot onto this course. Next to the helm, on a counter, was the bottle of Chivas he'd told Veronica to bring with her, and next to that a glass. He opened the bottle and raised it to his lips for a long, masochistic pull. Then he filled the glass halfway before turning the bottle on its side, allowing the brown ambrosia to spill across the counter and drip onto the carpet.

The widow Veronica Wallace just watched. He couldn't tell what she was thinking, whether she was admiring his boldness or confused by it.

His final action was to flip off all the ship's running and cabin lights.

"We're outta here," he said, stalking past her again and heading out of the cabin and down the ladder. She followed, and by the time she climbed down to the swim platform he was already in the ski boat waiting. Another rope was secured to the opposite cleat leading straight down into the water, taut under the weight it carried. Dead weight, indeed.

A very dramatic suicide. Something a creative and passionate individualist like Hamilton might stage. Live large, die big.

He helped Veronica step down from the platform onto the side of the ski boat, a treacherous task, maneuvering between two moving objects of unequal physics shifting according to the whim of an uncontrollable ocean. Once she was aboard he hopped back onto the swim platform, holding the rope tightly as he undid the knot on the yacht's other cleat. He then tossed the rope back into the ski boat and leaped confidently into the open bow in front of the windshield. He moved quickly behind the wheel, put the boat into reverse and hit the throttle, backing them rapidly away from the yacht. The *Picki Nicki* was already moving into open sea, slowly heading north, a tiny white crest breaking at the point at which the sleek bow cut into the water.

Veronica put her arm around his waist as both of them watched for a moment, bobbing like a nautical buoy. It was the perfect plan—the suicide note left in the Jaguar, Wallace's suit and boating clothes left neatly hanging in the master suite, his naked body hanging by its neck in the water as it was towed toward oblivion. If it was found at all there was no telling what condition the body would be in, what manner of saltwater preda-tor would have found it interesting, what the continuous pressure of the rope would do to any forensic evidence around its throat. Quincy himself wouldn't be able to see through this one.

She thought it was a brilliant plan. Enough to make her doubt her own treachery in favor of a man who was perhaps even more dangerous than herself.

"She was a beautiful lady," Veronica said wistfully. "Too bad."

Dillon watched the big yacht slip away from them, as if hypnotized by the sight. After a moment he glanced down at the controls, feeling his partner watching him. When he looked over at her she was smiling, a cold and selfishly hungry affection, apparently quite pleased with what she saw.

Dillon was smiling, too. Because what she saw was certainly *not* what it seemed.

45

Dillon was sitting in Carmichael's waiting room when the door to the office opened at eleven-fifty the next day. He'd been there for thirty minutes, knowing there was someone inside, narrating her nightmares, unaware that she was feeding the doctor's own demons. Having had not a minute of sleep, Dillon was aware of an uncomfortable buzzing in his ears that was only slightly more irritating than the rumbling in his stomach. There was no receptionist, just two chairs and a pile of magazines dating back over a year.

When the door opened, Dillon registered the doctor's expression upon seeing him there. But neither of them could react because the patient, a young woman with tear-streaked cheeks and bleary eyes, was still talking as Carmichael shooed her out the door. Dillon wondered what secrets she had just revealed, and if they made the doctor squirm.

He was already standing and moving into the inner office when the door closed behind her.

"This is highly unusual . . . I have a patient in ten minutes." For all his keen insight into human behavior, Carmichael was nonetheless a bad actor.

"No, you don't," replied Dillon. "It's noon and you never deviate from your lunch pattern, even on Saturdays." Carmichael had made this point several times himself when Dillon's appointments had bumped up against lunch. And it was true even on Saturdays, which Carmichael liked to work in favor of taking Mondays off.

Carmichael calmly put on his coat, watching Dillon wander about the office touching things on the shelves, peering around corners.

"Where do you hide it?" Dillon asked.

"What are you talking about?" But Carmichael already knew.

"The microphone."

Dillon sat down in the chair behind Carmichael's desk, offering up a cocky smile. He leaned back and reached into his pocket, withdrawing several audio cassettes, which he tossed onto the desk.

"Steven McCoy, attorney at law. Likes to wear his wife's maxi pads when he plays golf with clients." Dillon watched the resolve melt away from Carmichael's face.

"Patrice Stapleton. Beside herself because her husband wants her to do him anally with a snap-on johnson, the notion of which, to her great surprise, you seem to approve of."

Carmichael couldn't look at him, but didn't seem to know where else to look. He appeared to be shrinking, folding within himself, his face turning a bright shade of crimson.

"Shall I go on? Barbara Parker's husband—you two never actually said his first name—fantasizes about camping with his paperboy."

"Where did you get those?"

Dillon put his feet up on the desk and entwined his fingers behind his neck. He let the moment play out, his face setting like concrete.

"Her game is betrayal, Doc. Not fun, is it?"

Carmichael had stopped his nervous fidgeting and gazed out the window, the shadow of truth dawning over him.

"You'll have to be more specific."

"Okay, how's this for specific—she's fucking you worse than she was ever going to fuck me. And she wants me to help her do it."

Carmichael slowly turned his head and looked at Dillon, his eyes glistening violently now. There was much they could tell about the way the woman cast her dizzying spells, lulling men to the heart of her darkness. She'd been hot for Dillon the night before, wanting him in the boat as they returned to the launch ramp, whispering unspeakable acts into his ear with hot breath. He'd tiptoed at the precipice of this temptation, enough to maintain his place in the game. He told her she'd have to wait for him, that when the business of survival was finished there would be more secrets to share. She seemed fascinated by his newfound coldness, so much like her own.

Dillon put his feet back to the floor, just in case Carmichael made a move at him. He was wiry and strong, and although Dillon was fit, he sensed the eyes of a madman behind the wire-rimmed reading glasses.

"You see, I'm the new man, Doc . . . and you're next up on her dance card. You've got a bull's-eye tattooed on your ass."

Carmichael closed his eyes, his shoulders slowly sinking. "What do you want from me?"

"A refund, for starters."

Dillon watched the doctor draw a deep breath, shuddering subtly. He wondered how someone could slap on the pads to play the game, yet seem so unprepared to take a hit.

"Confusing as hell, isn't it? Believe me, I know how it is. You suck her in like good dope. Then when you choke on it you're not sure what to think, because part of you knows you bought the ticket for just that moment. There's nothing closer to the heat than the match itself, is there, Doc? In the bondage of their wickedness we are set free. Been there, haven't you? You know what this is about better than me."

Carmichael raised his chin slightly, a too obvious gesture of trying to remain in control. "I don't know why you're here."

"I'm just here to help, Doctor."

Carmichael said nothing for a moment, filled with contemplation and near-panic. Then he whispered, "Why?"

Dillon leaned forward and placed his hands on the desk to put as much sincerity into his eyes as he could. Over the years he'd perfected the posture in his work, making a stock he really knew nothing about sound like the client's economic saving grace. He said, "I'll tell you why, and hear this clearly: If you lose, I don't get to win. If you go down, I go down, too."

He got up and started for the door. "Think about it. I'll be in touch."

Then he left, knowing that Carmichael's mind would seethe, and that when his blood cooled the first place he would go would be to Veronica Wallace.

46

Detective Timothy Rubin was surly when he was awakened that morning by a seven o'clock telephone call from Dillon Masters. It was Saturday, and if Dillon Masters had a brain in his head he'd know not to enlist the detective's support by disrupting what was probably his week's only moment of peace.

Dillon called to suggest that a morning of surveillance at Benjamin Carmichael's office might be an interesting exercise in both patience and prudence. Any time after nine would be good. So Rubin had hit Starbucks for three grande mochas, double shots, and parked at a meter across from Carmichael's office tower garage with the morning paper. He'd noted the doctor's arrival shortly before nine. About three hours later, shortly after noon, Carmichael's car departed the parking lot with great urgency.

Rubin followed his white Cadillac STS to one of Bellevue's nicest addresses, a place Rubin recognized because he'd driven by it many times in the past four years. It was the home of Veronica Wallace, socialite, smug bitch queen, closet murderess. And now the centerfold in a new case file on his desk.

Score one for Masters. Maybe the guy actually *could* help Rubin save his ass.

He had one room temperature mocha left. He settled in at a fair distance so that the Cadillac parked in the driveway was within clear view. He couldn't help but visualize what might be happening inside. Like it or not, and he definitely did not like it, he had to admit that Veronica Wallace was the kind of woman that made the old imagination twitch.

He allowed the visualization to play out in his mind. But Rubin had no way of knowing how things really looked in the dark.

ON the night Hamilton Wallace died, Carmichael had simply shown up unexpectedly in the bar of Wallace's favorite Vancouver hotel. Veronica knew her husband's routine, that he would go to the bar for two Scotches after the long drive and then retire to his room to order room service. The two men had met just a few weeks before in a carefully orchestrated setup in a Bellevue restaurant. Veronica had insisted that Carmichael join them for dinner, assuring her husband that an intimate conversation with her shrink might provide some kinky fun for all. Nothing had come of it, other than Carmichael telling a few amusing stories about some of his clients' more unusual tastes in sexual desire. Now, several weeks later in Vancouver, Carmichael had once again appeared unexpectedly, claiming to be in town for a psychiatric convention. He sensed that Wallace couldn't place him at first, but he broke the ice by commenting that this was his favorite hotel. Wallace liked it when people shared his tastes. The two had shared a couple of drinks in the most remote corner of the bar, Wallace's last cocktail laced with a chemical dropped among the ice cubes with a quick flick of a wrist when Wallace looked away. The timing had been critical, as the drug had to hit him in the elevator going up. When it did, Carmichael helped the suddenly delirious Wallace to the room registered in Dillon Masters's name and tied him up in the special manner known to him and Veronica. The manner and precision of the bondage had always been his, an unvaried and detailed blueprint from a dark playroom in his mind. He had been in the bathroom when Wallace came to. When he heard the inevitable struggling he returned to the bedside, masturbated while watching the dance of death, then ended it with the blunt edge of the ashtray. Carmichael never told her that her husband was already dead when he struck the blow. He'd reveled in every moment of Wallace's agonizing departure.

He had told her all of this in exquisite detail while making love to her a day later, bound in a similar fashion, suspended between agony and delight at the whim of his lover, the widow.

TODAY'S conversation took place in the same posture. But on this day the widow was more pissed than pleased, and the words had been filtered through a wet gag and uttered between gasps of very real, unfantasy-like pain.

It was about one-thirty when Carmichael emerged from the house, moving much like a tired old man. He got into his car and drove away, his driving noticeably more subdued than before.

Rubin didn't follow. Instead he checked his mouth in the mirror for traces of dried mocha before getting out of the Mustang and walking up the drive toward the entrance to the Wallace mansion.

47

Rubin admired the leaded glass as he knocked on the massive oak front door. He'd always liked stuff like that. The lady of the house answered wearing a brown robe with leopard-spotted fur collar and cuffs. She was holding a coffee cup in one hand. Her face was obligatorily pleasant, as if she were greeting the mailman. He could see the haze of sex around her, a flush about the mouth. As he flashed his badge her eyes failed to hide a sudden spark of alarm. She was processing data at an alarming rate with equally alarming cool.

"Is your husband home, Mrs. Wallace?"

She paused, as if just now sensing trouble. Or perhaps, finally recognizing him.

"He's working."

"It's Saturday, ma'am."

"My husband doesn't care what day it is. I believe he's on a trip . . . I'm really not sure."

"You're not sure if your husband is on a trip or not?"

"No, I'm not. Is that against the law?"

"May I come in?"

Their eyes locked. She really had no choice here, not without compromising her cool. Even now, with her eyes and her manner, she'd already hesitated too long. Yes, she definitely knew who he was. Her stare was cold as she stepped aside for him to enter. It was the same stare with which she'd sent him away four years earlier.

"Can I get you some coffee?" she asked as they walked into the house.

"No, thank you. But please, don't mind me."

He followed her through the foyer into a hallway lined with colorful artwork, all florals.

"How have you been, Officer?" She didn't turn around as she talked. "Saving the world from grieving widows?"

He didn't respond. To do so would be to betray anger, and with it his edge would slip away. But God, how he wanted to coldcock this bitch.

They emerged into a huge room that combined the kitchen with an informal dining area, adjacent to what appeared to be a family entertainment center. The sunken room was bordered on three walls with plush built-in couches. A massive screen consumed the other wall, with a projection unit suspended from the ceiling. The entire space was very bright, made even more so by the gleaming stainless-steel appliances. This was especially true of the largest built-in refrigerator that Rubin had ever seen, a Sub-Zero that would be more at home in a cafeteria or a cruise ship. The house was far beyond the Street of Dreams kitchens his wife used to drag him to each and every August, forking over seven bucks to view a way of life he'd never know.

"Well, Officer, what can I help you with?" She was pouring coffee, not looking at him.

"It's Detective," he said.

"Congratulations."

"It was Detective before, too."

She smiled, taking a sip, looking at him in an unsettling way. Everything she did seemed so damned calculated.

"So he's gone again," he said.

"Who is? Oh, of course."

He just nodded, his patience barely in check.

"He travels," she continued. "Leases a Gulfstream. Do you know what that is?" Her voice was as deliberately condescending as it was falsely cordial. "It's a business jet."

He felt his face redden in anger. He imagined what it would be like to pop her, just one time, a quick jab to the mouth, watching her flop to her back. It would almost be worth his career.

"That's not where he is," he said.

Her face showed very believable confusion.

"I checked with all the civilian flight services when the airlines showed no bookings in his name. The outfit your husband usually uses says the Gulfstream Four he normally books is out on another trip. By the way, he really should look into the Five—more headroom, seats sixteen, gives you an extra six hundred miles range. And I will take a cup of that after all, if you don't mind."

Her face was expressionless as she poured him a cup. Handing it over, she said, "He flies out of Redmond."

"That's where I checked." He saw her puzzled look. "We have access to a lot of information, Mrs. Wallace."

"Why would you do that? I told you, he came back home, safe and sound."

He eyed her over the rim as he took a sip, hoping the steel in his eyes might make her squirm. The years had been gracious to her, perhaps with the help of a scalpel or two. She was still a stunning woman, the kind that made you feel the weight of your own inadequacies. In a normal setting he wouldn't know where to point his eyes, because there was nothing natural about looking at her, no way not to stare and keep your thoughts secret. Including, as he'd just experienced, the image of her lying on the floor, bleeding from the nose.

"He disappears, he comes back, he leaves again. . . . Must be hard on you."

Her eyes drifted. "Very."

"His office says he's been missing in action all week. That's different than being gone on business."

"Maybe he just didn't check in."

"Maybe."

She turned away, the seeds of anger evident in her manner now. "Look, I told your people that we haven't been getting along. He's having an affair, if you want to know. So he doesn't tell me where he's going and where he's been, okay?"

He could tell she was trying to muster a few stray tears. He had trouble stifling a grin, watching it. The act would have fooled most, but not him. He'd seen this little performance before.

"I'm sorry. It must be very difficult for you."

"It is." She was biting the knuckle of a fisted hand, staring dramatically out the window.

"So you're saying that you don't know where he is."

"Perhaps he's on the yacht. He goes there sometimes. When he doesn't come home I assume that's where he is.

At least . . . until lately."

"That would be *your* boat? The *Picki Nicki,* I believe?"

She looked at him now. "That would be our *yacht,* I believe."

He nodded, took another sip.

"Do you know the woman he's been having an affair with?"

Her eyes twinkled as she finally looked at him again. "How do you know it's a woman?"

"That'd be a bona fide curveball, wouldn't it?"

She stared a moment, weighing options, in no hurry. Then she said, "It's a friend of mine, actually. A woman I recently met. It's sick and wrong . . . and you're right, it is difficult."

He set the cup down, pleased and a little surprised that the rich don't make better coffee than anyone else. There was actually some sort of metallic-tasting mint flavor to it.

"Will you give me her name?"

"No."

"Interesting. Where were you last Monday night?"

"At an auction at the club."

"You're sure that wasn't Tuesday night?"

She grinned. "I'm sure."

"Which club would that be? You belong to several."

"That would be the Bellevue Country Club. They play golf there, Detective. Little white ball? Bag full of sticks? I left about eleven or so."

Rubin took out a notepad from his breast pocket and clicked his pen. "Can anyone corroborate that?"

"About three hundred people, give or take."

"Did you come straight home that evening?"

"As a matter of fact, I didn't."

"Where did you go?"

"I met someone."

Rubin froze for a moment, then asked, "Can you tell me who you met with?"

"Someone to corroborate *this* part of my evening?"

"Something like that."

"No."

"No, you can't tell me, or no, you won't tell me?"

"A little of both actually."

Rubin was writing as fast as he could.

"Who's the bald guy in the Cadillac?"

Now she just looked at him, realizing the ice was suddenly thin.

"Would you like me to repeat that?"

"No. He's my doctor."

"I see. Benjamin Carmichael. House call? Oh, that's right . . . he's a psychiatrist, they don't make house calls. Do they?"

"You really do your homework, don't you, Officer."

He looked up, drew a deep breath as if impatient with a child who was forcing him to repeat himself yet one more time.

"I've been a detective for eleven years. Before that, twenty-two as a uniformed officer. I find that I've developed a certain sense about things. Especially bullshit."

She grinned defiantly. "And what are your senses telling you now?"

"Maybe it's you who's having the affair."

"I won't stand here and tell you I've been the perfect wife. But then, since you already seem to know so much, you probably already knew that, too."

"Don't need a computer for that, lady."

Her smile made him want to punt her through the massive plateglass wall behind them.

"Do you have an attorney?"

"Tax, estate planning, corporate, or domestic relations?"

She wasn't smiling now. Neither was Rubin.

"Criminal." He winked at her.

Her eyes narrowed—that one got to her. He allowed a small grin to appear at the corner of his mouth, just to indicate he considered the joust his.

"Your husband finds out about your affair . . . your only explanation is that the guy is some nut who has been following you around."

She was good. Her face barely registered a trace of nerves.

"Do you own a cellular phone?" he asked.

"You already know I do."

"Records show several calls, all around midnight, to a Residence Inn in Bellevue."

"Please go now."

He took a final swallow of the coffee, wincing to communicate his opinion of it.

"Four years ago you got away with it. You were brilliant, there wasn't a crack of daylight in the case anywhere. But you did it, and you know I know."

Several seconds passed, their eyes locked. He flashed on the funeral, the rain, the hat she wore.

"Check the boat," she said. "The smart money says that's where you'll find my husband. Very possibly with his dick in someone's mouth."

"I'll do that. And I'll be sure and let you know about the dick."

He started to leave, hesitating at the door. It was a calculated move, one that over the years had always made him self-conscious for fear the suspect had seen as many *Columbo* reruns as he had.

"He said you'd have a tattoo."

"Who did?"

"The man you say has been following you. We questioned him. He said that you have a tattoo, above your breast. Says you put it there for him. To drive him a little crazy. A sex thing. Says it's you who's been having the affair . . . with him."

"That's preposterous, of course."

"Of course it is. But I had to ask."

He turned and headed down the hall. He grinned when he heard her voice calling him back.

"Detective."

He stopped, and turned around to face her. Her hands were opening the front of her robe, pulling it down off her shoulders to reveal the entirety of both breasts. Surgically perfect, catalog-quality ta-tas.

She was smiling. It was a frightening effect, something from an erotic nightmare, strangely compelling. "I wouldn't want to leave a doubt in your mind." He made sure his eyes didn't flinch from hers. Even so, he could see that the skin above her breasts was smooth as cream, and that there was nothing there to see. The tattoo, had it ever been there, was gone.

DILLON met Rubin at a coffee shop off the freeway in Renton. Rubin wasn't saying much, and he didn't confess he'd been to the Wallace residence, which meant that the lack of a tattoo on her breast did not come up. Instead he wanted to stress that Dillon had forty-eight hours to make something happen. It wasn't a concession or a courtesy from the Seattle Police Department; it was the lay of the land in this case. Everything was circumstantial, and it was a weekend. The judge who normally did this sort of thing for the department was at his condo on Maui, and the other judges who might be persuaded to issue an arrest warrant on the merits of this vapor were known to prefer Mondays. So there were two days left before the clock ran out, game over.

Dillon was equally guarded in what he told the detective. He told him nothing about the gambit on the *Picki Nicki*. Only that he was in the middle of something big.

In the parking lot Rubin lost the attitude and got real.

"I can't urge you to go through with it," he said. "This is dangerous. Neither one of us knows how dangerous."

"I think we both know."

"What you think doesn't matter. What I think has to wait until Monday."

"You want her more than you want me. That has to be true or you wouldn't give me this much rope."

"I won't bullshit you."

"Please don't."

"Unless something happens, I'm taking you down."

"It'll happen."

Rubin pocketed his hand and looked to the sky, where yet another in an unending stream of airliners was climbing out of Sea-Tac for points south. Mexico, perhaps. He seemed on the edge of something, facing an unseen barrier to full commiseration, wanting to not be a policeman right now.

Then he turned, as if throwing caution to the wind.

"Get your wife out of the line of fire."

"She's not involved. And she's out of range," Dillon lied. Karen played a pivotal role in what was about to happen.

"Do you have a weapon?"

"No."

"Get one."

"I can do that."

"Give her some room. It's like fishing . . . if the line's too taut, it breaks. Let her run with it."

Dillon nodded. "How will I contact you?"

"Nine-one-one."

"I'm serious. You have to be there when the trap-door snaps shut."

"Call the station. I'm always there. If I'm not, they'll know where to find me." He could see that the answer wasn't satisfactory. "That's the best I can do. You're on your own, you know that."

"Just be there when I call."

Rubin saw the desperation in Dillon's eyes. He wasn't sure how he would hold up if he were in the man's shoes. This was where the road split, where you got to choose who you are. The choice would be more important than the outcome in the long run, because if you survived, you had to live with yourself. If you didn't, then there were other consequences to your choice. At least, that's what Rubin wanted to believe.

He liked this guy. He had balls the size of grapefruits.

"I'll be there."

Dillon nodded again. The look they shared said everything before Rubin turned and walked to his Mustang.

JORDAN was tired and slightly drunk when he switched off the engine to his Lexus and went inside his condo. Once there, his first sense of impropriety was an odor, a subtle perfume, and it hit him quickly and with familiarity. When he turned on the kitchen light, he saw that Veronica Wallace was standing in the shadows in the living room beyond, dressed in her long coat. Her arms were folded on her chest, her hands gloved, and she was smiling at him.

"Hello, Jordan."

Jordan advanced into the room with sudden clarity, feeling the anger rising in his throat like bile. He would throw this bitch out of here bodily and call Dillon, something he'd been afraid to do until now. It had been a mistake to sit on this—but how do you tell your best friend that you'd just handled the woman of his dreams, however unknowingly, and that his dream was in reality his worst nightmare? You just do it, is how. Jordan had been a coward about it. Until now.

As he passed through the threshold into the living room, the ceiling fell onto the back of his head. He went to his knees, when another blow rained down on him, sending him sprawling to the carpet. Through half-open eyes swimming in spilled colors he saw the pointed toes of Veronica's boots. One of them touched him under his chin, lifting his line of sight.

"I hope you don't mind that we let ourselves in. When I was here before, I borrowed one of your spare keys from your kitchen drawer."

When he looked up, she was holding it out with her leather-sheathed fingers.

"I'll be sure to put it back when I leave."

He tried to speak, but no sound emerged from his throat.

"I'd like you to meet someone," she said.

Next to her appeared a larger figure . . . had to be a man, skinny, light reflecting off a bald head, waving like a windblown tree. Then the whole room started to collapse into itself, and as the nausea took hold it all began to wash dissolve to black. Before it washed over him completely, Jordan had two unconnected thoughts:

Now he understood how rock stars choked on their own vomit, and he was curious what they were going to do with the rope the man was holding in his hands.

48

Dillon decided to spend the night at his house. With Karen in hiding he'd be alone with his memories and his hopes for a second round at life. It wasn't completely a nostalgic notion—if the Dark Lady wanted Karen, she'd find him instead. He'd immerse himself in the forgotten luxury of his own bed and watch television and eat ice cream, as if the world was once again sane.

The plan for redemption was in place. It had a time-table, a script, even a contingency sequence. All it lacked was a match to light the fuse. For that, the bad guys had to tip their hand. Perhaps tonight, in fact. In the meantime, Karen would have no way of knowing if Dillon had been derailed, and Dillon would have no way of knowing if Karen had surrendered to her pain and abandoned him. Or even betrayed him. Not until the end game began. It was a plan based on trust, forged in the fresh context of deceit and cloaked in anonymity. She needed to be invisible for it to work. What he didn't know he couldn't tell, even with a rope wrapped around his throat and running down his back to his ankles. He would die alone for his sins, rather than put Karen in danger's way.

He entered through the garage and walked into a dark house. He moved quickly through the kitchen, into the hallway, and up the stairs, heading straight for the bathroom and the family medicine stash kept under the sink.

He turned on the bathroom light, then stooped low to search below the sink for the Tylenol. He found it and shook out three tablets.

When he stood up he saw an image in the mirror. His heart froze, a familiar ice bolt instantly electrifying each nerve in his body.

The Dark Lady was standing in the doorway behind him. She was pointing a gun at his chest.

They stared at each other for an eternity, Dillon not knowing if she would simply shoot him, or if she was simply enjoying his facial expression.

"You should get more rest," she said very quietly.

He turned around slowly. She had on a navy blue overcoat, and she was wearing gloves. But this wasn't a social visit. Her short blond hair made her look older than her age, or at least his memory of it. She looked as tired as he felt.

A small black canvas athletic bag was on the floor next to her feet.

"Change of heart?" he asked cautiously.

"A woman's prerogative." She still wasn't smiling. "Benjamin told me what a bad boy you are."

"Benjamin made the wrong choice."

"I don't think so. He has the benefit of knowing what happens to the men in my life who betray me."

"I've *seen* what happens to them."

She bit her lip, considering whether to pursue this or move on to the real reason for her visit. Dillon read the moment and realized that the bullet in her gun didn't have his name on it tonight. She'd come for Karen after all.

"We have to talk," she said.

He sat on the edge of the bathtub, putting his hands into his jacket pockets in a failed effort to appear nonchalant.

"Let's talk about you and your wife," she said.

"She's not here."

"Don't patronize me."

"If you know that, then why are you here? How did you know I was going to be here? You didn't. You came for Karen."

She paused to smile. "It's *you* I want to talk to. . . . It's the two of you I want to talk *about*."

He ran his hands through his hair nervously and drew in several deep hits of air.

"Karen isn't involved. Not anymore. That's nonnegotiable."

"She's more than involved, and you know it. I think that when you hear what I'm suggesting, you'll understand how it's all in your best interest as much as it is in mine."

Maybe he'd done his job too well. Maybe she really believed he'd give up everything for her, that he'd even help her kill his wife. He glanced at the athletic bag, wondering what it contained. His stomach rolled when the thought occurred to him that Karen might already be dead, and that some unspeakable proof was in the bag.

He didn't grin back. "If this involves Karen in any way, it's just not going to happen. Just shoot me right now."

"Karen doesn't have to die anymore."

He looked up at her. "Who does, then?"

She grinned, something private. "I keep changing my mind about that, it seems."

"All these people disappearing around you . . . you must think the police are a bunch of idiots."

She ignored his comment. "Here's the problem. Benjamin is a detail man, the very definition of anal retentive. If he had his way, you and Karen would both be eliminated from the equation."

"You're going to kill *him*, aren't you?"

She looked to the side. Her unspoken answer was as obvious as a spike on a polygraph printout.

"We had it all worked out. Hamilton and your wife were having an affair. She tried to break it off, he went crazy, and killed her in a fit of rage. Unfortunately you got killed, too. Everybody who knows him will understand that it could happen that way. Unable to live with what he's done, having nothing else to live for, he commits suicide. He takes your bodies out into the sound, feeds you to the sharks, and then kills himself in precisely the same sick little way you invented for him last night."

"You should write a book about sick little ways to die."

"I'll consider it when we're in Monaco."

Veronica Wallace lowered the gun slightly as she leaned against the door. Her eyes drifted, but not enough to give him confidence that a sudden move on his part would stand a chance. She was looking at herself in the mirror.

She was right about one thing. She was the quintessential block of ice.

Her eyes suddenly snapped back to him. "What would you say if I told you that none of this was about you? That what really started this whole business was the fact that I caught my husband having an affair."

"I'd believe that."

"And would you believe me if I told you that the woman he was having the affair with just happened to be your wife?"

Her gaze searched his eyes now, looking for blood.

"I'd say that's bullshit."

"Is it?" Her expression taunted him, holding the question hostage.

"Not possible."

"Would you bet your life on it, Dillon?"

It was amazing how such a subtle shift could bring into focus what had previously been so unclear. He considered it, saw how it tied up with a body bag full of loose ends. He knew Veronica was capable of exacting her revenge in a slow and patient manner, aging it in a lovingly crafted vessel called seduction. Seducing him to balance the scales. Seducing Karen to get closer to the kill. Seducing Carmichael to do her bidding. Coming here tonight to cast a slow poison of doubt on Karen's role. Karen and Hamilton Wallace . . . rhetoric or fact? Was she making a point or firing a bow shot? Was she explaining her case or pleading it?

It was all about revenge, sweet and sculpted like a headstone.

She seemed to be reading his thoughts. His confusion, his emerging pain, was precisely what she'd come for.

Her voice was suddenly softer, almost a harsh whisper. "Would you be so chivalrous then, Dillon? What would *you* do? Would you be so quick to judge if it was you?"

"If she was fucking your husband, you wouldn't be here telling me she gets to live through this. She'd already be dead." He was breathing hard. "You make it hard to feel sorry for you," he said.

"We believe what suits us, don't we?" Her smile changed then, from gloating to wistful. "Unfortunately, it's not as clean as the original story. It was beautiful, really. The man who has been stalking me kills my husband and then goes over the edge, killing his wife before he commits suicide. His own doctor helps the police unravel it all. Tabloid quality stuff."

"If it's so beautiful, then why not just play it like that?"

"Because you brought your little lawyer friend into it. I had to improvise, and if I must say so myself, things have turned out rather nicely."

He stared a moment, realizing Jordan was either dead or somehow in on this with her. "I hope to God you're just fucking with me right now."

She smirked. "You said it yourself. The risk compounds with each disappearance. You've actually made things much simpler for all of us. It ends here. You and I had our affair, but now it's over. Hamilton found out about it and committed suicide. When asked, you will attest to the former and be absolutely horrified by the latter."

He squinted up at her, reminding himself who—and what—he was dealing with here.

"Except in this version," she went on, "you and I ended the affair before Hamilton did himself in. There was no motive anymore. That takes the heat off you, and focuses it on the suicide."

"What happens to Carmichael?"

"Dear Benjamin." She narrowed her eyes. A slightly sad expression washed over her as she said, "I'm afraid he's not part of my future plans."

"He can't walk away from this any more than I can."

"You both get to take something away from this that should keep you happy and quiet. In your case it's money. And, of course, memories that will never leave you. In his . . . it's me."

Dillon considered this a moment. It was the first mention of any money, and such a thought had never entered his mind. As for the Dark Lady and Carmichael, it didn't wash. When it came to love, Veronica Wallace required a gourmet buffet. Carmichael was strictly fast food, spicy and cheap.

As for the memories, some poisons are permanent.

He shook his head at her in disbelief. "I'll never believe you went through all of this for *him*. He can't possibly give you what you need."

"Benjamin is a puppy. He's smart, and he'll do anything for me. That's certainly proven useful, even attractive at times." Her eyes softened. "But he's not *you*, Dillon. He doesn't know how to touch a woman. Just between us, he disgusts me. Perhaps when we've been in Europe for a few months, when everything is quiet again and the money is all in place . . . perhaps then I will revisit the issue of our relationship." Her eyes sparkled. "The open sea can be so treacherous . . . a man too drunk to see straight might fall overboard and sink like a discarded wedding band."

Dillon shook his head slowly. "Have you ever met a man you didn't use up and then discard like a tampon?"

"Of course. I'm looking at him, and he's quite beautiful."

"Really? From where I sit, I'm still your biggest risk."

"You want to live. You want Karen to live. You want life to return to normal. It's really that simple. You'll finish what you've started because you're that kind of man. And I believe I can motivate you."

She reached down and picked up the athletic bag at her feet, opened it wide, and showed him the contents. It was jammed with cash, dozens of bundles of hundred-dollar bills secured with rubber bands.

His heart slammed up into his throat, the sight of which brought a delighted smile to her face.

"You're so cocksure of yourself, aren't you," he said.

"I'm cocksure of *you*, Dillon. I know what you do for a living."

"I'm not the same man you met a month ago. All bets are off."

"I'm a lot like you in many ways. In fact, I'm counting on it. And I'm not without a sense of fair play. Value for value, Dillon. I know you understand what that means . . . and what the alternatives are."

She wagged the gun slightly, the maddening smirk back on her face.

"Fuck you. I'm nothing like you. I still have a soul," Dillon said.

"We'll see. You get to choose."

Her smirk made him want to charge through an inevitable hail of bullets to get his hands around her throat. It would be interesting to see which of them would go down first. But he had a better idea. One that would place the lit match squarely on the fuse of his and Karen's plan. She had bitten down hard and was ready to run with the bait.

He lowered his head and started rubbing his eyes. It was an important moment; she had to buy into his confusion and his fear. She had to believe that she had won.

"Tell me what I have to do," he said, nearly whispering.

She came to him and stroked his hair gently. He

could make his move right now, take her down, make her hurt. But he wouldn't. Not when he had her precisely where he wanted her. Too many questions hung in the balance. Better to wait it out, give Detective Rubin all the answers he would need.

Then it would really be over.

"That's a good boy," said the wicked queen, very much back in the game.

The athletic bag contained roughly a million dollars in cash. She wasn't sure because she hadn't really counted it. Hamilton Wallace kept a sizeable slush fund at the house for his frequent and impromptu Vegas junkets. It was money that would never be missed.

The deal was simple. Dillon would admit to the affair but know nothing about Hamilton Wallace's fate. He would just keep to his story and live with the humiliation of being part of something that turned out ugly. The widow would endure the investigation and the suspicion, the length of which might depend on whether they ever find the wreckage of the yacht they'd sent cruising into the night.

A year later he'd get another million in cash. It would happen every year for the next five years, long enough to learn to live with the real truth. He and Karen would live, and live well, and if they were smart and not too showy they could sidestep any IRS suspicion. Dillon was, after all, a financial professional.

Meanwhile, Veronica Wallace moves to Europe. A few months later, Benjamin Carmichael closes his practice and disappears. There are no friends and no family to notice or care. A few months later, they would rent a yacht and set out on a romantic Mediterranean holiday on a treacherous sea.

Everybody who counts lives happily ever after. No

blood, no foul. There would be plenty of time for redemption later.

The alternatives weren't nearly as attractive.

Before Veronica departed, she dug into the athletic bag and tossed him one of the bundles of cash. A taste, she said, to whet his appetite for life.

Dillon watched the street from the bedroom window after her departure. He saw a dark figure walking briskly along the sidewalk, perhaps headed toward the Safeway lot several blocks away, where a Mercedes SL 500 could sit for hours without drawing attention, even at this time of night.

He waited until the silhouette disappeared from sight before reaching into the pocket of his jacket and withdrawing a handheld tape recorder. The spools were still turning, which made him smile.

AT approximately the same time Veronica was departing Dillon's house, Tim Rubin's dream of a sailboat floating high above the clouds was shattered by the sound of his telephone. He had fallen asleep in front of the television, a regular occurrence since his primetime viewing habits involved a prone position on a very broken-in sofa. Like any respectable veteran on the force, he kept a cordless phone on the coffee table next to a bag of Ruffles.

"Rubin."

Silk Stalkings was on the USA channel, a rerun. Sergeants Lance and Lorenzo were sleuthing amidst palm trees and hotel lobbies full of pastel sports coats, riding in convertibles and interviewing suspects wearing bikinis on their verandas overlooking the Intercoastal. You could almost smell the Bain de Soleil. Rubin sighed. The world in which he solved murder cases was filled with rain.

It was Valerie Roderick, his associate at the station, the tall ex-University of Washington starting forward with the killer smile and the sweet J.

"Got something for you."

"Make my day."

"Hardly. Jordan Chapman. Five-ten, one-ninety, drives a black Lexus, plates read LAWMAN. He's also, according to your file, the attorney for your boy Masters."

"Tell me something I don't know." He had brought Valerie into his confidence as far as watching the file when he was out of the office. His agenda, however, he kept to himself.

"They just fished the Lexus out of Lake Sammamish."

"And he was behind the wheel."

"In the trunk. Hog-tied like one of those poor little roping calves in the rodeo. Somebody won the belt buckle with this guy."

Rubin didn't say anything at first. He was picturing what she had described, trying to link it to something, anything, remotely related to the cast of characters whose names were also in that file.

"Coroner run anything yet?"

"Nope. They're bringing him in as we speak. I thought you'd want to know."

"You thought right."

"Anything I can do?"

"Yeah. Tell me who did him. Have that on my desk by nine, would you?"

"That's why *you* get the big bucks, Mr. T."

He grinned—it was her nickname for him and he liked it.

"You coming in?" she asked.

"I don't think so. He'll still be dead in the morning."

"Coroner doesn't work Sundays."

"Is this a great country, or what?"

"What's going on with you?"

"Nothing. I'm sleeping on the couch like any self-respecting man my age should be doing," Rubin said.

"McCormick says you're a loose cannon with this."

"That's why *he* gets the big bucks."

"He used your name and the word 'revenge' in the same sentence."

"Maybe he should have used 'justice' instead."

"Don't fuck up. You're the only one in this place I can stand."

"Thanks. Really."

He hung up and closed his eyes again, wondering if Dillon Masters was still alive.

49

"He's on his way."

Dillon had been sitting on the floor in the darkest corner of the bedroom of his house when the call came. His father's shotgun, which hadn't been cleaned, much less fired, since Nixon resigned, was in his hands. It was unloaded but appeared lethal enough. A lethal bluff was all he had. The handgun he'd taken from the nightstand in the Dark Lady's house was with Karen.

He wondered if she had the backbone to use it. If a defining moment came, would she step into the mouth of fear? He only wondered a moment. Karen was still pissed off enough to shoot somebody.

The plan called for her to fade into the shadows to watch the kettle boil, and cover his back from the safety of an anonymous distance. It was dangerous, but knowing the movements of Veronica and Carmichael was the only way to anticipate their next move. That part, at least, had been her idea. Dillon's preference was that she hop a plane to anywhere until it was over. She convinced him that if they dropped out of the game now they would forfeit any chance they had of coming out whole. It was a curious and sudden turnabout, her going from noisy skeptic to eager recruit. Dillon needed her, and they both seemed to like how that felt.

And now, Carmichael was coming for him. The plan seemed to be working.

"Are you all right?" he asked.

"Don't worry about me," she said. "I'm fine."

"You'd be amazed if you knew how much I worry about you."

"Somehow that doesn't mean as much as it would have before."

"We can't go back to before. I'm sorry."

After an uncomfortable moment she finally said, "I don't think you want to go there right now."

She was right. Not when death was en route to his doorstep.

"Where is Carmichael now?" he asked.

"I'd say about a three-iron from you. He was at his office, then he went to the Wallace house. She arrived ten minutes after he did—I don't know where she'd been. Ninety minutes later he leaves and drives over here. He parked in the Safeway lot, went inside, and when he came out a few minutes later he walked right past his car down Castle."

The Safeway store was four blocks from their house. Castle Street would lead him into the cul-de-sac.

She had cut it close, and she hadn't needed to. Something in her tone made sure he knew not to take her partnership completely for granted. She was toying with him, flashing her control over the moment. She was reminding him that forgiveness was a long-term investment and she was in a day-trading frame of mind. He would deserve whatever her darker instincts might initiate under the guise of impulse. He'd taken her attitude as a sexual taunt, a promise of sorts. But now, thinking back, that had been his choice of interpretations.

. . . we believe what we need to believe . . .

The same tone made him decide not to tell her about his visit with Veronica Wallace earlier that evening. About her dangling the prospect of Karen's affair with Hamilton Wallace, the thought of which he couldn't completely shake off sitting here in the dark waiting for Karen's call. There would be plenty of time to dissect that discussion later on. It would take time to talk away the sickeningly sweet scent of doubt.

"You're ready?" she asked.

"It's set up." He paused, then asked, "Are *you* ready?" Her next move would be to call Rubin and get him over there ASAP. This would be it. They were nearing the closing bell.

"I have to be, don't I."

"I don't deserve you."

"We both know that's true."

"I'm serious."

"So am I."

"When this is over—"

"Dillon, don't."

"We'll go somewhere. Maui. Make a baby."

"Carmichael's probably in the backyard by now."

"Karen, I . . ." He drew a deep breath, leaving the thought hanging.

"I know," she said. "Be careful."

"*You* be careful." Anything could happen on her end. Veronica would be left unattended, which meant that everyone was at risk.

He hung up suddenly when he heard a noise downstairs.

His instincts had been right. Everything Veronica had told him earlier that evening had been a lie.

THE bedroom door was closed. Dillon saw the levered handle twist slightly. He watched the door push open slightly, then stop. A flashlight beam sliced through the dark and pointed directly at the bed, where a fetal-shaped lump could be seen. Then he saw the gun held in a gloved hand, extending through the door. It was followed by Carmichael, who eased into the room toward the bed. He stopped a pace away and brought the gun up.

The flash was blinding. The weapon apparently had a silencer of some kind, and emitted a muffled pop.

The bullet hitting its soft target made more noise than the gun itself.

The lump on the bed jolted but otherwise didn't move.

Carmichael moved closer, training the flashlight beam on the bed. He reached down and pulled the covers back—the light illuminated a pile of pillows arranged in the shape of someone sleeping.

"Drop the gun, Doctor."

Benjamin Carmichael jolted erect at the sound of the voice behind him. For a moment Dillon thought the man might have a cardiac arrest—his breathing seemed to freeze and his face contorted in a sort of silent scream. If he pivoted and fired, defying the bluff, Dillon was dead.

Dillon got to his feet, keeping the useless shotgun steady.

"I said drop the gun, you son of a bitch."

Carmichael moved in slow motion, extending his arm, dropping the pistol onto the pillows. He pivoted slightly so that he could see Dillon, who now stood in the doorway to the bathroom with the shotgun leveled at the doctor's chest.

His heart thundering, Dillon inched close enough to snatch the pistol from the bed, resisting the urge to drop the useless shotgun and point the loaded pistol instead. But that would be an acknowledgment of the bluff, and this was no time to show weakness. The real player, the one with the balls to play to win, simply turns over his hand and quietly collects his money.

He'd keep the pistol within reach, nonetheless.

"Fucked in the ass again, Doc." Dillon felt a new sense of rage that overpowered his fear. Adrenaline pounded through him now. He wanted to taunt the man, to slap him around awhile, make him bleed. There would be several minutes before Karen and Rubin arrived, and anything could happen.

Carmichael looked down at the bed as if unconvinced that he'd just been had.

Dillon didn't want him to get too far with that notion.

"I gotta be straight with you . . . your career and your life are now both officially in the toilet. No more jerking off to tapes of patient sessions, no more boffing desperate women on your little couch. No more HMO referrals, Doc. Now *that's* the shits." Carmichael didn't respond. Instead he took in his surroundings, nervously checking out his options.

"There's been a little change in plans," continued Dillon. "It involves a friend of mine at the Seattle P.D.

and his pal the D.A. You know, you just might be able
to cut yourself a deal that keeps you out of prison for the
rest of your life. Hell, I'm no lawyer, what do I know?
But that's what I'm thinking."

When Dillon saw the confusion on Carmichael's face
he couldn't help but allow a tiny smile to show through
his anger. This wasn't supposed to happen. The man
was wondering how Dillon had known he'd be here,
ready for him.

"Pisser of a day, isn't it? She stops by to make sure
I'm here, to get me to drop my guard, so you can show
up and lower the curtain on me. Very close to the original plan—stalker goes nuts, offs the husband, commits suicide. Shrink testifies, case closed. Very clever."
He paused a moment. "Makes you wonder what went
wrong, doesn't it?"

Carmichael looked up with sudden defiance. "The
two of you think you can pull this off. But she'll betray
you, too. Down the road, after some time has passed
and you finally think you can relax, she'll do it. You
won't know it's coming because she'll make you believe
you're in her heart."

"I don't think so. She'll be the one on death row, and
you'll put her there."

They kept their eyes fused. Carmichael was working
it out, realizing from Dillon's comment that Veronica
hadn't betrayed him at all. It was Dillon who was taking
the initiative again, just as he'd been doing since Vancouver. Dillon was going for it all, betraying him *and*
Veronica this time.

"Who's fucking whom, that's the big question, isn't
it, Doc?"

Watching Carmichael squirm, a sudden and quite
unexpected contradiction descended upon Dillon. There

was something about the doctor's eyes as he stared into the abyss of betrayal. Dillon could at least acknowledge Carmichael's pain without taking pleasure in it. What he had to do now was more like shooting a dog that had to be put down for killing the neighbor's bunny. Necessary and just, yet still a little sad.

He picked up the handheld tape player and pressed the button. The sound was thin, but audible enough to tear Carmichael's world apart. It was Veronica's voice, and it was cold.

. . . he doesn't know how to touch a woman. Just between us, he disgusts me. Perhaps when we've been in Europe for a few months, when everything is quiet again and the money is all in place . . . perhaps then I will revisit the issue of our relationship. The open sea can be so treacherous . . . a man too drunk to see straight might fall overboard and sink like a discarded wedding band.

The room was silent for about a minute. Dillon could see that Carmichael's breath was quicker, and that his gaze was fixed on something in the dark. He could almost hear Carmichael's heart breaking in two.

Dillon had a touch of compassion in his voice. "She thinks her husband is shark bait somewhere off the San Juans. She wants me to do the same where you're concerned. Same scam, different roles. It's you who goes ballistic, kills the husband, commits suicide. As for me, I'm just the guy she was fucking the whole time. But guess what—the game's not over yet, Doc. Your job is to figure out which color your uniform is. We're going to have a visit with my detective friend at the Seattle Police Department to talk about a trade."

Carmichael's forehead was furrowed with lines. He closed his eyes, as if the choices were too few, or perhaps too many. "You think you're different than me. I only wonder which of us is the bigger fool," he said bitterly.

Dillon raised his eyebrows. "Well, I know which one of us has the bigger gun, and I wouldn't go pissing him off right about now."

Carmichael looked up with a forced smile. "You're not going to shoot me."

"You know, you could be wrong about that. You fuck with my life, you serve me up on a platter, and then come here to kill me. Shooting you might just be the best idea I've had in a long time."

"No one will believe you."

"No? You've got a motive to try and kill me—I'm the man standing between you and the object of your obsession. It's me who's been having the affair with her, not you. There's a string of witnesses all over the city. She chose me and she rejected you. You're just her shrink, you're a fucking vendor. It ate at you that she didn't want you, enough that you tortured and murdered her husband, thinking you could frame me for it. But she still rejected you. Here you are—snap goes the shrink." Dillon glanced down at the gun in his hands. "Looks like self-defense to me."

"That's closer to the truth than you know," said Carmichael.

"The ending's not written yet. In one version the burglar gets shot. In another he cops a plea."

Dillon watched Carmichael's face closely for a reaction.

"Of course, in *her* version you just disappear." Dillon saw the wheels turning behind the doctor's eyes.

"So where's the body, Dillon?"

Dillon started to respond, but didn't. Carmichael didn't need to know to what lengths he had gone to get the body of Hamilton Wallace out of the water and safely into his freezer downstairs, hidden once more under the cross-rib roasts.

Carmichael saw his hesitance. "That's your ante in, isn't it. You give the police a body and a story, and they cut you a deal."

Dillon tried to keep as much information out of his eyes as possible. After a moment Carmichael grinned at him, sure of his guess.

"Why didn't you just crumble like you were supposed to?" he said.

"For starters, I'd say you're a shitty judge of character, especially for a shrink." Dillon paused before he added, "It was you, wasn't it? In Vancouver? *You* killed Wallace."

Carmichael's face was made of stone. Dillon smiled, certain *he* was right this time.

The doctor suddenly looked up and squinted. "You're not this good."

"I keep hearing that, and it's starting to piss me off."

"You're playing poker."

"Easy game with all the aces, Doc. Ask yourself how I knew you were coming here tonight. Ask yourself where I got the shoot-the-burglar idea. How could I know? How could I be ready for you like this?"

Carmichael's eyes narrowed into a scowl, then slowly relaxed into an expression that was strangely pleased. "Your bluff—consider it called," he said.

"I'm not bluffing, asshole."

"Really? Then why did you tell me she set me up tonight to be shot, when you just played me a tape that says she's going to shove me off a boat?"

Dillon felt the heat rising in his cheeks. "Let's just call it a woman's prerogative. I'd say she had a better idea."

Carmichael shook his head. "Don't fuck with me. I'm a professional in the fine art of bullshit. It's a game you can't win, I assure you."

Dillon realized his guest was right. It was time to end this hand while it was still his deal. He tucked the pistol into his belt, realizing he had no idea where a safety switch might be, fearful that he just might just shoot himself in the crotch. He backed up, keeping both his eyes and the shotgun fixed on Carmichael, who was watching him like a coiled snake.

Without looking, Dillon felt behind him for the camera tripod, on which was mounted his eight-millimeter Sony Handycam. He pulled it out of the shadows of the closet, making sure it remained pointed at Carmichael. The tiny red light glowed dull through a piece of masking tape that Dillon had put over it to prevent it from being seen. Admissible or not, the tape would at least seal the bargain with Rubin.

"It's a little dark in here, but this thing is amazing in low light." Grinning, giddy with his victory, he added, "You really should get one."

Dillon moved around the foot of the bed to the end table, giving Carmichael a wide berth. He sat down, reached for the telephone, and began punching in Karen's cellular number. She'd have alerted Rubin by now and the cavalry would be on its way. They'd all go downtown and listen to tapes and watch a little video. Then the men with badges would disappear into private rooms to chat and he and Karen could begin their healing.

When he was finished punching in the number, Dillon said, "Once you told me that when a man has a chance to save his soul, he should take it." He paused, listening to the dead space that always seems to occur before a cell phone begins to ring. "You still believe in the soul, don't you? I do."

The ringing began.

"I don't, as a matter of fact," said Carmichael.

"Big surprise there. That's what she said, too."

Carmichael grinned sadistically. A new thought came to him, and with it there was hope.

"She killed your lawyer friend, you know."

Dillon pulled the receiver back from his head a few inches. He could feel his blood surge in his veins, accompanied by an immediate sense of nausea.

Carmichael seemed satisfied with the effect of his announcement. "She did him the same way I did Hamilton. I know, I saw it happen. It was her thing—she taught it to me. She and Hamilton were into it. I guess maybe you could say she was into it a little more than he was."

The ringing continued.

"When you brought Jordan into this, it upset her applecart. You couldn't be an anonymous stalker if you had a witness who knew you weren't all that anonymous. So she adapted—she's very good at that, like a quarterback scrambling to save a broken play." He paused to gauge Dillon's attention. He could tell from his eyes it was complete and full. Dillon had lowered the phone from his ear unknowingly.

"Where do you think she was while I was in Vancouver doing her dirty work? She was in bed with your friend, giving him the ride of his life, not to mention giving herself a pretty brilliant little alibi with no holes in it. There's a whole trail of witnesses who can substantiate her claim that she was fucking your lawyer, having a very open affair with the guy. Same plan she had for you, only now with a little twist, one that you forced on all of us by bringing Jordan into this. Then, when the bodies start turning up, she admits to a previous affair with you. There are plenty of witnesses to that, too. Based on evidence, it's obvious you can't take the betrayal when she dumps you for Jordan. So you kill her husband *and* your friend, using a bondage technique that you and she shared in a more subdued version. And, you also kill your wife, I might add . . . all before you kill yourself under the unbearable burden of your grief, the fact of which I, as your doctor, will testify to."

Dillon's breath was shallow, his eyes glazing. Then, realizing he'd abandoned the call to Karen, he punched the Redial button and waited.

Carmichael's smile turned sarcastic and venomous. It reminded Dillon of the way the Dark Lady smiled when she sensed the proximity of pain. You can't fake evil this pure, even if you're a professional in the discipline of bullshit. Jordan was dead, and Dillon realized that it was his fault. His gloating about her, the invitation to the ill-fated lunch, had sealed Jordan's fate.

Karen's cell phone kept ringing and ringing. Something deep in Dillon's gut twisted a little tighter with every unanswered pulse. Everything he'd heard was unthinkable, so much so that it was brilliant. Every contingency had witnesses. The Dark Lady was sitting in the middle, able to point to whichever victim she chose.

Then again, maybe this was yet another bluff on a night dedicated to posturing.

Dillon raised the pistol at Carmichael. His hand was trembling slightly, and he could see that Carmichael's smile remained steady, strengthened by the blood that he'd drawn.

"I'm starting to warm up to the burglar idea," Dillon said.

If Carmichael wanted mind games, Dillon was up to it.

"You should know something, too," Dillon said. "She laughs at you. She thinks you're a chump. She says you're impotent and weak, calls you her little clown. She talks about you being dead, and she can't make up her mind if it's hilarious or if it makes her hot. Based on my experience, I'd say it's the latter."

The ringing stopped. A voice answered. His heart dropped and shattered.

It was Karen's voicemail. She was supposed to be in her car. She was supposed to either be with Rubin or rendezvousing with him. It was her job to find Rubin and bring him here. They were to wait for his call, and then they were supposed to come. That had been The Plan, and The Plan was clear and rehearsed and immune to screw-up.

Something was wrong at the worst possible time. It had to be the Dark Lady or a car accident or, God forbid, the sudden resurrection of Karen's feminine pride. She wasn't where she was supposed to be. Which meant Rubin wasn't where *he* was supposed to be. Which meant Dillon was quite alone in the darkness that he had imposed on himself.

Carmichael read Dillon's sudden confusion. It was only a moment, a lapse in presence, but the doctor pounced on it like a hungry jungle cat. He lunged forward, lashing out with an arm to divert the pistol's line of fire.

Carmichael connected with a roundhouse to Dillon's nose, sending him reeling backward over the nightstand, knocking the lamp and the phone to the floor. He was on Dillon instantly, pummeling his head with a flurry of fists, his face contorted with what looked more like anguish than rage. Dillon knew where the pistol was, but his arms were too busy fending off blows to reach for it.

Carmichael used one hand to grab the telephone cord and began wrapping it around Dillon's throat. The useless shotgun had been kicked aside, and the sudden blows had rendered Dillon weak, as if he were absent from his body, unable to fight back with any effectiveness. The pressure on his throat increased and his hands turned to rubber, devoid of strength. Carmichael was getting blurry and his words sounded as if they were coming from somewhere far away. His face was that of a child given over to animal rage.

"Who's . . . fucking . . . who . . . now . . ." were the forced words Dillon heard through a thunderous rushing in his ears. The strobing checkerboard pattern before his eyes soon gave way to an approaching wave of deafening blackness.

50

Detective Rubin was putting on his jacket to leave for the station when his telephone rang. He couldn't get back to sleep after the call about Jordan Chapman. Dark images filled his head, colliding with riddles and reminding him of the career risk he had invited into his life. His years on the job had caused him to conclude that a ringing telephone was an evil sound, especially at this hour—it almost always meant someone was dead. This time it was probably Dillon Masters. Or it was someone Dillon Masters had killed in a flailing attempt to save himself. Or it was another nightmare altogether. The city was full of them, each with a new twist on an old story.

He considered not answering. He would be at his desk in twenty minutes, and whoever was dead would still be that way when he got there. But he reconsidered—

it was just another night when injustice was unleashed and running wild in the streets of the Emerald City, and the innocent might be in need of his help.

"Detective Rubin?" The voice was female, midthirties, college-educated, very sharp, but somewhat shy. A little afraid, certainly nervous. She was on a cell phone, but the car wasn't in motion.

"This is Rubin."

"Thank God. This is Karen Masters . . . you're working with my husband . . ."

"I know who you are, Karen. Is there something wrong?"

"I don't know. Maybe. Everything's so . . . complicated."

"Calm down. I'll help you, but you have to tell me everything, nice and slow. Where are you?"

"I'm at this park, south of Tacoma. You have to meet me . . . I have to show you something."

"Be more specific."

"I'm at a place called Northwest something or other . . . where they have all the animals."

Rubin knew the place—Northwest Trek, a natural habitat turned into a zoo full of exotic animals that wouldn't hurt you if you stayed in the tram. In his mind he saw the body of Hamilton Wallace in the middle of a field, a pack of hyenas fighting over his testicles. He saw Dillon Masters behind the wheel of his Cherokee parked near the gate, eyes and mouth gaping open, a fresh black hole in his temple. His mind flashed to the twisted carnage that used to be Jordan Chapman and wondered if Dillon had met the same fate.

None of this made any sense. Northwest Trek, this hour of the night—it just didn't add up. Because any such news would reach him before a call from Karen Masters could possibly do the same.

Rubin switched the phone from one ear to the other.
"What is it you want me to see?" he asked.

"I can't explain . . . you just need to come. It's important."

He closed his eyes. What could this be? Subtle nuances were hidden between her words, messages trying to get free. Her tone betrayed the face value of her words. It was a little too cool and contrived, yet convincing. The fear was real, but something else was not.

"Are you alone?"

"Just come . . . soon."

"Say the word 'please' if you're not alone and in trouble. Work with me here, Karen, I can keep up. I'm with you. Say 'please' if you're in trouble."

A pause. Then, "You have to come right away . . . *please.*"

She told him to meet her near the park's gate. He asked her what kind of car she would be in, and she told him to park in the visitors' lot and she'd find him. He said it would take him close to an hour to get there, and just before she hung up she said the words, "I know."

Rubin called in from the car as he pulled onto I-5 South doing over eighty. He'd placed his portable red-blue flash on the dash to keep the state boys off his ass. He'd almost told Roderick to call in some backup, but instead he told her to cover for him if anyone else wondered where he was, and that he'd explain later.

He'd go this alone for one more inning. Hell, he'd been waiting for this to come down for the last four years.

KAREN was indeed on her cellular telephone. Except she was still in Bellevue, nowhere near Tacoma or the park called Northwest Trek. As she disconnected from Detective Rubin her heart was pounding, and a voice deep from within her most conservative memories of right and wrong told her there was no turning back now. The game was on, but the rules now were altogether different than those her husband believed they were playing by.

Dillon's plan never had her commitment or her endorsement, because it was all wrong. Not only would it in all likelihood fail, it was soiled by convenience. It had no moral compass. The same vaporous spokesperson for right and wrong who whispered in her brain told her that her way was a much more appropriate course of action. She could see it clearer than Dillon. Her plan was not only righteous, it had style. Ironically, it was a style her husband might appreciate—it was calculated and cold in a feminine, hell-hath-no-fury sort of way.

That's why she'd called Rubin and told him to meet her at the park. Because it was an hour south of where *her* plan would unfold, and it would take him another hour to get back into the game once he realized what she'd done. That would be enough time to do what she had to do.

Later, when it was over, she'd say that Veronica Wallace had held a gun to her head and forced her to make the call. It would be a story beyond refute, because Veronica Wallace would be dead.

Her former friend was so right. Men were so easy to manipulate once you knew what buttons to push.

51

Veronica Wallace sat in an impossibly comfortable chair imported from Turkey. She was in the den of the home her husband had built for her, facing a fine fire that burned in a gargantuan hearth finished with rare stones shipped from the Rhine in Germany. All the lights in the house were turned off, and she felt as if she were the center of the universe, a glowing star surrounded by the quiet blackness of eternity. She sipped a glass of Pinot Noir from a nearby vineyard of international repute. Sitting like this with the wine, she thought back to the night when her first husband died. He'd known the consequences of sin, too. It was amazing how stupid some men could be, despite their station in life. Somewhere out there was a man who could both afford her and keep his ego in his pants.

It seemed so long ago now, literally another life.

She also thought about her most recent husband. Like the one before him, Hamilton deserved to die. It was that simple. None of this was about her astounding greed or the homicidal manipulation of a sociopath who knew not what she did. Hamilton understood the rules. He broke them anyway. Now he was dead. In her mind it was that black and white. Whatever steps she had to take to protect herself in the process of implementing her very personal brand of justice were simply details. And whatever satisfaction she derived from it all, the fact of which she could not deny, was simply a by-product of human nature. Humans, she had come to learn, are inherently vengeful creatures. The ability to inflict wanton pain as an act of will rather than hunger is what separates us from the beasts. To squeeze the essence from every moment, bright and dark . . . that was the secret of living well.

She smiled, realizing she was alone again. Except for Benjamin, of course, but that was temporary. She wondered what might be next for her once this business was smoothed over, which, with a few carefully crafted stories, it certainly would be. Europe would be nice—the men were intelligent and generous, and the women were just as delicious. Yet it was a somewhat depressing and lonely thought, because no man really stood a chance. Not against her. No man was strong enough to be her equal. Not even Dillon, who had shown such promise with his brave and unaccepting response to his death sentence. Even he had taken the Judas coins and wept for forgiveness.

She had discovered Hamilton's sordid little affair the old-fashioned way—her female intuition. About a month before she found out for sure, she began to suspect that there was someone else in his life. It was an array of little circumstantial things that after a time became an equation with only one solution. There had been subtle shifts in his behavior, alternating gestures of uncommon attention and absentmindedness. His travel habits shifted, and suddenly there were clients in places he'd never spoken of, who were demanding unlikely meetings on weekends. They were usually in Tucson or Cabo San Lucas or Grand Cayman, from which he'd return with a tan and stories full of too many meaningless details. He began to buy her gifts, expensive jewels, the SL 500, all of them reeking of guilt. The clincher had been when she'd simply asked him if he was having an affair. There would be no escaping her ability to see the slightest trace of deceit in his eyes. She knew before she asked, which made the question an exercise in rhetoric and torment, watching his body chemistry react, sensing the delicious cracking of the foundation of his secret world. He said it was a preposterous notion. But she knew. How well he spoke the lie made no difference whatsoever.

Soon thereafter, when he had the gall to take another weekend trip to Mexico without her, she hired a private detective through a friend. The friend happened to be an attorney she'd met in a bar with whom she shared an affection for collectible wines and extended sessions of oral sex. While their own affair had lasted only a few months, their friendship, based on an honest appreciation of each other's personal moral code, had endured. Using a lawyer to hire out the tracking of her husband's movements would allow the process to remain shielded from any district-attorney types who might later be looking for stray motives. Her attorney couldn't and wouldn't talk, and she didn't even know the name of the detective he had hired to follow Hamilton. If anyone ended up dead, which was the likely outcome of the unearthing of any indiscretion not to her liking, the private dick and the attorney would never enter the picture. With the proper remuneration they'd erase her name from their Rolodex.

Hamilton was meeting a young actress from L.A. in whichever city his business took him. It began when members of *Premiere* magazine's 100 Most Powerful Players in the movie industry suddenly started calling Hamilton for money to invest in new projects, and he had been unable to resist the warmth of Hollywood's blindingly bright lights. He'd met the actress at a party in Pacific Palisades. According to the detective, rumor had it she'd arrived with a rock star and left with Hamilton, and the two had been doing a tango ever since. He and the bimbo would rendezvous in a city and check into the same hotel under different names, and after the dinner hour she would move into Hamilton's suite for the night. They always slept in his room, in case the phone rang. The private investigator followed her out of L.A. for three consecutive weekends with the same results, then called in some airline industry favors to backlog her tickets for the previous two months. Her travel had coincided perfectly with Hamilton's itinerary over the same period. They never flew together—Hamilton leased a jet, the bimbo flew commercial.

So it was simple. Hamilton had to be punished, and she had to be free. It wasn't just about the money, only a fraction of which would be hers in the event of a divorce. Hamilton had the best prenuptial lawyers money could buy. Divorce had never been an option. The fact that as his widow she'd collect exactly half of the considerable estate was merely a bonus. At least, that's how she felt now. This was about justice and revenge, which were just as delicious.

She had loved him in her way, but everything changed when he crossed the line. And the line had always been clear. She'd told him that she'd kill him if he ever betrayed her, meaning every word.

She grinned as she took a sip. He should have believed her.

It simply wasn't her fault. She'd given him everything a wife could possibly give. The sex had been mediocre though frequent, but that had from the beginning been his doing, not hers. From his perspective, she was an expensive whore, which had been his favorite vice once he'd come into his money. She would do anything, the darker the better. Of far greater value to him was the fact that she had been his social godsend, countering his awkwardness around his rich and powerful peers. She had an ease and grace that became his meal ticket with the Seattle philanthropic crowd. As for her own indiscretions, she worked hard to ensure that he never knew her appetite for fresh and often dangerous stimulation, the younger the better. There were plenty of men who could appreciate competent and sincere whoredom for the art form it truly is.

And now it was almost over. There would be questions, especially from that irritating detective. Such a funny, odd little man. She sensed how badly Rubin wanted her, imagined him thinking about her while he was alone at night. Touching himself. She liked that. Men had no clue when it came to hiding their desire. If Rubin hadn't been such a vulgar cynic he'd be attractive in a Neanderthal sort of way, a way she sometimes liked. Men like that were appreciative in bed. They practically turned inside out once they got you naked. It wasn't Rubin's knowledge of the truth that made him unattractive. He was certainly smart and tough enough, two very sexy things in a man. It was his sadness. It sucked the energy from the air around him.

And then there was the dead lawyer. She'd taken her time with his execution, primarily for Benjamin's benefit, who sat nearby stroking himself, obeying her command not to come until the climax of the deed itself. Jordan had been the easiest of all to read. She'd been at a bar several days prior to putting on the wig to capture Dillon's attention, watching Dillon and his friend navigate the waters of the singles scene. She had come to observe Dillon, having followed them there, but she'd noticed Jordan, too, wondering who he was, liking the cut of his suit. She'd seen the way his eyes worked the room, noticing who caught his attention and who didn't. His preference seemed to lean to the sophisticated side, the executive woman sitting quietly at the bar rather than the bimbo circulating the perimeter. He liked his women confident, and above it all, women who didn't come to play at it, but who came to get *to* it. *All you had to do was watch their eyes, and you knew everything.* Too bad for him, he was really a rather sweet young man. His role as her alibi had evolved into that of the victim, a new lover who would die at the hands of a jealous previous lover. Whether that previous lover would be her husband or Dillon or even Carmichael, had not solidified until very recently, when Dillon showed his hand. It was Dillon who had killed Jordan, when you looked at it that way. She was only doing what she had to do.

Somewhere in the depths of the dark house a door opened and closed. She heard it, felt a familiar instinct in her stomach. It would be Benjamin. Such a kinky, delightfully sick man, especially for a psychologist.

She smiled, took another sip, and enjoyed the warm, rich sensation on her gums before swallowing.

God, she was good. If He indeed dwelt in the details then she had a job waiting in heaven. That twit Rubin had thought he'd caught her on the issue of the cell phone calls to the Residence Inn. He would discover that they were calls to her lover. Calls that a jealous husband could conceivably discover. Details such as that would push the poor man over the edge. Perhaps Rubin would go there himself before this was over.

It had come full circle. Dillon Masters had murdered her husband, then disposed of the body using the victim's own yacht in a pathetic attempt to fake a suicide. He'd done it to have the woman of his obsession to himself. But she'd ended their affair shortly before the murder, and that's what set him off. When she wouldn't have him back, then no man could have her. Not her husband, not him. He'd shot himself in his own bed.

Karen's story would sound ludicrous. Nothing about it would hold water, because nothing about it was real. It had all been smoke.

She turned, seeing a dark doorway into the house and the shadows of the foyer beyond. She started to get up, but froze when she realized she was no longer alone in the room. Someone was standing in the corner, and it wasn't Carmichael.

A female voice, soft and full of velvet sarcasm, said, "Honey, I'm home . . ."

She could hear her own breath rushing in and out of her mouth. Nothing moved for several moments. The dark silhouette remained a statue. When it finally advanced into the room, it was pointing her own stolen gun at her.

Veronica Wallace's next thought, involuntary and surprising, was that the soft light was kind to Karen. She even looked dangerous in a Dark Lady sort of way.

*   *   *

DILLON opened his eyes to pain. For a moment he wondered if his neck might be broken, because his first attempt to lift his head from the carpet brought a stabbing jolt that made him gasp aloud. He used his arms to push himself upright, taking care to keep his head steady. He leaned back against the dresser and tried to relax his shoulders. Slowly, not sure what would happen, he forced his head to the side. It hurt like hell, but he was at least capable of movement. He touched his face, the skin slightly numb but sensitive just beneath the surface. The shit had been thoroughly and competently kicked out of him, but apparently he was not seriously injured.

The light in the bathroom was still on. In the doorway stood the tripod, right where he had left it. But the camera was gone. The tape inside of it held not only tonight's feature, but all of the surveillance video Karen had shot of Carmichael and the Dark Lady's movements.

Dillon pulled himself to his knees, then placed his hands on the dresser and pushed himself upright. He picked up the telephone and hit the Redial button. The phone rang and rang and rang before Karen's voice again asked him to leave a message. He started to, but couldn't find words. He'd try other options first.

He punched in another number, one he'd only recently memorized as a contingency for a moment just like this. This time his call was picked up inside of two rings.

"Homicide, Officer Landers."

"I have an emergency call for Detective Rubin."

"One moment."

Muzak, that saccharine pabulum for victims of crime, filled his ears.

Another female voice picked up the line. Young, possibly black. He remembered his escort when he'd gone to see Rubin and guessed this was the same person.

"Detective Rubin is unavailable. . . . Who's calling, please?"

"My name is Dillon Masters. It's important that I talk to him as soon as I possibly can . . . is he reachable? Who am I talking to?"

"Officer Valerie Roderick. What is this in regard to?"

"It's critical that you deliver a message to Rubin *now*. Tell him it's done. Tell him it's out of my control, that he needs to take over. No more bullshit game-playing. Tell him they tried to kill me. I'm done fucking around."

There was a short silence, during which Dillon assumed the long and lean Officer Roderick was frantically scribbling a note.

"Have him call me on my cell phone." He dictated the number.

He heard her tone of protest but wasn't sure what she was saying as he hung up and ran painfully down the stairs to the garage. He had to get to Karen before Carmichael did. In a clusterfuck of this magnitude, the next bullet had no name on it.

On his way out of the house through the garage he had the sudden impulse to look inside the freezer. His nerves told him what he'd see, or *not* see in this case—except for several packages of frozen beef wrapped in white butcher paper, it was empty. Carmichael had taken the body of Hamilton Wallace away with him.

52

The Dark Lady just stared at Karen for a moment. She tried a what-are-you-doing-here smile, followed by a flash of indignance, but neither of them was in the mood for bullshit.

"What is this?"

"Payback," said Karen, her eyes fixed and angry. "Upstairs. Your room."

She motioned with the gun, noticing the puzzled look on her captive's face. Karen followed her into the massive foyer, up the curved staircase to the third level, and into the magnificent master suite.

"In the closet," said Karen. When her host seemed hesitant, Karen raised the barrel of the gun to her eyeline for emphasis. Veronica backed up through the doorway into the closet, turning slightly as she entered and flipped on the lights.

Despite the task at hand, Karen couldn't help taking a moment to examine the room. It was done in blond woods, with extremely bright track lighting from overhead. There was a scent, a mild musk, probably some sort of moth repellant, or perhaps the collective residue of half a million dollars' worth of fine fabric. The clothes were neatly arranged by color. Karen shook her head slightly in amazement. It was as sick as it was extravagant.

"Over there," she said, motioning with the gun to the opposite wall. "Sit on the floor."

Veronica didn't move. Karen stared at her for a moment, then allowed a tiny smile to emerge. "For a woman who understands the application of drastic measures to monumental emotional problems, you should think twice about whether I'd use this thing or not." She gestured with the gun. "You've been a complete and total pain in the ass . . . Now sit the fuck down."

As Veronica lowered herself to a sitting position on the carpet, Karen backed off, maintaining eye contact, until she was next to the rack of black clothing. Each piece was further arranged by designer name, and Karen recognized them all.

The sound of a ringing telephone seemed out of place here in the closet. It was coming from Karen's coat pocket. Both women looked toward the sound, then at each other. Neither of them moved.

"Aren't you going to answer it?"

Karen's eyes narrowed. "No." They remained still until the ringing stopped. Veronica eyed Karen warily as she withdrew the phone and checked the digital readout to see who'd called. Satisfied, she then turned her attention to the lineup of clothes on their racks, assigning meaning into the unanswered call.

Thumbing through the rack, Karen calmly said, "Take off your robe." She looked to see if Veronica was complying. She was, slowly.

Karen found what she seemed to be looking for—a pair of black leather pants. The expensive stuff, Italian and soft. She pulled the hanger from the rod and tossed it to the floor in front of Veronica.

"Get dressed."

"I've got cash. . . . I've got it right here. Lots of it. You can have it."

Karen stopped and stared at her.

Veronica sensed a nibble. "Nearly a million. Small bills, untraceable."

"Show it to me."

"It's in that bag." She pointed to the black canvas athletic bag not far from where Karen was standing. Taking care to keep the gun trained on its target, Karen stepped toward it, bent low, and looked inside at the bundles of hundred-dollar bills.

"There's more where that came from."

Karen looked at Veronica and smiled.

"Never too thin, never too rich," she said.

For a moment it was as if they were intimate friends again. Then Karen returned her attention to the clothes.

"This, too." She had selected a black cashmere sweater, tossing it to the floor as well. Then she squatted to inspect the lineup of shoes displayed on racks under each designer section. "With heels, I think."

"What's this all about?" The Dark Lady was naked, pulling on the pants, still sitting on the floor.

"I told you. It's payback."

The Dark Lady shifted to her knees to pull the pants over her hips. When she was done she reached for the sweater and put it on. Karen watched it happen, holding the gun in one hand and a pair of black pumps in the other. When Veronica had the sweater over her head Karen tossed the shoes in front of her.

Veronica seemed nervous, not remotely used to facing the business end of a gun. Nonetheless she stepped into the heels with practiced ease. Then she fluffed her hair reflexively after pulling on the sweater.

The sight ignited a thought. Karen looked at the rows of boxes on the shelves above the clothes. Hatboxes. Shoe boxes. And one tall, round box, which would be the one she wanted. She pulled it down, allowing it to crash to the floor. A plastic head spilled out. The black wig that had been on it lay on the carpet like roadkill.

Karen used the toe of her boot to flick it toward Veronica.

"What the *hell* is this about?" said Veronica, not moving for it.

"It's about Dillon."

"We're going to see Dillon?"

"In a way we are."

Veronica's face tightened.

Then Karen said, "We're going to *kill* him." She grinned. "Payback."

Slowly, a trace of pleasure found its stage on the Dark Lady's lips. Fascinating. Like Dillon, Karen was proving to be a complete contradiction from the woman she thought she'd played like a hand puppet. Too bad they were too steeped in their own shit to discover it in each other. Sometimes a marriage can rally around the darkness and save itself.

Karen grinned as wickedly as Dillon might have wanted her to in such a moment. "He'd appreciate it if at least one of us was dressed for the part, don't you think?"

With a flick of the gun they departed. Karen picked up the athletic bag before leaving, turning off the light behind her.

Veronica did not see Karen remove a white envelope from her pocket and leave it on a shelf in the closet.

DETECTIVE Rubin was doing eighty and he was seriously pissed off. It dawned on him after only five minutes of waiting in the empty visitors' lot at Northwest Trek that he had been duped. He got out of the car and walked across the parking lot, opening his ears to the utter silence of the night. He wondered how many feral animals were watching him from the darkness of the hillside beyond. He thought about calling for backup in case anyone showed up, but didn't yield to that impulse. It was still too early to sign his name to anything that had to do with Dillon and Karen Masters.

Besides, no one would show. He knew that instinctively. And he knew why. Something was going down. Most likely somebody was getting killed. He'd been sent on this submarine watch to move him out of the way. It was Karen Dillon's role in it that had him puzzled. Maybe when she'd said "please" it was all she could do—Veronica Wallace had a gun to her head and a script for her to read. Then again, maybe this had been Karen's show from the outset. How or why was anybody's guess, but he'd seen it before. Revenge, the dish best served cold. Except some people, some women especially, liked to age it like fine wine.

He was back on I-5 again, heading north this time. He hadn't decided where he'd go first—the Wallace estate or Dillon's house. He was weighing these options when the cell phone rang. The sound made him jump in his seat.

"Rubin."

"Masters called." It was Roderick. "Sounds like it's hit the fan."

"Is he okay?"

"He wants you to call him. Said to tell you it's finished, that you need to take this over. Said they tried to kill him. You know what he's talking about?"

They. Benjamin Carmichael and Veronica Wallace. Veronica Wallace and Karen Masters. Karen Masters and Benjamin Carmichael. Somewhere in the midst of it all was the deceased lawyer. It was a gangbang with several potential outcomes, and right now he wasn't sure where to place his bet.

"I'm afraid I do. Where is he?"

She read the cell number. "You want backup this time?"

"No. I'm on my own for a while. Stay close to the phone though, will you?" He couldn't very well summon backup for an operation that was as rogue as it was illegal.

"You know I will."

He clicked the End button, then punched in Dillon's number.

53

Dark Lady drove. They were in the Jaguar, the sight of which clarified the depth of this deception for her. It occurred to her that her husband's body might even be in the trunk instead of Puget Sound. Nothing would surprise her now. Obviously, her world was not as it seemed, not remotely as Dillon had painted it for her. But she'd seen the *Picki Nicki* heading out to oblivion with her own eyes, trolling what remained of her husband behind it like bait. How the Jaguar figured into Karen's payback was still a mystery.

Karen had her shoulders turned toward Veronica, the gun on her lap but nonetheless pointing the same way. She'd made Veronica put on her long black Vacco coat and black leather gloves, and was trying to put herself in Dillon's head as she watched her drive. The wig was too Anne Rice, the clothes too cliché. Then again, a fetish knows no cliche. Dillon's bewitchment was more complex than simple fashion . . . it had to be. It had to be the connection between psychic elements and childhood experiences she couldn't comprehend.

Veronica glanced down at the gun. Her gun, from the drawer of her nightstand. She used to shoot it at a range she and Hamilton went to when he'd bought it for her protection for when he was away. She liked the way it kicked in her hand, as if it were alive and its power was hers to control. She used to imagine placing the barrel next to his ear when he was asleep.

She imagined shooting it now, wondering if she might get the chance if Karen's focus strayed for a moment. She wondered how uncomfortably loud it might be here inside the car.

"I like your real hair better," said Karen. "You look older in that . . . thing."

"Dillon didn't think so."

"Dillon was thinking with his dick."

"I'd feel a lot better if you'd put *that* thing away."

"And I'd avoid any potholes if I were you."

They were on I-405, making the transition to I-90 heading into town.

"When will you tell me where we're going?"

Karen didn't answer. They drove for a full minute in silence, the gentle purr of the Jag marking the time. The gun dampened any reasonable social expectation that comes when two people occupy the same confined space.

Karen's pocket began to ring again, bringing an anxious glance from Veronica. Karen was already staring at her, a gaze she held without moving while the cell phone continued to ring. Finally it stopped. "Somebody needs you," Veronica said.

"Somebody fucked up," replied Karen.

For a moment the Dark Lady seemed to be regarding a menu of options.

"So . . . you want your husband dead. Don't we all."

At first Veronica wasn't sure this comment was the right strategy. It was one of those old brother-sister truisms: I can say anything I want about my sibling, but if you disrespect my blood I'll tear your eyes out. When she looked over at Karen she saw that it wasn't the comment that was maintaining the silence. In fact, Karen seemed to be wearing a tiny, mysterious grin.

"You've never killed anyone, have you," said Veronica.

"That's a ridiculous question." A pause, then: "I suppose you have."

Veronica stared straight ahead. "I suppose."

More quiet. They were on a long floating bridge, the water on either side electric with fickle ghosts of city lights.

"Talk to me, Karen. I'll tell you everything, but first you have to tell me what this is about."

"I don't have to tell you anything," said Karen. "And I know everything I need to know . . . more than you think I know."

Veronica glanced over, unsure what to make of the woman whose coldness and absence of passion had made this entire affair possible. She wondered if Dillon had any idea who she was, if the irony of her being every bit the deadly woman Dillon craved was new or simply a glorious emergence of something that had been hidden deep inside the cocoon of her psyche. "Exit here," said Karen.

Several more long minutes of quiet followed. Then, breaking the mood, Karen continued.

"Dillon's betraying you," Karen said.

"Of course he is. I know more than *you* think I do."

"Oh? Did you know he's taking tape recordings of the two of you to the police?"

Karen watched Veronica's face, seeing the nerve she'd just hit.

"When you visited him in his office. He's got the whole thing on tape."

Veronica bit at her lip, eyes fixed on the road ahead. "He's also got Carmichael in his pocket. The district attorney is talking immunity if he sings about you." She paused, grinning now. "Dillon calls it a clusterfuck. I kind of like that . . . how about you?"

"I believe he picked that up from me."

"Whatever." Karen grinned, enjoying the feeling of her thumb on this bitch's future. "There's more."

"I'm sure there is." Veronica's tone was dismissive. The Dark Lady didn't want to play anymore. But then, Karen had already won this game of who's-fucking-with-whom. Both women now looked straight ahead as they drove on. A light rain began, and the Jag's wipers began their inverted rhythm, smearing oily residue from the road in an arcing pattern.

Finally Veronica, unable to accept the outcome, tried again.

"You said you're going to kill him. You dress me up . . . the least you can do is tell me why."

"I think you look hot. So will he."

"Just tell me, damn it."

When Veronica looked over at Karen, she saw a reflection of herself, something evil, taking prideful pleasure in the moment.

Karen's voice grew quiet. "I think you, of all people, will understand why."

Karen's grin was gone now, the darkness that was uniting them replaced by the unmistakable mask of betrayal, the steely countenance of a woman scorned.

"Just drive," Karen said quietly. "Before I change my mind."

DILLON answered on the first ring, as if he'd been waiting with his cell phone in his hands. He was heading toward the city, to the only place he could think of where Karen might be.

"Rubin?"

"Talk to me. What the hell is going on?"

"Where are you?"

"The curves in Tacoma. Is your wife with you?"

"No—she's supposed to be with *you*, for chrissakes."

Rubin paused, unsure if the comment was connected to the Northwest Trek charade or to something else. He wouldn't go into it now. There was a very good chance Dillon didn't know what his wife was up to.

"I'm losing my patience," said Rubin.

"She sent Carmichael to my house to shoot me."

She. Which she? For the moment both women were the same—equally lethal.

"Veronica Wallace did?" asked Rubin, prompting a confirmation.

"We fought. I had enough time to tell him how the bitch was using him, and that he was going down the same way Hamilton Wallace did. I offered him a shot at a deal with you, then he jumped me. I don't know why he didn't do what he came to do. I just know I got the whole thing on video."

"Inadmissible, but it might help your cause with the D.A."

"Not with him in possession of the cassette, it won't."

"Wonderful. I suggest you keep your day job, son."

"Let's just say I lost the fight. He has the tape. We've got to stop them."

"Stop *who*? Christ almighty, I need a program here! Where are *you*?"

"Heading to the marina."

"What marina?"

"Where Wallace keeps his yacht."

"You mean where Wallace keeps *her* yacht. The *Picki Nicki*. Cute fucking name."

"You know about the yacht?"

"Oh, yeah." The yacht had been a bit player in the drama of several years before. He remembered it sadly, since it had been a gift to Veronica from the husband she would murder.

Dillon plowed ahead. "Karen was supposed to bring you in when I had Carmichael in my pocket. But she isn't answering. She's AWOL . . . something's wrong." Rubin remembered she had used the word *please* with an urgent tone in her voice. But he still wasn't cashing this check at face value.

"Maybe she just left town," he offered. "Maybe you crossed one too many lines."

"I think Veronica Wallace has her. And if she does, I think I know where she's taking her."

"The yacht."

"That's right."

It was Dillon's only theory, his only hope. Veronica had discovered his treachery, his intent to betray her to Carmichael. It wasn't a change of heart that brought her to his house with a gun and a bag full of money. It was her realization that he'd duped her, that the *Picki Nicki* was back at its mooring slip and her husband's body was once again up for grabs. Somebody could have told her that her yacht was back, perhaps the harbor master or someone staying on a neighboring yacht. One can never assume a city is too big when one's life depends on anonymity. Maybe Carmichael went back to Veronica and told her that Dillon was selling her out, maybe she put it all together then.

If Veronica had Karen, this would be where she'd take her to kill her. Because she'd still be trying to pin the murder of her husband, and now Karen, on Dillon, and the yacht would be the place it would all come down. She'd simply finish the plan Dillon had started, the death-at-sea scenario, only this time there would be two bodies and some sort of incriminating evidence on board with his name on it. That was why Carmichael had searched for and then taken the body from his house—they needed it to finish what had begun as Dillon's idea, only with a sick new twist. This time around they'd *find* the boat and the bodies, and Dillon, the obsessed and insane stalker-psychopath, would be toast.

"I don't suppose you'll tell me why," said Rubin.

"Just get there . . . fast. I'll tell you everything when I can."

Dillon gave Rubin directions to the marina. Rubin said he knew the place and would be there inside twenty minutes.

"Call for backup," suggested Dillon. "We'll need it."

"I can't do that," said Rubin. "You know that. We're on our own on this." The ensuring pause punctuated the implication. "I'll be there as fast as I can."

By then, Karen might be dead and Veronica Wallace could have taken the *Picki Nicki* out to sea. If she knew how to helm the yacht, then she probably knew how to get ashore in the yacht's power landing craft, as well.

Dillon had to hurry. Twenty minutes would be much too late. Which meant that Rubin was all too accurate—he *was* on his own now.

54

Veronica Wallace deduced their destination several miles before they arrived at the marina. What she couldn't imagine was why they had come here. She pulled the Jag into the same stall where she had left it two nights ago with Hamilton's suicide note on the seat. She turned off the purring twelve-cylinder engine and drew a deep breath.

"I don't understand."

"Out," Karen ordered, motioning with the gun. They exited the car simultaneously, Karen motioning toward the ramp. She walked several paces behind Veronica until they were at the locked gate that led down to the docks and rows of Seattle's finest luxury yachts. She carried the athletic bag in the hand that wasn't holding the gun.

"Stop here."

Veronica turned to look at Karen, who was using her eyes to indicate the boats in front of them. Her expression darkened when she saw what Karen was pointing to.

The *Picki Nicki* was back in her berth.

Karen heard Veronica Wallace gasp as she bit down on one of her gloved knuckles. It was a satisfying sound.

"I told you I knew everything."

"This . . . is impossible."

"Witchcraft," said Karen in a venomous whisper.

"This can't *be!* I was *there!*" Now she turned to face Karen, realizing the extent of Dillon's deceit.

Karen looked her in the eye and with a dark smile said, "I was there, too."

DILLON had found the keys to the yacht in the Jag's glove box, and this had, in fact, been the genesis of the plan. He'd duplicated the keys and given a set to Karen when they worked through the details of the operation together the night before.

According to the plan, Karen arrived at the marina an hour before Veronica. The dock was nearly deserted in the cold darkness. It was hardly the yachting season— the owners of these grand cabin cruisers were more likely settling into their winter homes in Palm Springs. One of the keys fit into the lock of the *Picki Nicki's* engine room hatch, which was in the aft bulkhead, accessible only from the swim platform. The tiny doorway was under the N in the name painted across the back of the boat. She simply lifted it, went in, pulled it shut behind her, and waited.

A tiny porthole enabled Karen to see the walkway leading down from the parking lot. At the appointed time she saw Veronica walking quickly down the ramp, and after a moment coming around the corner toward her. She knew the Jag would be left in the lot to be found later, with a suicide note on the seat. She saw the way Veronica looked around, nervous and hurried, heard her footsteps as she climbed the ladder from the swim platform to the deck above. The next sound came moments later when the massive blowers were turned on, just inches from her head, followed precisely two minutes later by the ignition of the two massive MTU diesels. Veronica Wallace had been well-schooled in the procedures of starting up her pet yacht. The sound was deafening in this tiny space, which was not designed for co-occupation with the engines while they were operating. This was a repair and maintenance space only, and her head was pounding within minutes.

It was here, while she suffered for her husband, that the blueprint for an alternative outcome was created.

Karen kept her face close to the porthole as she heard the shaft click into place and the yacht began to inch backward. The compartment was heating up and the smell of exhaust threatened to choke her. Surely the space would be sufficiently ventilated. Otherwise she'd have to open the hatch, jeopardizing the entire operation.

The droning of the engine continued for over half an hour before their pitch descended to an even idle. Karen couldn't see much through the tiny side portals, but she knew Dillon was right behind them in their little boat, with the body of Hamilton Wallace lying on the floorboard hatch over the ski locker.

The next several minutes were an eternity of visualizing the scene outside, accompanied by the sound of footsteps and muffled voices, which were barely audible over the idling engines.

Finally the hatch cracked open. Karen remained at the rear of the compartment in shadow, just in case Veronica was standing next to Dillon. The crisp marine air was sweet and cool on her face.

Dillon squinted into the hatch's gloom. Seeing her, he put his finger over his mouth to indicate the need for quiet. She watched him haul Wallace out of the Wellcraft and hoist him onto the *Picki Nicki's* swim platform. Then, after catching his breath, he stuffed it through the hatch into the engine room. In the dim light she saw that it was naked, with a rope tied around its throat. It was a surreal vision, more like a prop hanging from the ceiling of the Planet Hollywood restaurant that had recently closed downtown after only a year or so in business.

Dillon blew a kiss her way before closing the hatch. She couldn't remember if she smiled back or even acknowledged him. She was alone with the body of the man her husband was to be accused of murdering by the woman with whom he had acknowledged having an affair, all because of some silly affection for gothic romance and the mysteries of feminine power. Not to mention a little harmless fetishism from the darkest corner of his libido. But right now jealousy or revenge was the least of her feelings. Right now she was frightened, wondering if she could pull off what had to happen next.

The motion of the yacht idling in the open water was making her sick. But she had no place to go. She would remember this as her darkest moment, and she used her fear and her anger to nurture the alternative scheme that was still developing in her mind.

There were more footsteps, more inaudible voices. Then the engines changed their pitch as the forward gears engaged. The boat began to move slowly through the chop, the confirmation of which she had to ascertain by looking out at the surface of the water, rather than trusting her own sense of motion. Her stomach was inflamed, ready to empty itself, and she was dizzy. Closing her eyes helped, but only slightly.

Dillon brought the Wellcraft alongside the yacht for a moment, as he said he would, enabling her to see that everything had gone down according to plan. She was alone on board now. She refused to look at the dark form of the body, which was barely visible in the dim ambient light of the engine compartment. Instead she stared out the tiny porthole, keeping her face in the shadows. Dillon was sitting on top of the driver's seat behind the Wellcraft's wheel, and Veronica was standing behind him with an arm around his waist, her chin on his shoulder, starting almost wistfully at her condemned yacht. Karen remembered standing that way herself once upon a time, when they'd used their boat in the short Seattle summers, when touching each other was still a pleasure.

She waited ten minutes before moving. It was critical timing, because she needed to be sure the Wellcraft was well away, yet the shoreline would still be visible.

Crawling over the dark form in front of the hatch, she'd pushed the door open and moved cautiously out onto the swim platform. It was a sensation unlike anything she'd ever felt, the slap of the air, the new tone of the engines, the sensation of being alone with her destiny.

There was so much to do now. She was surprised how, despite the circumstances and the proximity of death, she was reminded of her father, of cold mornings on the sound as she sat in her father's lap and steered the big Owen's cabin cruiser into the waves. Later he'd let her take it into the marina, resuming command after she'd lined it up in front of the mooring slip. That had been a time when her father still laughed, when the smell of diesel exhaust and the tug of a salmon on a nylon line was a little piece of heaven for both of them.

She could do this. She *had* to do this.

First order of business was to untie the rope that was lashed to the mooring cleat on the side of the boat, extending heavily down into the water, tied to the Wellcraft's anchor. She let the rope play through her hands until the end disappeared into the black water, taking the Wellcraft's anchor—rather than Wallace's body—to the bottom with it.

Then she climbed up the ladder onto the deck, sliding open the sedan doors to the main salon and up a short flight of steps to the pilot house, where the helm was located. Everything was as Dillon had told her it would be, the throttles pushed slightly forward. She shoved them even further ahead, feeling the increased pitch of the engines. She gradually turned the nose of the yacht toward land, keeping it steady until the boat swung back. The plan was to parallel the shoreline until the marina came into view, then bring the yacht to a full stop to collect herself before beginning the careful process of inching it through the corridors of docks and into its assigned slip.

They had driven to the marina before dawn to memorize the layout of the docks and the precise location of the *Picki Nicki's* berth. He had talked her through every move, having her close her eyes to visualize the controls, the cut of the shoreline, the feel of the throttles. There was a soft wind now, and she wondered if this would impact her ability to complete the docking.

Everything had been planned and discussed. But nothing had been able to prepare her for the reality of moving a twenty-ton yacht through a thirty-foot alley with a ten-knot breeze at her broadside.

She nudged the dock several times trying, one of the impacts sending the bow around at an impossible angle. It was the type of moment that would have normally beaten her, caused her to cover her eyes with her hands and wait for rescue, for someone to listen to her explain how impossible it was. But she was alone with the wind and the need to survive, and somehow she moved the *Picki Nicki* nose-first into its berth and shut down the engines.

She tied the vessel as securely as she could before she turned her attention to the body of Hamilton Wallace, waiting for her in the engine room.

At first she was certain it couldn't be done. She'd position the shopping cart she'd left near the stern of the yacht right next to the swim platform. She spent a very still minute surveying the area. Several of the yachts were live-aboards, and one or two cabin lights were still illuminated, probably a late-night reader of the latest Grisham blockbuster, or perhaps just a security measure on a timer. The sound of a yacht docking at this hour had to be out of the ordinary, so she studied every boat and every light, waiting several minutes, giving whoever might be out there every chance to investigate before returning to bed. But nothing moved. The air was full of the sound of the sea, the wind singing through the rigging of a few twelve-meter competition sailboats slumbering nearby.

She dragged Wallace out onto the swim platform. It took all her strength, and she was aware of the effect of adrenaline on her ability to work miracles. His eyes were the worst part—dry and distant, yet still somehow human, empty vessels that had once cried out for mercy.

She tried to pull the body upright, full-nelson style, but the weight was too much. There was an odor, too, even here in the night breeze, an unmistakable and gag-inducing smell. The heft of it, even for the small man that Wallace had been, was shockingly leaden. Her chest was heaving as she lowered it back to the platform, unsure what to do next. In the event she couldn't move it she was to tie it to the dock and dump it overboard for Dillon to retrieve later. But that would be risky and would have to be attempted in daylight. She had to try everything in her power to get it out of there tonight. Everything depended on the body.

She was about to find a rope to tie it off when inspiration found her. The swim platform was almost precisely even with the walking surface of the dock. She tipped the cart on its side, sliding it so the edge bridged the space between the dock and the swim platform. Then she literally slid Wallace into it, the limbs stiff and unyielding. Standing on the dock, she used her body weight to lean back while tugging on the side of the cart, slowly, with excruciating effort, pulling it upright.

Moving quickly, her hands clammy at the touch of dead flesh the temperature of thawing hamburger, she went back up into the *Picki Nicki's* master suite to fetch a sheet from the bed.

If anyone had bothered to look at the stern of the yacht, the cart with arms and legs protruding toward heaven, there would be no story available to cover it. It was an exposure of less than a minute, but it was still her fault—she'd forgotten to fetch the sheet ahead of time.

Using all her strength, she pushed the cart up the gangway to her car, which was parked inconspicuously at the side of the lot. Several other vehicles were nearby, belonging to the marina residents who, she hoped, were all sound asleep and, God willing, had heard and seen nothing.

The Jag was still there, too. She didn't bother to check to see if an envelope was waiting on the seat. She didn't remember seeing it later on when Dillon asked about it. She was soaked with her own sweat, exhausted and trying not to think about what her husband and Veronica were doing at that very moment.

If she visualized too much too vividly, she just might change her mind.

She drove the Jag away to stash it in an obscure parking lot in Renton, where it would play a role in her own plan to end it all.

VERONICA Wallace stared vacantly at her yacht the entire time Karen relayed the story of its return to the marina. Karen watched her just as intently, hoping for some reaction that would signify her understanding. She wondered what Veronica thought about her now, hearing how she had carved the heart out of her future and tossed her dead husband's body around like a sack of lawn manure.

"It can still work," said Karen after letting a minute go by to allow the full weight of the new reality to sink in.

Veronica slowly turned her head, her face genuinely confused and more than a little impatient. She squinted a moment before she spoke, the sense of deja vu tormentingly subtle.

"What are you saying?"

Karen smiled, comfortable with the moment. In fact, this was all going to turn out just fine.

"Let's go on board and have a chat," she said, shoving Veronica rudely in the small of her back, liking how it felt.

55

Officer Valerie Roderick was reading a six-year-old case file when the call came in. It was the reason she worked the swing shift—the detectives were home with their wives and the phones were slow. And when one rang, it was usually something interesting. She had created the facade that the paperwork left for her every evening by the homicide staff—computer work, actually—was both challenging and rewarding. For the two to four hours her presence overlapped with theirs, she was head down in it. It was completed, filed, and properly distributed within half an hour of their departure, leaving her free to pursue her hidden passion. Roderick was a closet mystery writer. It was why she joined the force following her glory days as a University of Washington power forward and English major honor student. A tryout proved she wasn't WBA material, so police work was the next best step. She was here in search of raw material, the deader the better.

"My name is Benjamin Carmichael," said the caller, who had asked the operator to speak to the detective in charge of the Hamilton Wallace case. It was an interesting request, since Hamilton Wallace wasn't, as far as the police were concerned, even missing anymore, much less a case.

"I have a message for the detective investigating the disappearance of Hamilton Wallace. It's critical that he receive it within the next few minutes."

She immediately registered the word "he." Sexist bastard. If it were a woman investigating the disappearance of Hamilton Wallace, chances are the guy would be in a cemetery by now and everyone would be going back to work.

"What is this in regards to?" asked Roderick, wedging the phone between her shoulder and her ear as she typed notes onto her terminal. She was the only person in the building who did it that way.

"Tell him to come to my office. Everything he's been looking for is there." He gave his address, which Roderick entered carefully.

"I'm not sure I can reach the officer assigned to this case tonight, sir. I can send over someone else, maybe a black and white. Is this an emergency?"

There was a pause, and when the voice returned it was softer, either slightly amused or slightly saddened, she couldn't tell which.

"Yes, in a way it is." This made her stop typing, a quizzical look alighting on her face. Two Hamilton Wallace calls in one night—Rubin would want to be the first to know. It'd be up to him to call in more firepower.

The line went dead. She keyed in the code for the automated digital trace, and a second later a phone number and name appeared on her screen.

Carmichael was calling from his office in Bellevue.

RUBIN picked up his cell phone on the first ring.

"You know a guy named Benjamin Carmichael?" Roderick asked him.

"Oh, yeah," he said.

She could hear traffic noises over the line. "Where are you?"

"Just south of Sea-Tac. You just calling to say hi, or what?"

"You got another wacko call. Some guy named Carmichael says you'll find what you're looking for at his office." She read the address to him.

"Jesus. Get me some backup on this, I'm on it. And do me a favor, too, okay? Send a black and white to check out the marina north of Ballard. I'm not sure of the name."

"You got it. What are they looking for?" she asked.

"A champagne Jaguar XK Eight. If it's there, tell them to call me immediately."

"You got it, boss," she said. But he had already disconnected.

56

The walk down the marina gangway was as surreal as any span of time Karen could remember. The night air was thick and completely still, and even the water was uncharacteristically quiet. The planet was holding its breath, wondering what might happen next. The moon was backlighting a thin veil of clouds, casting an eerie glow down onto the stage where the final curtain was about to rise on this drama. The marina was spotted with ramp lights that turned the mist around them into illuminated ghosts, bouncing reflections off the windows of the yachts that melted into the black water. Karen walked a step behind Veronica with a hand in her pocket, where she loosely held the gun. The sound of high heels on the concrete decking was out of place, like the tapping of a pencil during a funeral prayer. The crisp night air amplified every sound.

It was a walk toward the end. Whatever that would be, it was minutes away.

Karen tossed Veronica Wallace her husband's keychain and motioned for her to step onto the *Picki Nicki*'s swim platform and mount the ladder to the aft deck. Veronica removed her heels before the climb, her eyes burning back at Karen with a combination of wariness and disapproval. Karen waited until she was up on deck before she cautiously followed, sensing this was a vulnerable moment. She glanced at the aft hatch where she'd hidden two nights earlier.

Once on board she motioned toward the door. After a few wrong choices Veronica found the right key and slid open the portal to the yacht's elegant main salon.

"Wait," said Karen. Veronica froze, then turned. "Take off your gloves."

Veronica squinted but didn't move.

"Do it." Karen held out her hand to accept them.

Keeping her eyes on Karen, Veronica removed her gloves and handed them over. She watched as Karen put them on.

"Know your audience," Veronica said sarcastically.

"Know your neighborhood fingerprint technician is more like it," Karen replied, pulling them tight. "Go on." She motioned for Veronica to step inside.

Karen had never hit anyone before. She wasn't sure how much force to apply—she didn't want the blow to be mortal, yet it had to be sufficient to buy her the time she'd need. She opted to abandon restraint and slammed the butt of the pistol as hard as she could down on the base of the back of Veronica's neck.

Veronica fell forward into the center of the pure white carpeting. For a moment Karen watched her struggling there, stunned and disoriented and obviously suffering. Karen was tempted to hit her again, if not for the sheer satisfaction of it, then simply to further incapacitate her prisoner while she called Dillon and ended this once and for all.

The cabin was dark with the shades pulled. It had been the last thing Karen had done when she'd brought the *Picki Nicki* home. There was a musty smell mingled with the scent of fine wood and spilled Scotch.

"You don't have to do this," said Veronica, the words melding with spasms of pain.

Karen ignored her as she closed the cabin door and peeked through the shades on either side, making sure no stray lights had suddenly come on from within one of the neighboring boats.

"You can take the money . . . There's more—I can get it for you."

"This will do nicely," said Karen.

Veronica managed to raise herself on an elbow, the opposite hand clutching the back of her head. Her eyes were wet and half closed, the lids fluttering slightly.

"I don't get you . . . or your husband," she said.

"That might be the first thing you've said that I can appreciate," replied Karen as she sat down in one of the yacht's satin-upholstered chairs. She held the gun in one gloved hand, while removing the cell phone from her pocket with the other.

The pain was not too much to stop Veronica from furthering her point. It was instinct, the reflex to create your own options by pressing on the opponent's soft spot.

"You get close to the fire, and integrity abandons you. You're losers, both of you. You deserve each other."

"Integrity? Who are you to even speak that word?"

"You confuse integrity with morality. It's about being true to yourself. You and Dillon . . . you get too close, and you lose it. You're smart enough to see your shot but too weak to act on your instincts. To do the really tough work. That's what I mean by integrity. You don't have the stomach for this."

"I wouldn't be so sure about that," said Karen. She frowned when the cell phone connection misfired. She punched in the number a second time.

"All those years together . . . Dillon never knew what he had." Her forced and bitter smile held more satisfaction than humor. The Dark Lady's fetish was irony. "You have to live with the fact that this was all your doing. If you hadn't been so afraid of the truth . . . always so proper, so selfish . . ."

"I don't know what you're talking about."

"I'm talking about intimacy. It's women like you who drive your men to women like me. You have no idea what intimacy is . . . what a man *really* wants."

"And you do?"

"I should think that's obvious."

Karen drew a deep breath. If she was going to shoot the woman, now was the moment. Oh, God, she wanted it to end that way, she really did. And with any luck and more guts than she thought she could summon, it would.

"Don't press your luck with me."

Karen's hands were trembling. Still trying to call Dillon, she punched in a wrong digit, cursed to herself, and started over.

Veronica seemed to gain a flush of strength. "It's not me you hate. It's that part of you that *is* me. We're the same . . . it's just that one of us knows who she is."

Karen hit the Send button. "We're not the same," she said quietly, listening with relief to the sound of the ringing of Dillon's phone.

Veronica smiled viciously up at her. "No?"

Karen's eyes narrowed as they locked onto the woman who had seemed so perfectly suited to the role of a badly needed, trusted friend. It seemed so long ago, a time when Karen *wished* that it was true, that they were, in fact, the same. Perhaps, given the circumstances, it was truer than either of them realized.

But Veronica was wrong about one thing. Karen Masters now knew exactly who she was. She had rediscovered herself in the defining moment when she faced her husband's betrayal.

Dillon answered on the first ring.

"Rubin?" His voice was high-pitched, anxious.

"It's *me*," said Karen. She could hear static over the line and knew Dillon was in his car.

"Honey, are you all right? What the hell—"

"Shut up and listen to me, Dillon."

A quick moment passed before he repeated with a significantly calmer voice, "Are you okay? Talk to me, Karen."

"I'm fine. But you have to listen to me . . . You have to do *exactly* as I say."

From the floor, Veronica said through a new and truly amazed smile of realization, "You incredible bitch . . . you're going to kill us *both*, aren't you?"

Karen leveled the gun at her head in warning.

"Who's that?" asked Dillon, his voice on edge again. "You're with her, aren't you? She's there."

"I'm changing everything," said Karen.

"I'm in contact with Rubin. Carmichael's got—"

"Shut up and listen to me."

She could hear Dillon taking a long, deep breath.

"Bring the Wellcraft out to the point. The same place as before."

"You've got her there?"

"Yes."

"Jesus, Karen, what are you thinking?"

"Your way won't work! It can't. You really think your little police detective friend will just turn the other way? You're an accessory to *murder*, Dillon." She paused. "There's a better way. *My* way."

"What are you saying?"

"As long as Veronica Wallace is alive, this will never be over." Karen looked down at Veronica, hoping she'd understood the words. But her eyes were closed as she rubbed the back of her head. If she'd heard, there was no reaction.

"You want us to kill Veronica Wallace," repeated Dillon.

"That's right, Dillon. I want her dead."

"Jesus, Karen!"

"Just listen to me. The two of you have set it all up already. I left a note at her house tonight. It's a suicide note, Dillon, from Hamilton Wallace. In it he says he found out about your affair. He confesses to killing his wife in a fit of rage over it, that he can't live with what he's done, and that his life is over. He promises the bodies won't ever be found. The yacht—"

"Karen, listen—"

"No, *you* listen! The *Picki Nicki* may be found, it may not. Either way, nobody will be aboard."

He was shouting this time. "Listen to me! I'm trying to tell you . . . Carmichael's got Wallace's body, for chrissakes!"

Karen paused. On the floor in front of her, Veronica Wallace still had her eyes closed, slowly rotating her head in circles. She seemed not to have heard her death sentence.

"What do you mean?" she asked with alarming calm.

"Carmichael showed up. We fought . . . I lost. When I figured out where I was, I checked downstairs. The body is gone! He's got it. This won't work."

Now Veronica was looking up, sensing that Karen's plans just hit a pothole. She was smiling slightly at the notion.

Karen drew a deep breath and momentarily closed her own eyes. Obviously, this changed things. If Hamilton Wallace's body turned up somehow, perhaps as part of some plan of Carmichael's, then her carefully arranged setup was busted. Or perhaps the body would never materialize, but then Veronica Wallace would be dead and Carmichael would be as free as she and Dillon. With Wallace in his trunk and some obscure plan of his own in his head, all bets were off. They had to find Carmichael before he ruined everything. They had to convince him that they had already solved the problem and that Wallace's body simply had to disappear.

Or maybe she'd arrange something for Carmichael, too. Once you started, perhaps it got easier to stomach. What the hell . . . she'd make it up as she went along. The one thing that hadn't changed was the need to eliminate Veronica Wallace. The need for equity. As long as the Dark Lady breathed, their lives were forfeit.

"We'll have to do something about that, won't we," said Karen.

"Like what, for chrissakes? Karen, you just can't—"

"Stop. Carmichael needs a way out of this as much as we do." She reflected a moment. "It's too late. I'm committed. *We're* committed."

That's how you get away with it, by being a fucking block of ice . . .

"I need to know you're with me, Dillon. Isn't that what you said to me? That you needed me? That you needed to know you're not alone?"

"Yes, but my God . . ."

"Well, you're not alone, Dillon. I'm here for you. I need to know that we're in this together. Otherwise, it's all just been a fantasy, hasn't it."

Silence hung between them. Karen noticed Veronica's smile had vanished.

"Karen, listen, I'm with you, sweetheart—you know that. But think about this for a minute. Why would Carmichael cooperate—"

She cut him short. "Because I'll *convince* him, that's why." Her voice was full of a new confidence.

I can make a man do anything I want, once I know what his buttons are . . .

A moment passed. Then Dillon said, "You sound . . . different."

"Maybe it's you who's changed," she said.

"You can count on that."

"Maybe you haven't been looking close enough."

"You're talking about *murder*, Karen."

"That's just a word." A pause. "It's justice. Cold, swift, and in our case, very convenient."

Several seconds passed before Dillon said, "Remind me never to piss *you* off again."

"I'm doing this for *us*, Dillon."

There was something about the way she said it, a dangerous gentleness in her voice, that made Dillon squirm. Even now, in this goal-line stand with destiny, he could feel the chemistry of it, the sex of it. Deep in his stomach butterflies were scurrying about in a state of panic that was strangely delicious. Of all the outcomes, this was the most unexpected. His wife had turned out to be the darkest and strongest player of all.

"Sometimes you have to make up your own rules to survive," she said.

Dillon wondered if she was smiling on the other end of the line. She was pushing his little buttons for the first time, and he hoped she felt it, too.

"I'm ten minutes from Ballard."

The Wellcraft was on a trailer in a storage lot north of the city. No one would be there at this hour, and while it would look a little odd to be hauling out a ski boat in the middle of a winter night, it could be explained away. If anyone asked he'd say he was a fisherman. He hoped no one would ask.

"The Jag is in the lot," she said. "Just turn back the clock, Dillon . . . it's all like we left it."

"You've thought of everything, haven't you?"

"You thought of it first. Just hurry."

"It'll take an hour, minimum."

"Are we together? Tell me now if we're not . . . before I cross a line from which neither of us can ever return."

Veronica was listening intently, and from her eyes Karen could tell she was already formulating her alternatives. Karen sat up a little straighter.

"You're amazing."

"I know."

"I love you," he said.

"Just hurry, Dillon."

She hung up and lowered the phone.

"Well, well, well," said Veronica.

Karen just smiled down at her. It was easy, once you got the hang of it.

57

Dillon held the cell phone to his ear for another mile, listening to the dial tone. He was conscious of the way his body was reacting to what Karen had just said to him, and he knew it was as much for the *way* she'd said it as anything else.

She was willing to take this to the limit. To do whatever was necessary to save his ass and their relationship. To risk everything. To *change*.

And, to kill for him.

Nothing would be the same again. Everything and everybody was different than they were before. In darkness they had found a new beginning. He wondered what they had lost along the way.

Thinking about it, turning it inside out and back again, somehow it made a sort of mad sense. Karen had never approved of his strategy to trap Carmichael and Veronica and turn them over to Detective Rubin. Videos and hidden audio recordings . . . it was all too thin a margin for error when your life was on the line. She'd cross-examined every idea, every move, and she'd never backed away from her skepticism. She thought it was ludicrous. Something stronger was called for here. Something desperate and unexpected. He'd taken her response as fear, seasoned with a cynicism that was as understandable as it was easy to patronize. She had a right to her attitude. He'd betrayed everything that was sacred between them, and now he was asking her for redemption far beyond the call of forgiveness. He owed her all the venom she felt she needed to spew his way. He would swallow whatever jagged pill she needed to ram down his throat.

And of course, there was human nature to consider, that particularly feminine brand of outrage. What woman wouldn't want to kill an adversary who had given her husband something that she'd refused to give? Only the depth with which that primal urge had been buried kept it unspoken and unacted upon. He wondered if she was truly doing this for them, or for herself. Either answer made his skin tingle with a secret electricity that was hardwired to his imagination.

He prayed that somehow they'd get out of this. The rest of his life suddenly had new and unknown potential. The barrier between dreams and reality had cracked, and the view to the other side was full of black and compelling shadows surrounding a dark and mysterious woman. Beyond any hope he'd ever dared to consider, she just happened to be his wife.

The exit approached. He'd have to alter his present course to pick up the Wellcraft and meet her at the point of land where they'd staged their grisly charade before. He was less than ten minutes from the marina, twenty from the storage facility.

What to do . . . mercy or murder . . . survival or sacrilege? Which siren song licked at his mind now? Which voice was his own? Even considering it was intoxicating.

But what if it was all a lie? What if, in the end, he was about to receive precisely what he was asking for? What if the justice she referred to had nothing to do with Veronica Wallace?

The unknown . . . that was the *real* narcotic.

He swerved back into the lane at the last moment, missing the exit. He'd be at the marina in minutes, hopefully in time to stop Karen from doing what she'd intended. Before she crossed that line from which there would be no return. She'd changed into someone more potent than before. She had moved beyond him, yet she'd not left him behind. What she was *about* to do made no difference, really. The declaration, the heart of it, was the thing. To lose her now would be to abandon everything he'd been fighting to save. His future, his fantasy, his very soul. He'd found the woman he'd always dreamed he'd find . . . the kind of woman who always seemed to belong to someone else.

She had done it for *them*. That was enough. No matter how it turned out now. It was enough.

To save her, he'd have to betray her one more time.

The cell phone rang from the seat next to him. He looked down and saw the red light flickering with each ring, every button brightly lit. The digital readout showed that the call was coming from Karen's phone. He reached down for it.

Somehow he knew before he answered that the rules of the game were about to change yet again.

*   *   *

"**WHAT** to do, what to do," said the Dark Lady.

Karen just stared at her, seeing Veronica's eyes twinkling with a new idea, buoyed by hope, fueled by desperation.

"You should shoot him in the heart, I think. Besides the poetry of it, there'll be time for him to see your eyes . . . you can watch him drift away."

"Shut your fucking mouth, you cow!" Karen's emotions were betraying her now. She raised the gun, and both women saw that it was trembling.

"No one understands how it feels until it happens to them. Betrayal . . . the unforgivable sin. No one understands what you have to do." Veronica paused as her eyes raised to engage Karen's once again. "But *you* do, don't you, dear? You understand."

Karen closed her eyes for what she intended to be only a moment. She needed to be alone with what Veronica had said, if only for a heartbeat.

It was reflexive, involuntary, and just possibly fatal.

Veronica Wallace sprung like the lioness that every man who had ever known her suspected she was. She was on Karen in a fraction of a second, before Karen could remember the gun in her hand, before she could ward off the fist and then the elbow that crashed against her temple, knocking her from the chair to the carpet. She didn't feel the gun releasing from her grip, didn't see Veronica snatch it out of the air as she fell to her side on the floor. The butt of the gun's handle crashed against Karen's temple, and the darkness blocked out all sounds except the blood rushing in her ears and the scratching of the carpet against her ear.

All she had seen was the look in the Dark Lady's

eyes, wide and hungry. Not those of Dillon's deliciously evil queen, but those of a frightened animal who knows no other path to freedom. Whose only instinct is to kill.

"Karen?"

Silence. Dillon checked the readout again—the call was definitely coming from Karen's digital phone.

"Karen!"

He could hear that someone was holding the cell phone at the other end. Listening to him call for his wife.

"Hello, Dillon."

The Dark Lady. He knew immediately from the tone of her voice that the worm had turned. These were her favorite moments of the game.

"Shit . . . if you hurt her—"

"I've already hurt her. I may hurt her some more to pass the time until you get here. And if I see any other cars pull into the lot I'll kill her."

He didn't say anything.

"Come alone. Remember, lover—it can take a long, long time to die . . . especially at the hands of someone who knows what she's doing."

And then the line went dead.

58

Two black and whites were already parked in front of the Belmont Building when Rubin and the young officer arrived. One had its lights on, signaling to the world that Seattle's finest were here and protecting the public.

Rubin flashed his identification unnecessarily to the Pinkerton security guard in the lobby, who simply pointed toward the elevator and said, "Twelve" as they strode past without hesitating.

Carmichael's office door was open. A uniformed female officer stood sentry, standing back slightly as they approached and went inside.

The three other officers who preceded them all looked up. One of them, a career uniform Rubin had worked with before said, "Door was wide open. Un-fucking-believable."

Another officer was stooped over a desk, facing the other way as he read something on the PC screen. The one who had spoken to Rubin stood on the other side of a high-backed leather chair by Carmichael's desk. He was looking down at something Rubin could not see, given that the chair was facing toward the wall.

"Fucker's ripe, too."

Rubin walked around the chair to look. A naked body was positioned in it, limbs stiff, skin like waxed paper. The eyes were open and fake-looking, the hair straight and stiff. The body was still frozen. Only the very outer layers of clammy white skin looked as if it might be soft to the touch.

"You need to see this," said the other officer, still leaning down toward the PC screen. Rubin noticed the man had his reading glasses on.

"Read it to me," said Rubin, who wanted to use the moment to scan the body for details, for any subliminal and seemingly unrelated factoids that might pertain to what was proving to be an unbelievably twisted case. It was an old habit that had served him well.

The bespectacled officer began to read from the screen:

> *My name is Benjamin Carmichael. The man in the chair is Hamilton Wallace. I believe you may have been looking for him. I have been engaged in an affair with his wife, Veronica Wallace, for several months. Other people have been involved, but none of them had anything to do with his death. The responsibility is mine alone. This is my full and complete confession to the murders of Hamilton Wallace and Jordan Chapman. Details follow, in case you harbor any doubt. It is a responsibility*

*I can no longer bear. Unfortunately for you, you
will not find my body. May God, if he exists, forgive me for what I have done, and for what I must
now do. Benjamin Carmichael, Ph.D.*

The room full of police officers exchanged looks
with shaking heads.

"You believe this fucking shit?" asked the first
one. He was reading further text that detailed the
agonizing death of Hamilton Wallace in a hotel room
in Vancouver.

"Yes, I do," said Rubin, pulling the young officer
who had brought him here by the sleeve toward the door.

59

Karen concentrated on maintaining the muscle control that would keep her alive. Within the first minute she had discovered a demanding yet tolerable middle ground in her struggle to survive, a compromise between straining to loosen the pressure on her throat and relaxing the muscles in her back and hips, which were throbbing in agony. She was lying on her stomach, naked, her hands bound behind her. She knew the gloves had been removed because she could feel the bindings, whatever they were, digging into her wrists. They were apparently tied around her ankles, too, which had been pulled impossibly high behind her, up toward her buttocks. Something thin and cutting, she couldn't tell what, was wrapped about her throat and was connected to where her hands and ankles met in a confluence of unyielding knots at the small of her back. Breathing was possible only by arching her back in a manner not accounted for in its anatomical design, the effect of which created a hard-won slack in whatever was being used as a rope, which in turn loosened the pressure on her throat. The arch could only be maintained for several seconds before the unbearable muscle cramping returned, forcing them to relax, which in turn began to strangle her. Only the middle ground could sustain life, and like life itself, it was a finite and hopeless fuse, a brief respite from certain struggle. It was ultimately, and quite by design, destined to fail.

She couldn't see Veronica sitting a few feet away on a vanity bench, her gloved hands held in front of her face as if in prayer, watching the drama unfold before her on the bed. The master suite was filled with the sounds of Karen's breathing, gulps and gasps scoring precious seconds of fully committed effort, followed by increasingly longer intermissions of complete silence as the panty hose tightened to constrict Karen's windpipe. Veronica liked the irony of it, the fact that the gasping occurred in the moments when she could breathe. It reminded her of a night years earlier when death first raised its black curtain for her entertainment. Only this was better, because her partner was deserving rather than simply ignorant. This was a sipping wine with depth and character.

When she saw that Karen was alert, she moved closer and sat on the side of the bed. The only light came from oval portholes on either side of the hull. A ramp light just outside the bow filled the cabin with sufficient illumination so that they could see each other's eyes clearly. In any other context the setting would have demanded soft music to make love by.

"I want you to know that I wanted to believe you.

The part about killing Dillon, I mean." She ran her finger along Karen's cheek. "That's the secret to a good lie, isn't it . . . rooting it in something that we both understand. It almost worked. I wonder if you believed it yourself at some weak moment along the journey that got you here."

Veronica felt herself smiling. "I do hope he hurries," she said. "I wouldn't want him to miss a moment of this."

Karen could say nothing. She could only concentrate, every breath a critical project independent from the last. The work was too intense to allow fear into the moment. Her only emotion was rage, which had to ride shotgun next to the urgency of her presence of mind.

And she was afraid. All of the bravado, her arrogance, was gone. She had failed, and now she and Dillon would die. And while she had certainly intended that Veronica believe that this was her desire where Dillon was concerned, in her heart, despite its pain, she knew this was never a serious consideration. A fantasy, perhaps, one that led her to tonight's splintered plan, in fact. She considered the irony as she concentrated on the muscle control required to survive the next minute.

The silence was broken by the muted sound of shattering glass from the deck above.

The Dark Lady picked up the gun from her lap, running her leather fingertips lightly along Karen's thigh and hip as she moved into position. She leaned down to Karen's ear, close enough to smell traces of the morning's fragrance.

"There he is now," she said, allowing her lips to brush Karen's temple.

60

Dillon's Cherokee skidded to a stop next to the Jaguar on light gravel in the moorage parking lot. Dillon got out and ran around to the back. He yanked open the rear door and began tearing at the carpet, unable at first to find an edge or a fingerhold. After a moment he achieved his goal and pulled the carpet back, revealing the spare tire compartment. From it he extracted the tire iron and sprinted off, leaving the door open behind him.

At the locked gate he leapt high, inserting a foot into the wire fence mesh and using his momentum to vault over the top. His knee caught one of the triangular spikes placed there to prevent just such a move, and he felt fabric and skin ripping open with equal protest. As he hit the ground on the other side he heard the Cherokee's interior alarm beeping notice that he'd left the keys in the ignition.

The *Picki Nicki* was as dark as all the other yachts in the marina at this hour, hibernating behemoths dancing softly to the gravity of the moon. As he rounded a corner and ran, he focused on the stern and the letters painted there. The concrete walkway was illuminated by a series of overhead spotlights that made the surrounding water appear thick and black. Without slowing he jumped from the dock over the swim platform onto the third rung of the ladder leading to the aft deck. He scrambled topside and peered in after trying the sliding glass door, which was locked.

The stillness and the darkness inside the cabin made him hesitate, a shoulder-tap of paranoia. To bring him to the wrong place would be something she would do, leaving him to frantically wonder what was happening somewhere else. Then, partially illuminated by a shaft of light coming in at a side angle, he saw Karen's purse on the carpet next to a plush chair.

Dillon swung the tire iron, shielding his eyes with his forearm as the glass shattered at his feet. He kicked out a few protruding shards and carefully reached in, unlatching the doors and sliding them open.

He moved quickly through the cabin and descended three steps from the ship's galley into the hallway leading toward the guest staterooms and, at the end of the passage, the master suite. What had been a frenzy of movement was now careful grace as he virtually tiptoed down the passageway, chest heaving, his heartbeat hammering in his ears. Doorways to the berths appeared as rectangles of black. A place for death to hide.

From one of them he heard a sound. Gasping, frantic breathing. Suffering. Then silence. It came from straight ahead, from the end of the hallway. From the master suite, the door to which was only slightly ajar.

A few quick steps later he was kicking it fully open. In the dim light he saw the trembling body on the bed, recognizing the bound posture, knowing without seeing that the ropes were there and that time was short. He heard the gasping again, and only then did he comprehend that he was looking at his wife.

A quick, reflexive glance told him that the room appeared to be otherwise empty. He dropped the tire iron and quickly went to work at what he discovered to be an electrical cord that joined her ankles to her wrists. He bent low to use his teeth to try to pull some slack into the knot, but there were several of them, tied with amazing and perplexing creativity.

As he rose back up to take a breath, something cracked into the side of his head from behind, striking squarely over the ear.

The blow knocked him to the side, and as the deck under his feet began to rock uncontrollably he slid off the end of the bed onto the floor, grasping fistfuls of bedding to break the fall. He was kneeling on the floor half slumped over the mattress, and the pain arrived as blood rushed out of shattered capillaries in and around his ear to resurrect numbed nerve endings. It was a throbbing sensation that mirrored his pulse, and it burned like acid on a jagged wound. The blow had been levied on precisely the same spot Carmichael had belted him earlier that night.

The cabin light suddenly clicked on.

The Dark Lady was standing in the doorway to the head where she had been hiding. Leathered and gloved and intent on evil, she was a vision that in another time would have whispered hot breath into secret corners of his brain. The gun he had stolen from her nightstand—the one Karen had been using—was in her hand, held at the beltline, pointing at him.

He only looked at her for a heartbeat before his eyes went back to Karen. Her face was bright red from the effort of staying alive. Streaks of moisture, indistinguishable between tears and sweat, ran from her eyes to the mattress, leaving a gray mascara trail.

It was a perfectly satanic stalemate.

"Moment of truth, Dillon." Veronica's voice was smoke.

"Don't do this. Please . . ."

"And they say chivalry is dead." A sly grin appeared on her face.

"Let her go. Take me. This is about you and me anyway."

Her smile reflected madness.

Dillon's mind scrambled for an angle. "You're trapped," he said. "There's no point to this now . . . don't do this . . ." The words caught in his throat.

"You're right about that. No more options. Nothing more to lose."

"Please . . . I beg of you . . ."

She raised her eyebrows slightly. "This is what you asked for, isn't it? What you've dreamed of? And now it's here—you can taste it, Dillon. It's real, it's happening. I wonder how it feels, having your most exquisite dream unfold before you."

"I never wanted this."

Her smile was layered with implication. "You wanted *me* . . . all that I am, and I've given it to you. You asked for the fire and the madness, Dillon. Complete and utter freedom to indulge yourself in the unspeakable. To lose yourself in the passion of it. All the rules are gone. If the consequences are out of your control, then there are no consequences. You're free, you can do anything."

Dillon quickly surveyed the room. Reasoning with her held no hope—she was over some insane line where hope no longer existed.

"I'll do anything you want," he said.

He wished he still had the tire iron in his hand.

"I know." Her smile lost its focus for a moment. "I've transcended fear, you see. What an amazing feeling, having no fear. We should *live* that way."

Her eyes glazed, then she suddenly snapped back into the moment. "There *is* something I want from you," she said.

"Tell me."

She looked at Karen, as if pausing to listen to another round of her gasping before the silence of held breath returned.

"I want your soul, Dillon. I suppose that's what I've wanted from you all along. It's what every woman wants from her lover in one way or another."

He couldn't believe what he was hearing. The contradiction in her words was frightening. How could a woman who so earnestly rejected the notion of heaven suddenly foster an interest in the currency of the soul? It was the answer, which came to him in a flash masked as fear, that made him realize just how much danger he had been in since the day she had walked into his life. Like the fallen angel himself, she already knew her fate, it was written long before she fell from grace. The only pleasure and purpose of her existence was to take as much human suffering to hell with her as she could. She called it passion and a gusto for life, but it was only selfish greed, the purest of all evils.

Her grin changed slightly, moving on to the next moment. "There is one and only one way out. Not for her, I'm afraid, but for you."

A sharp sucking sound caused them both to look at Karen. Her entire torso was trembling at the effort it took to create even the slightest slack in the bonds. White foam was forming at the corners of her mouth, and her eyes were clenched tightly closed, every muscle in her face committed to staying alive.

"You get to choose, Dillon. Karen dies, just like this. But you . . . you have a chance to live! The choice is yours. It is my gift to you."

"You fucking bitch."

She chuckled softly. "What is it that Benjamin says? When a man has the chance to save his soul, he should take it. But at what price, I wonder? Interesting dilemma, don't you think? Your life or your soul. I wonder what you'll do."

Karen struggled for another breath while they both watched. There could only be moments left now. Dillon felt rage rising within him, a sympathetic tightness in his throat, his eyes filling with helpless emotion.

Veronica tilted her head back as if listening to the passionate angst of the Phantom of the Opera's final aria as he accepted defeat with melodic perfection.

"The money, the freedom . . . it's all yours Dillon. They'll believe Hamilton did this, to get back at you because of our affair. Then, as we've planned all along, he'll be unable to cope with what he's done and then he'll kill himself. The yacht, the body that may or may not wash ashore . . . nothing has to change. Your idea was brilliant, it had so many options, and it can still work with this one."

She paused, proud of her words.

"All you have to do is step back and watch it happen with me."

"You can't play God," said Dillon through his anguish.

"Oh, but I'm not playing."

"You'll kill me anyway."

"There you go again, not trusting me. Your wife *deserves* this! Don't you have any clue why she's here? To betray you! This whole thing was her plan, calling you here—she wanted you dead, because you wanted me! She wants what you can't give her, she wants what I could give you—something ravenous, unwilling to compromise! Your wife's a class-A bitch, Dillon! She's selfish and strong and on fire . . . just what you've always wanted in a woman. Isn't that ironic? She's just like me, actually. We could have been friends, if women like us *had* friends. Our world is black-and-white, you see. We have allies and we have enemies. We have those we can use and those we must punish."

She paused, making sure the words had time to penetrate.

When Dillon started to move she jerked the gun up to within inches of his head. He froze, eyes on his wife. Precious seconds ticked away. Karen seemed unable to breathe, her head now involuntarily pivoting back and forth.

"Just turn away, Dillon."

The choice was now. The defining moment.

Dillon closed his eyes.

He lunged. He heard the gun, felt himself being lifted slightly off the floor as the impact of the bullet spun him around like a blindsiding bus. His shoulder was an instant explosion of ice, cold liquid spreading like an arctic wave through his body to his hands and feet.

There was no pain, really, just a strange sensation of separation as he spun full-circle, facing her again, falling on her, his arms grasping for her shoulders, then her throat, twisting, dragging her down with him, the two of them entwined as the floor rose up to swallow them.

Suddenly he felt another blow to his head, followed by a set of powerful hands on his shoulders. Pulling him back. Sending him crashing against the wall. This time there *was* pain . . . the shoulder had melted and now the fire remained.

He saw a man with no face as he looked back through spotted circles of fight. The man was bending to pick up the gun from the floor. The angel of death.

The Dark Lady was on her hands and knees now, struggling to get up.

The angel of death had no hair and wore glasses.

Carmichael.

The doctor put his arms under Veronica's shoulders as he helped her to an upright sitting position on the bed. He knelt in front of her, gallant and tender as he touched her face, brushing her hair back from her eyes. She seemed dazed by Dillon's attack, and after a moment responded to her supplicant by putting her hands on his shoulders and rewarding him with her best thank-you-for-saving-me smile. In any other moment it would have been sweet.

Dillon glanced down at his left shoulder. Blood had already soaked through his jacket, and he could see a pea-sized black hole in the fabric where the bullet had entered. He had no idea how badly he was injured. Judging from the searing pain, his freethrow days were over.

When he looked back, the gun was pointing directly at his eyes. Carmichael was breathing deeply, as if the decision to shoot required every ounce of his concentration. He was still on his knees, sitting right in front of Veronica.

The Dark Lady was looking at him, too, her face smoldering with victory. If he died now, he knew he'd take that image with him, that it would have a place on his wall in either hell or heaven with equal distinction. Her black hand massaged the back of Carmichael's neck as if to comfort whatever demon made him hesitate. She leaned down close to his ear.

"End it . . . kill him . . . for us . . . for me."

Carmichael began to stand unsteadily, pushing himself up with one hand on the mattress. When he was upright he put both hands on the gun in a classic firing stance, ready to shoot. He stepped back and slowly closed his eyes, a strange sound emitting from his mouth.

Her smile widened. It had come to this.

Then Carmichael suddenly pivoted and fired a bullet into Veronica's lower abdomen.

Behind the palpable ringing in his ears Dillon heard himself yell. For an instant he thought the bullet was intended for Karen, who was right behind Veronica on the bed and was no longer moving. Veronica had fallen back onto her, her hands clutching her midsection.

Carmichael moved fast. He had withdrawn a pocket knife, expertly extracting the blade. It took him only a few seconds to slice the twisted panty house from Karen's throat and wrists, followed by the extension cord wrapped around her ankles. Dillon could hear Karen gasping urgently for air as the doctor cradled her face with his hands, checking her pupils, holding her in an upright position.

He spoke to Dillon without looking away from her. His voice was businesslike, patient yet urgent.

"Take her clothes. Go quickly."

Dillon felt a wave of nausea as he struggled to his feet, his left arm pinned to his rib cage. Karen's clothes were in a pile at the foot of the bed, and he grabbed as much as he could with his healthy hand. Bending over made his bloodied shoulder scream.

Karen was staring right at him when he finally stood upright, the first time their eyes had met since his arrival on the yacht. She was sobbing, struggling for balance. As Dillon approached she opened her arms to him, falling against his chest. He supported her with his functioning limb, her clothes bunched in its fist.

Carmichael was already on to the next task. He was positioning Veronica onto the bed lengthwise, where Karen had been. He arranged her head on the pillow, as if this was just another mortician's day at the office. Her gloved hands still held her abdomen, blood seeping out from between her fingers, the moisture making the smooth kid glisten.

"Take that with you," Carmichael said.

A flick of his eyes indicated a black canvas athletic bag on the floor. Dillon hadn't noticed it before and wasn't sure if that was what Carmichael had been referring to.

He didn't need to be sure.

Karen instantly pulled away from Dillon's one-armed embrace and snatched it up. She shot him a strange glance as she took her clothes out of his hand and moved into the hallway without looking back.

Carmichael was looking at Dillon with sad, hopeless eyes.

"I don't know what to say to you," said Dillon.

"Say you'll do what I couldn't."

"I don't know what you mean."

"Forgive the unforgivable." His eyes softened.

Dillon looked at Veronica. Her eyes were half open, fluttering softly. She was trying to say something, but she had no strength left to make a sound.

"A night with no dawn and no God," Carmichael said, his eyes glazed over; a madman's reverie.

Dillon used the moment to measure his distance from the door, less than confident with the timing of his exit. The gun was still in Carmichael's hand.

"This is what we both wanted all along, isn't it?" Carmichael said, suddenly returning to the room. "To imagine all the foolish and misunderstood little dreams that define us and bind us to the dark. How they turn out really makes no difference in the end, does it? It only matters that you taste it, that it was real."

Then he turned away and began to stroke Veronica's face with a terrifying tenderness. Dillon knew it was over, that he needed to get out of there before the insanity changed its course yet again, like a mindless storm. He shuddered at the thought of how the doctor might bid the Dark Lady a final good-night.

He took a few steps into the hallway, then heard Carmichael's voice.

"You know what the trouble with this world is? Nobody trusts anybody anymore." Carmichael grinned slightly, as if they were just two guys in a bar setting the world straight.

Then he winked before turning back to his dying lover, his hand continuing to stroke her forehead, her mouth still trying to form words, her eyes full of the worst flavor of fear.

Then Carmichael kicked the cabin door closed.

Dillon bolted down the hall into the main salon, where Karen was frantically getting dressed. It was difficult because she continued to hold on to the handle

of the athletic bag as she worked at the buttons of her
jeans.

THEY were nearly at the top of the ramp when they heard
the deep rumble of the *Picki Nicki's* engines. They stood
arm in arm as they watched Carmichael appear on deck
and toss away the mooring lines before he disappeared
back into the cabin. Moments later there was a shift in
the tone of the engines as the boat began to back out
from the mooring slip.

They said nothing as they watched it maneuver out
of the marina into the open water of the sound, cruising without running lights. Several minutes later it was
swallowed by the night and its quiet shroud of nocturnal fog. The drone of the diesels continued for a few
moments after the yacht's silhouette dissolved into the
waterline.

The *Picki Nicki* would never be heard from again.
Not a trace of her would ever be found, adrift in an endless night with no consequences and no God.

A police car wheeled into the lot, lights flashing.

Dillon took Karen by the hand, and in silence they
walked toward the parking lot. Tonight was the first
night of the rest of their lives, and they had much to
talk about.

61

Eleven Months Later

Detective Rubin pulled up in front of the Masters' residence and turned off the motor of his new department-issue unmarked Chrysler, letting the radio play on. The fifth game of the World Series was being broadcast, Indians at San Diego, and while he truly didn't give a shit about baseball, there was something about the Series. Funny thing, context. Changes how you look at everything. That and a twenty-dollar bet on Cleveland made Rubin a certifiable Mr. October.

It was one of those glorious Seattle days on the cusp of fall, the swan song of a summer that never arrives until late in June and finally commits itself by August. In four out of every five years it gives November a run for its money, with perfectly golden afternoons spiced with just a wisp of fall air. They called it an Indian summer,

which made Rubin laugh because someone was peti-
tioning the state legislature to mandate banning the use
of the term in the media due to its obviously offensive
ethnic slur. If the folks in Cleveland ever got wind of
that, who knows what they'd start calling their baseball team—the Cleveland Native Americans, perhaps.
Seattle's fuck-you-money Palm Springs crowd, none of
whom had signed that particular petition, was just now
thinking about heading south for their winter in a fair-
way condo.

Rubin wasn't sure where Dillon and Karen were
off to. Parked half a block away, hidden from view,
he watched Dillon loading suitcases into the back of a
brand-new Lexus SUV. A FOR SALE sign was the centerpiece of a much too perfectly groomed yard. Seems
Dillon and Karen Masters had sprung for a little professional landscaping this summer in anticipation of the big
move. Not bad for someone who'd lost his job in a jointly-
backed SEC-NASDAQ investigation a few months before, the outcome of which had rendered Dillon among
the dishonorably unemployed. The NYSE had also
jumped into the affair and stripped him of his Series 7
license. The SEC ruled that Dillon had acted on insider
information relative to a stock called Applied Software
Technology Systems, a venture-capital-backed high-tech
start-up that had filed Chapter 11 and 13 bankruptcy
papers that spring. Rather than defend its employee,
who admitted he'd received information on ASTS from
the wife and soon-to-be widow of the venture capitalist who had been the primary flushee, his company had
simply sent him packing. The fact that Dillon had admitted during the SEC hearing that he had been having
an affair with the woman, and that his name had not yet
been cleared in an investigation into the man's bizarre

death, didn't exactly endear him to the suits in White Plains. Even Janis turned cold in the face of a corporate blackball. Her ass was next on the chopping block, and for that Dillon felt genuinely remorseful.

Rubin got out of the car and walked toward the cul-de-sac and Dillon's driveway, enjoying the warmth of the sun on his face. He pulled his sunglasses out and put them on, pocketing his hands. It was a great day. The world was right again because the case of Hamilton Wallace was, as of that morning, finally and officially over. Justice, in all her blind and in this case highly intuitive wisdom, had somehow prevailed. The system, in all its equally blind and in this case inept mediocrity, had somehow worked as well. God bless America.

Dillon looked up when he sensed someone approaching. Rubin stood a few feet away, running his hand along the new vehicle, much as Dillon had done the first time he first saw Veronica Wallace's SL 500 in a restaurant parking lot the previous winter.

Dillon thought about those days more often than he'd admit, now that things with Karen were on a roll. Not about the trouble, but about the high. A scrapbook full of nasty little images that would never go away. It seemed so long ago now.

"Looks like someone won the lottery," said Rubin.

"It's a lease."

The money had never come up during the investigation. Veronica Wallace had been right about that much—it would never be traced.

Dillon closed the back hatch and extended his hand to Rubin in greeting. They looked at each other with knowing and respectful eyes, brothers from a war who shared something that the rest of us could never understand.

"House hunting?" He nodded toward the suitcases, which filled the back of the SUV.

"Second honeymoon. Maui. Maybe make a baby."

Rubin just nodded, a smile barely contained behind his public official's countenance.

"Shoulder seems okay."

Dillon nodded, rotating his arm slightly, which he did whenever anyone asked. Then he grinned. "Steroids. I can get you some."

The bullet had grazed his deltoid muscle, ripping half of it away but doing little serious damage other than to a perfectly good raw silk jacket. He'd been lifting weights all summer, building it back up, and it was nearly restored. Meanwhile the effort had put him in the best overall shape he'd been in since his twenties, and Rubin could see it. Dillon looked like he was ten or fifteen pounds lighter, which brought out some facial character that wasn't there before. Like Dillon needed any help with his face. He had the glow about him of a man trying to impress a woman.

Rubin bit his lip, unsure where to begin. It was an awkward moment familiar to every school kid who had finished with his carefully rehearsed small talk and faced the moment of coming out with an awkward invitation for a first date. Except now there was nothing at risk, nothing for Dillon to reject. Rubin simply wasn't sure how to say it, because it meant everything to Dillon.

"The D.A.'s decided to let it go."

Their eyes locked. Birds sang, a Boeing was climbing out for points east. After a moment Dillon nodded. Something deep inside him was melting, a knot of energy that had been sticking in his gut for more months than he'd bothered to count. He'd known it would turn out this way because Rubin had promised him it would, but living his life in confidence rather than certainty had kept the knot pulled even tighter. Now, as the tension released, he felt the sudden freedom in his throat and behind his eyes. He was surprised at how the emotion of the news affected him.

"They finally wrote it down and stamped it," said Rubin. "It's all on ice in a file someplace. A crazy doctor murdered his lover's husband. Same crazy doctor tried to murder a former patient, the wife of the man with whom said lover was having yet another affair on the heels of dumping him. Then the crazy doctor kills the lawyer that he suspects has also been sleeping with her during their relationship. The man cracked. He sees no way out, so he takes the object of his obsession to hell with him in her boat, which we cannot locate and therefore assume is somewhere on the bottom of the sound. Murder followed by attempted murder followed by murder-suicide. A lot of questions, not enough answers. But no one cares anymore."

Rubin stopped and adjusted his sunglasses. Then, without looking up, he said, "It's over, Dillon. You're a free man."

Both men stood in silence for a few moments, remembering.

THE story had coalesced that night in the fog as Dillon and Karen stood in the parking lot of the marina talking to Rubin. As he approached in the squad car, seeing them standing arm in arm at the top of the ramp, Rubin knew it had ended. And that the real work was ahead of him. He'd told his young uniformed driver to remain at the wheel and to call for backup. He got out and met the couple as they walked toward their car, more than a little dazed and confused.

"What happened to your shoulder?" had been Rubin's first question.

"It collided with a twenty-two-millimeter bullet."

"Who was it?"

Dillon didn't answer, but his eyes promised a story. It was then that Rubin studied Karen, whom he had never met, and whom he intuitively understood should not listen when Dillon told him what happened. She looked as if she'd been dragged from the bottom of the ocean, her hair soaked, eyes smudged and red. The collar of her coat was bunched tightly around her throat, and she held it there with her hand. With her other hand she clung even tighter to a black canvas bag with an Adidas logo on the side.

"Tell me who shot you."

"I think I should talk to an attorney."

"Your attorney is dead."

Dillon only hesitated for a moment, feeling a tug in his throat but not sure how to play this one with Rubin. He nodded, avoiding the detective's eyes.

Just then a second black and white entered the marina lot. The young officer from Rubin's car got out to greet them.

Rubin looked out toward the marina. He'd never been here, didn't know which slot had been the *Picki Nicki's*, and therefore didn't yet realize it was gone.

"Where's Mrs. Wallace?" he asked.

"I'm not saying anything to you."

But their eyes were engaged in a raging conversation. Each space between words, the subtlety in their tone, was a volume of the unspoken. It was Karen who sensed it and asked if she could sit down. Rubin put her in the back of the squad car, and after instructing his partner to call an ambulance returned to Dillon, who was shivering as he waited, standing in the headlight beams.

"Talk fast," said Rubin.

Dillon did, every move, every word, everything. He tried to look casual, knowing the other officers were watching. Once, when he started to break down, Rubin told him to keep it straight, try for a smile. He wasn't a suspect, so don't look like one. At this point staying strong was a requirement of survival. Looking strong was the best strategy money could buy.

It was then, in that moment, that Dillon understood how this would go down.

Rubin listened with his eyes on the ground, concentrating hard as he chewed his knuckles, pacing a perfect triangle. He appeared more guilty than Dillon, which later, upon reflection, would seem appropriate.

When he was finished Dillon wished he could disappear somewhere. "I can't go through this again," he said. "I'm done."

"Yes, you can and you will. You'll tell it straight. You'll just leave a few things out. If you make shit up, you'll slip. So don't do it. Just be clear on what *didn't* happen."

"I don't follow you."

"That's good. Don't try to follow me. Just tell the truth. How you met her—which, by the way, was in the waiting room at Carmichael's office. That's very important. Talk about what you liked, how she lit you up. The games, the sexual liaisons, including the little incident in which you were caught peeping behind her house. Tell it like it happened. It was all a game, all very perverse and hot, and it's all the truth. When you get to the Vancouver trip, say she was a no-show, so you came home.

No murder, no corpus delicti. You didn't even check in. They were framing you, they had your card number. You with me here?"

Dillon nodded, noticing the burning intensity in Rubin's eyes.

"You were pissed, you were hurt. She tried to end it the next day, said she had someone else. You couldn't know about the dead husband, the frame-up. So you went away. Hearts and flowers, very sad. Then a few days later Carmichael came after you. Said it was your fault he and Mrs. Wallace were splitsville. Said he'd make it square, make you pay. Just like he did the other guy, the lawyer."

"Wait a minute," said Dillon, waving his hands for emphasis. "It was me who introduced Jordan to her. I'm the common factor . . . that'll never fly."

"You introduced them when you were having an affair with her and you wanted to show her off. She slept with him behind your back. You didn't know."

"Like maybe he was the guy she was dumping me for."

"Not bad. It could have happened."

Rubin thought about that one for a moment before clicking back on track.

"You didn't know Carmichael was targeting Karen when he said he'd make you pay. You didn't know shit. It'll be me questioning you on all this, so whatever you say, I'll back you. I'll work around what doesn't fit. Just be clear on what didn't happen and don't get too creative with what did. Including tonight. You understand?"

Dillon nodded, less than convincingly.

"Look at me, right here in my eyes. There was no dead body. You didn't get a room. Everything else was as it happened. Are we clear?"

Dillon nodded, feeling like a child with a concerned

adult.

"Talk to your wife. Can you trust her?"

Dillon glanced at the car. He could see Karen inside, holding her forehead in her hands. The young officer was talking to her, and he wondered what she might be saying to him.

"I wouldn't dare *not* trust her." Dillon looked back at Rubin. "Why are you doing this?" he asked.

The question seemed to halt Rubin in his tracks. He raised his eyebrows and his gaze drifted out to the water.

"Someone has to."

Then he looked back at Dillon, who tried to muster appreciation in his eyes. He was certain, however, that all that showed was his uncertainty.

"You have to trust me," said Rubin. "And you have to trust your wife. Your life depends on both."

No one trusts anybody anymore . . .

Rubin tried a smile. "Nine parts truth and a little righteous creative license and you're home." He paused. "That's the way it's gotta be."

THE investigation, the meat of it anyway, lasted only a month. Rubin was always there, always the one asking the questions, filing the reports. Always fixing things. Dillon played his role precisely as Rubin had scripted it, telling it straight, knowing what to leave out, mixing in carefully prescribed and exquisitely timed curveballs. He'd met the woman of his dreams at a time when he most needed a woman's touch. His marriage was breaking up, he was vulnerable, and there she was, equally vulnerable. They were seeing the same psychiatrist, shrinking the same demons. They came together easily, the heat was spontaneous and irresistible. There were games to be played, elaborate mind-fucks, little public humiliations doubling as foreplay but always an end unto themselves, sometimes but not always followed by sex. She was dark, she was the devil, a hard drug for his willing vein. And then it all went to hell, suddenly and without explanation. That was the Vancouver thing. She simply didn't show. They were finished. She was bored, she'd found someone else to play with. He'd thought that was that, and under a cloud of guilt turned his attention back to saving his marriage, seeing if there was anything there to resurrect. And then Carmichael came, with his outrageous idea that Dillon had ruined his life. He's broken into Dillon's house, threatened him. Told him he'd take his wife from him, shatter his dreams. Then came Karen's call for help. Carmichael had her and Dillon needed to hurry. He'd kill her if Dillon called the police. And so he'd gone to the *Picki Nicki* as instructed, found Karen there with Carmichael and Veronica Wallace, who was tied up and in excruciating pain. Carmichael was drunk or high on something, completely out of his mind. There had been a struggle, the gun had gone off. Dillon had been hit in the shoulder but managed to knock Carmichael down in the ensuing brawl. Under the cover of chaos Dillon had grabbed Karen's hand and ran like hell, expecting a bullet in the back. The next thing he knew they were standing on the marina's ramp, watching as the yacht fired up and headed out into the darkness.

   . . . *a night with no consequences . . . where no one could hear her screams . . .*

   That was all he knew. And he knew it and said it that way over and over, precisely the same every time.

   He and Karen rehearsed it countless times. Rubin had questioned her alone and with others, sometimes for hours. Dillon never really knew what she'd told the detective, whether it differed depending on who was in the room with them. He only knew that she seemed, in a subtle yet strangely deliberate way, to enjoy Dillon's asking about it. She never tried quite hard enough to take his anxiety away.

There were details, hundreds of them, that led to nowhere. There were things that were never written down, things that became clear without being spoken. There were trails that tied in knots, knots that led to trails. There were witnesses who'd seen Dillon in Veronica Wallace's shadow, but none had seen them talk or touch. There were records and names and notes in Carmichael's office linking all of them to his patient chair and its box of Kleenex. There were phone records and credit card receipts and a million other things, all placed on a palate for the pleasure of the artist, lawyer, and detective alike.

In the end it was all about context. After a lifetime of studying those who kill and steal and then conspire to ravage the truth, in hundreds upon hundreds of courtrooms where the highly trained and highly paid plied their sleight of hand, Rubin had become its master manipulator. Rubin was the Johnny fucking Cochran of context.

There were secrets, too.

Rubin never told Dillon—or anyone else—about a tape he'd found in Carmichael's office safe. On it Karen had talked about her need to be at the center of things, her need to control her childhood friends, and when she got older, her need to control men. She talked about how she'd learned to temper this dark part of her personality in order to keep people in her life. Over time she'd come to learn that men needed the control, and to have

them, she had to give it to them. In time she'd learned
how to make them think they had control when in fact
they were shadowing her will. She'd almost forgotten
how strong she was, the vast extent of her power. She'd
talked about how that same sense of power had left her
marriage, because Dillon was controlled by something
else that was not of her design. The control *had* to be of
her design. It had to be about *her.*

That was her own drug, her own fetish. When she
thought about it, it was neither better nor more inexplicable than Dillon's. It simply was.

Rubin also didn't tell anyone about what he'd found
when he placed Dillon's and Karen's recent spending
habits under close scrutiny. It wasn't exactly a case study
for the IRS, but the gradually emerging appearance of
cash flow wasn't bad for an unemployed stockbroker
with a wife in career crisis. Anyone who looked could
see it, but because it was Rubin's job to look, no one else
did. And because it didn't change Rubin's world or the
rules by which he evaluated the strange case of Hamilton Wallace's death, what he learned about Dillon and
Karen's money stopped with him.

They'd found sadomasochistic pornography in
Carmichael's house. Some of it, in particular a pirate
amateur video label obtained through a London mail-
order house, had depicted a form of advanced bondage
precisely like that which had been used to kill Jordan
Chapman, right down to the knots. Pathologists had
reported ligatures and wounds on Hamilton Wallace's
body that were congruent with precisely that style of
bondage. Later, after a court order allowed Rubin to
open Carmichael's safe-deposit box, they'd found In-
stamatic snaps of Veronica Wallace and himself in the
exact same position. Apparently they'd taken turns,

tasting the bittersweet ambrosia of suffering before the hungry eyes of a lover who understood the pleasures to be found in the dark.

Whatever.

Rubin found one other thing to be curious. It didn't seem to pertain to the case, so like so many things, it never made its way into the case file. But Rubin noticed, because it spoke to him in a way that made him sad, made him expand the scope of his perspective on Benjamin Carmichael. In Carmichael's closet, in a box sealed long ago with yellowed tape, Rubin had found an orange stuffed panda bear wearing a baby's denim bib overalls. Written in a child's unpracticed hand on the vest, using what appeared to be black crayon that was nearly completely faded after the decades, was the name Sammy. The animal had a name, and it looked sad and abandoned.

The only other thing inside the box had been a keychain with a tiny airplane attached to one end.

Even monsters came from mothers. Even those who kill once dreamed in shades of white.

The forensic boys found traces of Hamilton Wallace's blood in the back of his Jaguar. Matching traces were found in Benjamin Carmichael's trunk, and on clothing found in his hamper. A little digging turned up a Greyhound bus ticket to Vancouver paid for in cash on the night of the murder, with an employee who recalled marveling at the sheen on Carmichael's bald head that night as he lurked at the fringes of the lobby.

An ashtray speckled with dry traces of the deceased's blood had been found in a hatbox in Veronica Wallace's closet. This cemented speculation that she and Carmichael had been partners in her husband's murder, a fact corroborated when a second employee identified

Carmichael as having been at the Fraser Hotel on the night of the murder. One positive ID makes you suspicious, two makes you place a bet. Detective Rubin had handled all of the employee interviews at the Fraser by himself, including that of the bartender.

What wasn't necessary wasn't kept. What didn't add up was set aside. Because so much did add up, and when viewed under the light of Rubin's contextual microscope, the conclusion was palatable, if not completely solid. It was an election year, and the D.A. was hungry for a close. If it didn't happen soon, it couldn't help the cause. And if it was ever going to solidify, it wouldn't happen soon.

So that morning, on the day Rubin visited Dillon as he was loading the new SUV for their trip, the D.A.'s office called Rubin in and told him they'd decided to write it off. It was over.

They never thanked him for his hard and diligent work on the case.

Very early during the investigation Karen confessed to Dillon that she liked the way he was handling himself. They were in bed, and she'd said it as she turned him over and took the top position, something she hadn't done in years. She said she saw a strength in him that she'd thought was gone, obscured in the shadow of the man she'd married. She liked the way he was fighting for their lives, the way he was shielding her from the world's harm. And behind closed doors, she liked it that he was a little afraid and unsure, a man vulnerable to the world yet strong enough to confront it. She said everything that had happened had caused her to reevaluate her life, that it returned to her feelings she'd thought she'd lost. That night she asked him to come back, to live with her in the house on the cul-de-sac, if nothing else for the appearance of solidarity as the investigation ran its course. In the meantime they would talk, they would make love, they would see what remained of hope. And for her, she would see how it felt to be in control again, the caretaker of his fear.

And in bed, in the embrace of darkness, she said it all made her hot.

THERE were also things that Rubin *didn't* know.

He didn't know just a month earlier, long after the business of Dillon's dismissal from the firm had become old news and the death of Hamilton Wallace seemed like a foregone conclusion, Dillon had returned to his office to pay a short visit to one of the ladies who worked on the administrative side of the business. No one else knew he was there that day—he'd come during lunch and left a mere half-hour later. The first question he'd asked his friend was about the balance in the IRA account of the young stockbroker to whom he'd given the hot tip about Applied Software Technology Systems. He had two dates in mind—the day before he'd bought the stock, and the day after the bottom fell out of it. The account had only fourteen thousand dollars in it before the trade, seventeen hundred a few days later.

When Dillon left the office that afternoon, the young broker's IRA balance was in excess of twenty-five thousand dollars, and it was composed of precisely the same stocks that had been there before he'd liquidated everything to buy Applied Software. Of course, the new money was after-tax dollars, which was an unavoidable compromise and the reason for the excess over the amount that had been lost. Later that day the confused young broker started to ask about it, but a wink and a kiss on the cheek from the bookkeeper told him all he needed to know. He was never tempted to ask about it again. In this business, you took your money where you found it. Somewhere down the line, the IRS might want to know where the money came from, or they might not. That wouldn't be Dillon's problem anymore. One by one, Dillon's problems were being paid for in full.

The other thing that Rubin didn't know, because he hadn't bothered to check, was that Jordan Chapman's headstone in a cemetery overlooking the Olympic Mountains had been paid for by an anonymous donor who had requested the word LAWMAN be carved onto it in large letters. Jordan had been well insured, so his elderly mother and his only sister were nicely taken care of. That same donor made an equally anonymous contribution of twenty-five thousand dollars to a local boys' club to support their basketball team and other programs. The contribution had been made in Jordan Chapman's name.

"**WELL**, I guess this is it, then," said Dillon.

"I guess it is. Congratulations." Rubin didn't offer a handshake, rendering the comment rhetorical rather than sincere. The nongesture seemed to make Dillon uncomfortable. He just nodded at him very slowly.

"I suppose I should say thank you," said Dillon, "but that seems . . . I don't know . . . wrong. Maybe just inadequate."

Rubin nodded. "Some people get to choose what they believe. It's what they do about it that makes you who and what you are." Now he grinned, trying to erase Dillon's obvious discomfort "Tell your baby that someday."

"I'll do that," said Dillon, blushing slightly.

"So what's next? I mean, after Maui."

"I don't know. I was thinking about going back to school, maybe doing some coaching, work with kids. I'm not in a big hurry. Right now I'm really into my wife, I guess."

Rubin just nodded, and Dillon wasn't sure he'd heard the answer to his question.

Rubin had indeed heard, but he'd already moved on. He was feigning further interest in Dillon's new car, but he was actually just passing the moment, once again looking for an entry point to something bigger on his mind. Something he had to say, even though perhaps it went without saying. Because despite what he knew, it was what he didn't know that still kicked around in his mind. For Rubin, closure was like context. It was one of life's necessities.

"Who was fucking whom, that's the real pisser," he said without looking up. He continued talking; anybody watching would have assumed he was doing a thorough checkup of the vehicle. "Mrs. Wallace working you against the doctor . . . him working you against her . . . you working him against her . . . what'd you call it—a clusterfuck, I think you said. I like that. A world-class, take-no-prisoners clusterfuck."

Just then the door inside the garage opened. Both men looked, seeing a woman carrying a flight bag coming toward them. Karen didn't look at all like the frightened woman Rubin had met that night at the marina, or the nervous woman he had questioned for hours here at her house and at the station. This Karen had been competently overhauled. The housewife hair was now much more Hollywood chic, shorter, wealthy and hip. Her nature-girl freshness was now a testimonial for

Max Factor and his peers. She wore a short, tailored black leather coat, tight at the waist. A white crew-neck ribbed cotton top was tucked into black stretch pants, which were inserted into short, square-toed boots with a thick and stylish two-inch heel. This Karen was more appropriate for a little spin down Rodeo Drive than a ride to Sea-Tac in an SUV. The look was topped off with a pair of expensive sunglasses.

It was the earrings that caught Rubin's attention. Two, maybe three carats each. Worth more than the Lexus into which she climbed after politely shaking Rubin's hand, like two old friends who didn't like each other much dispensing with an obligatory moment.

Dillon walked her around to the passenger side, opened her door, and held it as she climbed in gracefully. Then he closed the door and returned to the driver's side. Before opening his own door he turned to shake the detective's hand.

The detective grinned, an old friend with an old truth.

"I just hope you know who *she* was fucking," said Rubin quietly, his smile remaining bold despite the in-your-face substance of his words. It was as much a question as it was a declaration of that which had never been spoken.

Dillon said nothing and got in.

Rubin would remember Dillon's responding expression. It was a brave and genuine smile, but it straddled certainty. Maybe it didn't matter anymore. Maybe the woman he once knew and had nearly lost, forged and tempered and changed by the fire they'd survived together, was less important than the woman he now seemed to cherish. The saucy little witch with the attitude in the front seat, putting lipstick on using the rearview, oblivious to them both. The kind of woman that always seemed to belong to someone else. A rich man's woman.

Maybe.

Whatever.

The new Lexus backed into the street. When Karen waved goodbye to Rubin, the detective saw that she had put on a pair of short black leather gloves. He'd remember that little touch, put it in the thinly veiled psychological thriller he and Valerie were writing together based on this case. A story about people bound by the darkness they create for themselves and others, and their power to choose their outcome. About how to survive a clusterfuck.

Inside the vehicle, a full minute passed before either Dillon or Karen spoke. They both stared ahead, conscious of what they were leaving behind and how close it had all come to trapping them there. The silence felt good, but like all pleasures, it eventually surrendered to reality.

"So . . . what'd he want?" Karen finally asked.

"I think he came by to wish me luck," he said.

He reached for her hand, brought it to his mouth to touch the soft, fragrant leather to his lips. When he looked at her she was smiling at him from behind her sunglasses, and he smiled back, holding tightly to her hand.

Something that lived in the space between his imagination and his spine blew secret icy-hot kisses into his ear, and he shivered slightly.

"I love you," he said.

She continued to smile at him, then turned her eyes to the road ahead.

"I know," she said softly, the smile lingering.

1

PORTLAND, OREGON

October, 2012

Don't get me started.

No one with a modicum of sense—and please, just shoot me if I ever actually use the word *modicum* in an actual conversation—could blame me for being pissed off about things in general. The airlines want a hundred bucks to change from a flight with a waiting list to another flight that is only half full, and thirty bucks to load your bag. One commuter line wants a hundred dollars for a carry-on. Thank you for flying Trans Sphincter Air. My HMO announced their annual forty-five-percent-rate hike on the day a pro athlete I once admired got busted—again—for beating up a hooker and his wife on the same day, which earlier had brought us the news of a senator tweeting his junk to yet another hooker. The IRS wasn't buying my deduction to The Society for the Prevention of Cruelty to Copywriters, one of which I once was. Reality television hadn't gone away, nor would Britney or Lindsay Lohan or The Donald, who continued resisting a sign-off on the restructuring of his hair.

Grease was no longer The Word. *Bullshit* was.

Far beyond the boundaries of my claustrophobic little world, the Democrats wanted us to forget that half the working population, which was shrinking, is on the public dole. Meanwhile, the Republicans wanted us to overlook the fact that, among all those senators and congressmen and governors with right-leaning tendencies and greasy palms, not to mention dropped drawers in low places, a guy who looked like a blowup doll and with no memory was the best they could come up with for the next Presidential race. That someone could actually be named after a catcher's glove. And because of a book and a movie, half the planet actually believed that Mary Magdalene lived out her days as Mrs. Jesus H. Christ, while the other half—including those with rags on their heads and bombs under their vests—are still quite convinced that God is on their side.

At least Saddam and bin Laden were dead, with no bounty of vestal virgins anywhere on their eternal horizon.

Bring the boys home? Not that simple, Sparky.

What's a thinking man to do, give Newt the vote? I don't think so.

In my case, the answer was sanity itself. In my abundant spare time I wrote a column for a liberal local weekly—I'm no liberal, by the way, but it was the only paper interested—entitled *Bullshit in America*. Somehow calling it out for the consideration of my thinking brothers and sisters made it all the more tolerable. Maybe people would realize they are not alone in their frustration at being jerked around.

There remains no shortage of material.

Then, just when I thought I was safe from the stench of my own indignant cynicism, the next chapter in my heretofore vanilla but suddenly very strange existence was about to be unleashed.

Or, perhaps better said, *unhinged.*

After one dance as an undercover facer for the Feds, a chin for hire, the last thing I ever thought I'd do was once again take up arms as a designated seducer of women at the behest of someone with a badge. A strange destiny indeed for good cheekbones and a few years modeling underwear for the local metropolitan daily.

My name is Wolfgang Schmitt, and I'm here to confirm the rumor that shit really does happen.

MY dear, sweet, institutionalized mother looked at me and said, "I *love* your new show!"

Which, had I been some talking-head movie reviewer on local-access cable—almost got that gig back in the nineties—would have been sort of sweet. But I was a happily unemployed advertising hack who had just come into a buttload of under-the-table federal money—I'll explain *that* later—so my smile was at once forced and sad.

My mother thought I was Chuck Woolery with shorter, cooler hair.

She wasn't the first person in recent memory who thought I looked like a gameshow host, but she was the only one who could attribute that fine opinion to Alzheimer's. Okay, maybe the resemblance was there, but I preferred the occasional George-Clooney-meets-Owen-

Wilson comparison I used to get in bars. We were sitting in what had once been a bedroom in a Victorian mansion overlooking the Willamette River—which no one born east of Idaho has ever pronounced correctly—but was now a private nursing facility that charged five grand a month for round-the-clock apathy and food with all the charisma of car wax. The first thing I did with the aforementioned money—earned via the seduction of a billionaire's wayward wife under the threat of being audited to hell and back—was move my mother out of the state-funded hellhole into which I had originally, and naively, deposited her in the hope that someone wearing a starched white uniform would give a shit.

That notion proved to be an airball. This place was about as therapeutic as the funeral home it had once been. But that was about to change. I had an idea, and I had the cash.

"I'm not on television, Mom."

"Oh, did they cancel you? Who do I write to?"

"I'll look it up for you. For now, besides that, you seem happy today."

Maybe if I told her she looked happy, she'd buy it. My mother was constantly smiling, a trait I'd hoped would endear her to the staff until I remembered this was Planet Dementia. She wore a sweatshirt with the words *My Grandma Can Beat Up Your Grandma*—purloined when the woman in the next room died with no relatives willing to pick up her things—over a baby-blue flannel nightgown and fuzzy purple Barney slippers. The sweatshirt and the slippers both hid an excruciating irony—my mother had no grandchildren.

As her only child, that was, of course, my fault.

According to the staff here in hell's little waiting room, from time to time my mother believed she was on a cruise ship. And that she was the cruise director. One day I arrived to find her leading a geriatric line dance in the foyer to the tune of "Achy Breaky Heart," everyone wearing robes and black knee socks. After forty-nine years of living with a man whose favorite word was "goddamn" and whose idea of a family vacation was going clamming in the rain, I didn't have the heart to tell her otherwise. The day my father died, seven lost years earlier, was the first day she forgot who either one of us was.

The universe is funny that way, trading one purgatory for another.

I visited my mother three times a week. We no longer had the past in common, so there wasn't much to discuss, this being a blessing for both of us in many ways. Since I could not impose the needs of my recently broken heart on her motherly sensibilities, I found myself trying to convince her that the captain and crew really liked her, and that, yes, those new folks on *Hollywood Squares* really couldn't hold a candle to Paul Lynde and his dead cronies. Somehow Whoopi Goldberg in the center square just didn't cut it for Mom. The meaninglessness of the banter had given me a chance to look critically at the accommodations, and the closer I looked, the less I liked what I smelled. A faint scent of urine always greeted me upon arrival. Sometimes there was spilled food and what I feared was vomit on her bedding—it wasn't easy to tell the difference—and that blue flannel nightie never seemed to get a day off. The staff assured me that laundry was a daily exercise and that it was taken quite seriously, and oh, by the way, that urine smell was my imagination. This was not true, however, of the crumbs that accumulated on the floor in the corners of her room, luring the occasional undiscerning cockroach.

I don't think they liked me all that much, actually.

The administrator was quick to flash his certificate of compliance from the state board of nursing home auditors, but frankly I didn't appreciate his attitude. He reminded me of that guy who married Liza Minnelli, the one who looked like an exhumed extra from the *Dawn of the*

Dead and got another few minutes past his allotted fifteen sound-bite minutes when Michael Jackson died. If someone had told me the guy running my mother's nursing home was a holdover from the old funeral home days, I'd have bought it.

I should have checked her out of here weeks ago.

Then one day Mr. Formaldehyde sought me out to announce that, with deep regret, he was closing the home. I had a month to find my mother a new ship in which to cruise. Something about unreasonable regulatory pressures for sanitary upgrades—his look told me he thought I might have had something to do with that one—and the increasingly hostile and unfair reimbursement policies of those bastard Republicans politicizing Medicare. He casually mentioned he hadn't been able to find a buyer, adding that the building required significant capital improvements and that, frankly, none of it penciled out. Cheaper, he said, to shut the doors. It was at that very moment, as I visualized the aforementioned pencil penetrating the membrane of his inner ear, that a lightbulb with the wattage of a Tom Cruise smile illuminated my near-term investment strategy.

And so, being the good and newly moneyed son that I was, I decided to buy the place.

CPSIA information can be obtained at www.ICGtesting.com
Printed in the USA
LVOW13s0904161013

357171LV00001B/3/P